Dark Side of the Mirror

By

Elaine Meece

Michelle,
Enjoy the read!
Elaine Meece

Author -Elaine Meece

Sassafras Publishing
686 Brinsley Cove
Memphis, TN. 38017

Published May 2013

ISBS-13:9781489523327
ISBN-10:1489523324

Cover Art by Valerie Tibbs Design

This book is a work of fiction. Names, characters, places, dialogue and events are products of the author's imagination or are used fictitiously, and any likeness to actual person, living or dead, business establishments or locales is entirely by coincidence. References to any real places, groups, or organizations are intended to only provide a sense of authenticity and are fictitious in use.

Dedication

In memory of my grandmother, Mary Francis Stallings. She gave birth to three sets of fraternal twins—Tio and Abner, Earl and Shelley (my father), and Ruby and Ruth. My Aunt Ruth is the last one living and has just turned a hundred and one.

Acknowledgement

I want to commend the U.S. Marshals Service for having a great website and also a friendly public relations department that is willing to share information.

I want to thank critique partners Dee Julian and Ellen Stucker. I also want to thank my daughter, Valencia and my husband, Geoffrey for their help and support on this book.

Chapter One

Deputy U.S. Marshal Braden Wolfe wanted to be the first.

First of the multiple fugitive task force formed to apprehend Selena Menendez, who'd been profiled on *America's Most Wanted*. Someone had called before the show had finished airing and claimed they'd seen her. He wanted to be the one to cuff the bitch who'd left Senior Deputy Marshal Charles Williams dead. He rubbed the scar on his upper arm where Menendez's bullet had grazed him, reminding him he'd show this coldblooded killer no mercy. None, whatsoever.

This time she wouldn't get away.

He glanced at Marcy Hill, who sat to his right on the commercial jet. She had moxie and could hold her own with the guys. Still he watched out for her. He'd come to think of her as a little sister and would go to any length to protect her. He liked having her on his team. Sometimes criminals confessed much faster to a woman. "Look out your window."

She craned her neck to see around Braden and Darrel. "These mountains are huge. It's July, yet they're still covered with snow. That's awesome."

"Anchorage is on the other side. That's where we'll meet up with Marshals Reuben and Kneller who formed the task force. As soon as I heard about Selena, I called Marshal Reuben."

Marcy smiled. "Did you beg?"

"No, but I would've. Luckily, I didn't have to. After I explained my history with Menendez, he invited us to their party. If she's captured today, she'll be the U.S. Marshal's Catch of the Day."

"Try not to go in and take over. You're not the lead on this."

"When have I ever—"

"Try Phoenix and Oklahoma. You're going to get a reputation of being a bully. Why do you think no one ever wants the FBI involved?"

"Okay, you've made your point."

"I'm surprised Darrel and I got to come along."

"That took some doing." He rubbed the back of his neck. "I convinced Chief Deputy Reiner it'd take more than one person to haul Menendez back to Kansas. Then I mentioned it might be helpful to have a woman aboard. That's where you came in."

"Thanks. I've never been to Alaska."

"Well, get a real fast look at it, because we won't be here long. Today's Saturday. We'll be home by Monday night. Trooper Henson and his pilot will fly the task force to a helipad about ten miles from Moose Head Resort."

"And then?" Marcy asked.

"We're hooking up with park rangers. They're giving us a lift to the lodge. Menendez is about to get a wakeup call. They obtained a *no-knock* warrant. Good morning, Miss Menendez."

"How'd they swing it?"

"Alaskan State Police have a DNA match and the fact that she's murdered a federal marshal along with several others, it was easy. There's no doubt she'll be armed and dangerous. Remember that."

"Who was brave enough to get a DNA sample?" Marcy asked.

"The lodge owner snagged a hair sample from Selena's brush when she delivered linens. Remind me to hug that lady."

"What about prints?"asked Darrel Johnson—a huge black man who looked like a linebacker wearing Vanquish sunglasses with a diamond stud in one earlobe. He sat to Braden's left.

"Once the DNA results came back, prints weren't needed. The marshals have a surveillance team that drove out earlier. There'll be more troopers on hand as well. I told local units to hang back. I didn't want the target getting hinky and disappearing on us again. They'll only move in if she attempts to bail."

"Is her gang with her?" Darrel asked.

"Nah, which isn't like her. Wolves usually travel in packs. But we'll still go in with the ballistic shield and long guns. Selena won't go down without a fight. I guarantee that. I'm ready to do this."

"Well, contain your excitement," Marcy stated. "It won't come as a surprise if you end up going home empty handed. Not after the last time."

Braden rolled his eyes. He didn't want to think about Phoenix. The time when Selena gave a task force the slip. "I'll bet ya two hundred that I nail her and haul her ass to jail this time."

"I don't bet," Marcy added. "It's a frivolous waste of money."

"I sure the hell do. You're on, Wolfe," Darrel said. "You have to get Selena Menendez behind bars or you owe me two hundred."

"Deal. I'm gonna hate taking your money, Johnson. As soon as we extradite Selena back to Kansas, we'll head to your bank and get *my* money."

Darrel leaned forward and glanced at Marcy. "Was he this confident last time?"

"Yep."

This is different. Selena won't know what's hit her.

Braden couldn't wait to leave the enclosure of the jet. He didn't like sitting sandwiched between Marcy and Darrel. Also Marcy's sweet perfume made him nauseated.

She brushed her short brown hair behind her ears as distress showed on her face. "Oh, snap."

"Something wrong?" Braden asked.

"No, well, yes. I forgot to tell Alex that Brittany and Erica's soccer games were moved up an hour. I'll leave him a message."

"Good Lord, I'm glad I'm not married with a house full of kids." Braden tried to stretch his legs to get comfortable. "And I plan to stay single."

"Two kids isn't a house full." She flashed him a generous smile. "I have a friend coming from Atlanta. I'll pay for the dinner if you'll take her out."

"No, thanks. It'd take more than a free meal to entice me."

"Come on, please. I don't want to fix her up with someone who'll be hitting on her all evening for a wham-bam-thank-you-ma'am."

Darrel laughed. "She doesn't hold a very high opinion of you as a man."

"No, she doesn't." Braden grinned. "Now, angel, how do you know I wouldn't try to persuade your friend to have kinky sex with me before the evening's up?"

"Maybe she's heard you can't keep it up long enough to make a woman happy," Darrel said, then chuckled.

"I've had no complaints. Hell, I'm only thirty-three, and everything's still in perfect working order. And if I took your friend out, she could very well end up in my bed. I like sex as well as the next man."

Marcy blushed, then glanced around to see if anyone was listening. "I didn't mean for it to sound like you don't. It's just that you've never mentioned anyone. That's a loss. You're a handsome man. I've never seen eyes as green as yours. And if you'd let your hair grow instead of wearing it in that military style maybe more women would be interested."

"First of all, I like my hair just fine. I've worn it like this since I was a Marine." He ran his hand over his hair. "Second, I know plenty of willing women. I'll share a few secrets. I'm not gay. And I'm no monk. I just like keeping my personal life private."

Marcy's intense scrutiny made him edgy. "Who was she?"

He decided to play dumb. "She who?"

"The lady who turned your blood to ice water."

"I don't know what the hell you're talking about."

"Were you married to her?" Marcy asked.

"Mind your own damn business, Hill." Braden stared straight ahead, ignoring her.

Despite his warning, she continued. "But I'm right. There was a woman?"

He lowered his voice. "There are lots of women. Whenever I have the urge, I pick one up in a bar, and after a few drinks I take her to a motel, meet my manly needs, and then drop her off where I found her. It's that simple."

Though crude, this method kept him at a *safe* distance from having any kind of relationship. He had *no* intentions of becoming involved with one woman on a regular basis. *Never* again.

"Really, Wolfe? Hookers?" Marcy asked.

"Hell, no. Trust me, angel, I don't have to pay for sex."

"That's what you made it sound like. Besides, you seemed fond of that nineteen year old streetwalker. Red hair. She wore tall purple high heel boots. Used to hang out over near the stadium. Wasn't her name Summer?"

"You never told her?" Darrel asked.

Braden shook his head. "Less people who know the better."

"Know what? You have to tell me now," Marcy insisted.

"Can I?" Darrel asked like an eager kid.

Braden nodded. "Sure, knock yourself out."

"He gave the girl enough money to go back home and go to beauty school."

"Ah, Braden. You do have a heart after all. Why didn't you want anyone to know?"

"Because someone who knew would assume Summer did something in exchange. I only take out consensual women over twenty who want to indulge in hot sex with no strings attached."

"Pathetic. You need to find a nice woman and settle down."

"Yo, momma, you'd better stop jammin' on the man," Darrel warned.

She glanced around Braden and scowled at Darrel. "It's dangerous to have casual sex."

"So is being a marshal," Wolfe commented. "You gonna quit?" He knew Marcy's husband wanted her to find a job that wasn't dangerous and didn't require so many hours away from home.

"That's different. This is my job."

Darrel grinned. "Someday, you'll get a chick home and find she has an Adam's apple." He chuckled. "I'd like to see that."

"Real funny, Johnson."

Shit, these two won't shut the hell up.

Braden released an aggravated breath. "Why can't you put on headphones and watch a movie like everyone else on this flight?"

"But who'd drive you crazy?" Darrel asked.

"What about getting AIDS? Or herpes?" Marcy forged ahead with her interrogation. She wouldn't let it go.

Holy freaking crap. He thought about gagging her and requesting she be put in the cargo section. *Now that's evil.*

"I use name-brand condoms." Braden paused while the jet hit some turbulence. He grinned. "Think I'd stick my little man just anywhere without protection?"

"Little? Is that a confession?" Darrel slid his shades upon his head.

"Not at all. Trust me, he rises to the occasion. Makes me proud every time."

Darrel chuckled. "Does this little man have a name?"

"He does, but I'll never tell the likes of you."

Marcy's cheeks burned red. "This has gone too far. The last thing I want to know is your appendage's name."

"Aw, hell, what the heck," Braden said, teasing her. "I'll tell you."

She covered her ears. "Don't! Don't say it."

"This should teach you not to pry into my private life."

"I should file a sexual harassment suit," Marcy said with a hint of laughter in her voice. "You're incorrigible."

He laughed, knowing he'd gotten the best of her. For a few minutes he stared out the window as they dropped in altitude. He wanted to change the subject. "How'd your girls like the dolls I picked up in Mexico?"

"They loved them. You should receive their thank you notes soon."

He nodded, then leaned back and closed his eyes. Before he could stop himself, his mind slipped into the black zone—memories he tried to keep buried.

Daddy, are you coming? You promised you'd take me to my game.

Braden clenched his fists, wanting to punch something or someone. He forced Andy's voice away and choked on the knot in his throat.

An image of his five-year old son lying in the small casket surrounded by his favorite teddy bears and toys flashed in his mind and squeezed the muscles inside his chest.

God, I miss Andy. I miss his smile and laughter, miss the way he'd crawl into my lap and rest his head against me.

Braden's breath hitched for a moment as that old haunting pain sliced through him. Not a day passed that Braden didn't think of Andy. Because when it got right down to it, he could have prevented it.

He hated his ex-wife as much as he hated Menendez. Hate and his desire for revenge were the only two things that kept him sane, the only reasons he wanted to continue living. It'd be a life *without* children. Because when you lost one, there was no greater heartache. Marcy had hit close to the source of his pain.

◆◆◆

Sarah Mason pulled the long, touring kayak onto the bank beneath the conifers, then stopped, and breathed in deeply. The strong pine scent along with the cool, crisp summer air made her feel alive. Something she hadn't felt in a long time. She gathered the gear and walked toward her cabin. Overhead an eagle cried out as it soared through the gray sky.

The hair on the back of her neck rose, and she stopped on the path surrounded by tall pines, sensing that someone was watching. It wasn't the first time she'd had the eerie sensation. She felt like Little Red Riding Hood on her way to Grandma's house. Was the big bad wolf lurking nearby?

Alaska had a lot of predators besides wolves. Bears. Mountain lions. Either one might consider her a tasty lunch choice.

"Let's get one thing straight. I am not on today's wildlife menu."

She jingled her bear bells on the hike back to Moose Head Resort. Confronting a grizzly wasn't on her list of top ten things to do while in Alaska.

She sighed with relief when she reached the resort. Inside the cabin, she flipped on the mp3 player, letting the classical music ease her troubled mind before turning on the shower. She slipped from her clothes and stacked them neatly on the toilet lid.

A dog barked nearby, but she ignored it, tuning out everything but the rich baritone and soprano voices singing in *La Traviata*. She stepped in the shower.

No doubt, she appeared antisocial to the owner and the other guests, but she wasn't here to make friends. She came to this isolated spot to get away from the heartache she'd left in Tennessee where constant reminders of the life she'd had with her husband and son haunted her daily.

She wanted to decide what to do with her life, and she had. She wanted another child. Another child could never replace Tristen, but at least she'd have someone to love and wouldn't be alone. But how?

Adoption? Would they let her adopt? She was single now. She didn't necessarily want an infant. Surely, there were children who needed homes and someone to care about them.

She'd check into it when she returned home at the end of the summer.

After her shower, Sarah padded barefooted to the kitchen. She removed a ripe tomato, lettuce, and turkey from the refrigerator and proceeded to make a sandwich. She dropped the tomato, and it rolled.

Oh, fudge. Come back here, you sneaky tomato.

She retrieved it, rinsed it off, and made the sandwich.

Her stomach growled reminding her she hadn't eaten breakfast. She'd taken to the lake at daybreak and kayaked through the misty morning. But pulling out early had been worth it. Remembering the mother moose and its twin calves at the lake's edge, she smiled.

Simultaneously—the front and back doors *burst* open.

Sarah's heartbeat rocketed!

Uniformed men swarmed the cabin.

Their weapons aimed at her.

Fear shot up her spine.

She screamed.

Her sandwich fell from her hand.

Sweet Mary, mother of God. What's happening?

Possibilities rapidly flashed through her mind.

Her lungs deflated. She gasped for breath.

"U.S. Marshals! Let me see your hands!" shouted a tall, lean man wearing a dark jacket and a blue cap. "Now!"

"Police," another man shouted. "Get your hands up."

"Drop to your knees," a large black man ordered. The other officers shouted commands faster than she could comprehend them.

She dropped to her knees and placed her hands above her head.

"Selena Menendez, I have a federal warrant for your arrest. Lay face down, and put your hands behind you," the tall marshal demanded.

Sarah's mouth gaped open in shock. It took a few moments to find her voice. "I haven't done anything. You have the wrong person."

Before she could say another word, the marshal slammed her body on the floor, then jerked her arms behind her. His knee rested in the center of her back, pinning her down.

Her heart hammered.

Pain shot through her arms.

She cried out, "You're hurting me."

"It hurts?" he asked. She nodded. "Good," he said. "Guess those cuffs are on tight enough. What do you think, Johnson?"

The men laughed. Then she heard a woman's voice. "Don't go overboard, Wolfe. She has rights."

"She has the right to go straight to hell as far as I'm concerned," the green-eyed marshal said. He lowered his mouth to Sarah's ear. "I won't have a moment's peace until I see this cop-killing bitch executed."

His warm coffee-scented breath sent chills through her.

Sarah inhaled deeply as she tried to raise her head. "There's been a mistake. I haven't done anything."

His hand immediately slammed her face back to the floor. "Don't make me tase you."

Pain surged through her cheekbone as it made contact with the shiny hardwood. She whimpered.

Oh, God.

Why is this happening?

◆◆◆

Braden had a really weird feeling about this entire takedown. It'd been too easy. What kind of game was Menendez playing? Leaning close to her, he breathed in her fresh, clean scent. Soft and sweet like cotton sheets from a clothesline. "Angel, I didn't tell you to move. You do what I say when I say it." He gripped her arm. "Am I clear?"

"Yes," she said her voice strained and weak.

Braden had waited a long time for this moment. He stood and glanced around the room. "What's that racket?"

"Opera. Haven't you ever heard opera?" Marcy asked.

"Yeah, I've heard it, but what in the hell is she doing listening to it?" He turned to Darrel. "Grab her other arm."

As they lifted her to her feet, her robe parted open, revealing two of the most beautiful breasts he'd ever seen. Her dark olive skin tone shimmered in the light and large round nipples hardened when the cold air touched them. He raked his gaze down the front of her naked body several times before he reminded himself who this woman was and what she'd done. His resentment for her prevented any lustful thoughts.

She held her head low, and her cheeks burned red. Her reaction surprised him since it wasn't in her nature to embarrass easily. He studied her closely. Definitely Selena. Beautiful but deadly.

"What a rack," one of the men said.

"Please close my robe," she asked, shame illuminating her face.

Braden frowned at the man for the crude remark before grabbing the sides of the robe and pulling them together. His fingers lightly touched the exposed skin on her stomach—soft and smooth like fine silk, and a charge of heat shot up his arm as he thought of her as a woman rather than a fugitive.

Remember Charlie.

He tied her sash and stepped back.

He only wanted to feel disgust and hate for this woman certainly not desire. As a true siren, she used her beauty to mesmerize men before she killed them. She'd count on his male libido to cloud his mind and distract him, giving her the opportunity to strike. He cursed under his breath for his physical response. "You've worked as a stripper. Why go shy now?"

Marcy gave him a cool glare that was a warning he'd taken things too far. She didn't understand how venomous Menendez was.

"Give her even an ounce of compassion, and it might cost you your life. Think about that." He turned his attention back to his fugitive. "Selena Menendez, you're under arrest for ten counts of grand larceny, distribution of illegal substances, five counts of first degree murder, and a firearm violation." Her expression revealed sheer horror as if shocked by the charges. He finished reading her offenses. "Lady, you got some kind of rap sheet." He read her rights. "Do you understand?"

Her face tightened. "I haven't done any of those things. I'm not Selena Menendez."

Despite his effort, he couldn't stop staring at the single tear rolling down her cheek. He'd witnessed Selena confronted before in an arrest attempt, and this wasn't how it'd gone down. Instead, she'd fought and shouted profanities. Why this change?

He reassured himself this was his fugitive, the woman who'd boldly fired on him. She *had* to be Menendez. It was the face he'd seen in dreams, the face he hated.

"I want to run her prints," Marshal Reuben said.

Braden scowled at him. "No need for it. This is our girl."

"Something seems off," Marshall Kneller said, siding with his partner.

"Go for it. But you're wasting time."

"Our scanner's in the helicopter, did you bring one?" Reuben asked Braden.

"Didn't see the need. Besides, it's your show."

They asked one of the state troopers. He returned with the device and opened it. "It wasn't recharged."

Braden grinned. "Looks like none of us came to the dance with our dancing shoes on. As soon as we reach Anchorage, we'll run her prints through AFIS. If this isn't our girl, I will apologize, and you can return her to this wilderness paradise."

He stared at his fugitive for a moment before pulling a picture of Menendez from his pocket, comparing it to her. He studied her high cheekbones and finely sculptured straight nose before his gaze moved to her perfect lips and almond shaped brown eyes. The woman in the picture had lighter hair with a reddish tint to it. This woman had long dark hair, but hell, maybe she dyed it.

This had to be Selena Menendez.

Despite her outward beauty, a vile darkness harbored within. A malevolent and sadistic nature. She had no heart—only a black soul that'd make the devil proud.

When he showed her the picture, he ignored her stupefied expression. After all she was a damn good actress. She'd fooled the best of them, including Charlie. As she stared at the photo, her breathing grew rapid. Her breast crested with each breath, rising just above the top of her robe.

Liquid heat funneled through him, arousing him, but his own desire repulsed him. Until they could run her prints through the system, they'd have to assume this woman was Menendez.

He glanced over to Trooper Henson, who stood near the mp3 player. "What other files does she have?"

"Madame Butterfly. Verdi. Beethoven's Greatest Works."

"Any Santana or Latino music?"

"No. Just classical."

"It doesn't fit her profile," Marcy stated.

Braden stared into the woman's eyes. "What's your name?"

"Sarah Mason."

As he noticed the monogramming on her robe—S-M, he grinned. "How convenient to pick a name with the same initials on your robe, Selena Menendez."

"Now you hear me! My name is Sarah Mason. I don't know anyone by the name of Menendez. I live in Germantown, Tennessee outside of Memphis, and I was a nurse at the Methodist Hospital there until recently. Call them. They'll tell you."

They'll all be in bed in that part of the country. What's your driver's license number?"

"I don't have it memorized," she snapped. "My purse is under the bed."

"I'll fetch it," Marshal Kneller offered.

He returned with a huge black bag.

"Nice purse," Marcy mumbled. "I can't afford Coach."

Braden dumped the contents on the counter. It contained the usual female crap—brush, makeup, billfold, sunglasses, and phone. He opened the wallet and removed her driver license. "Sarah Mason." He studied the picture of a man and boy together. Then he tried using her phone. "No service."

"I don't have coverage here."

"Need a better service provider, angel. What's your social?"

She rattled off the numbers, then gave her address.

Braden jotted down the information, pulled out his phone, and called his headquarters. "Run a name and social. Also, see who pays the utilities for 555 Neshoba Bend, Germantown, Tennessee. Text it to me." The information came back almost immediately. He looked at the other officers. "Social and address belong to Sarah Rachel Mason, age twenty-nine."

"I told you I wasn't Selena Menendez."

He called his office back. "Pull a photo from the Tennessee DMV for Sarah Rachel Mason and send it to my phone."

He didn't have to wait long before it came back. The lady in the picture had the same face as his fugitive. The same face on her license. He grinned and held his phone up. "So what'd you do with Sarah Mason after you stole her identity? Murder her?"

He really didn't need the prints to know this was his fugitive.

"I'm Sarah Mason. Please, believe me."

Braden flashed her a grin. "Until we reach Anchorage and can verify your story, you're stuck with me."

"Look, my maiden name is Sabatini."

"Italian? Yeah, right. And I'm Chinese."

He could tell the others had their doubts about this woman being Menendez. How could she be anyone else? Then he remembered the birthmark.

"There's one way to end this." Braden jerked the robe over her shoulder and revealed a birthmark that resembled the shape of Florida. "That birthmark tells a different story.

You're good. And the Academy Award goes to Selena Menendez."

The woman lifted her chin bravely and glared at him. "Until you know for sure, you have no right to treat me like an animal. No right at all. I'm innocent until proven guilty. Isn't that what they say?"

He laughed. "Lady, in my book, you're guilty until proven otherwise. And that's how it's gonna be."

"Braden, it's still innocent until proven guilty," Marcy reminded.

Marshal Reuben still didn't look convinced.

Hell, it'd kill Braden if these goobers let her go. That could happen. The final call belonged to Marshal Reuben. He thought of what Marcy had said about being a bully and taking over. Well, maybe he was being pushy, but he didn't care. He'd waited a long time for this.

"I saw her kill Charlie," Braden said. "I don't need a jury to tell me she's guilty."

His fugitive's face paled, and her eyes filled with tears, making her appear vulnerable and frightened—not what he expected from her.

When her legs buckled beneath her and her eyes closed, Braden caught her in his arms, lifted her, and lowered her to a small sofa. Could she be faking? He touched her cheek and saw she was out cold. He checked her pulse and felt the small thump of life as blood flowed through her veins.

Aw, crap. She's fainted for God's sake.

He expelled a heavy breath to ease the tension.

Unconscious, she appeared so peaceful and innocent, which made it difficult to believe she had a witch's heart.

Darrel folded his arms as he studied Selena. "It looks like her, but something doesn't seem right. Her ID info checked out."

The two Alaskan marshals nodded in agreement. The troopers appeared more amused over the dilemma.

Braden frowned. "Stolen identity. Hell, the real Sarah Mason is probably in a shallow grave somewhere. If it looks like a duck, quacks like a duck, then it's a damn duck. End of discussion. You're just hoping it's not her, so you don't have to cough up the two hundred. I won. Admit it."

Darrel grinned. "Nah, you haven't. The bet stated you have to get her behind bars. So, it's far from being over."

"She's running scared to have hidden here and go as far as taking someone's identity," Braden stated. "As we say, you can run, but you can't hide."

"I'd hide too if Dagastino had a contract on my head," Marcy commented.

"She should've known killing his only son and stealing his shipment of coke would piss him off," Braden said. "And if he gets wind of her capture, he might try to take her."

"Kansas won't be the only state wanting her," Marshal Kneller added.

Braden grinned. "Well, let them get in line. We were here first."

"But what if she's the wrong woman? What if she really is Sarah Mason?" Marcy asked. "I've always heard everyone has a double."

He held out the picture for her to see. "Her DNA was a positive match. She has the birthmark. She looks exactly like the picture except for the hair." When he saw she wasn't convinced, he sighed. "Aw, damn. She's faked seizures. This fainting spell could be just another attempt to stall us until she can figure out how to escape. Do you really think this could be anyone but Menendez?"

Marcy shook her head. "I guess not. But she doesn't have a Latino accent, and no weapons have been found."

"She dropped her accent. It's all part of her damn act. She thought she was safe being this other woman, this Sarah Mason." Right now he didn't care about accents or guns. *Damn it.* This was *his* fugitive.

"Since we have the DNA match, we'll take her to Anchorage," Marshal Reuben said, trying to show some authority. More than likely the guy feared Braden was right, and he'd never live it down if he let her escape. "Let's do this and get the hell out of here."

Braden walked over to the sofa and knelt down. "Menendez, wake up." He patted her cheeks. "Wake up."

Finally, her eyes blinked open. She appeared disoriented and confused for a moment until recollection of her situation showed on her face. "I was hoping maybe I had dreamt it all."

"No darlin', it's no dream. But I assure you that I'm your worst nightmare." He jerked her to her feet. "Hill is going to help you get dressed. Frankly, I don't give a rat's ass whether I drag you to Kansas buck-naked. So if you try anything, you might find yourself still wearing that robe."

Shards of ice shot from her eyes, revealing the anger and hate she felt for him. Good, that's what he wanted. A black bruise had already formed where her face hit the floor. A small surge of guilt bothered him for a moment. He'd been raised not to manhandle women, but this was different. This woman was a killer, a heartless psychopath.

Trooper Henson removed his wide brim navy hat, then rubbed his forehead with his arm. "You need any help?"

"I can handle her," Marcy replied.

Braden scowled. "Give me your hardware until you come out."

Marcy didn't argue and gave up her weapons.

He turned to Selena. "Now Johnson and I will be just on the other side of that door."

Ten minutes later when Marcy opened the door, Selena Menendez walked out dressed in jeans and hiking boots. She raised her eyes to his. "Aren't you going to pack my things?"

"Hell, no." Braden rubbed his hand over his hair, then looked at Marcy. "Shit...grab a couple of changes of clothes for her. But that's it."

"My toothbrush, please."

"Grab that too," Braden said, with a frustrated sigh. Showing this woman any consideration, any compassion whatsoever pissed him off. He didn't want to go soft. He wanted to make this woman's life a living hell. If he hadn't gone soft on his ex-wife, Andy might still be alive. His blood heated, rising to a boiling point. He wanted revenge for Andy and for Charlie, but he had to keep his hostility buried. He forced the old anger down and uncoiled his fists before breathing in several deep breaths.

"Thank you," Selena whispered.

He stared into her deep brown eyes and saw she truly meant it. She had slanted, exotic eyes with long thick lashes. He didn't want this woman being appreciative.

"And my jacket."

"Don't push your luck."

Marshal Reuben glanced at other marshals who'd driven in and been there all week on surveillance. "Kneller's riding back with you. Can you box up her belongings and bring them back with you?"

"Yeah, we'll take care of it."

◆◆◆

Sarah couldn't believe what was happening. She had to try one more time to convince this marshal who seemed to be in charge that she wasn't his fugitive. "Look, I'm Sarah Mason. I've never even had a speeding ticket. I'm not a criminal. Can't you just look at me and tell I'm not the type to break a law, let alone murder someone?"

"Apparently, the person who called your name into *America's Most Wanted* thought you were." U.S. Marshall Braden Wolfe sneered. "You fooled Charlie right before you shot him at pointblank range, but you won't fool me, so shut the hell up, Selena."

How could he believe she was this Selena Menendez? The *idiot* wouldn't listen. Of course she had to admit, the picture he'd shown her of this Selena woman could've been her. While they shared the same dark slanted eyes and hair, the other woman had a harsh expression and cold eyes.

But they also shared the same birthmark. How?

"I'm *not* that woman in the picture."

"Save your breath. We have a DNA match."

Sarah's stomach rose into her throat.

She had been raised an only child. Someone with the same DNA and birthmark would have to be her twin. The possibility of having a sister left her speechless. How? It would mean she'd been adopted. For now, she pushed the thought aside and studied the jerk calling the shots.

Despite the marshal's masculine, attractive face and his piercing green eyes, he was a number one ass. His height and proud stance intimidated her more. And each time he glared at her, she could feel the hate radiating from his eyes. Dangerous eyes that made her feel as though he was strangling her each time his burning gaze landed on her.

"This cabin is mine for the summer," she stated. "I doubt my money will be refunded."

"Don't you worry, angel. We'll give you the best accommodations money can buy. Cozy little eight by ten cell with its own urinal and sink." He grinned slyly and winked. "With a good view."

She wanted to claw his eyes out. "I plan to sue you."

"You go right ahead, darlin'." Amusement danced in his green eyes, and he flashed a nasty, sarcastic grin. "Johnson, put the waist chain and leg irons on. "

God, I despise this man.
Rotten low-down jerk.

She had no choice but to go with him.

Surely, in Anchorage, she'd be able to prove her true identity. While twins shared the same DNA, they had their own set of fingerprints. First thing, she'd contact an attorney.

"Trust me, you're better off with me than Dagastino," Wolfe said. "When the state buries you, you'll be in one piece. If he catches up with you, he'll slice and dice you into a thousand pieces and then use you for fish bait."

Sarah's entire body tensed. If the cops believed she was this Menendez woman, so would this other man, this Dagastino.

The man who would turn her into *fish bait.*

Chapter Two

Braden hoped the news of Menendez's arrest wouldn't make it to the lower forty-eight. The *America's Most Wanted* film crew shot the footage of her being escorted from the cabin to the car, but that wouldn't air until next week. By then, Selena would be behind bars.

As he escorted Menendez to the blue and white AS355 Twin Star helicopter with the Alaskan State Trooper logo on the side, he kept a tight grip on her upper arm. She had a difficult time staying in step with him because of the shackles.

Inside the chopper, Darrel claimed a window seat.

Braden placed Selena in the middle seat behind the cockpit and secured her shoulder restraint and lap belt. He'd forgotten how tight choppers were. He glanced back at Marcy and Marshal Reuben in the narrow space in the rear, sitting on a bench seat. She'd been stuck in the same spot coming down.

Trooper Henson climbed up front with Dan, the pilot.

"Nice chopper," Braden shouted to the front.

Dan twisted around. "Yep, she's our newest addition. Twin engines with a lift off of 6.6m/sec. Holds the pilot and five passengers with a payload up to 6,172 pounds. She's sweet. You fly?"

"Planes. Helicopters are too complicated. How are things looking?"

"There's a front moving in, bringing a lot of cloud coverage. Right now we have a visibility ten miles or less. I hope we'll be back in Anchorage before it hits."

Damn. Of all the rotten luck. Braden wanted Menendez behind bars as soon as possible. He didn't need this delay. He didn't want her getting a *Get Out of Jail Free* card. He placed his headset on. "Let's lift off."

The rotor on top came to life. The blades cast shadows inside the interior. Dan kept the chopper hovering low while building speed, then lifted upward in one swooping motion.

Thirty minutes into the flight, the sky and earth seemingly joined by a white haze of thick clouds. Being a licensed pilot himself, he didn't like the conditions. "That front is moving in fast," he said loudly into his mouthpiece. "You got any idea where we can put down?"

"There's a large hunting lodge nearby with a helipad," Trooper Henson replied.

"How far?"

"About fifty miles." When they neared the lodge, Henson glanced at him. "You call it. Want to stop?"

Braden stared at Selena and thought about all the things that could go wrong. He'd never live it down if somehow she escaped. But he couldn't risk the lives of everyone aboard. "Considering our visibility is decreasing rapidly, take it down."

The pilot radioed the lodge and announced their arrival.

After Braden stepped from the helicopter onto the helipad, ducking beneath the blades, he walked toward the lodge's office. The rustic lodge, constructed of pine and fieldstone with a covered porch wrapped around it, appealed to him. He paid for the remaining vacant rooms, then returned to the chopper, climbed upon the landing skid, and glanced through the door.

"We have three rooms. Two connect. Hill and Menendez will share a room. Johnson and I'll take the connecting room. Henson, Reuben, and Dan will take the other. Let's get settled in our rooms and rest a few hours before dinner."

◆◆◆

Braden knocked before opening the connecting door into Marcy's room. Selena sat on the edge of one bed while Marcy rested on the other. Hill glanced up and smiled. "This is small but comfortable. I love it here."

A muscle twitched in his jaw. It irritated the hell out of him that she acted like this was a vacation. "Don't forget this isn't a damn slumber party. Secure her to the bed or a chair."

"She's in full restraints with a padlock. Where can she go?"

"You'd be amazed at what she's capable of." He walked over to Menendez and pulled her up from the bed. "Move it, lady. Up toward the headboard." He jerked the pillows from beneath the bedspread and stacked them against the decorative bars. "Sit up and lean back."

She obeyed. A whimper escaped her lips as he secured her to the headboard using a sit-belt for extra security. The wide leather strap would hold her.

"I brought this all the way from Kansas just for you."

At first her icy glare made him flinch, but then he reminded himself that's what he wanted, for her to loathe him. Any time she thought of hate, he wanted her to see his face.

◆◆◆

"Daddy, you promised."

"I know I did, Andy, but we have to do what the judge said."

"But I don't want to live with Grandma and Paw Paw.

"My lawyer is working on it. Hang in there, buddy."

Braden grimaced from the painful memory. He opened his eyes and stared at the ceiling. Had he been dreaming about Andy? Is that why the haunting words were the first thing that came to mind?

The aroma of cooked beef drifted up from the small diner connected to the lodge. He sat up and rubbed the back of his neck before he stood. His stomach rumbled, reminding him it was dinnertime.

He glanced over at the other bed. "Wake up, Johnson. Naptime's over. Let's go eat."

Darrel yawned and stretched. "All right, man. I'm awake."

"Get the others while I wake Hill." Braden walked to the connecting door and knocked. "Marcy, I'm coming in."

She sat up and stretched. "What time is it?"

"About eight. Let's grab a bite to eat before the diner closes," he said, then gave Menendez a hard glare. "Okay, sweetheart, you're going out on the town. Behave, or I'll find some closet to lock you in."

He freed her from the belt that held her against the bed's railing and witnessed the intense pain on her face when she attempted to move her stiff arms.

"You had it too tight." Marcy scooted by him and quickly massaged each of Selena's arms. "Is that better?"

She nodded. "Thank you, Marcy."

"Now isn't that sweet. Girlfriends." He jerked Marcy around. "Hill, you'd better keep your guard up and toughen your heart. Because she doesn't give a damn whether you see your family again or not. Charlie made the mistake of showing this bitch an inch of mercy, and it landed him six feet under."

◆◆◆

Sarah had never been so humiliated as when she entered the small diner.

Silverware clanked against plates as people stopped eating and stared with condemning eyes at the cuffs and ankle restraints linked to the waist chain. She hobbled beside Wolfe like a geisha. But the savory aromas reminded her she was about to get a hot meal, so she ignored the stares.

The pilot and state trooper sat at the counter.

Wolfe guided her to a table and pulled out a chair. "Sit."

Once the marshals were seated, a waitress brought out menus. Her face paled as her gaze lingered on Sarah's cuffed wrists. With her pad in hand, she glanced at Wolfe first. "What's it gonna be?"

Wolfe shifted his gaze to Marcy. "Ladies first."

She glanced up from the menu. "Grilled chicken sandwich, a garden salad, and sweet tea."

Johnson and the other deputies ordered.

Wolfe released a tired breath as he stared at the menu. "I'll have a steak-medium rare, with fries, and rolls. Give me coffee with that. Go ahead and bring me that slice of apple pie I saw in the case. I'll eat that while I wait."

"Ma'am, what will you have?" the waitress asked Sarah.

"I'll have—"

Wolfe spoke for her. "What's on the blue plate special?"

"Meatloaf, potatoes, and white beans. But, this late I'm not sure there's any left. They've already started cleaning the kitchen."

"Scrap the bottom of the pan and give her the blue plate special with a tall glass of tap water."

I hate this man.

"Wolfe, let her pick something," Marcy said.

"So long as a meal is provided, I'm within the guidelines. It doesn't specify what kind of food. Hell, she's lucky I'm following the rules today."

Sarah wanted to clobber Wolfe over the head with the heavy salt and pepper shakers.

The waitress returned shortly with Braden's pie. Sarah couldn't tear her gaze away from it. It smelled heavenly. She could almost taste it.

The rest of the food arrived, and the lingering aromas overwhelmed Sarah, causing her stomach to growl loud enough that Wolfe looked at her. "Hell, woman. You should've eaten lunch." He flashed a devilish grin. "Enjoy."

Ass.

Her stomach clenched into a painful knot. She couldn't resist glancing around the table at the delicious looking hot food on their plates. Her gaze stopped on the dried out meatloaf, a lump of hard potatoes, and beans that had been heated so much they looked like a dried out desert floor.

Wolfe polished off his pie before cutting into his steak and taking a bite, chewing it slowly with his eyes closed. "Damn that's good and juicy."

Sarah refused to show any reaction to his taunting. Her restraints were designed so she could raise her hands to the table. She managed to grab the fork, break off a bite of meat and raised it to her mouth. She scowled at the taste. *Disgusting*. She tried a bite of potatoes, but couldn't swallow the thick, cold clump. A sharp pain inched down her throat when it went down. She gagged and coughed.

Wolfe held the glass to her lips. "Drink."

She gulped down the cold water. "Thank you."

His eyes held her gaze for a moment.

Please look at me closely. Please see that I'm not this Menendez woman.

He dropped his gaze to his plate and shoveled down a few more bites and swigged his coffee before looking at her again.

He had *that* nasty grin on his face, the one she despised.

Marcy stopped eating. "That food looks like it was left over from lunch. You're being a bastard, Wolfe."

"Hill, there's nothing I could do that would be bad enough to this woman. Every time I look at her, I'm consumed with hate, and I think about Charlie. About his wife and three kids who don't have him in their lives anymore because of this bitch. Don't lecture me again."

Johnson glanced at Marcy. "Did you ever leave that message about the soccer game?"

"Yes. I hope Alex got it. I'd hate for the girls to miss their games. They'd never forgive me."

Memories of soccer games flooded Sarah's mind, and she envisioned her son's giddy face after winning a game. She swallowed back the pain. She glanced at Marcy. "How old are your girls?"

"Nine and seven."

Sarah gave Marcy a faint smile. "My son loved playing soccer too."

Wolfe stopped eating. "I don't recall you having a son, Menendez. I know you've had like four abortions."

"I've never had an abortion. Never! And I did have a son. The picture of the boy in my wallet was my son, Tristen."

"So where is this kid now?" Wolfe asked a confident smile on his smug face.

"He's dead." She breathed in several deep breaths. "He and his father were killed in a head-on collision about a year and a half ago. It'll be two years on Christmas Eve."

They stared at her unsure of whether to believe her, maybe unsure of what to say. Wolfe stared the longest and for just a moment his hard, uncompassionate eyes softened, and a degree of tenderness showed in his expression. For just a moment, she caught a glimpse of a different man—a gentler man with regrets.

She reminded herself he was still the same thoughtless ass who continued to treat her like crap. In Anchorage when her prints didn't match Selena Menendez's, she wanted to have a front row seat. She wanted to watch the shock and confusion on his face when he realized he'd arrested the wrong woman.

Damn, that'll be sweet. One epic moment.

Sarah would make him pay once the truth was known. Not only did she plan to sue him for all he was worth, she wanted him fired. She put her fork down. "I'm done."

"Hell, don't eat," he said. As if changing into a different mask, his face tightened, appearing hard and merciless again. "I don't care."

Somewhere beneath Wolfe's gruff exterior was a tender, softer man. Why did he work so hard at hiding his emotions?

"I'm going to order her something else," Marcy said and waved at the waitress. "I wouldn't feed that blue plate special to my dog."

"You don't have a dog, Hill. If she were really hungry, she'd eat it."

Marshal Reuben eyed everyone at the table. "We need to turn in early so we can leave at dawn."

Wolfe glanced at his watch. "Finish up." Then he tossed a twenty-dollar bill on the table for the waitress and stared at Sarah with a stern expression. With his large hand grasping her arm tightly, he jerked her up from the chair in one lifting motion.

It angered her that his touch caused a feverish heat to spread through her. Sensual in nature. And the idea of feeling anything for this man of stone alarmed her.

Scared her.

Confused her.

But mainly, it embarrassed her.

He yanked her several times almost making her fall while escorting her through the lodge. Back in the room, he secured her to the headboard again. "Where the hell is Hill?" He shouted into the other room. "Johnson, where is Hill?"

"Don't have a clue."

The door off the main hall opened, and Marcy entered. "I called home using my calling card on the lodge's phone. My cell won't work this far out." She stood beside the bed. "Isn't there some way of securing her so she can lie down?"

"Probably, but I want her to sit awake all night and think about what little mercy she's shown all the people she's killed."

"I've never killed anyone. I couldn't," Sarah said, wishing Wolfe would see who she really was and know she couldn't be his fugitive. "Please, let me lie down to sleep. I'm so tired," she pleaded.

"Hell, no." He stalked around the beds toward the connecting door, then paused and stared at her. His gaze moved over her face in slow motion and again his eyes mellowed. Pity perhaps. He walked back to the bed and removed the belt that secured her tightly to the headboard. "I'm doing this for Marcy, not for you."

Strange, but she knew he was lying. The man had a heart. Maybe a teeny teeny tiny one like the Grinch, but nevertheless a heart.

"Lay down."

She did.

"Don't try to leave."

"Thank you," Sarah whispered.

"Don't thank me. I just don't want to listen to all your bellyaching tomorrow." With that said, he walked from the room, stopping in the doorway. "Hill, don't trust her. You let her get away, and you're making good on my wager with Darrel."

"Hey, that's not fair." Marcy griped.

"I have a bad feeling about this," Wolfe said, pinning Sarah with a hard look.

"Go. Everything is under control," Marcy assured him.

Relief trickled through Sarah when Wolfe finally left. Besides making her angry, he made her nervous and edgy. And she knew why, though she hated to admit it. Several times her blood had raced with heated sexual sparks when he stood near her or when his breath kissed her cheek. How could her body respond to him? Not only did she still love Mark, she despised this man.

Marcy removed a wrapped sandwich from her purse. "I was afraid he'd smell this. Then there'd be hell to pay. It's just a cheeseburger."

Sarah smiled and breathed in its aroma. "You're a saint. Thank you."

Don't get any ideas that because I'm nice, I'm a pushover. I'd hate to be forced to shoot you. Am I clear?"

"Yes, I understand. So why the concern?"

"I didn't enjoy my food because your dinner looked horrible. He should've made them return it to the kitchen."

"It was cold and yucky."

"Braden can be a real bastard."

"Because of his friend Charlie?"

"I'm not sure. He's been this way ever since he was assigned to the Kansas City District. We learned quickly he doesn't like to talk about himself." Marcy unfolded the foil and held the burger to Sarah's mouth. "But he's good at his job. And he'd give his life for any of us."

"What about family?" Sarah asked, then took another bite.

"He never mentions anyone. He's single. I know his parents are alive, and he has some brothers. For some reason, he never visits them. When I found out he was all alone on Christmas and didn't have plans, I invited him to my house, but he thanked me and declined. Later, I overhead him tell someone he ate a chicken potpie for Christmas dinner."

It reminded Sarah of her holiday meal—a turkey TV dinner. She'd been invited to dine with friends, but Christmas was a difficult time for her.

After Sarah finished the sandwich, Marcy wadded the foil and tossed it in the trashcan. Then she removed her phone.

"I thought your phone wouldn't work."

Marcy grinned. "I'm amazed Wolfe bought that. There's a tower behind the lodge. I couldn't tell him I was hanging back to order you something."

Sarah laughed, for the first time feeling a little relaxed.

She tried not to listen to Marcy's private conversation while the lady marshal cheered over her daughters' victories and expressed her love to them before disconnecting.

The thought of family and home stirred up memories of Sarah's husband, Mark, and her son, Tristen. Tears sprang to her eyes. Mark's last words to her had been, *Love you. See you later.*

Later never came.

♦♦♦

Until there was proof otherwise, Marcy had to assume this woman was a fugitive who would read her kindness as a weakness that she could use to her advantage to escape. Marcy had to remember what Braden had said about letting her guard down around this woman. She pushed her doubts aside about this being someone besides Menendez.

She snapped off the light and pulled the blanket over her shoulder. The heavy drapes kept out the dim light of the Alaskan night, making the room dark.

Marcy's thoughts returned to her own problems. At least Alex left his love nest with Tiffany long enough to take the girls to their games. It seemed like months since he proclaimed his love for another woman and moved out, but it had only been three weeks. She drifted to sleep thinking about the child she carried. A child she hadn't told Alex about. The bastard didn't deserve to know.

During the night, Menendez's soft sobs woke Marcy. Obviously, Selena had some regrets for the things she'd done. Or maybe she was upset because she'd been caught. "Try to sleep. You got yourself into this mess."

Marcy couldn't allow herself to feel pity for this woman who placed no value on human life but her own. Marcy's emotions could get in the way. At the wrong moment, it could cost her.

The sobbing stopped. "It's not what you think. Yes, I'm upset over being arrested and treated like this, but I should be able to prove who I really am once we reach Anchorage."

Marcy didn't reply at first. She recalled what Selena had said about her son and husband. But Menendez had never had a family. If this woman were Menendez, they would've found guns in the cabin. Again the unnerving thought entered her mind.

Maybe this isn't Menendez.

She'd never convince Braden.

"Tell me about your husband," Marcy said. She turned on the small lamp on the nightstand.

"Why? You wouldn't believe me."

"I might." Then another possibility occurred to her. "Did you have any siblings growing up?"

"No, I was an only child. My father was a butcher in Austin, Texas. He owned his own shop, and Mother taught piano lessons."

"Do you play?" Marcy asked.

"Yes, I do."

That explained the classical music. "I always wanted to play the drums, but my parents ignored my musical aspirations."

Selena laughed. Or was it Sarah? Marcy mused over the two very different women. "Explain the birthmark?"

"What?"

"The birthmark. You have Selena's birthmark."

"Let her explain it. She has mine." They both laughed, then she continued. "That bothers me. How can two people be so much alike unless we're twins? When I studied genetics, I learned that identical twins can have the same birthmark."

"Twins separated at birth," Marcy said. "Your DNA was a match. If your prints are different, there's no other way to explain it."

"This might sound crazy, but I want to meet Selena when she's finally captured. I've always wanted a sister. Of course, she's not exactly what I had in mind."

"Please just stop." Marcy couldn't listen to any more. What if Selena was playing her for a fool? "Just wait until we get to Anchorage. Like you said, we'll know the truth then." But as she thought it over, she had a really strong feeling this woman wasn't Menendez, and Wolfe would have to eat humble pie and admit he'd been wrong. He'd be in one hell of a bad mood.

"After I sue Wolfe, I hope he ends up on the side of the road with a *Will Work for Food* sign in his hands. I want him digging in trash cans and pissing in alleys."

Marcy's laugh turned to snorts as she envisioned the things the woman across from her said.

"All jokes aside, if Selena and I turn out to be sisters, it means I was adopted. There's no way my mother would've given up a child, so how were we separated?"

"You'll probably never know."

"I wonder if Selena knows I exist. There used to be an old Christmas movie Grandma Sofia had about two sisters who performed in nightclubs together. Every Christmas I watched it with her."

"White Christmas," Marcy said. "My grandmother insisted we watch it every year. George Clooney's aunt, Rosemary Clooney was one of them. She ends up with Bing Crosby. Everyone overacted. It was so corny."

"True, but I liked the song they sang about sisters. Every time I heard that song, I'd wished for a sister." After a few moments of silence, the woman claiming to be Sarah began to sing softly. "Sisters, sisters."

Marcy joined Sarah, singing in unison. As they sang, their voices grew louder.

"Lord help the mister that comes between me and my sister, and Lord help the sister that comes between me and my man."

The connecting door burst open. Wearing only boxers, Braden stood in the doorway, an angry bull ready to charge. "What the hell is going on in here? A damn variety show?"

For a moment, Marcy could've sworn Wolfe turned purple as he exploded into the room like a rocket.

"Get up. Move over behind her," he said. "I'm sleeping in this one. You're in here laughing like a couple of sorority sisters. Hell, this woman's a coldblooded killer, and you want to be her BFF. What's gotten into you, Marcy?"

"You've got the wrong woman."

"Like hell."

◆◆◆

Braden couldn't believe the camaraderie between the two women. He waited until Marcy climbed in the full-sized bed behind Menendez before reaching for the light. Just as he was about to click the switch, he caught a glimpse of something shiny in the trashcan. He leaned over, lifted it out, then unfolded the foil and saw the mustard and dried cheese on it.

"I'm not believing this, Hill. You went behind my back and bought her something to eat."

Marcy sat up and looked at him. "I did, and I'm not sorry, Wolfe. I won't be inhumane to anyone even Menendez."

He wanted to shake some sense into Marcy.

"We'll discuss this tomorrow, Hill." Braden turned off the light and laid in the dark room, outraged. *Shit.* If it hadn't been for the damn fog, they'd be in Anchorage.

"Did you see his face," Selena whispered.

"I thought his eyes were going to pop out of his head," Marcy whispered back.

Selena giggled. "Like one of those cartoon characters when their eyes bulge a foot out of their sockets."

This is too much.

Braden cleared his throat to attract their attention. "Hill, I don't want you working with me anymore."

Marcy sat up again. "That's not fair."

"You could jeopardize the lives of everyone on the task force because you're too soft for the job."

"I'm not soft. I just don't believe this woman is Selena Menendez."

"She's playing you, Marcy, just like she did Charlie. Once we're back, I'm writing a full report on your inappropriate behavior, and I can't see you moving up from a GL9. Hell, I can't guarantee you'll have a job."

"Bastard," Selena whispered. "Don't let him upset you. Once my identity is known, he'll be the one looking idiotic. When he's fired, you'll have the last laugh. You might even get his job."

Marcy's sniffles turned into soft giggles. "Shh...you'll have him trying to sleep between us. Besides, maybe it's for the best. I'm pregnant. Go to sleep, Sarah. We have a long day ahead of us."

Something in Braden's heart jolted as he heard Marcy actually refer to Selena as Sarah. Damn, if Selena didn't have Marcy bamboozled. Then Marcy's confession of being pregnant played through his mind, and his anger toward her dissolved.

Again, he thought of Selena Menendez and the profile *"America's Most Wanted"* had done recently. Then he mentally reviewed the other profiles he'd read about her.

"Marcy, you weren't there when Charlie died. He was about to cuff Menendez when she fell to the ground and started convulsing in tremors with her eyes rolled back in her head. Charlie, thinking she was having a seizure, leaned over her to see what he could do. She grabbed his gun and shot him point blank in the gut before turning it on me."

"I'm aware of what went down."

"She can be so believable. You're not the first one she's tricked."

"I see a difference in them. Sarah's nose is more slender, and her eyebrows have more of an arch than in the picture. I don't think it's my imagination."

"You're delusional." He paused for a moment. "How long have you known you're pregnant?"

"Only a week. I'm about four weeks along. I'd planned to request a desk job."

He rolled on his side, facing the other bed. "I won't say anything if you'll request the desk job."

"Thanks, Braden. I'm sorry. But something tells me Darrel's gonna be two hundred dollars richer."

"We'll know in Anchorage." He plumped the pillow up and closed his eyes. He fell asleep assuring himself that the woman was Menendez.

◆◆◆

Where are you?" Dagastino asked his nephew, Michael. After his son's death, he decided he needed someone to continue the Dagastino family's reign, especially with a weakening power structure due to so many Latino, Asian, and Russian gangs moving in. He chose Michael. It required some lies and underhanded maneuvers to make the kid give up his life and come willingly. This was the kid's first job, and after this his soul would belong to the family business.

"We had to land in a riverbed about a mile from the lodge where they're staying," Michael replied.

"You got everything you need for the job?"

"Yeah. We're good."

"Who is going in?"

"Lenny."

"Tell him to get in and out without being seen."

"Will do. He's leaving now. We'll be right behind them tomorrow. As soon as they make an emergency landing, we'll land, and while they're still dazed, we'll take Selena. By this time Wednesday, you should have your hands on her," Michael said.

"Don't count on it. The bitch is luckier than hell."

Chapter Three

Daddy, can we go to the monster truck show? Ben and his dad are going. Can we? Pleeeease.

If I can arrange to be in town.

Braden traded assignments with a guy and made Andy the happiness kid in the world. They left the show and stopped at Five Guys for dinner.

He had lain awake for only a few moments but as usual haunting memories filled his mind. He bolted upward from the pillow into a sitting position. He pushed the blanket back, then checked the time. Five A.M.

He turned on the lamp before glancing at the bed beside him. Menendez slept facing him. The image of Selena's distorted face as she cursed profanities played in his mind. Just for a second he thought this woman wasn't Selena, but then his common sense kicked in. He wouldn't be as gullible as Marcy.

"Wake up, ladies. Look alive." He yawned and stretched. "Because of your late night antics, I feel like shit." He shook Selena. "Rise and shine." He pinned Marcy with a harsh look. "Don't take any chances with her."

Braden slipped into the other room and dressed.

Fifteen minutes later, he returned to the women's room. Selena sat on the edge of the bed with her hands cuffed and feet shackled. He glanced at Marcy and noticed the cell phone next to her ear.

"Liar," he whispered.

She had the nerve to smile at him.

"Listen, Mom. I think Braden's ready for us to pull out. Give the girls my love." After she put her phone away, she turned to Braden. "I'm hungry. I hope we have time to eat."

"Nope, Trooper Henson is grabbing some coffee and doughnuts to go."

On the wide front porch, Braden stared at the blue sky. He stretched his arms up over his head and breathed in the fresh pine-scented air. He thought about taking some time off and returning here when he finished this job. Do a little hunting or fly-fishing. Relax for once. Of course anytime he let his guard down, guilt over his son's death tormented him.

Visibility wouldn't be a problem today. He spotted Dan at the helipad about ten yards away, doing the preflight check.

"How's it looking?" he shouted.

"We're good to go."

Darrel stood from the large Adirondack chair and joined Braden at the edge of the porch. "Hill's husband might not approve of you sleeping with them."

"Hell, if I hadn't, Selena would've convinced Marcy to turn her loose by morning."

"Hill's usually a real good judge of character."

"Yeah, I thought so too before this. I'll get Menendez aboard."

After relieving Marcy of Menendez, Braden walked her to the blue and white chopper. The others entered behind him.

"Okay, I rode in that cramped cargo section yesterday," Marcy complained. "Someone else needs to sit back there today."

"But you fit, I don't," Darrel argued.

"It makes me motion sick," she countered.

"I'll take the back again," Marshal Reuben offered.

Braden gave Darrel the look.

"Aw, man." Darrel frowned. "I can't see out the window from there."

Marcy smiled. "Live with it."

Darrel squeezed in the small space in back of them.

Braden leaned over his prisoner, pulled the shoulder harness and lap belt into place. He couldn't help but feel her breath against the side of his face. She smelled feminine. As soon as his safety restraints were in place, he leaned back, closed his eyes, and pinched the bridge of his nose for a second.

Henson slid into the copilot's seat, then turned and offered a box to Marcy. "Sunday morning special. Doughnuts and coffee."

She selected one and passed the box to Braden.

"Thanks, man." He offered one to Selena. "If I don't give you one, Marcy will just sneak it to you later."

"I heard that," Marcy said.

Braden passed the box to Darrel and Marshal Reuben. Then took the coffee and passed it around.

Selena held the doughnut like it was an exquisite porcelain piece and raised it to her mouth. Her tongue darted out and gracefully licked the chocolate from it.

Braden couldn't help but stare. Liquid heat poured into his groin, and he stifled back a groan. She had an inviting mouth with full, soft lips that'd make a man fantasize all the different ways she could use it. He looked away quickly not wanting to find anything about this woman desirable.

"Ummm. . .I love chocolate," she said, letting out a long stretching moan of pleasure.

He inhaled a sharp breath, trying not to think about how sexy she sounded. But he couldn't. His mind asked the question before he could stop it. What would she sound like having an orgasm? Would it be the same soft erotic sound? Hell. He didn't want this.

He finished off his coffee before shouting to Dan. "Take it up. I'm ready to leave Oz."

Johnson and the others laughed.

"Wolfe, you're the closest thing I've seen to a winged monkey," Marcy said. "Fly yourself back to Kansas."

Braden laughed. "Cute, Hill." He glanced at his prisoner. She was scrutinizing him as though he were a germ under a microscope. He grinned. "What? Does it surprise you that I have a sense of humor?"

She shrugged. "Why should I care? I just want to reach Anchorage where you can run my prints and find out I'm not this Menendez woman. And then I never want to see you again." She paused a second. "With the exception of court when I sue you."

"I'll see you in court all right, but you'll be the one in the hot seat." Braden slipped on the headset.

Dan put the main rotor into motion and taxied forward, hovering above the ground.

Braden always enjoyed the first moments when the huge mechanical bird lifted into the air. Within seconds, it flew through the valleys of lush conifers between the tall snow covered peaks, slowly lifting.

He leaned his head back and closed his eyes. Again he mentally reviewed Selena's files. He remembered something he'd read. She couldn't eat chocolate without a reaction, and she'd just eaten a chocolate doughnut.

Like a crocodile, he cocked one eye open partially and studied Selena's long thin arms but didn't see the slightest redness. Flustered, he sat upright and frowned. "Let's talk chocolate."

"Chocolate?" she echoed. "You don't exactly look like Betty Crocker."

"Left my apron at home. How long before your skin breaks out?"

She stared at him with a baffled expression. "What are you talking about?"

"You're allergic to chocolate."

"No, I'm not," she retorted.

Braden glanced at his watch out of habit before staring out the window at the wilderness they glided above. The blades cast a shadow against the landscape below like a large eagle scouting for a kill.

Marcy cleared her throat. "Maybe she's not getting the rash because she's Sarah and not Selena. If memory serves me correctly, allergies are caused from environmental factors rather than genetics. Does Menendez play the piano?"

"Just what the hell are you talking about?" Braden inquired.

"Sarah plays the piano. Her mother was her teacher, and that's why she loves classical music."

"Well if I had a damn piano in here, I'd let her play Chopsticks," Braden snapped. "That'd just prove everything." He didn't want to listen to reason, because he didn't want to be wrong. Because if this wasn't Selena, he'd have a lot to account for—probably in court. His head ached behind his eyes.

"You're being unreasonable. Totally close-minded about the possibility of this woman being Sarah," Hill mumbled.

A loud blast loud rang out.

The explosion jolted the helicopter.

Braden's head whipped back from the motion.

Marcy and Sarah screamed.

The remaining piece of the tail boom shook.

Braden's pulse quickened as realization hit him.

The main rotor whipped around causing the helicopter to spin out of control.

Black smoke rose from the back, filling Braden's lungs. His eyes burned. "The tail rotor was blown away!" Braden shouted to Dan.

Johnson and Reuben coughed from the seats behind him, choking from the fuel's strong odor as it pervaded the cabin.

"We're going down!" Dan yelled. "I can't control it! Brace yourselves!"

When the body of the helicopter hit the top of the timberline, Braden gripped the shoulder harness, holding him in the seat.

Branches split and cracked.

The chopper flipped over. Gravity pulled on his body, but the seatbelt jerked him back.

The helicopter came upright again. Tree limbs beat against the outer pod, causing its doors to fly off.

The deafening noise blared in his ears.

One of the main rotor blades flew through the air like a boomerang.

Marcy threw up while the men in back cursed. Beside him, Selena prayed, prayed to God and to the saints. But the prevalent sound he heard was his own heart pounding through his chest.

Hell, he was scared.

Really scared.

The chopper slammed against the ground, smashing its nose and causing the front Plexiglas to bow. The force shoved the control panels against Dan and Henson in front. They screamed in agony.

Gravity kept the momentum of the chopper's body in motion, sending it rolling like dice on a casino table. It went over the rocky edge and tumbled down a hill.

"Hang tight!" Braden shouted as the remainder of the tail boom broke off, exposing the fuel tank and engine.

Shit. We could burst into flames any moment.

"Oh, God. We're going to die," Reuben shouted.

"Christ, this can't be happening!" Johnson added.

"Heavenly Father, please protect us and keep us safe," Selena whispered. "Even Mr. Wolfe."

If the situation hadn't been so bleak, he would've laughed.

Branches and debris outside the chopper passed before him in a solid green haze. Then the bottom fell out from under his stomach as the metal pod took a drop from one ledge to another.

Braden managed a brief glance at Selena who sat with her eyes closed, gripping her hands together. Marcy's sobs filled the cabin as they continued to move.

He braced himself.

Behind them, the men cried out in desperation. "We're breaking in half!" Darrel Johnson shouted over the mayhem.

Braden glanced back. The rear section, containing the fuel tank had ripped off.

When the bench seat they shared blew out, Johnson and Reuben gripped the back of his and Marcy's seats.

Braden unfastened his restraints. He crawled into the narrow aisle, then braced himself on his knees. He extended his hand. "Johnson, Reuben...Don't let go. Grab my hand."

Both men hung on for dear life. The fear of dying showed in their eyes.

"Give me your hand, Johnson!"

But he couldn't.

Marcy cried out. "Grab hold!"

"Oh sweet Jesus. No!" Braden shouted as the two men vanished through the opening. His heart moved into his throat. He turned and tried to make it back to his seat, but when the chopper shifted directions, the impact threw him forward.

Large branches protruded through the openings and broke off. The bending and twisting of metal screeched loudly. As inertia kept the wounded chopper sliding over the ground, Braden's body hit against the inside walls like a pinball. Then everything went black.

◆◆◆

Horrified, Sarah gasped as Wolfe's body was slung around.

Tree limbs battered the outer frame, flogging what was left of the helicopter, and its momentum kept it plowing forward. Pieces of the outer panels flew off the top. If they flipped or turned too quickly, he'd be thrown out.

With a huge jolt, the pod crashed into something and stopped.

Her body hurled forward, then slammed back as the seatbelt and shoulder restraint held her in. She waited expecting the movement to continue, but it didn't.

Her heartbeat still raced.

The scent of burnt rubber, heated metal, and vomit permeated the small space. Though the crash seemed endless, it had only lasted seconds.

Sarah would've never dreamt that she'd be alive after the crash. She thought of all the times she had wished she'd died with Mark and Tristen, but not now. Now it was good to be alive.

Thank God.

Her heart tightened when she thought of the men who'd just died. "Marcy, are you all right?"

Marcy removed her headset. She placed her head between her knees. "I think so. I hope the baby is all right."

"Any abdominal pains or vaginal bleeding?"

"No. I'm just nauseated."

"Fetuses have been known to survive serious accidents." Sarah turned her attention to Wolfe. His limp body lay in a mangled heap of debris near the front. The men in the cockpit appeared severely injured and unconscious. She glanced back at Marcy. "Wolfe needs my help. You've got to free me."

Marcy straightened up, still appearing dazed and disoriented. The death of her comrades had left her speechless. As she comprehended what Sarah said, her expression became guarded. "I can't free you."

"I'm not Selena. You said it yourself. Don't start to doubt your own intuition. Wolfe is injured."

Marcy unfastened her safety restraints and made her way over the debris to where Braden laid. A look of alarm shadowed her face as she stared at him. "I'm not sure he's alive."

She dug through his pocket and retrieved his keys before making her way to Sarah and unlocking the padlock, then freeing her hands and feet.

Immediately after dropping the chains, Sarah crawled over to Braden. After removing his headset, she placed her fingers on his neck. "He's alive!" She first noticed the swelling and redness on his forehead. "He's got a nasty knot. No doubt, he'll have a concussion. Hopefully, it won't be severe."

"Please just don't let him die," Marcy whispered, tears edging the rims of her eyes. "I've lost Darrel. I don't want to lose Wolfe too."

"I'm sorry about your friend and the other men. I'll do what I can for Wolfe." Sarah examined his limbs to make sure no bones protruded through the skin. "No compound fractures. That's good. Of course that doesn't mean he hasn't broken anything. There's a chance he could have pulmonary problems or internal bleeding."

Marcy drew in a ragged breath. "I hope not."

"He has a nasty laceration on his thigh that'll require stitches. I need something to clean it with." Sarah doubted there was anything on board. "Got anything that's liquid?"

"No—yes. I have some saline nasal solution."

"That'll work."

Marcy glanced around at the disarray. "If I can find my backpack. It might've blown out."

Sarah realized her purse was probably gone.

Marcy retrieved her bag from under the seat where she had crammed it and pulled out the container, then handed it over. "This is a new bottle."

"Good." Sarah squeezed the liquid over the bloody gash, removed her shirt beneath her sweatshirt, and secured it around his thigh.

She left Braden to check on the pilot and the trooper but quickly discovered they were dead. She said a brief prayer before returning to Braden. "It's too late for them."

Marcy blotted more tears away with her shirtsleeve. "We just met Dan, Reuben, and Trooper Henson. Still, I can't believe they're gone." She sobbed a moment, wiping away a new wave of tears. "They were really terrific guys. They had to be. They put up with Wolfe."

"Do you think there's a chance the two in back survived?" Sarah asked.

"It's not impossible. Just very unlikely."

"I'm sorry." Sarah hated seeming cold, but Wolfe needed attention. She placed her hand on Marcy. "There's nothing we can do for them, but we can save Wolfe. He shouldn't be moved, but I need more room and better light," she said, as she glanced around for something to use as a stretcher. Her gaze swept over what was left of the top. "Help me push this loose panel off."

The task required the strength of both women. Marcy's face paled as she helped lower the heavy slat, and her hands shook.

"Maybe you should lie down," Sarah said.

"I'll be all right. I'm just queasy."

After clearing the debris, Sarah scooted the metal panel beside Wolfe. Though the chore was slow and tedious, they managed to roll Braden unto the makeshift stretcher. They transported him from the wreckage, set him on the ground, then collapsed beside him, catching their breaths.

"The helicopter should have compartments under the front seats that may contain medical supplies and tools," Marcy said.

"Good. We need to see what's left that can be used," Sarah said.

"What about the pilot and Trooper Henson? We can't just leave them."

"We'll decide what to do with them once I tend to Wolfe." Without saying more, Sarah crawled back inside what remained of the helicopter's cabin.

Marcy entered the shattered pod behind Sarah. "Keep your eyes peeled for a flare gun. There should be one in here."

Ten minutes later, they carried two metal utility boxes off the helicopter like a couple of proud war-torn pirates who'd hit the mother lode. Sarah opened the first box. "First aid supplies." She pillaged through the items and sighed with relief at the sight of alcohol, bandages, pain pills, and an emergency thermal blanket. "This has things in it I'll need for treating Wolfe."

Marcy discovered tools in the other box. "What we need now is food and water. I'll keep looking."

While Marcy returned inside to search, Sarah arranged the supplies needed to work on Braden. But Sarah couldn't do it alone. Leaving Wolfe on the panel, she stood and walked back to the helicopter and leaned in the twisted doorway. "Marcy, give me a hand."

"I'm on my way."

Sarah turned back around. Her heart jolted in her chest. "Put the gun down."

"Drop to the ground, Selena." Wolfe lifted his head and aimed his gun at her. "Now!"

◆◆◆

Braden struggled to keep the gun aimed at his fugitive. What had Selena done with Marcy?

She didn't move. "I am a nurse. You're hurt. You need my help."

"Like hell," he snarled. "At the count of five if you're not on the ground with your hands in the air, I'll pull the trigger without a moment's regret."

Marcy sprinted from the helicopter and jumped in front of Sarah. "Lower the gun, Wolfe."

"Get out of the way, Marcy." Why wouldn't she get out of his way? Damn her. "Where are the others?"

Marcy hesitated. "Dead."

Pain, anger, and sorrow clouded his eyes. With all his strength he managed to raise his head and glare at Selena. "You're the one who should've died, Menendez."

"She's not Menendez. Think about it," Marcy said. "If she were Selena, we'd both be dead, and she'd be gone."

His head flopped back as another intense pain hit him. Perhaps the dizziness caused it, but he was starting to believe her. He waited until the throbbing pain eased for a moment before meeting her gaze again. As his hand trembled, he dropped the gun. Marcy was right. Selena would've been gone by now. He'd been wrong.

Marcy grabbed his gun. Selena, no Sarah moved to his side. He stared at her in disbelief.

She offered him a smile. "You can close your mouth now."

He studied her features. Selena's face. God, he'd been so sure. "Sarah."

"Yes, Sarah Mason."

Marcy crouched beside Wolfe. "Sarah and I talked about it last night. We decided they had to be twins separated at birth. Like in the movie *The Parent Trap.*"

"You didn't know?" Wolfe asked Sarah.

"No, I didn't. But we can discuss it later. Right now I need to determine the extent of your injuries."

Shit. Braden's head spun. Excruciating pain surged through his knee, and he cried out.

"Where is most of your pain centered?" Sarah asked.

"My knee and lower leg."

"I'm going to cut your jeans, so I can get a better look."

She lifted a knife, and he flinched. But instead of stabbing him, she cut the denim straight up his pant leg.

She folded back the excess material. "Your knee is swollen but the patella seems to be in place. That leads me to believe you have an ACL injury. You've torn some ligaments or the meniscus. When we return home, you may need surgery. Is the pain only in your knee?"

He shook his head. "Lower leg." She pressed her fingers gently down his leg. He grimaced when she touched one spot.

She pushed on the larger bone in his calve. "Any pain?"

"Only the smaller bone."

"That's good. I need to find something to elevate your leg. I hate we don't have any ice for your knee."

"Where's a glacier when you need one?" Marcy asked.

"Take this—it will ease your pain."

He opened his mouth and managed to swallow the bitter pill without water.

"Are you dizzy? Blurred vision?" Sarah asked.

"All of the above." He grimaced.

She shined a flashlight in each eye. "Since you're not throwing up and I don't see any danger signs, I'd say your concussion is mild. Do you hurt anywhere besides your leg? Stomach? Chest?"

"No, I don't think so."

"I'm going to examine you. Tell me when it hurts. And give me an answer using one through ten. Ten being severe." She pressed her fingers firmly on his clavicle bone, then worked her way down. "Any pain?"

"None." But when she pushed on his ribs, he drew in a quick breath. "Six."

"Can you move your left arm?" she asked. He lifted it, and she smiled. Good. Now raise your right leg, just a little."

He managed to lift his good leg. "Did I pass?"

"Not yet." She removed his shoes and socks and checked his feet. "You're still warm. You don't have any paralysis as far as I can tell. Maybe a cracked rib. Take a deep breath does it hurt to breathe?"

He did as she requested. "No, just when you touched it."

"You're probably bruised."

"The pain in my knee and leg is a ten." He stared up at Sarah. "Is my leg broken?"

"Difficult to say. I didn't feel anything out of place. If you have a break, it could be a small fracture in the fibula."

Braden hadn't been able to take his eyes off Sarah. It still unnerved him how much she looked like Selena.

She raised her gaze to his. "Has the Hydrocodone started working?"

"I'm not sure. My leg still hurts like the devil."

"That gash presents the greatest danger. Getting an infection out here wouldn't be good. I'll close it up first."

"With what?"

"I found a needle in the emergency supplies, but rather than use regular thread, Marcy has dental floss. It's stronger and sterile."

He nodded.

"I need to see how deep it is." She gently pulled back the torn skin. "After I stitch you, I'm going to wrap your knee tightly and make a splint for your leg." She glanced at Marcy. "When that pill kicks in, I'll start."

"Start now. I'll deal with the pain." The pain in his leg didn't compare to the pain striking his chest every time he thought about Darrel and the other men. All dead. No doubt, his fault. He wanted to be the one to tell Darrel's family. He pushed his grief aside and tuned back into what Marcy was saying.

"Wolfe, I remember what a baby you were that time you had a toothache. You'd better hope that pill kicks in."

Sarah waited beside him like an angel of mercy, holding his hand in hers and stroking his forehead with her other. He could envision her as a nurse, her camaraderie with her patients, cheering them to raise their spirits. He really saw her—Sarah not Selena. Somehow, for just a second, he'd seen past the facial features and viewed a different woman. Her smile brought a rush of warmth to his chest.

Stop it.

Don't even go there.

Surely it was the pain pill causing the irrational feelings.

"Please stop staring at me. Try to sleep," Sarah said. "You're making me nervous."

Braden managed a smile before closing his eyes and drifting off.

Later he awoke and stared into the canopy above him, studying the patches of blue sky. His mind wandered down a familiar path.

Can we ride it again? Please, Daddy.

If we keep riding it, Andy, you're gonna throw up your corndog.

Together they rode the mini-rollercoaster three more time. Then Braden played a basketball game and won Andy a big green dinosaur that ended up being called Freddie Dinosaur.

Braden pushed the memory back. Nearby, Sarah and Marcy talked. He lay still listening. From the popping, sizzling sounds and the scent of burnt wood, he comprehended that the women had managed to start a fire.

"Sarah, what are your plans now that we've spoiled your summer?" Marcy asked.

"I'm not sure. I could demand the cabin I paid for, but personally, I don't want to see the woman who more than likely called *America's Most Wanted*."

"I'm surprised no one has mistaken you before for Menendez."

"Since Mark's death, I don't get out a lot."

"Will you return home?"

"I suppose. It doesn't seem like home without Mark and Tristen. I'm not sure where I'll go. I've been thinking of other places to live."

"What about your parents?"

"They died years ago. I have a few relatives in Texas, not anyone I'm close to. Knowing that I was somehow adopted explains a lot."

"Such as?" Marcy asked.

"There were things said about me that I never understood and my mother wouldn't explain. Like one Christmas. I think I was eight, maybe nine. Uncle Eddie showed up at Grandma Sofia's Christmas dinner, sporting a new wife, his third or fourth. He handed my two cousins who were about my age beautifully wrapped, long boxes and gave me a little square box that had been hastily wrapped. I found myself gasping when I saw the beautiful bride dolls he'd given them. I knew mine couldn't be a doll, but I expected something equally as nice." Sarah paused for a moment.

"Well what did he give you?" Marcy asked.

"It was a cheap plastic comb, hairbrush, and mirror set. I remember how disappointed I was."

"Surely you didn't thank him. Did you?"

"I guess I would have, but Grandma Sofia snatched the box from me and started beating Uncle Eddie over the head with it. And that's when he said, 'It's not like she's really family.' My mother's eyes filled with pain."

The fire popped for a moment as a breeze stirred the air, sending chills through Braden.

Then Sarah continued. "I asked, 'Why did he say that?' Mother never explained it. Never. She only told me Uncle Eddie was a two-bit gangster that would end up dead someday."

"Did he?" Marcy asked.

"Yeah, he did. But not for another ten years. Later Christmas Day when I overheard Grandma Sofia and mother arguing in the kitchen, I heard my mother say, 'If not for Eddie, we wouldn't have Sarah. And my Grandmother turned away and stormed upstairs."

"So Uncle Eddie must've been the one who arranged the adoption."

"Probably. And now that I've been spending time musing over the fact I'm adopted, I realize no one ever mentioned my resembling anyone in the family like they did my cousins, Gina and Francesca."

"You went home without a doll. That's so sad. Damn Uncle Eddie's lousy hide," Marcy said.

Sarah laughed. "Actually I ended up with the best present. Grandma Sofia returned downstairs carrying a very old porcelain doll with long dark curls that had been hers as a child. She gave it to me."

"Ahhh, that's so sweet. So how did Eddie finally get it?"

"All I know is that some pimp shot him for trying to shortchange one of his girls." The talking ceased.

Though Braden fought feeling any emotions, her story had touched him. He didn't want to feel anything for anybody, especially someone who looked like Selena Menendez.

While Marcy and Sarah continued talking, different thoughts roamed through Braden's mind.

What had caused the explosion? He doubted it was a malfunction with the troopers' new chopper. He explored different possibilities before coming up with only one conclusion. During the night, someone had managed to plant an IED. Which meant it'd been detonated from somewhere nearby. Probably with a remote control or phone. Who was behind it?

Dagastino. But how had he known about their takedown of Menendez? He couldn't think about it now. Now he had to concentrate on what the kingpin's immediate plans were.

There was a possibility he'd want to see the wreckage and proof that Selena was dead. If that were the case, Braden knew it wouldn't be long before they had company. And like him, they'd believe Sarah was Selena.

Shit.

Sarah Mason probably thought her ordeal was over. She didn't have a clue her problems were just beginning. Braden would bet a year's wages that right now paid killers were searching for her—dead or alive.

If they found her alive, they'd return her to Dagastino. And keeping him and Marcy alive wouldn't be beneficial to them.

Chapter Four

Braden decided he'd remain behind with the wreckage and insist the women try to make it back. He'd only slow them down.

He claimed responsibility for Andy's death, and now he was responsible for the deaths of the men. But how had Dagastino known? *Shit.* Someone had to be leaking information concerning Selena Menendez back to the mob boss.

He wondered if the mole was connected with *America's Most Wanted.* Then another disturbing thought entered his mind. They hadn't known about the DNA match. Could it be someone from his office? Different people who had the information came to mind, but he couldn't imagine any of them selling out.

"Hill!" he managed to shout. The pain had returned. Between one and ten, it rated a twelve. He called Marcy's name several times before she glanced his way.

She stood and walked over to where he lay. "Hi, stranger. Welcome back."

"I need to speak with you and Sarah. Now." Despite the mild Alaskan summer climate, sweat beaded on his forehead. "This is important."

Sarah joined them and knelt beside him, placing her hand on his head. "You're too pale." She turned her attention to his leg. "Have you noticed my handy work?"

He managed to raise his head and take a glimpse of his leg braced on both sides with two small limbs and wrapped in duct tape. "Very creative."

"Duct tape. Never leave home without it. My stitches are a little ragged, but the needle didn't want to cooperate," Sarah remarked.

"Wolfe just has tough skin," Marcy said, then grinned.

"It should hold until we can get you back to civilization."

"I'm not going. You and Sarah can make it back faster without me."

"We're not leaving you," Marcy said.

He looked at Marcy, then Sarah. "Whoever planted that bomb is going to want proof Selena's dead."

"I would if I were him. Selena has nine lives," Marcy stated. "She always lands on her feet."

"I'm glad you're finally convinced I'm not her," Sarah said to Braden.

"Yep, I was so damn sure you were Selena." He thought about apologizing for the way he'd treated her but now wasn't the time. "Don't move the men in the cockpit."

Marcy frowned. "We can't just leave them."

Sarah chimed in. "We can cover them with stones to keep large animals away."

"Then Dagastino's men will know someone survived. If you leave them untouched, he'll think our bodies are scattered over the Alaskan landscape."

"What about search parties. Don't we want them to know we're alive?" Marcy asked.

Braden sighed. "I'd bet my sweet ass that Dagastino's men are already combing the area. They'll be a day ahead of any search party." His face contorted. "Aww, God! My leg."

"Tonight will be your worst night," Sarah commented as she removed the Hydrocodone from her pocket and twisted the top off. "I'm going to give you another pill, but that will only leave four."

To his amazement, she held up a bottle of water. "Where'd that come from?"

"From inside one of the side compartment along the seats that remained in tack."

Regardless of his agony, a smile curled his lips. "You geniuses come up with any food?"

Sarah shook her head. "No, but we will."

"How long was I out?"

"About four hours," Sarah replied. "I stayed with you while Marcy scouted the area."

"Neither of you have any business going out alone."

"Wolfe, we can't stay here."

"She found a cabin," Sarah added.

"Well, that's stretching it. It's not much, but it'll keep us safe," Marcy confessed. "I think God intended it to be a cave, but then someone enclosed the front, trying to convert it into a cabin. I doubt it's an idea they got off Pinterest."

Sarah laughed.

Braden frowned. "I don't have a clue what you're talking about."

"Pinterest. It's a girl thing. You wouldn't get it," Marcy added. "As soon as that pill kicks in and takes you to Neverland, we're going to move you."

"You're sure this shelter is deserted?" Braden asked.

"It doesn't look like anyone has been there for a long time. It's not that far, but we'll have to get you down a steep hill."

"How in the hell do you plan to move me?"

Sarah winked at Marcy but kept a straight face. "Dragging him through this brush has possibilities. It beats trying to carry his sorry ass."

Marcy grinned.

Braden looked at Sarah. "You just want to get even with me."

Sarah gave him an exuberant smile. "Not yet. Just remember, Wolfe. Paybacks are hell. Maybe later when you're not expecting it."

"I guess we could use the stretcher Sarah made," Marcy said, smiling at her.

Braden stretched his neck again trying to see what Marcy was talking about. He studied the two long branches that ran parallel linked together with horizontal placed strips of gray duct tape doubled so neither side was sticky. He only hoped it was strong enough to hold him.

"First Aid 101. Constructing it kept me busy while Marcy was gone."

"Sarah will stay while I go for help."

"Damn it, Hill. Listen to me. Sarah and you need to take what you can carry and try to make it back. Together you stand a better chance."

"Like I said, you're out voted. We're not leaving you."

"Marcy, that's crazy. Think of your baby," he said, speaking as a friend.

"You accused me of being soft. Well, I'm not. We're still a team. And I'm making sure you're safe before I leave."

He scowled at her. "You alone? No way. It's my fault the others died. I should've had someone guarding the helicopter at the lodge. I don't want to be responsible for your death as well."

"Wolfe, Marshal Reuben should've made that decision. Yes, you pushed your way in and took over, but it wasn't your decision to post someone at the helicopter. Now, one of us has to go for help. I'm not a nurse. I can't take care of you."

Sarah sighed. "As much as I dislike your company, Marcy and I decided I should stay behind."

Marcy intercepted. "If Sarah walked into a police station who do you think they'll mistake her for?"

"Selena," he mumbled.

"Right. And they'd take her into custody."

"Well, the sorority sisters have the whole damn thing worked out." He doubted he'd be able to change their minds. Actually, they'd thought out the situation carefully, but he couldn't stop worrying about Marcy. What if she ran head-on into Dagastino's men? Or even a bear or a pack of wolves? Before another thought crossed his mind, Braden's eyes closed, and he could feel the magic of the pain pill floating him on a cloud.

◆◆◆

Sarah studied Braden. He was out cold. His pain would double while they attempted to move him to the stretcher, so they had to do it while he slept. "I'm going to roll him toward me, and when I get him up, shove the stretcher under him."

Marcy pushed the stretcher beneath Braden. "You make that look easy."

"If you've worked in a hospital, you get used to doing it. Let's get him to the shelter, then we can come back for the supplies."

"There's an upper compartment in the helicopter. I didn't mention it because I wanted to make absolutely sure you weren't Selena. But there should be some rifles stored there. We'll grab them when we get back."

"Why wait? What if we run into Dagastino's men or a bear?"

"I have my service gun and a Ruger .22 semi-automatic. The Glock .40 might stop a bear." She paused as if thinking. "You're right. Wait with him. I'll hurry."

Marcy returned shortly carrying a really big gun and walked to the end of the stretcher. "This Remington 700 might stop a bear. It's actually a sniper rifle." She placed it beside Braden. "Hope we can lift this."

"We'll manage."After positioning herself at the rear of the stretcher, Sarah started the count. "One, two, three, lift."

"Damn, this is heavy."

"Maneuver around those huge leaves."

"They look like they belong in some tropical jungle. What are they?"

"Devil's Club. It has poisonous thorns. It was mentioned in a safety film the resort made me watch along with bear safety."

They tramped through the endless conifer forest toward the deserted cabin. Two hyperactive squirrels scampered up a tree as they approached.

A fire burned in Sarah's arms and legs, and the thin mountain air stung her lungs. "Lower him. I have to rest before I drop him."

"Damn, he's heavy," Marcy complained.

"It's like hauling a dead pig." When Sarah thought about what she'd said, she laughed. "I swear I wasn't referring to him being cop."

"I didn't take it that way." Marcy giggled. "Just remember, at least a hundred pounds of his weight is ego."

They both laughed.

After they set the stretcher down, Sarah wiped her forehead on her sleeve. Maybe they shouldn't have moved Wolfe. Should Marcy be attempting such a physical feat? She didn't want to do anything that would put Marcy at risk for a miscarriage.

It was a little late to be debating what to do. They couldn't turn back now.

Sarah rubbed the back of her neck. "I can't wait to reach the cabin and rest."

"Don't get your hopes up about this place."

"Well, at least it'll shelter us from the rain and animals."

Marcy stood at the end of the stretcher. "Let's keep going. If he wakes up, he'll be a pain in the ass."

Sarah gritted her teeth. Ignoring the stinging ache in her arms, she lifted her end of the stretcher. They needed to reach the shelter before the drizzling rain started up. Since being in Alaska, the skies had been mostly gray, and it had rained a little each day. She didn't want Wolfe getting too damp. "How much farther?"

"Not far. Just beyond those trees and down the slope." Marcy stopped after another five minutes. "Lower it. I'm frazzled."

Sarah rubbed her sweaty hands on her jeans. "This cabin is a God-send. Did you find any food?"

"There are some old cans, but I doubt we'd consider eating any of it."

Sarah sighed. "My stomach isn't happy to hear that."

After the brief rest, they lifted Wolfe and continued on. They stopped and started six times. Each time Wolfe seemed heavier. Sweat dripped down Sarah's face, and blisters had surfaced on her palms from gripping the stretcher. The open sores stung, but still she held her end.

They left the woods. The barren landscape looked like something from photographs of another planet. Boulders of all sizes covered the mountain side. In the distance high snowy peaks rose skyward. Thank goodness they had crashed on a lower slope.

At the top of the hill's steep incline, they set him down. Marcy grabbed her lower back while Sarah tied her boot strings. They rested ten minutes before undertaking the risky task.

"Okay, let's take it slow and easy," Marcy said.

Sarah studied the base of the hill and wondered how they'd get Wolfe over the boulders. Hopefully, there was a path. She insisted on being in front, to carry the bulk of his weight. Marcy didn't argue and switched places with her. Slowly they inched the stretcher around the rocky incline, while trying to maintain their balance.

Rocks shifted.

Sarah's feet slid.

The stretcher tipped, and Sarah gasped. Her reflexes kicked in, and she dropped to her knees, managing to stabilize it. "That was close."

"Too close."

"I'd never convince Wolfe it was an accident."

"Well, you're the one who admitted you plan to get even with him."

In the small clearing at the base of the hill, they lowered Wolfe to the ground. What should've been a thirty minute hike through the woods ended up being a two hour ordeal. Sarah stared at the shelter built into the stone hill, realizing how primitive it was. "Who lived here? The Flintstones?"

Marcy giggled. "I told you it wasn't the Hilton."

"You called that one right." Leaving Wolfe just outside the door, Sarah followed Marcy through the entrance. "It's cool in here."

"At least it'll maintain the same temperature."

"I'm sure some bear returned for the winter and was irate to see his cave transformed into a cabin," Sarah said.

Marcy laughed. "That explains what happened to the person who lived here."

"What's that?"

"The bear got even."

They both chuckled.

Sarah stood just inside the door, looking the place over. It smelled stale and musty. A natural crevice existed in the top of the cave allowing for ventilation. Whoever lived here had chiseled out a fireplace in the sidewall of the original cave beneath the crevice. She pivoted around. Across the front, logs had been placed and filled in with sod or mud and had two dingy windows, one positioned on each side of a heavy wooden door, letting in a little light. "It has possibilities."

"Yeah, for a caveman." Marcy propped the front door open allowing more light to enter. The light revealed old wooden crates, traps, and a stack of pelts.

"Wolfe qualifies as a Neanderthal. It's the perfect home for him." Sarah checked out the bed by the fireplace. She pulled old decayed blankets back and winced when dust exploded around her face like a small atomic bomb. She peeled back a thick mattress pad. "It's a freaking slab of stone." On the far side of the room, a cast iron bed stood in the corner. "Wolfe needs the lower bed."

"Let's get him settled and head back."

Though exhausted, they managed to transfer Braden from the stretcher to the bed. Sarah eyed the rustic chairs and table someone had made, then turned to Marcy. "Do you need to sit and rest?"

"We'd better go if we want to be back before he wakes up. We can use the stretcher to haul things back on."

Sarah nodded. "Good idea. At least we don't have to worry about it getting dark. When I first arrived, I'd expected it to be bright and sunny all night, but it's more like an overcast day."

"It takes some getting used to," Marcy admitted.

Before leaving the shelter, Sarah pushed a small stone in front of the door, so it wouldn't swing open. "He should sleep another two hours. I just hope he doesn't roll off the bed. That's one hard floor."

At the wreckage site, Sarah and Marcy found the crashed helicopter and the bodies of the two men undisturbed. No one had been there. With the pilot and other deputy still inside, an eerie feeling settled over Sarah. Then she reminded herself this was about survival. She studied the inside of what remained of the helicopter and spotted the compartment Marcy mentioned.

Marcy and Sarah each unhinged a latch, then opened the long narrow compartment revealing several more guns.

"We should grab both of the Mossberg .12 gauge shotguns and ammo," Marcy said. "And maybe another rifle."

"I know very little about guns. You select. But we'd better hurry. Wolfe will be waking up soon."

Back outside, Marcy inspected the load. "This is going to end up heavier than Wolfe."

"Let's try to make it with everything." Sarah stepped inside the desecrated aircraft and scanned the wreckage once more for anything useful. "Help me remove the shoulder restraints from this seat."

"What for?" Marcy inquired.

"I can use them to make arm pads for Braden's crutches."

"Smart thinking."

But the removal required a sharp knife and cost them some time. They swept away their footprints with branches before heading back to the shelter.

◆◆◆

Michael Dagastino couldn't swallow. His heart had moved into his throat when the blue and white Alaskan State Trooper helicopter had gone down in a billow of black smoke. From the air, he realized the debris and passengers would be scattered over miles of thick forest. He ordered his pilot to land in a dry riverbed south of the crash.

His Uncle Leon, who sought revenge, would prefer Selena be alive. With so much debris, Michael didn't expect her or any of them to have survived the crash.

Recovering her body wasn't going to be easy.

Right now, he didn't have time to dwell on what went wrong or the consequences it caused. Right now, he needed to find her body and get out of there before a rescue party found the crash-site. He figured they had a good head start—at least a day.

◆◆◆

Grandma took me to ballet class. I was the only boy there. I had to wear girly tights. I don't like dancing. I want to take karate like Corey.

Braden remembered getting in his mother-in-law's face and shouting about turning his son into a sissy. The next week Andy started karate at Corey's dojo. Of course, Braden never told Andy his mom made him take one session of Irish step dancing. He pushed the memory aside and thought about the men who'd died. It darkened his mood even more.

He tried to wet his cracked lips, but his mouth was too dry. His knee and leg throbbed as the pain medication began to wear off. Finally, he opened his eyes and glanced around taking in the rustic, primitive shelter. His leg rested on a stack of rotted blankets and furs.

The popping of a blazing fire drew his attention to the fireplace. His gaze swept over the rocky ceiling, and he realized the shelter was a cave of sorts. He felt like a guest in a hobbit's cottage. But where were the two hobbits who'd left him there?

Sarah came through the door, carrying two straight sticks equal in length and width. She flinched. "You scared me. I didn't realize you were awake. How's the pain?"

"Not too bad for now. Where's Hill?"

"Hunting."

"You're kidding?"

"Don't tell my stomach that. Marcy told me she used to hunt with her father and brothers. I just hope she gets back soon."

"What day is it?" he asked.

"Still Sunday. We're in the land of the midnight sun. It's difficult to distinguish one day from another."

"Feels like it's been days." He paused for a moment listening to the fire popping. "Why'd you pick Alaska for a vacation?"

Sarah moved one of the chairs to the fireplace and sat down. "It's not a vacation. I was escaping. I googled Alaska and thought it might be a great place to hide from my memories. Boy, was I wrong."

Braden stuffed the faintly soured smelling feather pillow under his head, propping himself up. He wanted to apologize but would she think he was being contrite to avoid a lawsuit? "Guess we ruined your trip. I'm sorry for the way I treated you."

"I'm sure you are. I have a good case against you."

The sparkle in her eyes gave her away. He'd let her play her game, pretend she'd have her day in court, but the lady had already forgiven him. He wasn't sure why. He paused for a moment. "You're still grieving?"

"Not really grieving. It's easier to let go when you don't have constant reminders around. I'll always love Mark, but I've come to terms with his death. As far as Tristen, losing a child is something you just can't get over. It still hurts."

Endless pain.

Braden thought of Andy. He considered sharing his grief and what had happened but wasn't able to force the words out. He'd never spoken to anyone about it. Instead, he changed the subject. "If Marcy kills something, I doubt she'll know how to dress it?"

"We made a deal. If she kills it, I'll skin and butcher it. My father owned a butcher shop, so I've had a little practice. I just hope she doesn't bring back a grizzly or a moose."

Braden smiled at the thought of little Marcy coming in hauling a grizzly over her shoulder or dragging a dead moose by one leg. Studying the shaved, smooth sticks again, he motioned toward them. "What are those for?"

"Your crutches. I don't think you should put any weight on that knee. You could cause more damage." She grabbed the poker and stirred the logs until flames shot up.

"Too bad the crutches aren't ready. I really need to relieve myself."

"I still need to pad the top, so it doesn't hurt your arm. Think you can lean on me and hop?"

"Yeah, I'll manage."

Sarah pushed the chair from their path and propped the door open before helping him stand on one leg. When he draped his arm over her shoulder, he breathed in her woman's scent. The raw natural smell made his groin stir with need. But the moment he forgot and stepped down on his injured leg, pain shot through it, making him regret he even had a penis.

Outside, he leaned against the cabin, standing like a flamingo.

"I'll be just inside," Sarah said as she stepped back through the door, giving him some privacy.

Braden fought the dizziness. Surely, they had been missed. He wondered if rescue teams were searching for them yet. "Sarah, I'm ready."

Sarah stood beside him, letting him drape his arm over her shoulder. His gaze lingered on her cleavage, and he experienced a jolt of lust. He recalled how beautiful her breasts were and how her large, dusty brown nipples hardened to the cool air.

She eased him down onto the bed. Her breasts brushed against his chest, making his little man rise beneath the covers. He took her hand and held it in his. "Thank you, Sarah. If our roles were reversed, I doubt I could be as forgiving as you."

She shrugged. "Who's to say I've forgiven you?"

"I wouldn't blame you if you don't. I behaved like a number one asshole. I don't want you thinking I treat women like that. It's just that Menendez—"

"Is different than most women. I know she wounded you and killed your friend. You really don't need to explain it." When the door opened, Sarah let her hand slip from his and turned to face Hill. "Did you kill anything?"

"A ridiculous looking bird."

"Please tell me it's not a buzzard," Braden said.

Marcy laughed. "It looks like some type of game bird."

"Let me see," Sarah said as she darted across the small room and snatched the bird from Marcy. She held it up by its feet. "It's big."

Braden thought she might start eating it before plucking the feathers. His inner humor dissolved once a pain ripped through his knee, making him grimace.

"I hope it's not on the endangered species list, and we all end up arrested." Marcy rested the rifle against the wall.

"Can't see that happening," Sarah said, "I don't plan to leave a shred of evidence behind."

The women giggled.

The bird had a black head, with red around its eyes and a white ring around the neck. The body had red, brown and gray feathers.

"I think you're safe. It looks like a pheasant," Wolfe said.

"You entertain Wolfe, while I pluck our little friend."

Marcy stepped in front of the fire, warming herself. "Great fire. Sarah swings that ax like a pro. She has enough firewood piled up to last a day or so."

He motioned to the branches leaned against the wall. "She's making me crutches."

Marcy smiled. "The way you treated her, you're lucky she's not hacking on you with that ax." She turned her backside to the blaze. "I spotted a stream with salmon in it. I'm going to repair the net I found with my dental floss and see if I can catch anything."

Braden's chest felt empty. "It seems wrong to be concerned with food, thinking about the men who died. One of us should've guarded that helicopter during the night."

"Hindsight." Marcy sat in the ladder-back chair by the fire. Neither spoke for a few moments. "On the floor, Sarah and I discovered a hole chiseled in the stone and figured it was probably used to keep food cool. There's a thick wooden plank with Styrofoam on the bottom that fits over it. Once the space is filled with salmon, I plan to leave."

"Marcy, take Sarah. I can manage alone."

"And when the pain pills are gone, will you manage then? And what if you fall?"

He didn't argue. Marcy's mind was already made up.

"Besides, I'll probably run into the search party. Hell, no one will find you in this cave."

Sarah returned inside with the featherless bird.

Braden couldn't help but feel proud of the two women for using their survival skills. "How long before it's ready to eat?"

"Maybe an hour," Sarah said. "I'm not sure how long it takes something like this to cook over an open fire." She continued to prepare the bird. "I found some things we can use. Grant you, I have no earthly idea how old these items are."

"Like what?" Marcy asked while stepping around the make-shift counter someone had made from stacking old wooden crates.

"Salt and pepper. I also found coffee, baking soda, tea, vinegar, and sugar. I'd be afraid of the flour, and the rice has weevils."

A short time later, Sarah placed the well-done pheasant on a tin camping plate she'd discovered and set it in the middle of the table. "What's your preference?"

"I'll take a leg and a thigh," Wolfe replied.

She sliced through the tender meat. "It's hot."

His mouth watered as he smelled the roasted bird. Nothing had ever tasted so good. By the time they finished only a pile of bones remained.

♦♦♦

Braden drifted in and out of sleep. The pain in his leg had lessened. A cool bundle of rags rested on his knee. The charred smell of burnt wood and meat filled the air while a flame sizzled and danced in the fireplace.

He mainly concentrated on Sarah and Marcy's conversation, enjoying their friendly chitchat. And oddly enough, he found himself wanting to know more about Sarah. He liked her stories involving Grandma Sofia. With each story, his interest in her grew.

Marcy threw a log on the fire. "So how'd you meet Mark?"

"My first nursing job was at a doctor's office in Dallas. Mark came in for his yearly checkup. My heart couldn't stop beating when I stood beside him taking his blood pressure. He was so handsome. But he was a patient, and I didn't say anything."

"So who made the first move?"

Sarah sipped the coffee, then continued. "In a week, he returned for an insect bite. The following week, he dropped by for a twisted ankle. I wanted to flirt or say something, but I couldn't. Then the next week, he jogged up beside me at the park. His ankle had miraculously healed. He asked me out and the rest is history. How'd you meet Alex?"

Marcy smiled. "I sat by him on a trip to New York. We talked the entire flight. Then we ended up sharing a cab. Strange but true—we'd booked the same hotel, and he ended up across the hall. We were both from St. Louis and our paths had never crossed. But after that, we were an item."

"Fate. You were destined to be together."

"Think you'll ever remarry?" Marcy asked.

Braden waited to hear her answer.

"I haven't dated anyone since Mark."

"Time heals everything. Maybe you'll fall in love again."

"I'm not looking for love."

Neither was Braden. The last thing he wanted, if history repeated itself, was to be tied down with one woman who'd end up ripping his heart out.

Although his body had responded to Sarah's, she wasn't a threat to his heart. Sarah's grief ran deep, too deep for her to fall in love with another man. As far as him falling for Sarah, he couldn't. He'd never be able to love her, considering she had the same face he'd hated for the past five years.

When he awoke, Marcy sat by the fire, apparently grieving for the men who'd died or maybe missing her girls. He didn't interrupt her.

He turned his thoughts to the pilot. Had he turned in a flight plan? Maybe they should've stayed with the helicopter. Had the other officers who drove back reached Anchorage and wondered where they were? If the rescue teams tracked the wreckage using the helicopter's GPS, they would assume their bodies had been blown out like Darrel and Marshal Reuben. Would they continue searching?

◆◆◆

"Hey, Selena. Get your ass in here."

"Stuff it, Carlos," she snapped.

"I'm serious. They're talking about you."

"Besa mi culo," rolled the profanity off her lips. Selena flushed the toilet, pulled up her jeans, and hurried to the den. She sat beside Carlos, then turned up the volume."

"And now this breaking news," the *America's Most Wanted* host said. "Last week we profiled American's bad girl, Selena Menendez. Before our program ended, a viewer called our tip hotline and reported seeing her. Federal Marshals formed a task force with other Alaskan officials and cornered Menendez."

"Alaska? Cornered me? This can't be fuckin' real."

They played actual scenes from the arrest across the screen.

"The bitch has my face."

"That's far out. She's identical to you."

"Shh. Listen."

"After making the arrest, federal marshals escorted Selena aboard a helicopter. They were forced to land during heavy fog at a nearby lodge. The next morning, they lifted off, heading toward Anchorage. The flight never made it. Rescue teams have formed and are trying to get a GPS location on the helicopter. Our prayers go out to the officers and their families."

"So if she dies in this crash, even Dagastino will think she's me. I don't give a shit who she really is. Just so long as she's dead, and my name is on her grave."

"I wonder why she looks like you. You got any sisters?"

"Have I ever mentioned one, shit for brains?"

"Well, no. But she could be you."

"Freaking amazing, isn't it? This could be my biggest break."

"What if she survives and her real identity is discovered? Dagastino will put his jefes back on your trail."

Selena stared at the television set before turning her gaze to Carlos. "If she survives, I want to know where I can find her. We can set her up to be killed by Dagastino's guys. They'll think they've killed me."

"How do we keep her from talking?"

Selena ground her teeth while thinking. "I'll cut her tongue out if I have to. You can pretend you're betraying me for the bounty he's offered on my head. Then we'll take his money and disappear with a new identity."

"You're a wicked woman."

Chapter Five

The morning after the crash, Michael Dagastino stared at the body of a man, a U.S. Marshal they'd come across in the vast wilderness. His stomach knotted. No one was supposed to die.

Shit.

This made Michael an accessory to the crime. Had Uncle Leon insisted he head up this trip to make it impossible for him to ever return to his old life? If there'd ever been a chance of walking away from the family business, his involvement in this venture had sealed his fate.

One thing in their favor, the clouds hung low in the sky. No rescue team would chance flying in this.

"The bitch isn't here," Lenny shouted.

"If you'd done the fuckin' job right, we'd have Selena and be on our way to Jersey," Sergio nagged.

"Stop busting my balls over it," Lenny retorted.

"Find anyone else?" Michael asked Lenny.

"No, just this white dude and lots of debris from the chopper."

Michael swung his backpack to the ground. "Let's bury the body."

"Shit no," Sergio said—the oldest wise guy and his uncle's lieutenant. "You do that, and it won't look like an accident. Leave him."

"We have to eliminate any survivors," Chase added, a thirty-two year old soldier in the crime family, one who seemed sharper than the others. His uncle referred to him as the hammer. "No one can make it back alive to tell what happened."

Michael studied the heartless men with him. Did any of them have even a shred of conscience? He doubted it.

How long would it be before he became desensitized to murdering people?

◆◆◆

The cool pack on Braden's knee eased the pain, and he had slept through the night. But now chills racked his body. He could only raise his head enough to see Sarah and Marcy sitting at the table, weaving string through the aluminum frame of a fishnet. His lightheadedness made him drop his head back to the pillow.

"It's cold in here," he managed to say.

Sarah stood and crossed over to him. "Good morning." She placed her hand on his forehead. "You don't have a fever. The pack on your knee is causing your chills."

"Take it off."

After removing it, she lightly touched his knee. "The swelling's gone down. How's the pain?"

"Barely tolerable."

"I'll bring you a pill."

Braden took the pill from Sarah. Not wanting to be in the Twilight Zone for three to four hours, he snapped it in half and put part of it under his pillow for later. Hopefully, half of it would be enough to dull his pain. He hunkered down beneath the ragged blankets, shivering.

Sarah returned with the cover from the other bed, tossed it over him, and smoothed it out. Her gentle hands comforted him. "Better?"

"Much." He reached out and gently grasped her wrist. "Thanks, Sarah."

"No, you don't." Though she pretended to be hostile, amusement filled her eyes. "Don't think you're talking your way out of a lawsuit."

"You think we could settle out of court?"

Her facial muscles relaxed into a soft expression. "What'd you have in mind?"

"Steak dinner."

"You think I can be bought that easily?"

"I was hopin'.."

Sarah smiled. "Does that include a piece of chocolate pie?"

"Anything you want. Hell, I'll buy you the whole damn pie."

Marcy set the net down before she stood. "Enough talk about food. You guys are making me hungry."

"There are some blueberries left," Sarah said. "I'll pick some more tomorrow."

Marcy joined Sarah at Braden's bedside. "You could eat a thousand of them and still be hungry. I'm going to the river and try catching our supper."

"Take Sarah and a gun."

"And what about you?" Marcy asked.

"I'll manage."

"I really need to examine your wound and make sure it's not infected," Sarah argued. "Maybe I should stay."

"It can wait until you come back," Braden insisted, wanting time alone.

"He's right," Marcy argued. She grabbed the net. "Besides, I need you to herd the fish."

"A Salmon roundup. Sounds epic." Sarah gently brushed the side of his face with her hand. "When we come back, I want you to try using your crutches. Don't attempt it while we're gone. Understand?"

"Yes, ma'am." He closed his eyes, pretending to doze off. He didn't want to sleep. He wanted the quiet time to reflect on his co-worker and the men who'd died.

He blamed himself for the men's deaths, just like he blamed himself for Andy's death.

Guilt weighted him down like an anchor. Maybe he was a Jonah—always bringing bad luck to the people around him.

◆◆◆

Sarah gazed on Braden's sleeping face totally aware she'd become attracted to the marshal. Why was her attraction for him so strong? An image of her hands and legs cuffed and chained popped into her mind. She'd never felt so dominated by a man and powerless to control him. Instead of being repulsed by it, a sensual heat radiated through her.

Hell, no.

Bondage is not my thing. Don't even go there.

And it was more than just a sexual awareness that frightened the hell out of her. She faced Marcy. "Let's go. I want to be back before he wakes up."

"You're not starting to grow fond of him, are you?"

"Nope, he's just another patient," Sarah lied. She'd spent too much time by his bed while he slept, studying the masculine lines of his unshaven face. She wondered about the tenderhearted man beneath the rough exterior. She'd only caught glimpses of the man who spent Christmas alone every year—the man who had family but never saw them. What had wounded him so badly it'd hardened his heart?

"I could've sworn the two of you were flirting."

"Nurses always carry on with their patients. It doesn't mean anything." But it had. When his hand had touched her, she'd become breathless and filled with desire.

"Good. Braden is not a long-term relationship kind of guy." Marcy pointed to a wadded heap of burlap in the corner. "Grab a feed bag so we'll have something to put the fish in."

At the shallow river, Sarah marveled over the grayish salmon with tiny black ovals on their backs working their way up stream. "That's not even a face a mother could love."

Marcy laughed. "You won't think that when they're filleted and cooked."

Sarah couldn't argue. She wanted something to eat besides berries. When she left Alaska, she didn't want to ever see another blueberry-not even in a muffin or pancake.

"Grab a tree limb and barricade that side of the stream so they'll swim my way," Marcy instructed. She straddled over the offshoot—one foot on the bank, the other on a rock with the net positioned in the water. "I'm ready."

"That seems like cheating."

Like Marcy had predicted, the salmon searched for another passage. As they crowded the entrance of the offshoot, Marcy maneuvered the net over two large ones.

She dumped the first two fish into the burlap bag, then repositioned the net. "Oh, snap. This water is freezing my hands. I wish I had a longer handle."

Sarah pointed to a deeper section "I could sure use a bath. I smelled something horrible this morning. I kept looking for what had crawled inside and died, then realized it was me."

Marcy laughed. "I'm just as ripe, but my hands are stinging from holding the net. I can't imagine subjecting my entire body to this extreme cold."

"How 'bout we slip our clothes off and splash ourselves?"

"I'm willing to try it."

After catching a total of six fish, they walked to a point where the water was slightly deeper and formed an inviting clear pool.

"Funny, how once you have a kid you lose your modesty." Sarah removed her clothes and boots, then set them upon a boulder.

Marcy undressed and stacked her clothes on top of Sarah's. She stooped down, dipped her hands in the water, splashing her face and arms. "Crap that's cold." She smiled. "I've never been modest. My mom said I was a streaker at an early age. When I was two, I stripped down and ran into the front yard naked. Some sick-o neighbor called the cops."

Sarah laughed. "I hope you grew out of your need to streak." She cupped water in her hands, then splashed it on her body. She shivered for a moment. "Well, this isn't working," Sarah complained. "I still feel dirty. Think about this. Survivor Man and the Polar Club swim in icy water. It'd just be for a few minutes."

"They're idiots. Besides, the sun is nowhere in sight. You'll freeze your ass off."

Sarah smiled. "I'm going for it."

"Are you insane?"

Sarah took the leap into the frigid water and went under.

Oh fudge. It's deeper than it looks.

The cold water zapped her body like a lightning bolt. If she'd had a heart condition, she would've had a fatal heart attack right then. She popped up and twisted around looking for the fastest route out.

"Oh snap, what the hell!" Marcy slid in beside Sarah. "Shit, this is cold. She struggled to get out, but couldn't get a grip on the mossy rocks and kept sliding back in, splashing them. "We're trapped."

They both tried to get a grip on the slimy green rocks.

"Give me a push, Sarah. Then I'll help you out."

Sarah stood in the shoulder deep water, planted both hands on Marcy's butt and pushed. She didn't like the view. "You're derriere is in my face. You better not cut one."

Marcy giggled while pulling herself into the scruffy grass. She extended her hand and tugged Sarah out.

They both collapsed for a moment and laughed until a gust of wind whipped over their nude bodies.

Sarah shivered. "Oh, Lord. I'm freezing. Let's get dressed. I'm going to be a Popsicle."

"Bet Braden wouldn't mind licking a Sarah Pop."

"Marcy, you're horrid. Don't say that. The man can't even stand to look at me."

"Could've fooled me. I've seen his eyes glued to your ass."

"You're kidding, I hope."

"No, I'm not."

Sarah couldn't listen to anymore, and not because it appalled her. Instead, it made a pool of heat swell in her lower stomach. "I'm numb. We'd better dry off or we'll end up with hypothermia."

"Well, at least we'll die clean," Marcy said. "Maybe we can rig some type of curtain in the cabin. Then we'd be able to sponge off."

"I've already tried that."

A mother grizzly and her two cubs crashed through the brush on the other side of the river. The adult female rose on her hind legs and roared. The deafening sound echoed through the air.

"Bears! It's bears, Sarah! Oh my God! I forgot the rifle. Oh, God! What should we do?" Marcy asked. "What if she comes after us?"

"Stay calm," Sarah ordered. "We're in her territory. She's just warning us. We didn't surprise her. She smelled us miles away. Let's just slowly walk away."

The bear appeared to be searching for the best way to cross the river.

Marcy stood paralyzed until Sarah shoved her clothes and shoes in her hands. "What about the net?"

"We'll get it later," Sarah said. "If they come after us drop the bag. Maybe they'll eat the fish instead of us."

They each gripped a corner of the heavy burlap bag and carried it between them, holding their apparel in the other and walking as fast as they could away from the river toward the cave.

"Are the three bears following us?" Marcy asked a spark of humor in her voice.

Sarah laughed softly. "I can't believe you said that. This is serious."

"I know, and it scares the crap out of me."

"Good. So whatever you do, Goldilocks, don't run. That'll make her want to chase us. That's what my Alaskan guidebook said."

Sarah had goose bumps all over, and her feet hurt from the twigs and rocks. She glanced behind them. Not seeing the bears, she took time to slip her socks and boots on.

Marcy slipped her shoes on as well. "I think my butt's blue. I've never been this cold in my life. I can't stop my teeth from chattering."

"I can beat that. I think my nipples popped off a few yards back."

Marcy laughed.

"Shivering is good. It's when it stops that you have to worry." Sarah listened for the bears coming through the thicket, but only heard her heart pounding.

♦♦♦

Braden heard the women laughing and talking as they walked up the path. He eyed the crutches leaning against the wall and stood on his good leg, then hopped over to retrieve them. Using the crutches, he hobbled to the dingy window, spit into his palm, and rubbed a round spot on the glass to peer through.

His mouth dropped when he saw the two beautiful, wild and carefree nymphs walking toward the cabin. Marcy had a nice enough body, but it wasn't nearly as voluptuous as Sarah's.

The women stopped in front of the cabin and hopped around on one foot while slipping into their jeans. Boobs jiggled freely. He couldn't take his eyes off Sarah. After the women slipped their bras on, he hurried toward his bed, dropping the crutches off where he'd found them, and hopping the rest of the way back to the bed.

With his heart racing, he closed his eyes, feigning sleep but couldn't stop thinking of Sarah. A prize-winning boner appeared, and he had a difficult time not grinning.

He should've felt guilty for watching, but he didn't. And it sure in the hell had taken his mind off his pain.

When the door opened, he fought the urge to glance their way. He blew out a few heavy breaths to convince them he was asleep. He opened his eyes to narrow slits. Both women huddled in front of the fire, appearing very much like rotisserie chickens, rotating their bodies from front to back.

"That pain pill knocked him on his ass. He's still out," Sarah whispered. "I'm going to check his stitches. I also want to examine his knee again."

"I'll start on the fish. You go ahead. That's certainly a job I wouldn't want."

Sarah slid the blanket back over his knee, leaving his chest and arms covered. She lightly probed his knee. "It's better and not nearly as swollen. I'm amazed he's sleeping through this."

Her simple touch made his erection thicken. He had a difficult time not flinching as her fingers made contact with his skin.

As she peeled the blanket back and pushed his boxers above his upper thigh, she gasped. "Oh, my goodness. He's got a huge woody. It's epic."

"You're kidding?"

"No, for real. I'm impressed. I wonder what he's dreaming about." She blotted over the healing gash with a damp cloth, applied an antibacterial ointment, and put on a new bandage it.

"I'd love to take a peek, but I can't," Marcy confessed. "I'd never be able to look him in the eyes again."

When her fingers touched his flesh just below the groin, he almost released a sexual groan. He stifled the sound.

"He's a beautiful man. Mark wasn't nearly this endowed. "He must be having a hell of a dream."

Braden thought he'd explode. Finally, he opened his eyes and stared at her. "What are you doing?"

"Cleaning your wound and changing the bandage."

"I thought you were trying to molest me."

"Only in your dreams. But I'll show you a few knee exercises I think you're ready for."

"Sounds painful."

"No pain, no gain," she told him. "So, they say."

"Can't believe everything you hear." Braden lifted the band of his boxers and peeked inside. "Aww. . . hell. I guess you saw this."

"I'm a nurse. I've seen quite a few."

Marcy giggled.

"You didn't let Hill see me in this condition did you?"

Sarah grinned. "No. I invited her over, but she declined the offer."

"Isn't that unethical? You know, exploiting my body. Isn't that breaking some kind of nursing code?"

"Maybe if I'd sold tickets and made a profit. Who were you dreaming of?" The sparkle in her eyes indicated she was teasing.

Braden couldn't resist. He wanted to see her reaction. "You."

Her face flushed a deep red, and her eyes widened before she dropped her gaze to the floor. "That's not funny."

He gave her his serious look. "Actually, I dreamed Sofia Vergara was giving me a bl—"

"I get the picture." Again she blushed. She tugged his boxers back over the wound and stood.

"You sure embarrass easily for a woman who's seen it all."

"I must admit it's not every day I see something that could be the opening act in a freak show."

He peeked under the cover. "You hurt his feelings. My little man is sensitive to rude comments."

Sarah laughed out loud. "You're bad, Wolfe."

"Okay, you guys. Something is smoking in here, and it's not the fish. So cool it." Marcy soaked the salmon in a large pan. "Remember, you two don't like one another. Don't forget you're suing him."

"Bite your tongue, darlin'," Braden snapped. "That's settled. I bought her off with the promise of a steak dinner and chocolate pie."

"And I've forgiven him."

Braden's gaze locked with Sarah's as if they were the only two humans in the world. His chest tightened with a deep heating sensation, and his heartbeat quickened. He assured himself the feelings were due to her being his caregiver—sort of a Florence Nightingale Syndrome. That and being thrown together in a small space.

Sarah stood and carried the supplies to the table, then dumped the bowl of water out the door. "We have company."

Afraid Dagastino had already discovered them, Braden sat up. "Grab a rifle."

"I think they're just ambling through."

"Ambling?" Braden asked.

Marcy laughed. "Latch the door just in case." She glanced back at Braden. "It's a mother grizzly and her cubs." She glanced out the window. "Sarah, did you rub this spot on the glass?"

"What spot?" She joined her at the window. "No, that's a perfect circle. Hey, that wasn't there before."

Marcy and Sarah turned and faced him at the same time. Marcy led the charge. "Have you been out of bed?"

"I heard something, so I managed to get up."

"And what you heard didn't happen to be two naked women?" Sarah asked, with one brow arched in suspicion.

His face heated, giving him away.

Busted.

"Damn you, Braden. You sick pervert. I had the decency not to look at you. So how long did you stand there once you realized we were naked?" Marcy demanded.

Sarah frowned. "That meant you were awake while I worked on your leg. You phony."

"Sofie Vergara my ass." Marcy placed her hands to her hips. "You got that stiffy watching us."

"If it makes you feel better, I was watching Sarah."

"What's wrong with my body?"

"You're married, Hill, and I work with you. It'd be like looking at my sister."

Sarah shook her head. "You're pathetic. We should've left you at the crash-site."

"Come on. Don't be angry. I didn't know you were naked."

"But I bet you stood there, gawking until you realized we were coming in," Marcy scolded.

"I'm sorry." He paused. "No, actually I'm not."

Sarah frowned. "And as far as that steak dinner, keep it, I'm suing."

"Now we had a deal. It's too late to back out."

Braden needed to avoid Sarah. She had openly flirted with him, and he was very attracted to her. Truth was, she tempted him, but he needed to control his libido.

"Thank you, Sarah. I'm glad you're here to take care of me."

"I'd do it for *anyone*."

When she reminded him of Selena, hate and anger surged through his blood. But sometimes like now, he could look at her without thinking of Selena. Now he only saw

Sarah. He wanted to take advantage of her body and imagined how it'd feel running his tongue over her skin.

Being confined in the small cabin with her made his attraction worse. Marcy's presence had been the only thing stopping him from seducing Sarah. The feelings weren't one-sided. Sarah's eyes simmered with sexual heat anytime she looked at him—whether she'd admit it or not.

"I need to take a leak," he said as he sat up. "Do you think the bears have gone?"

"I checked a minute ago and didn't see them." Sarah fetched the crutches. "Use these."

He stood on one leg and positioned them beneath his arms before attempting the feat. After a couple of steps, he glanced back to Sarah. "Thanks for making these."

"Whatever you do, don't put any weight on that leg," she warned.

He nodded in agreement, then hobbled out the door and over to the side to relieve himself.

Overhead an eagle soared in the gray haze above the timberline in search of prey. Stalks of fireweed waved in the breeze. Instead of returning inside, he lowered himself to a boulder for a moment and sat, enjoying the fresh pine-scented air and scenery. He couldn't help but notice that the cabin offered no alternative escape route through the back if someone attacked.

The door opened, and Sarah stepped outside. "How'd they work?"

"Great. Damn resourceful of you to use the padded part of the shoulder restraint to make arm pads for my crutches."

"Every now and then I come up with a brilliant idea." She paused beside him. "You look lost in your thoughts."

"I was. Actually, I think we should go with Marcy."

"No way. Your leg needs to be elevated, and we're not carrying you. Besides, you took a hard blow to the head."

"If anyone discovers us, there's not a back way out of this place. It's sheer stone."

"Relax, you worry too much. Marcy will go for help, and we'll be rescued. That's how I see it going." A silent moment passed before she spoke up. "Marcy mentioned you're single. Have you ever been married?"

"Once. I'm divorced." Braden pushed up from the rock and stood. He didn't want her thinking there could ever be more between them than a little naughty fun while waiting to be rescued.

He let one crutch fall to the ground. Then he slid his hand behind her head and held her firmly as he pressed his lips against hers. The kiss was eager and forceful. Hard and unforgiving.

♦♦♦

Sarah's lips hurt under the pressure of his mouth. Her heart pounded from the kiss, not from desire but fear. What was he trying to prove or accomplish?

Once he pulled his lips from hers, he straightened to his full height and glared into her eyes, revealing his tortured soul. This man had issues. No doubt he was damaged goods.

When he freed her, she stepped back and picked the crutch up from the ground. She didn't know what to make of the kiss. It had been intended to intimidate and frighten her, not romance her.

She glanced up not letting him bully her. "You have demons. I'm not sure why or what you're hiding, but apparently, there's something in your past that's eating away at your soul. Whatever it is, you need to deal with it."

After handing him the crutches, she turned and walked toward the door as the truth confronted her. Despite Braden's crudeness, her body and heart responded to this man. If she were wise, she'd keep away from him, because he wasn't about lasting relationships. He'd offer her nothing but hardcore sex with no commitment. She reminded herself this man couldn't even look at her without feeling hate.

Be smart about this.

Despite the warnings, her body ached for his touch while her heart yearned to reach out to him—to free him from whatever held him captive.

Inside, Marcy glanced up from the table. "Dinner's almost ready." Her gaze lingered on Sarah's face. "What's going on between you two?"

Sarah shrugged. "Nothing, if I have half a brain."

"Keep that thought. I like Braden, but I don't think he's capable of showing love for anyone. At most, maybe a sense of responsibility."

"All he has to do is flash those deadly green eyes at me, and my body gets all hot and bothered."

"That bad, huh?"

"I'm afraid so."

"You'd better come up with a course of action, because I'm heading out in the morning. You'll be alone with him. Think you can handle that?"

Sarah sighed. "If the caveman will stay in his corner, I'll stay in mine."

◆◆◆

Dagastino sucked in a deep draw on his Cuban cigar then exhaled the smoke while listening to his nephew, Michael over the phone. "I need proof she's dead. Find her body."

"I'm telling you. No one could've survived the crash."

"Helicopter, right?"

"Yeah. So?"

"Survival rates of helicopter crashes are damn good. What have you got so far?"

"One body—Deputy U.S. Marshal Reuben. Scattered metal. The tail rotor and part of the boom. The wreckage has to cover several miles or so of rough terrain. We're not equipped to deal with mountains and endless wilderness."

"Quit whining and find her. You owe me, Michael."

"Okay, we'll keep searching."

"And Michael. If you find the chopper and her body's not there, you can count on the bitch being alive."

"I understand, Uncle Leon."

Dagastino hung up the phone and looked at the picture of Frankie. Menendez had seduced his only son and then murdered him simply to steal a shipment of coke.

And if they brought Menendez back alive, he'd make her wish she'd never been born. He thought of all the means of torture he'd inflict on her. He'd start by peeling off her skin an inch at a time while she was very much alive. And after he'd inflicted all the damage he could, he'd put her out of her misery, for good. The next time she opened her eyes, she'd find herself in hell, pleasuring the devil.

Chapter Six

Late Monday evening, Michael Dagastino stared at the helicopter's severely battered body a few moments before approaching it. It had taken all day to find it. One good thing about being in Alaska, darkness wasn't an issue. As he entered the remaining section, he hoped the sickening sweet odor meant Menendez was dead. But when a strong wave of nausea hit him, he paused, then turned away from the sight of the two decomposing bodies and stepped back out. "Sergio, go see who they are."

"You got a weak stomach, Michael? Surprised you entered the business."

"I've been sick most of the day," Michael said, not wanting to appear weak. He couldn't let them see how much he hated this job, or how much he despised them and his uncle. They were all scumbags.

But he had no choice. He'd accepted his uncle's help and money. Souls didn't come cheap. But now, he had Michael's heart and soul in his pocket.

"Could be altitude sickness," the Native American guide suggested.

After a few moments Sergio returned, and Michael glanced up. "Was she in there?"

Sergio rolled his sleeves up. "Nah, just the damn ass-wipes in the cockpit. The others probably blew out when the back came off. They gotta be dead."

Michael studied the outer shell of the helicopter before looking back at the men. "Uncle Leon said if her body wasn't here to figure she's alive."

"How could someone survive this?" Antonio argued.

"If we go home and she turns up alive, it'll be my head." Michael slung his backpack over his shoulder. "Don't get too comfortable. We won't stop until we find her."

"Come on, man. This blows," Lenny griped.

"You punks are lazy shits," Sergio added.

Chased and Antonio moaned and complained, then gathered their gear.

The distant sound of a helicopter could be heard. It had to be a rescue team searching the area.

Since it was heading their way, they needed to hurry. "You heard it too?"

"Yeah," Sergio said. "Don't sweat it. With the clouds pouring it, it'll head back soon."

Michael looked at the man guiding them. "Where do we go from here?"

The Inuit guide stared at the ground around the wreckage, looking for tracks. "If anyone left here walking, they covered their tracks."

"I noticed something sort of weird," Antonio stated.

"It's you, douche bag," shouted Sergio in his gritty gruff voice.

Antonio flashed the old wise guy a hostile frown. "I'm serious. One of the seats is missing the padded shoulder harness. What moron would want it?"

Michael decided Antonio could be on to something. He drew in a deep breath and held it before stepping inside to see for himself. He studied the chair with the missing shoulder restraint. The other remaining seats hadn't been disturbed. Back outside, he looked at the men. "Someone cut it. Whoever removed it walked away from here. We have to assume Menendez is alive."

Antonio shrugged. "Could be Wolfe."

"He could still have her," Lenny added. "The man would probably go to hell and back to catch her."

"Well, so would your Uncle Leon," Chase said.

"We'll take her from Wolfe. If he's alive, he has to die." Sergio insisted, the oldest of the group. "If no survivors make it back, this will be considered an accident."

Michael didn't correct Sergio. "I don't want anyone else to die over this."

Antonio coughed to clear his throat. "We're already responsible for those shitheads killed in the explosion. "

"Lenny's responsible."

"You're in charge, Mikey boy," Sergio added. "You're just as guilty as the rest of us."

"If Lenny had done the job right. My instructions were to cause a slight problem so they'd have to make an emergency landing—not blow the tail off."

"Shit, man. I was in a hurry. Quit riding my ass over it."

"Now's not the time to hash it over," Sergio said, cutting his eyes to the wide-eyed guide. "We're running out of time. Once the sky clears, the rescue units will be headin' this way."

Michael calmed himself not wanting to show how stressed he was. He wasn't a killer. But by talking openly, the guide's life was now in jeopardy.

The native guide glanced around the forest surrounding them. "We need to divide into two groups. Big Rock River runs east and west, and it has streams branching off. It'd make more sense for any survivors to follow the water source."

Michael studied the men who'd come with him. "I'll take Sergio and Antonio with me. Lenny, you and Chase go with the guide."

"And if the marshals get in our way?" Chase asked.

"You decide." Michael hated the possibility of someone else being killed over this woman, but he had to appear callous. He had to adjust to this way of life since he'd agreed to become a part of the family business.

As they walked off in different directions, Sergio shouted, "Keep your radios on. This isn't a fuckin' Boy Scout hike."

Michael's legs ached from the long hours of struggling through the undergrowth. He hated Alaska. The no-see-ums drove him crazy, constantly biting but not offering anything visible to slap at. Gray skies and light drizzle affected his mood.

Michael couldn't go back and face his uncle without finding Menendez.

He missed his old life and Amy, but he'd made a pack with the devil and was stuck in hell.

◆◆◆

Tuesday morning, Sarah stood in the doorway and prayed for Marcy's safety as she headed toward the forest. Was Marcy's leaving a mistake? There had been no alternative. Rather than return inside, she stayed outside.

The sky had cleared. Good, now maybe a rescue team could reach them. She grabbed the ax that had been left by the door and returned inside.

"What are you doing?" Braden asked.

She couldn't resist teasing him. "Now that Marcy isn't here to protect you, I thought it might be time to get even with you. After all, I am Selena's sister. I could chop you up and feed you to the bears."

He appeared guarded for a moment before his eyes lit with amusement and a smile spread across his face. "I'm yours for the taking. Of course, I thought you might want to use my body in a different way."

The innuendo didn't escape her, and her face heated. "I guess I'll keep you around. I don't want to be alone. So for now you're safe."

"So what's the ax for?"

"To cut the branches off a fallen tree."

"Why? We have enough firewood."

"Since Marcy took the flare gun, I thought I'd make a big pile of brush in the opening. If a rescue team flies over, I'll light it."

"The ceiling's been too low for a chopper to risk coming for us. No one will be searching until this front moves through."

"If you'd quit moping and get out of bed, you'd know the sun is actually shining today."

Braden's face lit with an exuberant smile. "Get the brush ready."

The task turned into more of a challenge than she'd expected. Once she was done, she stared at her work with satisfaction.

◆◆◆

Later that morning, Braden waited until Sarah went inside and closed the door to unzip his pants. He'd downed a couple of mugs of dark coffee. It had been so strong that he immediately rinsed his mouth out with baking soda. He could use a decent cup of coffee. He didn't feel like going back inside the musty cabin. Instead he sat on a huge, flat rock and breathed in the fresh scented air

His thoughts drifted to Sarah. Her elegant height and facial features indicated her father had probably been of European descent. Maybe a trucker passing through.

He managed to open the door and hobble with his crutches to the bed.

Sarah stood at the small counter, placing salmon on two plates. "Lunch is ready."

"Once we leave here, I never want to eat salmon again." He closed the door behind him.

"Or blueberries," she added. "Today when I go for more water, I'll see if I can find something else to eat." She set the tin plates on the rickety table.

"I'll skip lunch." He made his way to the bed and collapsed. "If you go out, take the gun."

"I will. Though I'm not sure I'd know how to use it."

Braden glanced at his revolver on the table. Hell, he hoped she wasn't one of those idiots who believed in gun control. "Bring my gun over. We'll start with something small, then try the rifle."

She carefully grabbed it and walked toward him as though carrying a dead rat. After handing him the weapon, she sat beside him. "Mark didn't want guns in our home."

Yep, idiots.

"Angel, out here you'd better know how to shoot. Grip it with two hands like this." He demonstrated how to hold the gun. "Line up this little U with the white tip on the barrel. Then slide your index finger over the trigger, hold your breath, and squeeze. Simple."

"It is for you."

"Try it." He offered her the pistol.

She imitated what he'd shown her. "Like this?"

"You're letting it drop." He leaned closer and placed his hand on her forearm, raising it. "Hold the barrel straight. The only place your bullet will go is into the ground."

He flinched as he breathed in her scent. It horrified him to think how badly he wanted her. He lifted the gun from her hands and set it aside.

"That's the extent of my lesson?" she asked.

"No, this is." He tilted her face toward him and slowly placed his lips over hers. Unlike the last kiss, this one was intended to seduce her. Heat moved from his mouth straight to his groin. He'd half expected her to push him away, but instead, she eagerly accepted his tongue.

After the kiss, he moved his mouth to her ear. "Do you want me to stop?"

"No," she whispered, breathlessly.

He moved his hand over her left breast and molded his palm around it. She whimpered with pleasure. He kissed a path down her delicate neck. Midway, his kiss turned into a sucking motion. He'd always thought passion marks on girls looked nasty, but in some primal way, he wanted this woman to wear his mark.

He leaned her back on the bed and raised her shirt and bra above her breasts. Damn the woman had the most gorgeous body he'd ever seen.

Using both hands, he held her left breast and outlined the nipple with the tip of his tongue before closing his mouth over the hard nub and sucking it. Her nipple tightened against the pressure applied. After a few moments, he changed to the right one, teasing it until he heard her moan with need.

Out of breath, he straightened and gazed into her eyes—dark exotic pools shimmering with desire. Suddenly, his breath hitched. This was the face he'd hated for years. "I can't. You're too much like her."

Immediately, Sarah's expression changed from desire to humiliation and embarrassment. After pulling her bra and shirt in place, she stood without a word and hurried to the door, then left.

Shit. Sonofabitch. Why'd I hurt her?

He'd sat for an hour, feeling like a bastard, wondering where she'd gone and worried sick about her. Just as he grabbed his crutches, Sarah opened the door. She avoided looking at him and walked to the fireplace. She rebuilt the fire before pulling a chair over and sitting in front of the blaze. "I don't want you to think I'm easy. My husband Mark was the only man who has ever touched me like that."

Braden gave her a slight nod of his head. "I know. And I'm sorry. I shouldn't have kissed you."

"I'm not Selena. You were kissing me not her."

"I'm sorry. It won't happen again. It was just a physical response. That's all."

"Maybe to you, but not to me."

He thought about her choice of words. Was she trying to tell him that she felt something for him? Something besides lust? God, that'd be horrible. Hell, they'd known each other for a few days. He didn't believe in that love-at-first-sight bullshit. Or destiny. Maybe she did. If that were the case, he'd have to stop that egg from hatching.

"Now, angel, I don't want a lasting relationship with any woman. It's not you. For me it's all about sex. No pet names for each other and Valentine Day's cards. None of that romantic crap."

"Then I pity you." She pushed a red-hot piece of charred wood that had popped out back into the fire. "Mark and I had a good sex life, but that was only part of it. He was my soul-mate and my best friend. There's so much more a man and woman can offer one another."

"Well, I don't want it. So if you have an inkling about there being more between us, forget it. It's not gonna happen."

♦♦♦

Sarah would never tell him how she felt. Despite his crude personality, she'd come to like him, to care about him. She doubted it was love, but she didn't want a relationship that couldn't develop into something more. She wanted more than sex with a man. Commitment and companionship. Love and devotion. Someone who'd stick by you when you were sick and fix you chicken soup.

Even if Braden were capable of a lasting relationship, he'd never be able to get past her face. Selena's same face. She'd been foolish and careless with her yearnings. Perhaps because of their situation and the care she'd given him. Maybe she just wanted to feel needed by a man though she suspected not just any man would do. She wanted to feel needed by Braden. Why? Nothing about it made sense, and he was so different than Mark.

Once out of this mess, she'd return to Memphis and never lay eyes on him again. And the little episode on the bed proved she was ready to start dating if the right man asked her out.

The loud choppy sound of a helicopter whizzed overhead. Sarah raced out the door. Outside she realized she hadn't grabbed anything to light the pile of dead brush. She jumped up and down waving her arms. "Down here! Down here!"

But soon the sound faded. Braden stood in the door, a frown on his face.

Tears gathered in her eyes when she realized the helicopter hadn't spotted them. She couldn't believe she'd done something so lame.

He started to speak, but she raised her hand, stopping him. "Don't even say it. I know it's my fault they didn't see us. I don't need you rubbing it in. What I did was stupid."

"No, it wasn't. I'm not angry with you. I'm just pissed the damn helicopter flew over so quickly. It's taken them long enough to get over this way. They're assuming no one survived the crash."

She couldn't hold back the tears. Tears for not being rescued, tears for Mark and Tristen, and tears because of her situation.

"Sarah, calm down." He moved closer to comfort her.

"Don't touch me." Remembering how he'd reacted earlier, she walked back inside by the fire. Dry ragged sobs caused her chest to ache.

Braden followed her and stood beside her. "Sarah, it's not your fault. That pilot cruised over way too fast."

"It's not that," she said, sniffling. "It's everything. I miss my husband and son. One day, you think life can't get any better and the next you've lost it all. Life is so fragile."

"Yes, it is. And I'm truly sorry about your son and husband." He offered his hand, and she slipped her fingers through his and squeezed. He gripped back even tighter. She had to pull back from the man before she got hurt. She couldn't explain the connection she had with him.

For the last few months, she'd suffered through sexual urges. She wasn't the type to lure a stranger into bed. This was different. Braden and she had been thrown together, and she'd never see him once they were rescued. Would she deny herself this opportunity to ease the sexual craving that bothered her often?

◆◆◆

Michael never wanted to hike through woods again. Finding Selena in this never-ending Alaskan forest appeared hopeless. If she had survived, it was as if the earth had opened up and swallowed her. Was Satan protecting his own?

"Yo, Michael, it's Chase. Come in."

Michael held the radio to his mouth. "I'm here. You find anything?"

"We backtracked around. You know that marshal we found this morning."

"Yeah, Marshal Reuben. What about him?"

"Somebody placed stones over his body, so the animals couldn't reach him. That means someone's alive."

Michael exhaled a breath of frustration. "Any sign of Menendez?"

"None, man."

"She's alive," Michael said. "Call it a gut feeling. Whoever buried this man, could have Selena. Perhaps Wolfe. We'll keep searching. We're going to move upstream. I heard a helicopter fly over."

"We did too. Seems the pilot was in a hurry."

"Probably thinks they're dead. But someone buried that deputy and cut the shoulder restraint from the seat. So someone survived," Michael stated. "And we'll find them."

◆◆◆

Marcy had walked since early that morning. She wondered how far she'd gone. Her arms and shoulders ached from carrying the rifle, and her thighs cramped. She rested against a fallen tree to catch her breath. Her gaze lowered to her stomach. "Hey, little one, I guess I'll tell your daddy about you when I get back. Not that the dickhead deserves to know."

If I make it back.

Her mind drifted back to the day she'd learned she was pregnant. She'd prepared a candlelight dinner for Alex and had shipped the girls off to her mother's, hoping for a romantic evening to spring the good news.

At nine-thirty, she blew out the candles and lifted the wine from the ice bucket. While taking it back into the kitchen, Alex walked in from the garage. He stopped and stared at her, taking in her short, black cocktail dress.

"What's the occasion?"

"I've been waiting for you since six. Your dinner's in the fridge."

"I've eaten."

"Where?"

Guilt shadowed his face.

"Who is she?"

Still he didn't speak.

"Alex, are you having an affair?"

"I want a divorce, Marcy. I'm sorry, but I'm not in love with you anymore."

The words pierced her heart, yet she fought the tears. "And what about Brittany and Erica? Do you not love them anymore?"

"You know I do. That's different."

"You didn't answer me." She inhaled a deep ragged breath. "Who is she?"

"It's the new woman I hired a couple of months ago."

"Tiffany, the receptionist who's going to night school?"

"Yes. I didn't mean for it to happen, but it did. It's more than sex. She's there for me. You're always gone. You're married to your job. It means more to you than I do."

"Go. Get out, Alex. Pack your things and leave."

The snap of a nearby branch brought Marcy back to the present. She quickly lowered the gun from her shoulder and aimed in the direction of the sound. Something big pushed through the brush. Her body tensed.

Stay calm.

Be ready.

She positioned her finger on the trigger and held her breath, preparing to shoot.

Chapter Seven

Marcy's heart raced, and sweat beaded across her brow. Whatever was coming toward her was breathing heavily.

Steady. Get ready.

"Son-of-a-bitch."

"Darrel?" she shouted as she eased off the trigger .

"Marcy?" Darrel stepped into the clearing.

"I was about to shoot you."

"Good God, I was afraid you all died! Anyone else make it?" he asked, his expression full of apprehension.

"Braden and Sarah. But Dan and Henson didn't. What about Reuben?

"Broken neck. I did the best I could to bury him." They both paused as if giving a moment of silence to show respect. Darrel broke the silence. "So, it's Sarah now?"

Marcy nodded. "Yes, not Selena."

"Does Braden buy it?"

"Yeah, considering she's nursing him back to health. His knee's pretty banged up. I hated leaving them together."

"Afraid he'll kill her."

"Not exactly. Let's say they shared looks that could boil water. I'm just afraid he'll break her heart. In the short time I've known Sarah, she doesn't come across as the type to sleep around with just anyone."

"I can't see it. Braden attracted to someone with Selena's face. God almighty, that's freaky." Darrel grinned. "Wolfe owes me two hundred."

"Yep, sure looks that way." Marcy pulled a canteen from her shoulder. "Want a drink?"

"Hell, yeah. I've been stomping around in these woods for hours. I'm burning up."

"The sky is dimming. Let's try to make it a few more miles before we stop."

"I'm good for it." He lifted the canteen, tilted it back, and wiped his mouth. He fastened the cap and held it out.

"Hang onto it. I have another one." Her attention shifted to the battered Coach purse draped over his shoulder. "Sarah's purse. I'm amazed you found it."

"Yeah, I thought it might be important. It took a beating, but it's intact." He reached his hand out. "Want me to carry the rifle for a while?"

"That'd be great. It's heavy." They walked a few yards in silence. "Braden is almost positive Dagastino caused the crash."

"No surprise there. Can Braden get around?"

She nodded. "Sarah made him crutches, so he's able to move around the cabin, but his leg isn't up to a major trek."

"You got any food?"

"A little." She pulled out a pouch. "I've kept it sealed to keep bears away." She handed him a large chunk of smoked salmon.

He gobbled it down like a hungry dog. "Thanks." He scanned the area. "You got a plan?"

"Actually, yes. I'm following the river. And if I'm not mistaken, this is the same river that runs by the lodge."

"That could be a hundred miles away."

"I know, but it seems like the best plan."

"Then let's move out," Darrel said.

◆◆◆

Wolves howled in the distance, sending chills over Sarah. Their howls made her feel isolated and lonely.

It had been warm outside, but that didn't change the cave's temperature. It remained chilly most of the time. The fire had died, yet Sarah continued to stare at the brilliant, red embers while thinking about everything Braden had shared. It seemed odd that he'd been raised on an Iowa farm. Corn country. She could envision him as a little boy, playing cops and robbers with his brothers. But what she found truly amazing was the fact that he'd shared his personal life, from his childhood through his years in the Marines and how he'd gotten into law enforcement. From what Marcy had said, he didn't like talking about himself.

"You'd better get to bed. It's late," she whispered.

Braden positioned the crutches and pulled himself up from the chair. "Why don't you take the bed tonight?"

"No, I'm fine on the small bed," she lied.

"It's not a bed. It's a flat rock."

She laughed. "It's not so bad with pelts on it."

"There's room for both of us on the bed. I'll sleep on one end and you sleep on the other. My brothers and I used to do that when we had relatives visiting."

"I'm not your brother." She glanced cautiously at the bed. She didn't want to put herself in a position where the intimacy between them would ignite again. "Sleeping in the same bed with you probably isn't wise."

"I promise, I'll stay on my side."

"Hmmm...Still risky."

"Desperate times call for desperate measures," he winked. "We're both adults."

She rose from the chair and approached the bed. She didn't trust Braden or herself. "Which end?"

"You choose."

"I'll take the foot." She crawled across the bed to the far side and stretched out on the opposite end from him. "It's lumpy, but it beats sleeping on stone."

◆◆◆

Braden eased down onto the mattress, propping his foot on the stack of old blankets. When he realized her bottom was slightly touching his thigh, lustful thoughts seeped into his mind. Despite fighting the fantasies, his dick hardened. Her icy feet touched him and caused shivers to spread through him, killing the erection. "Damn, your feet are cold."

"I'm sorry, but they're freezing, and you're like a furnace."

"Give me your feet."

Sarah rolled to her other side facing him and extended them toward him. He caressed one of her soft feet in his hands and rubbed it before blowing his warm breath on it. Then he did the other foot. After massaging both feet, he brought them to this chest, letting them rest against him. The simple interaction had him aroused again.

"Are they warm now?" he asked.

"Yes, thank you," she replied, her breath husky.

Had the contact affected her as well?

Before letting her feet go, he brushed his fingers over the bottom of both, and she jerked them away. "Don't! I'm ticklish."

"I see."

"They feel much warmer. Thanks."

He grabbed her foot, held it to his mouth, and kissed her toes.

"Don't do that. Please."

Braden released her foot, but couldn't fight the images of sucking each one of her elegant toes. She had soft slender feet. After a few moments of silence, he whispered. "I'm sorry I hurt you today."

"You were right. There can never be anything between us. I think I was more embarrassed than hurt. You gave it to me straight—the way things are."

"Sarah, I like you."

"Thanks. I like you despite your caveman persona. You'd better go to sleep. I'll need to check that leg in the morning."

Braden hadn't confided in anyone like he had Sarah. He had come close to telling her about Andy. He found her life interesting and sad. Sad because she had no one but two cousins left. It was her Grandma Sofia who impressed him. She must've known Sarah was adopted, yet from the things Sarah had said, the woman favored her.

He knew what Grandma Sofia saw. Sarah had a good heart.

My Sarah.
Shit, now that's crazy.
God where did that come from?

He had to be losing his mind from being cooped up in the cave.

Once he dropped Sarah off in Memphis, that'd be it. There'd be no need to ever see her again.

For a moment before falling asleep, he worried about Marcy. Then his thoughts drifted to the men who'd died. The guilt churned in his stomach over their deaths. Then Andy came to mind. Braden had promised Andy a beagle puppy when he was older. A promise he was never able to keep.

I told Corey and Todd that you're a U.S. Marshal, and they didn't believe me. Can you come to my school one day? Please, Daddy. Pleeease.

Braden showed up at Andy's school the next week, wearing his marshal's jacket, gun, and badge. Being a marshal, the principal allowed him to keep his gun rather than leave it in the office. Andy couldn't stop grinning long enough to eat his Happy Meal.

The whistling of the wind lulled Braden to sleep.

He awoke to find Sarah's ass against him while her feet cradled the back of his neck. He pushed aside the sexual impulses her sweet little bottom caused.

As much as he hated leaving the warm bed, he needed to relieve himself. After maneuvering his legs to the edge, he grabbed his crutches, pulled himself up, and hobbled to the door. A gray sky greeted him along with a fine mist that blew against his face. He hoped it cleared. Maybe another search effort would be made.

He didn't know how many more days he could stand being confined, especially with Sarah. He wanted her. His senses were heightened around her like a buck seeking out a doe in heat. Her deep natural scent kept him aroused.

He'd been a fool yesterday. Hell, he doubted Sarah would've stopped him. He didn't have to look at her face and think of Selena. But after seeing how hurt she'd been, he realized it'd kill a woman like her to have someone use her body and walk away.

Okay, I'll admit I care about her.

But it's not love. Damn-it. No one falls in love in a matter of days.

He sat outside on the rock, enjoying a gentle breeze.

Sarah pushed through the door. "I'll be back. Just rest while I'm gone."

"Sarah," he called, stopping her. "Take my gun."

"I've got it."

Her late husband would roll over in his grave several times if he knew Sarah had become a gun toting mama. Braden chuckled.

By the time Sarah returned, he'd rekindled the fire.

She came through the door, struggling to bring in a large bucket of water. "It's chilly out there."

"I was beginning to worry about you."

"I took the time to freshen up at the river." She set the bucket down, then wiped her hands on a feed bag. "You're probably due for another bath. It'll take a while for the water to heat."

"I'd like to rinse my mouth out," Braden said. "Do we have any baking soda left?"

"A little." She returned with a cup of water and a spoon of baking soda. "Don't spill it."

"Thanks."

She waited beside the bed to take the cup. "I shot at a rabbit, but missed. It looks like it'll be salmon again tonight."

"I'd rather not eat."

"Food equals energy. You have to eat."

Once the water heated, she placed the bowl in a chair beside the bed and dipped the rag into the warm water, then handed Braden the cloth. While he washed himself, she raised the blanket to clean his wound. Her hands touch his skin, sending heated urges through his body.

All he could think of was getting her beneath him.

When she giggled, he opened his eyes.

She pointed at the blanket and grinned. "It's alive."

His little man stood at attention raising the blanket like a tent. Heat flamed across his face. "Sorry."

"No, you're not."

Only one person could relieve the intense sexual arousal that continued tormenting him.

Sarah.

"Can you wash my back?" he asked.

"Sure. Twist a little so I can reach you better."

"Thanks. It's driving me crazy." He handed her the cloth.

The sexual electricity between them heated the air like a summer thunderstorm.

She dipped the cloth into the bowl and wrung it out before wiping over his back. If he wasn't mistaken, her hand trembled as she washed his shoulders. When she leaned closer, he breathed in her scent.

"That feels damn good. A little harder."

Sarah pressed down on his skin. Her nails scraped him.

When he moaned with pleasure, she stopped. Before she could move away, he grasped her wrist and pulled her into his lap. He wrapped his arms around her waist to keep her from jumping up. "Sarah, I need you. And I think you want me."

◆◆◆

Sarah didn't know what to say. Instead of answering, she closed her eyes and waited to see what he'd do. He inched his hand under her shirt. His hand tightened around her breast. Desire flowed to every sensual part of her body. Hell, she wanted this as much as he did. She lifted her shirt as a sign of her surrender.

She chose to ignore her inner wisdom. Instead she arched her back so his mouth could reach her beaded nipples. His tongue lashed over their tips, causing her to moan. He nipped her with the edge of his teeth. Sitting in his lap, his masculine flesh pressed against her.

Stop him.

But she couldn't. Her entire body burned with sexual need. He kissed her, then pushed her from his lap and guided her down on the bed. He crawled beside her and lowered his mouth to hers, allowing his tongue to deepen the kiss. He unbuttoned her jeans and tugged them down a bit.

Her body jolted from his intimate touch. She thought any moment she'd burst into flames.

He taunted her with his mouth and fingers, making her even hungrier to be satisfied. His thumb brushed over her most sensitive spot, sending erotic ripples through her. She was too far gone to be embarrassed.

Oh God, I can't believe I'm doing this.

It doesn't matter. Enjoy it. I'll never see him again.

He took time to remove her jeans. Her hands gripped his shoulders as his mouth worked its magic, sending her over the edge. Her entire body tensed in painful pleasure.

But the primitive desire to have him inside her kept her hot and needy.

"Turn on your side," he whispered, his voice raw with passion.

With her body pulsing with anticipation, she did as he said.

He pulled his good leg from his jeans.

When he eased behind her, their bodies fit together like puzzle pieces. His hot, bare skin ignited her passion as he nudged her right leg slightly, then slid in and started stroking her.

"Push deeper," she whispered.

Flesh met flesh as she pushed her bottom back to meet him in a primitive rhythm. His large hands clamped over her breasts while his lips nibbled her earlobe. His hot breath seared her skin with sensual heat. When she clenched her inner muscles around his masculine flesh, he cried out and stroked her even harder and faster, causing them both to scream out. He withdrew quickly. She felt cheated not being able to savor the moments of his release.

"I don't know if I pulled out in time. I think I'd already started coming. Are you by chance on the pill?"

"No. After Mark died I didn't think about birth control."

She flinched inwardly. A pregnancy wouldn't be good. Braden had made his feelings for her known. This was sex, not love. And she hated she'd given into her desires without any consideration to the consequences.

But I've considered adoption. If I were pregnant, it'd be even better. The child would really be mine.

She doubted anything would come from this but a guilty conscience and a trip to the confessional—followed by a lot of Hail Marys.

At least this time, Braden hadn't freaked out and stopped. But then Sarah realized why. He hadn't really looked at her the entire time. Had he used her body while pretending she was someone else?

Anyone but Selena's identical twin.

Her throat tightened.

She tried to remind herself that it hadn't meant anything to her either. He was a convenient stranger that she used to ease the intense sexual fever she had. But unlike him, guilt had edged its way into her mind, and now she wore shame like a wedding veil.

"Are you all right, Sarah?"

She nodded. "Sure, why wouldn't I be?"

"You look like you're on the verge of tears. Want to talk about it?"

She shrugged. "I'll be all right. I'm not used to sleeping around. That's all."

"Are you afraid you could be pregnant?"

She shook her head. "No. You don't have to worry either. Mark and I had a difficult time conceiving Tristen."

◆◆◆

Braden would never admit it to Sarah, but the thought of her becoming pregnant had surfaced only seconds after he started climaxing. Though he'd pulled out, he feared it hadn't been in time. And there'd be no way he wanted to ever be a father again, especially with a child that could be born with Selena's genes.

Sarah stared at him with hurt eyes. "Don't concern yourself. If I turn up pregnant, I'll deal with it."

"I'd be willing to pay for the abortion."

"You're a bastard." She searched for her clothes, then slipped them on. "I'd never kill my baby."

"Okay, I deserved that. But that's how you made it sound."

"I just meant I'd raise it without your help."

"I wouldn't want you to. I'd want to pay for my part of the kid's upbringing."

"You're only talking about the money aspect."

"Angel, I don't want to have children. Ever."

"Then you should've been better prepared."

"Hell, I wasn't expecting to be with anyone. This was just going to be a quick arrest and then back to Kansas. I didn't expect to end up over the damn rainbow. I keep a box of condoms in my truck. Usually, I'm prepared."

"Maybe I should be the one who's worried. Do you have any STDs?"

"No, I got checked about a week before leaving Kansas."

After slipping on his clothes, he hobbled outside on crutches and sat on a boulder. Guilt perched on his shoulder like a noisy parrot, scolding him about what a selfish ass he'd been. He used her, and he wasn't proud of it. The damn woman had turned him into pretzel. If he didn't care about her, why would it bother his conscience now?

So I do care. And if she has my child, would I care about it too?

No. He couldn't love another child. All his love was buried with Andy. He didn't have anything left to give in that department.

Tell her about Andy.

I can't.

Braden assured himself he was jumping the gun on this. Hell, she said she had a tough time getting pregnant.

He couldn't return inside and face her. Instead, he stayed outside. Squirrels scampered up trees, playing chase. A deer mouse darted beneath a pile of stones. Then two other deer mice scurried beneath the rocks. Something had frightened them. Perhaps a hawk perched nearby.

It wasn't until he felt a gun in his back that he snapped from the deep trance. His heart rate jacked up.

"Where the fuck is Menendez?" asked a deep gritty voice.

Chapter Eight

"I know you've got her," the man behind him said, the gun still pressing against Braden's back.

Two more men approached, and Braden's stomach tightened in knots. He hoped Sarah would glance out the window before opening the door. Even if she saw the men, there wasn't anywhere to hide or a way to escape.

"She died in the crash. Just a female deputy and I survived. She's gone for help."

"Then where's Selena's body?" asked the older man who had a rough edge to his looks, a typical old wise guy with a New York accent.

A very tall young man with movie star looks stood in front of Braden, studying him with a deep intensity. He figured the guy was in his twenties. The man with him appeared to be middle-aged—late forties perhaps.

"Marshal Hill buried her," Braden answered.

"He's lying, Michael," the older man said.

Shit, this was like being on the set of *The Sopranos* or *The Godfather*.

"I'll be the judge of that, Sergio." Michael shifted his gaze back to Braden. "Then why didn't we find her grave? And why bury her and not the two men?"

Braden swallowed the lump in his throat. "Hill took care of the body. She didn't have the strength to pull the men out, just Selena. Maybe the animals dug her up."

"Bullshit," shouted the man who walked up with the one called Michael.

"You're fucking right, Antonio," Sergio quipped. "He's feeding us some shit."

Michael studied the splint and bandages Braden wore from the knee down. "Your deputy would have to be an amazing woman to have moved you here alone."

"The smartass has Selena," Antonio said.

"I want the truth," Sergio demanded. "And if I don't get it, I'm going to break your other leg."

Braden let out a surrendering sigh. "Okay. There was a woman, but it's not Selena. I made a mistake."

"Her DNA matched," Michael said.

Braden wondered how the young wise guy knew. Obviously someone was feeding information to Dagastino. "I thought it was Menendez until we crashed."

"We'll decide that for ourselves," Sergio announced. "Where's the bitch?"

"I don't have her," Braden said. "She left with the female deputy to get help."

Antonio kicked the door in. It swung back.

Sarah stood just inside the cave with the shotgun aimed at the men. "Drop your guns."

Sergio gasped. "Sweet Mary, mother of God. It's Selena."

Michael glanced at his men. "Remember, Uncle Leon prefers she be alive." The young wise guy took a couple of steps toward her. "Put the gun down."

Sarah shook her head. "No, I won't. Don't come any closer, or I'll shoot. Now, let Braden go, then go back out the door."

Sergio kept a pistol aimed at Braden's head. He couldn't help her.

"Menendez," Antonio said, "if you don't lower that gun, Sergio is gonna blow the marshal's fuckin' head off."

"I'm not Selena Menendez." Defeat shadowed her face as she let the shotgun slide from her grip to the floor. One of the men grabbed it.

Sergio drug Braden inside, then shoved him to the floor.

Sarah ran to him and knelt beside him. "Wolfe, your leg! Are you all right?"

"It hurts like hell."

"Where are his crutches?" Sarah asked the three men surrounding her.

Sergio grinned. "He won't be needing them."

"That's my decision, not yours," Michael said, his voice stern.

"There's no fucking decision, Michael. We'll take Selena with us and the marshal has to die. If not, we'll all have federal warrants on our asses."

"I said I'm not Selena."

"If you're not Menendez, I'll shoot my own fuckin toe off," Antonio said.

Michael offered him a pistol.

"What the hell's that for?" Antonio asked.

"Go ahead, shoot your toe off."

Sergio appeared confused. "What you talkin' about, Michael?"

"This isn't Menendez. She would've pulled the trigger instead of dropping the gun. She wouldn't defend the man who wants to see her burn as much as Uncle Leon."

Braden met the young wise guy's gaze. "They're twins separated at birth."

Michael studied Sarah with an acute interest. "I've seen pictures of Menendez. This woman's face doesn't have Menendez's hardness."

Why couldn't Braden see the difference? But he had more important things to worry about like keeping Sarah and him alive.

"You want us to pop them now?" Antonio asked—a look of excitement on his face.

"Michael should do it," Sergio said. He turned to the younger man. "It'd be your first kill. The sooner you get it over with the better. Each time it gets easier. It almost becomes like a sport."

Sarah wrapped her arms around Braden.

Braden embraced her and kissed the side of her face to console her. He thought about the small Llama .22 semiautomatic in his boot. But it wouldn't be any good against three weapons.

"I'll do it. But I want them face down on the bed."

"Holy shit, Michael. Just shoot the motherfuckers in the back of their fuckin' heads," Antonio said. "And be done with it. Not all this drama."

"I don't want to see their faces. Both of you move to the bed," Michael ordered.

"We won't say anything about the crash. Please don't kill us," Sarah pleaded as Sergio forced her to the bed.

"Get your hands off of her," Braden shouted. He managed to limp to the bed and lay beside Sarah.

"After you ice them, we'll pull out a bottle of whiskey and celebrate. Think of this as an initiation into the family. Your uncle will be proud of you," Antonio said.

Braden lay beside Sarah on his stomach while Antonio bound their hands behind their backs. So much for reaching the .22 tucked in his boot. He turned his face toward Sarah. "I'm sorry for the way I treated you."

Instead of answering, she continued whispering a prayer.

"It won't hurt. It'll be fast," Braden assured her. As Michael moved toward the bed, Braden closed his eyes, preparing for the first shot. Sweat beaded on his forehead. "Close your eyes, Sarah."

"Braden. I'm so scared," she whispered.

"Don't you know nothin', Michael? You gotta shield yourself from blood spatter. Take that pillow and hold it over his head and shoot through it," Sergio advised. "Capice?"

Michael nodded and snatched the pillow, then held it over Braden. The pressure of the gun pressed through the thin layer of cloth and feathers.

Braden held his breath, waiting for the blast.

Any moment now.

The shot rang out.

His body flinched, and he smelled the fumes from the powder.

I'm not dead.

Though he wasn't sure what was going on, he didn't dare move even when Michael lifted the pillow. Another shot rang out.

God, Sarah. He killed her.

Braden's heart knotted as emotional pain vibrated through him. *Sarah.* But when she exhaled the breath she held, he wanted to cry with joy.

She's alive!

Not sure why Michael shot the mattress instead of him and Sarah, Braden turned his head toward the men just as Michael pivoted around with his gun aimed at the two thugs.

Two blasts of gunfire rang out—fast and efficient. First, Sergio then Antonio grimaced and crumpled to the floor.

Sarah screamed.

"Holy crap. I just screwed up," Michael set his gun down, then checked the pulses of the other two wise guys. "They're dead." He first untied Sarah then Braden.

Braden took the opportunity to pull the .22 from his boot and aimed it at Michael. "Kick your gun over."

The tall young man did it without hesitation. "You want their guns too?"

Braden shook his head. "No, if you were going to kill us, you'd have done it already. Why them and not us?"

"I couldn't kill *innocent* people. Until now I've never killed anyone. Antonio and Sergio are Uncle Leon's right hand guys. "

Sarah's body trembled. "Thank you."

"But what will I tell Uncle Leon and the others?"

"Others?" Braden slid the pistol in his pocket. He wanted it handy in case Michael changed his mind.

"Yeah, Chase and Lenny. There was an Indian guide with them. We split up to search. The guide must've wised up and disappeared on them. Sergio radioed them and told them to meet up with us here."

"Radio? How far does it transmit?"

"Not over twenty miles on a straight path."

"A rescue team might be within that range."

"Yeah, but it's set on one frequency. I don't have the code for the others. We rented the equipment, and the man preset our radios on one frequency. You use it and Chase and

Lenny will hear you. As soon as our helicopter lands, I'll send someone for you."

Braden had to go against his own code of ethics and let Michael walk away. If he didn't rejoin his group, the other men would show up at the cave. "When are you being airlifted out?"

"In two days at a pick up point."

"Contact the others. Tell them I killed Antonio and Sergio and that you barely escaped. Order them to meet you back at the pick up point."

"I'm not sure they'll buy it. They'll probably come after you for killing Antonio and Sergio."

Braden hesitated. "Tell them we were airlifted out."

"Lenny might be that gullible, but Chase isn't."

Sarah sat up and wiped her eyes. "Don't forget to mention that Wolfe's prisoner isn't Selena."

Michael nodded. "Still sounds half-ass, but I don't have an alternate plan." He explained what Lenny had done. "The guy's an idiot. Once you were forced down, we planned to grab Menendez. No one was supposed to get hurt."

"Still, you were in charge and four people ended up dead," Braden stated. Though Michael wasn't a natural born killer like the others, he was involved up to his eyebrows. Braden couldn't let it go, but at the same time he didn't want to push Michael into a corner. The guy might reconsider letting them live. "Radio the others before they show up here."

"After I contact them, I'll bury these guys." Michael stared at the bodies a moment before glancing at Sarah. "I'll clean up this mess, then bring you most of our provisions. There should be enough food to hold you over."

"So long as it's not salmon," she replied. "And, Michael, thanks."

◆◆◆

That evening Michael stood by the small fire inside the cave, dreading the lies he had to tell his uncle. You couldn't survive as a mob boss without being able to read people and know when they're lying. His uncle had perfected the skill.

Wolfe and Sarah gobbled down the canned stew as though they hadn't eaten in months. It amazed him the closeness these two had developed in such a short time. Michael suspected the deputy had strong feelings for this woman but worked hard to suppress them. It was a no-brainer that the woman seemed hopelessly in love with the marshal. Would they be this attracted to one another under different circumstances?

He thought about Amy. It burned him all the way down to his soul to think of her dating other men, knowing he could never be a part of her life. But he would never involve her in the kind of life he was now living. When the fire popped behind him, his mind returned to the present.

"Who designed the crutches?" Michael asked.

"I did," Sarah answered.

"Good work. Though I must tell you cutting the shoulder restraint from the helicopter made us realize someone had survived the crash."

Sarah appeared regretful."It never occurred to me that anyone would notice."

"We did. You never knew about Selena?" Michael asked Sarah.

"No, I didn't."

"Then I wonder if Selena knows about you," Michael commented.

"I'm not sure."

"Why the interest?" Braden asked.

"A thought occurred to me. It's probably best for Sarah if Selena doesn't know about her. She doesn't come across as the type who likes sharing, especially faces," Michael said. "She might resent Sarah for having a better life. Human nature is a peculiar thing."

"It's not like we live in the same state. This might sound insane, but I'd like to meet her."

"I agree with him," Braden stated. "I think it's best to stay away from her. Unless, she's behind bars when you visit."

"I know we're not exactly the Kardashian sisters." Sarah broke off a piece of bread and ate it before glancing at Michael. "How did you end up working for your uncle?"

"My mother was determined to keep me out of it. I was in my last year of grad school when she became ill. There wasn't enough money to cover her medical expense and care. About the same time, a professor accused me of cheating by submitting a purchased term paper. I was dropped from the program. Uncle Leon stepped in and covered the bills. He paid off my student loans. When he asked me to join the family business, I felt I owed him."

Sarah appeared intrigued. "What was your degree in?"

"Psychology. I was finishing up my masters at the time."

She smiled. "That explains your interest in human nature."

"It wasn't until later I realized Uncle Leon paid the professor to lie."

"That's a lowdown thing to do," Sarah replied.

Michael liked Sarah, but he wasn't too fond of the marshal. The guy would go after his own mother if she'd wavered from the law. He envisioned Wolfe slapping handcuffs on a little gray haired lady.

◆◆◆

Sarah joined Michael by the fireplace. "Is it too late to return to psychology? You could transfer to a different college. Surely, your uncle would understand. Wouldn't he want you to finish school?"

"You're either in the business or six feet under." Michael paused. "There's no turning back. A degree isn't needed to conduct the family business."

"You'll have to answer in court for the deaths of the deputies who died when that helicopter came down."

"Yeah, I figured I would."

Would Braden really involve Michael since he spared their lives?

Sarah turned her attention to Braden. The man had a face longer than a basset hound.

He's jealous of Michael.

And for just a moment, a glimmer of delight filled her heart. Then she realized his jealousy didn't stem from love, but from a case of primitive possession like a caveman protecting his turf. And she was the only woman in the village.

"Interesting the way you two met," Michael said. "Once you're out of here, do you intend to continue seeing each other?"

Sarah nor Braden replied. She knew Braden had no interest in seeing her once they left Alaska. "Excuse me. I need some fresh air."

Outside, she sat on the large rock by the door. It had become a makeshift lawn chair. The fact that she was alive exhilarated her. When the door opened, she'd expected to see Braden.

Instead, Michael approached her. "Mind if I join you?"

She shook her head.

"You sure? You seem upset."

She cleared her throat. "I miss my husband and son."

For the first time, Michael's face reflected his thoughts. Did he think she had a family somewhere? That she was an adulteress?

"I'm a widow. They were killed in a car accident two years ago."

"Oh, I'm sorry. Have you been able to move on?"

"I thought so." She glanced at the cabin. "Obviously, I moved in the wrong direction, and I'm feeling guilty. I wonder what my husband would think of me."

"It's not uncommon for people isolated together under stressful situations to become intimate with one another. You've both suffered a frightening experience with the crash. It's similar to Stockholm Syndrome. Though Wolfe isn't really holding you hostage, this isolation and the circumstance for being here has caused you to form a paradoxical emotional bond. It's a type of self-preservation mechanism."

"I think it's more a case of overactive hormones. Whatever, I'm feeling foolish. I could've used my willpower."

Michael chuckled. "Willpower is a complex matter, especially when affected by stimulus out of your control."

"Overall, Wolfe's a bastard."

"It's his defense mechanism to avoid getting too close to you."

Sarah enjoyed Michael's company. He possessed a silky smooth voice that relaxed her. It wasn't hard to picture him as a shrink. "Maybe you'll have an opportunity to finish up your degree someday."

Michael sat beside her. "I'd have to start the entire program over if I switched schools. The worst part of this was breaking up with Amy."

"Was it absolutely necessary?"

"Absolutely. I didn't want her involved in this kind of life. I called off our engagement a month before the wedding. Uncle Leon never knew about her."

"Maybe, you're totally wrong about your uncle," Sarah reemphasized.

"In his eyes, I'm a fly, and he's holding the swatter."

The door opened, and Braden stood in the doorway, staring at them, his expression distorted with anger. "Am I interrupting anything?"

Michael smiled. "No, pull up a rock."

For the first time, Sarah laughed. "Before you sit down, grab a couple of beers and the pretzels."

Michael laughed at her joke.

"Don't remind me. I'd kill for a cold beer." Braden stepped from the door, closing it behind him. "I need some fresh air."

Sarah saw through his flimsy excuse for joining them. He wanted to know what was transpiring between her and Michael.

"I'd better turn in. I set my tent up not far from here." Michael stood. "I'm heading out early. "Good night." He walked toward the forest.

"Good night, Michael," she called out.

Braden mumbled something under his breath.

Sarah and Braden returned inside and stood in front of the fireplace. She couldn't think of anything to say. Maybe she had been infatuated because of the situation. She hoped so. After all, when Braden thought she was Selena, he'd been heartless. The man knew how to be cruel. No, Braden wasn't for her. She'd return to Memphis and try to put Alaska behind her.

"Too bad, Michael can't be a psychologist," Sarah finally said to Braden, hoping to break the icy silence between them.

"Why's that?"

"He has a really good insight to how people think. Like knowing why you're acting like such a bastard."

"He doesn't know shit."

"Wolfe, I'm not expecting anything from you. I won't be waiting for flowers or phone calls. What we did shouldn't have happened."

"You got that right. I was thinking with my dick."

And I was thinking with my heart.

But she didn't say it out loud. "And if I'd been smart, I'd have chopped it off when I had the ax in my hands," she said.

"I'm sorry, Sarah. I hadn't intended for any of this to happen." He paused. "But you came willingly."

She nodded. "You're right. I did. I don't regret it. I think I would've stayed locked in a shell, hiding from life if you hadn't come along. Now I'm ready to start a new life."

She changed the subject back to Michael, hoping she could convince Wolfe not to charge Michael for the death of the deputies and only charge the others. "He spared our lives, and now he's in a tight spot with his uncle."

"He could possibly be facing a life sentence without parole. When I get back, the first thing I'll do is have a warrant sworn out for his arrest. They have to pay for the deaths of those men. There's no way around it."

Sarah's chest tightened in distress. "But Braden, he's not like the others. He had a future until his uncle interfered and pushed him into the family business."

"None of that matters. He joined up with the wrong crowd, and he's going down. He dug his own grave."

Chapter Nine

Marcy glanced at Darrel, who not only carried Sarah's large purse but also the heavy rifle. "Let me carry something for a while."

"I got it."

"Then let's take a ten minute break. I could use one."

They trailed off in different directions into the woods for a bathroom break. When Darrel returned, Marcy stood by the river, looking in both directions. "I wonder how far we've come."

Darrel shrugged, "Damned if I know. My concern is how much farther we've got."

"Good point."

She washed her face at the river's edge and smoothed her hair. Then she noticed a large grizzly, probably a male, on the other side of the river. "Darrel, you might want to have the rifle ready."

He twisted around and stared behind him. "Oh shit. Sweet mercy. Think he sees us?"

"He smelled us at least a mile back. And just because he looks as clumsy as you, he can outrun us."

"Think he's hungry?"

Marcy grinned. "I don't know. Why don't you go over and ask? While you're doing that, I'll find a tree to climb."

"You're real funny, Hill."

"Where's that chivalrous nature of yours?"

"The way he's looking at us, I'd say somewhere between my fatback and my rump roast."

The bear lifted his large head and sniffed in their direction, then grunted several times.

Darrel slowly removed the rifle from his shoulder and held it in position. "We need an elephant gun."

"He's not an elephant. If you shoot him between the eyes, it'll take him down."

"Hell, you do it. You're a better shot than me."

"Darrel, be a man. Hold that gun up. Think of him as a gangbanger who's about to shoot you."

"Bullshit. I've never had a gangbanger want to eat me."

Suddenly, the bear jerked his head as though listening to something before it darted into the thick brush and disappeared.

Marcy and Darrel glanced at each other.

He shrugged. "What spooked him?"

"Maybe he got a good look at your face." No sooner than she spoke the words, she heard what had frightened the bear.

◆◆◆

Braden sipped his coffee slowly. His conscience had bothered him about Sarah all night. What had transpired between them had been more than sex. It had been emotional, reaching to his soul. But he wasn't the man for her. She needed someone who'd be there for her instead of someone like him who'd be chasing down fugitives for months at a time.

Besides, he had too much baggage with Andy's death. And there was still the fact that she was Selena's sister.

He had to continue acting callous and cold to her, pretending he didn't care. He'd rather see her hurt now than later when things didn't pan out between them.

As for Michael, Braden had come up with a way to spare him. He didn't want to destroy the guy's life. He asked him to stop by before heading out.

When Michael entered the cabin, he smiled at Sarah. "You look better since you've eaten a full meal."

"I feel better. Thanks."

Michael turned his attention to Braden. "What did you want to talk to me about?"

Braden sat in a chair by the fire and folded his arms across his chest. "Turn federal witness against your uncle. I'm almost positive you could make a deal with the federal prosecutor."

"What would it involve?"

"You'd have to change your name and relocate. I'll request to be there for most of the transition period."

"It's my only way out of the family business, isn't it?"

"The only way other than in a coffin or going to prison."

Michael paled for a moment. "There's a girl I was engaged to. If Amy will still have me and be willing to come with me, can I bring her?"

"Probably. But she'd never be able to see her family. You need to understand that."

"I've never mentioned Amy to my uncle."

"When the heat turns up, he'll become very resourceful at knowing everything about you, trying to find a way to get to you. Trust me he'll discover your vulnerable spots."

"I'm not sure she'll agree," Michael said. "She has a large family. Would I be able to finish school, and could my mother be transferred?"

"Yes. Both could be arranged. You think about it. Contact me if you're interested, and I'll contact the necessary people."

"What about the charges for those men who died in the crash?"

"I believe you're telling me the truth. The others would be prosecuted."

Michael stared at Braden. "And if I don't turn federal witness?"

"A warrant will be sworn out for your arrest. You could end up serving life."

"I'll think about your offer."

"Try to learn as much as you can about your uncle. The more you have against him, the better. I'll take what you have to a federal prosecutor and judge."

"Michael, give Braden's offer careful consideration," Sarah advised. "This might be your only chance of escaping the pit of vipers you're with."

"I will. And I'll find a way to speak with Amy." Michael looked back at Braden. "You'll probably be hearing from me." He shifted his focus to Sarah. "It was a pleasure meeting you. I wish you the best."

"Thanks, Michael. Same to you."

Michael gave Braden a slight nod to say goodbye.

◆◆◆

Marcy heard the rotor blades of a helicopter whipping around and around. She shielded her eyes and stared at the gray, misty sky. "I see it!" She pulled the flare gun out and fired into the air. "There it is!"

"Down here!" Darrel dropped everything and waved his arms. "We're here! Don't you fly over us, you son-of-a-bitch! How could they have missed the flare?"

"How could they miss something as big as you? You really stand out against these gray glacier rocks," Marcy added.

"Maybe they just thought I was a black bear."

Despite the grimness of their situation, Marcy laughed.

"It's turning around!" Darrel shouted.

Again they jumped and shouted, waving their arms.

"It's landing!" Marcy yelled over the noise.

Once the huge silver bird landed on a patch of dry riverbed, they ran toward it. Then Marcy stopped.

"Darrel, wait. What if it's Dagastino's men?"

They waited as the helicopter's doors opened. The pilot and the man in the passenger seat stepped out. Marcy squinted her eyes, trying to get a look at them. The man appeared familiar. As he ran toward her, she recognized him.

"Alex! God, thank you." She limped toward him, her feet burning and stinging. "Alex! Alex! You came for me."

"Marcy," he said as he lifted her in his arms and held her next to him. "I knew you were alive." After kissing her forehead, he grinned. "You smell terrible, sweetheart."

"Yeah, I do." Her gaze held his. "You're the last person I expected to see."

"I love you, Marcy. I've been a idiot."

"Let's go. We'll talk later." She glanced toward the helicopter. "Are the girls with you?"

"No. They don't know about the crash. Your parents and I kept it from them. They're still at your mom's. I stopped by the house and packed you a bag. I'm staying at the lodge where you were."

They joined Darrel and the pilot. Marcy asked the pilot, "Can we go after Braden and Sarah? Braden has a busted knee."

"I don't have the gear aboard for treating a medical emergency, and it's clouding up," the pilot said. "I'll radio for someone to fetch them."

"Who is Sarah?" Alex asked.

"The woman we all thought was Selena Menendez. The other men with us were killed in the crash."

"God's that's tragic. It could've been you."

Alex helped her inside the helicopter. Darrel and the pilot followed.

The pilot radioed in concerning Sarah and Braden. Then he glanced back at Marcy. "Sorry, but your friends will have to wait until morning. Visibility is decreasing rapidly. That's not uncommon this late in the evening."

Marcy nodded, knowing there was nothing she could do for them tonight. After the chopper lifted, she unlaced her boots and slipped them off. Blood oozed from the blisters.

"Your feet are bad," Alex said.

"I've hiked for miles. I'll tell you about it when we get back."

Marcy's heart had only experienced this much joy when her daughters had been born. Alex had come for her. He was sorry. Would she be able to forgive him? Could she ever learn to trust him again? Though he'd had the affair, she couldn't blame him completely. How many times had she put the girls' activities and her job first? Too many to count. She had taken him for granted.

Despite the role she'd played in pushing him into the arms of another woman, she couldn't make things too easy on him. She considered the fact that he had traveled thousands of miles to rescue her only a start.

They reached the lodge an hour later. Marcy gave Braden and Sarah's exact location to the rescuers. One of the rangers had stayed at the cabin while on a hunting trip, so Marcy didn't see any point in going back in the morning.

She hated Sarah and Braden had to remain stranded one more night.

After calling her mom and daughters, she rested in the tub with her eyes closed. It'd been great hearing their voices. When Alex walked in, she offered him a smile. "This feels wonderful. I don't want to get out."

"Don't fall asleep. They had Neosporin at the front desk. I'll doctor your feet tonight."

She stood and stepped from the tub. Water droplets ran in rivulets down her body. She didn't miss the sexual hunger in Alex's gaze. It'd been a long time since he'd given her such a sensual look. She couldn't deny the effect it had on her body.

Alex draped a large towel around her, then pulled her into his arms. He held her for a moment before drying her. "Your breasts look larger."

"You just haven't seen them in awhile. I'm sure I've lost weight."

"The diner's closed, but they'll still do room service. Anything particular you want?"

"A steak, salad, and a loaded baked potato. If they have chocolate pie, I'd like a slice—no make it two."

Alex grinned. "You're entitled to eat all you want."

Still standing behind her, he paused a moment before placing his hands on her arms and leaned and tenderly kissed her shoulder, working his way up her neck. "Oh, Marcy. I've missed you."

When she thought about Tiffany, she pushed him back.

What had happened between Alex and his slut?

Until she knew whether he had walked away from Tiffany on his own, she had to keep her distance. If the bitch dumped him, Marcy didn't want him coming home like a rejected dog with his tail between his legs. "We need to talk. I'm not sure about us yet."

He spun her around and gazed into her eyes. "I love you."

"So you say. Where's Tiffany? Last I heard you wanted to marry her."

"I realized it's you I want, not her. She's no longer working for me."

"I need time, Alex. You hurt me."

"I'm truly sorry. I'll never hurt you again."

Yeah, that's what they all say.

"Like I said, I need to think about us and what I want for my life."

"Marcy, I can't live without you."

"But you did. It didn't kill you. I can't go through this again."

"You won't. I swear."

A cyclone of confusion spun in Marcy's mind and kept her from thinking clearly. Brittany and Erica had been miserable since Alex left, but her decision had to be based on what she felt. She wanted him back, but before making that decision, she had a lot to consider. Thank goodness this room had double beds. She needed to speak with one of the ladies who worked in Alex's office and find out what really happened to Alex and Tiffany's love affair.

And if Tiffany dumped him first, what then?

How would she deal with it?

Chapter Ten

The next morning, Marcy stared at the ceiling while hoping the fog had lifted and the rescue team had left to find Braden and Sarah.

Then her thoughts returned to Tiffany.

While Alex showered, Marcy removed his phone and pressed the office number. It'd be almost lunchtime, but perhaps she could catch Mrs. Beard before she left.

The old receptionist answered the phone. "Hill and Jones' Accounting Firm."

"Mrs. Beard, this is Marcy Hill."

"Marcy, you're alive! Good God! Alex lost it when he learned about the crash."

"He found me. I survived, but three others died."

"I'm sorry, but I'm certainly glad you're all right. I don't think Alex could've lived with himself."

"Speaking of Alex, I need to know if he left Tiffany or did she dump him?"

"He broke up with her. I'm certain of it."

"I want him back, but I have to make sure he's coming back for all the right reasons."

"I understand, dear. I really think he's learned his lesson. He became sidetracked and confused, but I never doubted his love for you. That Tiffany is a persistent young woman who is delusional. Basically I'm saying she's wired too tight."

The buzz of the electric razor stopped, so Marcy quickly thanked Mrs. Beard, disconnected the call, and put the phone back in his jacket pocket.

Alex stepped out dressed in shirt, vest, and jeans. He looked great. He smelled like a blast of citrus. "Coffee sounds good. Let's go eat."

In the diner, she sipped her orange juice making it last. The smell of the bacon and coffee made her stomach growl, but she decided to stick with just toast since she felt queasy.

"I'm surprise you didn't order coffee," he said.

She wasn't ready for him to know about her pregnancy. "I figured since I've gone without caffeine this long, I might as well give it up."

"Makes sense. You feel any better?"

"Much. I guess my stomach wasn't ready for the steak and pie I ate last night."

He grinned. "You had the appetite of a lumber jack."

Marcy flinched when someone dropped several dishes on the floor in the kitchen. It took her a minute to regroup her thoughts. Though she had the story from Mrs. Beard's perspective, she wanted to hear Alex's account of it. "Tell me what happened with Tiffany? I need to know before I decide whether to allow you to move back in."

"Like I said, I fired her. I realized I love you, and the more I thought about what I'd lost, the more I despised her."

Marcy wouldn't ask for any more details. His brief summary confirmed what Mrs. Beard had told her.

"Have you made a decision?" he asked, his eyes revealing eagerness.

She shrugged. "I'm working on it. Though I never stopped loving you, I'm not sure whether it'll work. I don't know if I can live in a relationship with someone I don't trust."

"Understandable." Alex blotted his mouth with his napkin. "If I can't move home, can we at least date?"

Marcy couldn't hold back the smile. "Yeah, we can date."

"Should I stop the divorce proceeding?"

A pain stabbed her heart. "You're the one who filed. Do what you want."

"I wish I could go back and change everything, but I can't. I can only try to make it up to you."

But you can't. You can never give me back my trust.

Marcy stood. "I'm tired. I'm going go upstairs and lie down. Please wake me if the rescue team returns."

"I will."

Upstairs Marcy pulled back the blankets and crawled into bed. She closed her eyes but couldn't sleep. She had to cleanse her mind of Tiffany or any reconciliation with Alex would only collapse like a house of cards.

◆◆◆

The fire had gone out, and the cave had cooled again.

After grabbing wood, Sarah returned inside and rekindled the fire. Soon a blaze danced, heating the cave. The smoke stung Sarah's throat and eyes. She walked over to the bed and touched Braden's forehead. His fever had returned, and his body trembled with chills. At least he hadn't thrown up again.

He opened his eyes and stared up at her. "Sarah, I feel like I'm dying."

"You're not. You're a survivor. It could be a touch of food poisoning from the turkey Michael gave us. You were the only one who ate it. I just stoked the fire. You should warm up."

The cabin heated like a dry sauna, but Braden still shivered. "Are there any more blankets?"

She'd already piled the pelts on him and her blanket. "No, but I have an idea."

Leaving her clothes on, she climbed behind him and slipped beneath the heap of covers. She could only imagine how ripe they smelled. She couldn't wait to take a long, hot bath.

"What are you doing?" he asked.

"Offering you a little body heat. That's all. So don't get any ideas. Turn on your side."

He did as she requested. Then she scooted her body in line with his, her breasts pressed against his back and her pelvis cradled his butt.

"You feel good," he whispered.

She draped her arm over him as her head settle behind his on the mattress. "Are you any warmer?"

"Yeah, I am. Do you do this for all your patients?"

She giggled. "No, just the ones with terminal stupidity like you. Now try to sleep."

◆◆◆

When Braden awoke, he thought of Andy.

I want to be just like you when I grow up. I want a marshal's cap just like yours.

The next time Andy stayed with him, he gave him the navy cap with yellow lettering. U.S. Marshal. It was an old cap someone had left behind, but it thrilled his kid.

He pushed the painful memory from his mind, but not before anger shot through his veins. He hoped the bastard who'd killed him was rotting in hell. The two hundred sixty pound creep didn't last six months once the inmates learned he'd killed a kid. The guy was found with his throat slit. Braden had wanted to hug the inmate who'd killed the son-of-a-bitch.

He had the sensation of something missing—an arm or leg. Something vital and then realized it was not having Sarah beside him that made him feel empty.

She stood by the fire. "Still chilled?"

"No, I think my fever is gone. I'm soaking wet, but I'm feeling almost human again. My stomach has stopped churning."

She walked to the bed and placed her hand on his forehead. "No fever. Good. I'm tired of cleaning up after you."

He pushed the piles of covers back and sat up. "Thought I was dying for a while there."

"Are you hungry?"

"My stomach's not up to it, but I wouldn't mind rinsing my mouth."

She rubbed her fingers over his beard. "You look real dignified."

"It itches. This Grizzly Adam's lifestyle isn't for me."

"My legs could use a few strokes of a razor. I might be mistaken for a sasquatch."

He chuckled then grew serious. "Thanks for taking care of me."

Sarah pinned him with a stern look. "You're my patient. That's all."

"I thought maybe you wanted me again."

"Think I'll pass, but I will bring you some water."

The whomp, whomp, whomp of a helicopterr sounded nearby.

"Helicopter! Sarah, light the brush. Now!"

She grabbed the bucket and scooped hot coals from the fire, then hurried outside.

In only moments, flames reflected in the dingy window. The fire blazed upward. Any pilot who didn't see it had to be blind.

The helicopter's rotor engine roared loudly as it passed over the cabin. Outside, Sarah jumped up and down, waved her arms, and shouted.

The scent of the burning brush permeated the air, and sparks floated in the breeze.

He wondered whether it'd been Michael or Marcy who'd made it back first. God, he hoped Marcy was safe.

Braden hobbled out on his crutches and joined Sarah. "They landed nearby."

She smiled and hugged him. "I told you someone would come."

◆◆◆

When Marcy heard the helicopter approaching, she pushed Alex aside. "Braden and Sarah are here!" She hurried through the lodge and ran outside and waited for it to land. The moment the doors opened, Sarah was helped out by the rescue team. Next several men carried Braden on a gurney through the door.

Marcy cried tears of joy and wrapped her arms around Sarah, then stepped away. Sarah smelled like the cabin—smoked wood and salmon. Marcy explained how Alex rescued her. "We notified the rescue unit of your location as soon as we could. I'm sorry it took them so long."

"I'm just glad to be back."

"Darrel and I haven't stopped eating since returning."

"Darrel? Alive?"

"Yeah, I found Darrel. I almost shot him for a bear. Unfortunately, Marshal Reuben didn't survive the crash."

"God, that's awful. I'm sorry about the marshal."

"What's this about Braden being sick?"

"He's over the worst of it," Sarah replied. "I don't think I could've stood another day there."

Marcy recognized the despair in Sarah's eyes. "Are you going to be all right?"

"I'm fine."

Marcy placed a hand on Sarah's shoulder for a second. "I hated leaving you."

"I know." Sarah walked toward the lodge. "I need a bath."

"They have a room ready for you. I placed some clothes that might fit you along with some other items on the bed."

Sarah gave her a weak smile. "Thank you, Marcy. Is there a way I can get my belongings back? My clothes and mp3 player mainly."

"Marshal Kneller took them. I'll see what I can do."

"Thanks." Before stepping through the doorway, Sarah paused. "As soon as I can arrange it, I'll fly home."

Marcy couldn't put her finger on it, but Sarah didn't seem the same. Distant. Sad. What had Braden done to her? She decided to confront him and hurried to his room.

As the doctor was leaving, Marcy slipped through the door. "How are you feeling?"

"Clean but tired and hungry. Where's Sarah?"

"Taking a long hot bath. I arranged for her belongings to be sent here."

"When?"

"Tomorrow. Marshall Kneller sent them with a guy that's passing this way on his way to Seward."

He nodded. "The sooner we get her home the better."

"Braden, you bastard. You messed around with her, didn't you?"

"She's a grown woman. I didn't make any promises to her. She chose to do it, knowing damn well there could never be anything between us."

"Sarah doesn't come across as the type for a one nighter. She finally opened her heart to another man, only to have you use her."

"I'll talk to her tomorrow."

"She's planning to leave as soon as she can arrange transportation to Anchorage."

"She's not to leave this lodge alone. There's a chance she could still be in danger. We'll make sure she gets home safely."

Braden gave Marcy a brief update on what happened with Dagastino's men at the cabin.

"But you said Michael Dagastino knows she isn't Selena. So what's the problem?"

"A comment he made."

"What's that?"

"He wondered how Selena would react once she learns she has an identical twin. He didn't think she'd be too happy. And I think he's right. I'd like to keep this away from the press."

"Too late. *America's Most Wanted* told how you brought down Menendez and reported the crash. Mom had to flick the television off before the girls saw it. Selena will be curious about this woman you mistook for her?"

Braden frowned. "No Doubt."

Chills washed over Marcy.

Sarah could end up a deadly double.

◆◆◆

Michael did as he'd promised and reported Marshal Wolfe and Sarah's location but received the news they'd been rescued. Chase and Lenny bought his story about the marshal killing Sergio and Antonio. But it was his uncle he dreaded facing.

Standing on the other side of his uncle's office door, he slowed his breathing with a couple of deep steady breaths and mentally demanded his body to relax. If he acted nervous, Uncle Leon would know he was lying.

Look him in the eye. Don't squint or fidget.

When he entered the lavish office, his uncle had a receiver crammed under his ear, reaching for a fat Cuban cigar from a silver plated box. The room smelled like rich tobacco and bourbon. Michael sat in a high back chair in front of the desk and waited for his uncle to finish his conversation.

"I want this shipment, but I'm not willing to pay their so called transport fee. Greedy bastards. Been dealing with them for five fuckin' years, and now they want to piss down my back."

Michael started to stand, thinking he'd come back later, but his uncle motioned for him to wait. He nodded and settled back in the chair. He'd practiced what to say until he almost believed it himself. Almost.

"Tell them they're not the only assholes importing coke, and if they don't drop the extra fee, I'm dealing with someone else." Uncle Leon slammed the phone down, then stared across his desk. "When'd you get back?"

"Last night, late."

"Is Selena dead?"

"No, but Sergio and Antonio are."

He stood from his chair. "What the fuck happened?"

Michael told the story Wolfe concocted.

"Son-of-a-bitch! Wolfe killed them?" his uncle asked.

He nodded. "When I realized I couldn't do anything for them, I left."

"Why the hell didn't you shoot back?"

"I did, but we were in the open. No one had a clear shot at Wolfe."

"Did he have Selena?"

"The woman wasn't Selena."

"How'd you get close enough to see her?"

Michael had just placed a size twelve foot in his mouth. He swallowed hard and thought carefully before answering. "I'm not going by her appearance. Think about it. There's no way Wolfe would give Menendez a loaded weapon. Why would Selena protect him? They worked as a team."

Uncle Leon lit the cigar, leaned back, and puffed on it. "You might be on to something. Wolfe has kept her on the run as much as I have. There's no way he'd trust her."

His uncle's expression still expressed doubt about the entire incident.

Michael's hand started to shake. Had his uncle noticed?

Calm down. Be apologetic.

"I'm sorry I let you down," Michael said, trying to sound sincere. "Sergio was your number one guy. He or Antonio should've been in charge, not me." He tried to keep his breathing even. "Though I'm not sure what Sergio would've done differently. We were totally taken by surprise."

Don't repeat the story unless he asks.

He'd caught himself about to say something lame like *I swear it's the truth.* The term was a red flag for lying.

His uncle shrugged. "Shit happens." He studied a paper in front of him before glancing back up at Michael. "The DNA taken from this woman's cabin was an exact match to Selena. If it's not her, it has to be a sister. I want to know more about her. She might come in handy someday."

"Maybe the lab screwed up the DNA results. Like you just said, shit happens."

The less his uncle knew about Sarah the better.

Michael could never be like this man. He thought of the deal Wolfe had offered. Could he pull it off?

Chapter Eleven

The next morning Sarah couldn't stop thinking of Braden. Did she love him? Was it possible? She pushed up from the huge Adirondack chair and made her way to his room. She pounded on the door.

"Come in."

She entered the room. "I just stopped by to see how you're feeling."

"I'll live." He turned his head on the pillow in the opposite direction, not looking at her.

When he didn't say anything else, she decided to leave. She wouldn't force him to talk.

"Sarah," he shouted.

"What?" She let the door close behind her.

"I didn't mean for you to leave. It's not you. My leg is hurting. The old quack took off your splint and put my knee into some type of contraption."

"And the laceration? Has it healed properly?"

He pulled the cover back revealing his thigh. "It left a hell of a scar."

"It makes you look like something that crawled off Frankenstein's table. Sorry, I didn't exactly sew a straight line."

"I don't care how it looks. He told me to keep my weight off that leg until I get a MRI." He paused a moment. "I want to make sure you make it home."

"Thanks. Marcy told me you're a little apprehensive over Selena learning about me. I doubt she gives me a second thought."

Braden rolled over on his back. "Don't count on it."

"There's a bus picking up a group in the morning to drive them to the Anchorage airport. I've arranged a ride with them."

"I'll see if they have room for us. You got the number?"

"Front desk would have it." She took a step away from him. "I better check to see if my things have arrived."

He gave a slight nod, mumbled something, and closed his eyes.

Outside his room, she paused by the door. The man was impossible, and her life would be a hell of a lot better off without his moody ass in the picture. Then why did she feel like crap?

Her luggage and mp3 player didn't arrive until late afternoon. She removed the one dress she'd brought, hung it in the bathroom, then turned on the shower, hoping the steam would loosen the wrinkles. She dug in her makeup case and set out the essentials. Tonight, she wanted to look her best.

Later that evening when she strolled into the diner, Marcy waved at her. It felt as if she were intruding on Marcy and Alex's reunion. Unsure of where to sit, she walked to their table. Marcy introduced Alex. The man was hot.

She'd expected Braden and Darrel to dine with them. But instead they sat a few tables over with a group of men.

Sarah sat on the other side of Marcy and opened the menu, then studied the choices, overlooking the selections of salmon. Once she laid her menu down, she made eye contact with Marcy. "Would you two prefer to be alone? I'd understand."

Alex spoke first. "No, we want you with us."

Marcy gave Alex an appreciative smile, then looked back to Sarah. "You clean up well. Every guy in the place glanced up when you walked in."

But there was only one man Sarah noticed, only one man who counted.

Braden.

She forced a smile. "Thanks."

After the waitress had taken their orders and served the drinks, Marcy looked at her. "I'd love for you to stay with us at Christmas. Come a few days early so we can shop."

"No, you have Alex and the girls. Christmas is a time for family."

"From what Marcy has told me, she's decided to make you the sister she's never had. She really wants you to visit," Alex stated.

"Marcy might not be up to it with the baby coming."

Alex choked on his beer, then cut a questioning look at Marcy.

Had she said something wrong?

"It's not like it's my first pregnancy. I'll be fine."

Alex beamed brighter than a star.

He sure seemed happy.

Sarah wouldn't allow herself to be jealous over Marcy, but she seemed to have it all—a handsome, loving husband who rescued her, two daughters, and now a third child on the way. No, she was happy for Marcy.

She wanted to steal a peek at Braden but didn't want to get caught gawking.

As they finished their salads, a group of fishermen entered the diner. An older lady from a tour bus group walked to the jukebox and dropped in coins and punched several selections.

Alex gazed into Marcy's eyes. "I believe they're playing our song."

"Do you mind?" Marcy asked Sarah.

"No, go ahead."

Alex and Marcy walked over to a small patch of shiny hardwood and embraced.

Shadow's in the Moonlight played as they danced.

Sarah tried not to be envious. Even if Braden were capable of dancing, he probably wouldn't ask her.

"May I have this dance?" asked one of the men who'd entered only moments before.

She nodded and stood. He escorted her to the dance floor. His height allowed her to fit nicely into his arms. But still there wasn't any heat. Not like the fireworks she experienced when near Braden. More than anything she felt awkward. They moved slowly to the music. She caught a glimpse of Braden. He watched like a hawk with glowing green eyes.

She didn't necessarily want to make him jealous. She just wanted a damn reaction from him. Something besides that smug arrogant expression he wore half the time. Some small way of knowing if he cared for her at all.

"I'm Daniel Gibson from Nebraska."

"Sarah Mason from Memphis."

"I wasn't expecting to see any good looking women out here in the middle of nowhere."

"Thank you." Her cheeks heated a moment.

Before the dance ended, Braden turned his chair away. Apparently, he didn't care if she danced with other men.

"You gonna be staying long?" Daniel asked.

"No, I leave in the morning."

"We could have tonight." He winked.

"I don't think so. I'm tired. Actually, I'm about to turn in."

After the music stopped, she thanked Daniel for the dance, walked back to the table, and sat alone. In a few minutes, Marcy and Alex returned. She placed her hand over Marcy's. "I'm going to my room."

"Your steak hasn't arrived."

"Would you ask them to cancel my order? I can't stay."

Marcy nodded, then directed her gaze to Braden for a moment before looking back at Sarah. "I'm sorry things aren't working out with him."

Sarah smiled trying to give the pretense that Braden's callous attitude didn't bother her, but it did. Damn it. It hurt. "I've never considered myself obtuse until now. I've been as naive as a teenager. I'll see you in the morning. Good night."

◆◆◆

Braden fought going after Sarah when she left the diner. No doubt Marcy saw him as a number one prick, but it wouldn't work with Sarah. Letting her down easy was worse than just cutting the rope now. But when Sarah danced with the man, jealousy had inched up Braden's spine, filled his stomach with bile until he thought he'd gag or burst into toxic green flames.

The man she'd danced with exited directly behind her, stopping at the bar only long enough to grab a bottle of wine and two glasses. Braden knew exactly where the man was heading.

He wanted to leave but couldn't until the waitress returned. Finally, he handed the girl his money and stood, grabbing his crutches. "Keep the change."

"Where you running off to in such a hurry?" Darrel asked.

"To check on Sarah."

"It's about time you treat her right."

"That's just great coming from a guy who's been married and divorced four times."

"I never treated any of them as badly as you're treating her."

"I'm doing what's best for her."

"You keep telling yourself that."

Braden made his way to the slow service elevator and then went up to the second floor. He hobbled down the hall. The door hadn't closed all the way. Voices came from her room.

"Daniel, get out," Sarah said.

"I thought that comment about turning in early was a hint for me to join you. Kitten, you won't regret it. I'll make you purr."

"I'm sorry you misread me, but I have no intention of sleeping with you."

"At least let me give you a sample of what you'll be missing."

"Let me go. Stop that."

Braden shoved the door back.

Daniel had his mouth over Sarah's, forcing her to kiss him.

Braden grabbed the man's shoulder and yanked him back. "Get your hands off her."

The guy whipped around on Braden. "I saw her first. You go find your own."

"She's under my protection."

"Protection?"

"Deputy U. S. Marshal Wolfe, Federal Marshals Service. Now you can leave willingly or in handcuffs. Those are your choices."

The man grabbed his wine and stormed out without uttering another word.

Sarah's eyes clouded with tears.

"You all right?"

She shook her head apparently unable to speak.

The man's rough kiss had smeared her lipstick. Braden grabbed a tissue and blotted the lipstick at the side of her mouth.

"Thank you," she whispered a tremble in her voice.

He couldn't resist wrapping his arms around her and pulling her next to him. "You look irresistible tonight. No wonder you have men following you."

"I didn't do anything to lead him on. I wouldn't have accepted the dance if I'd known he'd take it as an invitation for more."

"You have no idea how desirable you looked on that dance floor. If I could dance, I would've been next in line."

"Thank you. I've been ragged for so long I thought it'd be nice to dress up."

"I'd hoped you dressed up for me."

A blush glowed from her cheeks.

Yep, she wore the dress for me.

He leaned his head against hers. She smelled like mimosa blossoms. "Ah, Sarah. I do want you, but don't you see why I can't?"

She shook her head. "Not really."

"It wouldn't work between us. I don't want to ever settle down and you do. I live in Kansas and you in Memphis."

"And I look like Selena."

Explain about Andy. She deserves to know. I can't.

He nodded, agreeing. "So you see, angel, I can't offer you anything lasting."

Her eyes filled with yearning as she gazed up at him. "Then give me tonight."

"Sarah, tomorrow you're flying home. I won't be calling or coming for visits. It'll be totally over between us. Still want me to stay?"

"Yes, I do. My common sense has taken a nosedive."

He unzipped her dress and helped her out of it, then carefully tossed it over a chair. He kissed her bare shoulders and whispered in her ear, "You're going to regret this later."

She nodded and closed her eyes. "Probably, but I need to feel loved tonight."

"But tomorrow you'll wake feeling used."

"I know. But I don't want to be alone."

Braden had given her every opportunity to back out. Truth was, he wanted her again and was glad she hadn't changed her mind.

He lowered his mouth gently to hers, and for a moment, he simply touched his lips to hers before deepening the kiss. His tongue swept the depths of her mouth, tasting her.

"You smell wonderful," she said. "Like charred wood and spice."

Again he kissed a trail down her neck, then across her shoulder while pressing his pelvis into her. He stumbled a little.

"We'd better lie down before you fall," she suggested.

Braden didn't want to take another chance on becoming a father. A small chance existed Sarah could be pregnant though she'd assured him the possibility was almost nonexistent. Just the chance had him sweating bullets. "Sarah, I've got to go downstairs for a moment."

She appeared hurt.

"I'm coming back."

"Will you stay the entire night with me?"

"If that's what you want."

"It is. So grab your things."

"I don't have much but these clothes someone gave me and a sweatshirt and toothbrush I bought downstairs."

"Are you able to get downstairs and back without any help?"

Though he wasn't sure, he declined the offer of help and hobbled from her room. Just as he turned the corner heading for the elevator, Darrel emerged. "The bus driver said he has room for us and to be at the bus at seven A.M."

"Great. That'll get us back to Anchorage by two." Braden's knee ached, and the thought of going downstairs and coming back up didn't appeal to him.

"You need any help?"

He started to ask Darrel to go for him, but didn't. It would cheapen what Sarah and he planned to share, and it was no one's business. "No, I can manage. But thanks."

Darrel grinned. "See you in the morning."

Braden returned to Sarah's room with two foil packs and a toothbrush.

When he opened the door, she lay in bed beneath the quilt and sheet. In the dim light, she appeared like a Greek goddess. Beautiful and elegant. He closed the door behind him. "I hope you still want me."

She nodded and lowered the sheet, revealing her full breasts. Her nipples transformed from large flowers to hard buds while her eyes appeared as brown pools shimmering with desire.

He crossed the room and placed the condoms on the nightstand and slipped from his clothes before lowering beside her. His leg brushed against hers, and heat consumed him. Damn this woman had him bewitched. "When you walked in the diner, wearing that dress, I wanted you."

"I wore it hoping it'd have that effect on you."

He kissed her deeply, letting his tongue dominate her mouth, then rolled his body on top of her. He kissed her neck and worked his way to her breasts, letting his tongue tease her until she let out a sensual gasp.

She kissed his neck, under his chin, and his jaw line. Her hands gripped into his shoulder. She parted her legs and sprawled her hands over his bottom, then pulled him against her. "We can play later. I want this."

Proficiently, he popped the condom out and rolled it down his length. "Roll on your side. My leg is hurting."

She faced the wall, allowing him to ease behind her. His fullness filled her. She tightened her inner muscles bringing him to the edge. He stilled himself for a moment to regain control.

He raised her dark hair and kissed the back of her slender neck several times, then kissed her shoulders.

She felt so good. She knew exactly when to push, when to squeeze her muscles around him, and when to make those soft sexy sounds.

Braden held her in his arms while working his hips back and forth slowly. Something about this was special, not just sex. Not just gratification. They were fused together, body and soul.

"Braden. I think I'm going to die."

"Same here." He kissed the side of her face before picking up the pace and bringing them to the edge together. Sarah countered each of his movements, pushing her flesh against his. His breathing was harsh and ragged. She shuddered in his arms. He released immediately, joining her in the heated moment.

"You're beautiful, Sarah."

"You make me feel beautiful. For tonight just hold me, Braden."

He held her and savored the moment.

Again he had that completeness he'd felt before with her in his arms. But come morning, he would let her go. He clenched his eyes closed as his conscience tormented him. Never once had he lied to her about his intentions. So why in the hell did he feel guilty?

"Sarah, there's something extremely important I need to explain. It's something I don't talk about."

She turned over and faced him. "I'm listening."

"Valerie and I had one son Andy, who was five."

"Didn't you say you're divorced?" she asked.

"Yes, we are now. I'm not even sure where Valerie is."

"Does she have custody?"

"No. Andy died, and I'm responsible."

Her eyes reflected her confusion. "How?"

"I was separated from Valerie, and I had already filed for a divorce and full custody of Andy because she was an addict. Long story short, her parents asked for custody also and got it because of my job. I had weekends and holidays. Valerie was supposed to only have visitation with her parents present or a court appointee."

"But they didn't abide by the rules?"

"No. One weekend when I was out of town and couldn't take him, her parents trusted her with him." He paused and swallowed back the anguish the memories caused. "While he was there, she shot herself up and left him in the care of her boyfriend. When Andy wet on himself, the guy lost his temper and beat my son to death."

"Oh, Braden. I'm so sorry."

"After his lifeless body had been delivered to the morgue, the report showed several broken bones, extreme bruising, and a fractured skull."

A significant moment passed between them.

"Do you feel like you're to blame because you were out of town?"

"That and the fact that a month earlier, I found Valerie in a comatose state from a drug overdose, and I considered letting her die. Instead, I called an ambulance and started CPR. Now I regret not closing the door and walking away. I would've been attending her funeral rather than Andy's."

"I was angry when Tristen and Mark died. Angry with God, angry with myself, and angry with Mark, not that he could've stopped it. What if I hadn't changed shifts and worked Christmas Eve. We put off going to the movie until Christmas Day, but for them, Christmas Day never came. The only reason they were out was to buy me a jewelry box

I'd mentioned. Unbelievably, the jewelry box came out of the wreck without a scratch."

"But I could've stopped Andy's death. That's the difference."

"You should point the finger at Andy's grandparents who knew they were going against the court's order. Does Marcy or Darrel know about this?"

"No, it happened before we worked together."

"Thank you for telling me. It helps me understand why you keep yourself at a distance from any kind of relationship. But you shouldn't."

"I'll never marry, and I sure as hell never want a kid again."

He expected her to push away. Rather than leave the bed, she cuddled closer laying her head on his chest and wrapping her arm across him. Her long dark hair sprawled over him, feeling like silk against his skin.

She loves me.
She'll get over it.
But will I be able to give her up?

Chapter Twelve

Walking down the hall, Marcy paused by Sarah's door. She wanted to slug Braden for being such a jerk. Poor Sarah didn't realized she'd spilled the beans to Alex about her pregnancy. It had to come out sooner or later.

"Don't interfere," Alex advised. "She's a grown woman. She's not some naïve kid."

"No, but she's vulnerable and lonely."

Back in their room, Marcy turned on the hot water in the shower, then walked back in the bedroom. "What's wrong?"

Alex remained solemn. "When did you plan to tell me about the baby?"

"Once I made my mind up whether I want to stay married."

"You think you can manage the girls, a newborn, and work?"

"I've already asked for a desk job."

"You know you don't have to work. We might have to cut back a little, but you could be a stay-home mom."

She considered what he said. She'd wanted to stay home when the girls were little, but they hadn't been able to afford it. Tempting. "Maybe."

In the bathroom, she slipped from her clothes, then stepped inside the shower, letting the mist cover her. The soap slipped from her hand and landed by the drain. She leaned to grab it. When she rose, Alex stood behind her. His erection brushed against her thigh.

"Nice view."

She faced him. "Alex, I haven't given you my answer."

He pulled her into his arms, lowered his mouth to hers, and kissed her hungrily. "Ah, Marcy. Damn it, I need you. I only want you in my life. Please don't shut me out. Give me a second chance. I don't expect you to trust me for a while. I know it's something I'll have to earn."

"Alex, I still love you."

"Can I come back?"

"I'm not sure. I'll always worry that you'll dump me for the first skirt that walks by."

He placed a finger on her lips to silence her. "Never, love. Never again."

Alex kissed her as though it was their first kiss, slow and sensual before turning her toward the wall of the shower. Her body burned with sexual need. And she wanted him back, but would it work? She placed her hands on the flat surface and stood with her legs apart. With one thrust, he penetrated her. He wrapped his arm around her waist to steady her as he began to stroke back and forth.

Marcy's tears blended with the water pounding down on them. Bittersweet tears. Tears of joy and sorrow. Had she given in too easily? Though she had wanted this, wanted him to need her, it also terrified her. Had she made a mistake?

◆◆◆

The next morning Marcy and Alex entered the diner at six A.M. as Braden had requested and sat at a table. Braden sat with the group of men he'd been with at dinner. Where was Sarah?

"Order me the special. I'll be right back."

Marcy didn't find Sarah in her room but then remembered how much she liked sitting on the porch. Downstairs, she found Sarah outside in a huge Adirondack chair. "Are you all right?"

She smiled and nodded. "I've been remembering my time with Tristen and Mark. Vacations. School plays and soccer games."

Marcy sat down beside her and took the photographs Sarah offered. "Mark was a real hunk. And Tristen was a great looking kid."

"He was. Smart too."

"Did things work out between you and Braden?"

She shrugged while her cheeks turned pink. "Depends on what you mean by *work out*. Yes, we slept together. No, we're not continuing our relationship."

"I hate him. The coldhearted bastard."

"Don't," Sarah said. "I asked him to spend last night with me. He was completely honest about his intentions. He never led me on. So, don't blame him."

"But you're so perfect for him."

"He has his reasons." Sarah sighed. "It wouldn't be right for me to discuss it."

"Still, I don't understand why he'd give up any chance of being happy."

"He's afraid."

"Braden Wolfe isn't afraid of anything."

Sarah placed everything back in her purse and stood. "Everyone is afraid of something." She walked toward the door. "I'm going to grab some breakfast before we head out. Where's Alex?"

"In the diner." Marcy followed Sarah into the pine-scented lodge. She stopped her in the lobby. "There's something I haven't been honest about."

"What's that?"

"Alex and I have been separated. He left me for someone else and now he wants another chance. I've agreed to give it to him. And I'm afraid I've given in too soon."

◆◆◆

Sarah didn't ask the details of Alex's affair. She figured it wasn't any of her business. "I see. I hope it works out for you, especially with the baby coming."

Then she realized she'd said too much to Alex. "You hadn't told him about the baby, had you?"

"No, but it's all right. It's not like I could've hidden it much longer. My stomach pooches a little, and my breasts are enormous."

"Alex seems crazy about you. The man rescued you. I think he's worth taking a chance with."

"I hope so."

Marcy rejoined Alex at the table. Rather than sit with them, Sarah chose a seat at the counter and placed her purse on the stool beside her.

Her heartbeat quickened when Braden approached her. "Good morning," she said to him. "Do I have time to grab a quick bite before we leave?"

"A very quick one. The bus pulls out at seven A.M."

"In that case, I'll get a doughnut and glass of milk."

Sarah twisted a straw wrapper around her finger, waiting for her order. "That was really nice of Darrel to lug my bag through the woods."

He motioned at the waitress to bring him coffee. "Did anything fall out?"

Sarah glanced at her Coach bag. "Nope."

He grinned. "Still suing?"

She laughed. "I should, you know."

"I'm sorry for everything, Sarah."

"Don't be. I'm not quite sure when it happened, but I've come to terms with Mark and Tristen's deaths. Now, remembering them makes me smile instead of cry. So in a way, this trip has been a success."

"Good, eat that doughnut and let's get out of here." Braden turned and motioned to the others.

"I'll need to grab my luggage."

"Don't bother. Darrel will get it. Just make your way to the bus."

After eating, Sarah joined the others outside. The huge white tour bus with an Alaskan logo in red and blue had parked near the lodge's front door. Though the bus trip would take longer than flying, Sarah didn't mind. She was relieved they weren't going by helicopter.

Before climbing aboard, she glanced back at the lodge, remembering the night she'd shared with Braden

Sarah sat in back across from Marcy and Alex while Braden sat with Darrel a few rows up. Her flight left at three-fifteen P.M. and arrived in Memphis at six-thirty-five A.M. with two layovers. Tomorrow morning, she'd be home, and Braden would be back in Kansas.

She believed he had feelings for her. Obviously not enough to make any sacrifices or changes in his lifestyle.

Sarah glanced across the aisle at Marcy. "I'll miss you."

Marcy offered her a smile. "We'll stay in touch. Don't forget you're coming for Christmas."

"I'll be there. You have my email and phone number."

"Yes. I'll be able to keep you posted on Braden."

Sarah thought about her offer. "No, I'd rather you didn't."

"I understand. I'm worried about you."

"I'm okay, just exhausted."

"I'm joining you," Braden said, looming over her. "Scoot over."

Sarah flashed Marcy a quick smile, then moved to the window seat.

Braden lowered into the seat and placed his crutches in floor before fastening his seatbelt. He took her hand and laced his fingers through hers. Then he leaned and kissed her cheek. "You all right?"

She nodded. No, she wasn't all right. It would've been better if he'd sat away from her. His nearness made her wish for things that she could never have. But it surprised her how affectionate he was in front of the others.

Finally, the bus pulled out, weaving around the drive that made a loop in front of the lodge, and drove down the wooded road to the highway.

◆◆◆

Braden had intended to sit up front with Darrel, but at the last minute decided he'd rather spend the time with Sarah.

"You're a good nurse. Have any plans to return to work?"

She shook her head. "I received enough money from the insurance settlement and Mark's life insurance to live comfortably. I paid my house off, so I have very few bills. At least for the next couple of months, I'll just relax around the house, sleep late every day, read, and sit by the pool."

"Slacker. Must be nice to be a lady of leisure."

"Trust me, it came at a high price. If I could have my husband and son back, I'd work every day of my life without one complaint."

"You're still very much in love with Mark, aren't you?"

"Yes, but I've let him go. I'm ready to move on in my life."

Braden thought about her last comment. Was she trying to give him a subtle message, let him know she had room for him in her life? He wanted to remind her that he had no intentions of pursuing a relationship, but he needed to be just as subtle.

"Do you think you'll start dating?" he asked

Her fingers pulled from his like threads being ripped apart. "I'm not sure what I'll do. I wasn't just referring to seeing men. I was speaking of life in general. I won't go through each day grieving for them. That's all I meant."

She turned her head and stared out the window. Her body language told him she was slightly peeved at him. Eventually, she relaxed and stared toward the front. After a few moments, her eyes closed and her breathing grew heavier. Her head slowly tilted over until it rested on his shoulder.

They'd made love for hours into the night with long stretches of foreplay. Sarah was so sensual and willing.

Don't let her walk out of your life.

Rather than push the notion away, he considered what it'd be like married to Sarah. And what would happen when he finally came face to face with Selena? Would he be able to pull the trigger, seeing Sarah's face? A face he'd come to love.

Come to love?

The phrase caused a lump in his throat.

"Sarah's a lovely woman," Alex said to Braden.

Braden glanced across the aisle. "She is and kindhearted."

"You two seem well-suited for one another," Marcy said.

"I'm not suited for anyone. I'm a loner, and I plan to stay that way."

"The lone wolf," Marcy said. "That's a shame. I think Sarah could make you happy."

Frustration tightened Braden's jaw. "Mind your own damn business. My job is dangerous. She'd always have to worry about losing me like she did her husband. I doubt she could stand losing someone again."

"She's losing you now," Marcy whispered.

Braden didn't reply. Instead, he glanced at Sarah who still slept with her head against his shoulder. He had called the Memphis district of the Federal Marshal's Service and requested they have someone at the airport to drive Sarah home. When the bus hit some bumps, she woke suddenly and gripped Braden's arm. "What's happening?"

"Potholes. You've been asleep."

She straightened up in the seat, then stretched and yawned. "I didn't get much sleep last night." She smiled. "Not that I'm complaining."

"Any regrets?"

"Not really."

"Good. I worried you would." He stretched his legs out and reached in his pocket to remove his wallet. He pulled out a business card and offered it to her. "Call me if anything should come up as a result of our being together."

"Keep your card. You've made your point about us. I also recall you saying you don't want any children. So give me one good reason why I should call you?"

"To help financially."

"I've already told you. I have money. You won't be hearing from me, no matter what. Maybe this time, you were the one used. I don't need you, Braden. You can head back to Kansas without feeling any responsibility or guilt."

Braden's stomach twisted. He should be thrilled, but he wasn't. He couldn't put his finger on why her bluntness made him discontent, but it had. He'd expected a big teary scene. But Sarah had ironed up her emotions and hidden her true feelings.

Little was said in the next three hours. Braden's thoughts drifted to Andy and a pain caught in his chest.

Braden remembered his last Christmas Eve with Andy. His son sat on the sofa with his grandmother's camera in hand.

Jamey told me and Corey that Santa isn't real, so I'm gonna get a picture of him coming down the chimney and show old Jamey.

Well, Andy, Santa's not so easy to catch.

Not even ten minutes later, Braden set the camera on the table, lifted his sleeping child, and carried him to bed. He kissed his forehead, then covered him. *Good night, sport.*

The more you love someone, the deeper the pain is when you lose them.

He didn't want to love again. No one had come as close to his heart as Sarah. He hadn't intended for it to happen.

After checking Sarah's bags in at the airport, the marshals and Alex walked her to the gate for the Memphis flight and sat in the waiting area. Their flight didn't depart for another hour.

Sitting beside Sarah, Braden sensed her struggle to stay strong. Her eyes appeared shiny and sad. He slid his fingers through hers and squeezed her hand. She squeezed back. Her grip tightened as if trying to keep her emotions intact.

Her flight started loading. Shortly, they called her seating section, and she stood.

"Sarah. . ."

She shook her head and closed her eyes.

She was hurt more than she'd let on.

He didn't say any more, not even goodbye.

Marcy followed Sarah to the line and gave her a hug, then joined the others. She glared at Braden. "You're not going to say goodbye?"

He shook his head. "This is how she wants it."

Marcy's expression showed how displeased she was with him.

No doubt, she and Sarah had become close friends.

Sarah glanced back and stared. His breath hitched.

Go after her.

His throat burned. He bowed his head and closed his eyes as he battled internally whether to stop her. He thought about taking Sarah into his arms and asking her to be a part of his life. His determination to let her go, won. As he raised his hand to wave, she turned away and boarded the plane.

Sarah was gone.

His Sarah.

◆◆◆

The media vans and cars parked in front of Sarah's house came as a shock. She didn't want the publicity or the attention. All she desired was to climb in her bed and let all the tears she'd held back for so long flow.

The deputy pulled in her driveway. Reporters swarmed around the black SUV. Sarah stepped from the car. People crowded her and poked microphones beneath her chin.

"Mrs. Mason, do you plan to sue the government for this callous mistake?"

"Mrs. Mason, is it true you saved the deputy who arrested you."

Then one held up a picture of Selena. "Can you explain why you and this woman look identical?"

The deputy pushed the reporters back, allowing Sarah to make her way toward her house. He escorted her to the front porch before returning to his car for her luggage. As she unlocked the door, a man approached her. "Sarah Mason, I'm Russell Goldstein, attorney at law. Here's my card in case you're interested in taking legal action for the ordeal the government put you through."

"I'm not suing. It was a justifiable mistake."

After pushing her bags through the door, the deputy shook her hand. "I'll have some patrol cars drive by and get rid of these vultures."

Inside her house, she locked her door and closed her blinds. It wasn't long before several Germantown patrol cars arrived, dispersing the crowd.

The silence unraveled her nerves. For just a moment, she thought of Braden and could still smell his male scent she'd grown accustomed to. She remembered when Mark died how she'd take his robe to bed with her and breathe in his scent. But for Braden, she had nothing to remember him by.

Though it was morning, Sarah headed to the bedroom and pulled back the comforter. She curled up on her side and drew in a painful breath and let the tears fall freely. Her raw emotions stemmed from several sources, not just from Braden's rejection. But partly from exhaustion, partly from remorse over life in general and a little from apprehension of what the future held.

She finally made the necessary trip to the bathroom and laughed at her swollen eyes in the mirror. She looked more like one of the aliens from *Star Wars*. She splashed cold water on her face before walking into the kitchen where she searched for something to eat.

Unfortunately, her refrigerator and cabinets were as barren as the Sahara. Her stomach growled. Right now she'd even consider eating a camel—humps and all.

In her pantry, she discovered a few items. Rather than attempt to cook, she ordered a large Hawaiian pizza and a two-liter of Coke, enough to last for several meals.

She stared at the telephone, wishing it'd ring. Wishing it'd be Braden. Even if he were just checking to make sure she'd made it home all right.

When the phone rang, she flinched. "Hello."

No one spoke. She glanced at the caller ID, but it read private caller.

"Hello, can you hear me?"

Silence.

Finally, she heard a click and the dial-tone returned.

Had it been Braden? Had he wanted to hear her voice? Was he missing her as much as she missed him? Then an eerie thought came to her. Could it be the sister she'd never known?

◆◆◆

Braden wondered how Dagastino had learned about the arrest of Menendez in Alaska. Who had taken money in exchange for supplying the mob boss with the most recent information on Selena? It could be anyone from a clerk to a judge. He couldn't go in accusing and pointing fingers, but he would definitely stay alert.

When it got right down to it, this mole who'd sold out to Dagastino was responsible for the deaths of three men. Braden would make them pay.

It'd been a week since he'd seen Sarah. He glanced up from the piles of paperwork on his desk and stared at the telephone. He'd considered calling her. He'd called the Memphis marshal just to see if she made it home safely. She had. Though he didn't like the attention the mishap had drawn from the news media.

Hell. He wanted to hear her voice. His life had never felt emptier than when they parted at the airport. The impact had hit him hardest when he'd entered his lonely apartment, climbed between cool sheets, and stared at the ceiling for hours, missing her.

During the next month, he thought of Sarah less. After his knee surgery, he had so many cases backed up that he had little time for his thoughts to stray. His social life was on the verge of making the endangered species list due to the long, exhausting hours he put into his job. He stood from his desk and stretched.

A woman from the front office approached him. "Catch up, yet?"

"Nah, but I'm not sweating it."

She smiled seductively. "Since you don't have time to cook, why not let me cook for you Saturday night?"

He started to tell her no. Then he realized being with the sexy blonde might be just the cure for getting Sarah out of his head.

"Patricia, isn't it?"

"Yes, Patricia Green."

"Sure, what time?"

"Seven."

Saturday night Braden knocked on the apartment door. Patricia answered, wearing a tight fitting T-shirt and blue jeans. Her nipples bulged through the thin stretchy material. She wore toe rings and an anklet. She never looked like this at work. He stepped through the doorway. "I'm overdressed."

"Don't worry. I'll undress you in a little while."

Nothing like a woman who knows what she wants.

He followed her to the kitchen and sat at the table while she put the finishing touches on dinner. When she bent over to check the bread in the oven, her top raised revealing her ass in the low-riding denim. She wasn't wearing any panties. No, surprise there.

While they ate the cranberry chicken she'd prepared, she glanced up at him and unexpectedly asked, "So tell me about this woman you mistook for Selena Menendez."

He blotted his mouth. "What about her?"

"Do you think she plans to sue?"

He shrugged. "Probably not."

"Identical twins. Who would've known?"

Braden had accepted this dinner to clear his head of Sarah. "One reason I don't usually date someone from work is because I don't want to talk shop all night."

She placed her hand on his. "You're absolutely right. Sorry about that. It's just that I find it fascinating. Okay, no more shoptalk. Promise."

After dinner, Patricia took his hand and pulled him to the bedroom. "Time to make you more comfortable." First, she removed his tie and shirt. She rubbed her hand over his chest. "Feeling better?"

He stepped back. "I can't do this."

"If you're not ready for this, we can watch a movie."

"I'm sorry." He slipped his shirt on not taking time to button it. He grabbed his tie. " I can't stay."

"What'd I do wrong?"

"You didn't. Everything was perfect. It's me. There's something I've got to deal with. It's not you, Patricia."

He escaped from her apartment and drove to a nearby park, pulling over beside the lake. He leaned his head over the steering wheel and closed his eyes, fighting his desire to contact Sarah.

The next day at work, Patricia wouldn't speak to him. Hopefully, she wouldn't share the experience with her coworkers. That's the risk he took for mixing his personal life with his job. He'd never dated any of the women he'd worked with until Patricia. What a mistake.

Wanting to see Sarah's face, he pulled out a photograph of Selena. And as he stared at the picture, he didn't see Sarah. Instead he saw a harsh face, with squinted angry eyes. He saw Selena Menendez.

Two different women, with two different hearts and souls. For a moment, his resolve weakened, and he allowed himself to reminisce about his time with Sarah. Damn it to hell, he missed her. It'd been over a month, and she continued to haunt him.

On his way home, he picked up a fifth of Jack Daniels, hoping it'd block out his thoughts of Sarah and ease the empty ache in his chest.

Chapter Thirteen

Sarah entered the garage and closed it. She opened the door leading to the kitchen before returning for groceries in the car. At the store, several people recognized her from all the publicity she'd received.

Inside, the light flashed on her answering machine. She set the bags down and pushed play, but whoever had called hung up without leaving a message. She checked the caller ID and smiled when she recognized the Kansas City area code. Marcy had called twice. But this number wasn't Marcy's. There was a possibility it was Braden who'd called.

She dialed the number and waited.

He picked up. "Sarah?"

Her heartbeat quickened.

"Yes, it's me. Did you call?"

"I did. Just wondering if Selena has contacted you in any way. Has she?"

"No," Sarah said, choking back the disappointment. "Anything else?"

"No. Yes."

The line remained silent for a while.

"Braden, are you there?"

"Yeah, I'm here. Sarah."

"I'm listening."

"I've missed you."

"Oh, Braden. I've missed you. Not a day goes by that I don't think of you."

"Same here." He cleared his throat. "My knee is working again. I had outpatient surgery. I thought I'd be up and running sooner, but it took about a week before I could put my weight on it. I've been swamped with work. How have you been?"

"Just sleeping a lot. I've been exhausted lately. I need to get out and exercise, but it's been too hot. I'll be glad when September gets here. I'll start walking again. I've gained a few pounds from sitting on my ass and eating."

"You're not living on chocolate doughnuts, are you?"

She laughed. "No, pizza."

"Uh, angel. That'll make a fat woman out of you."

"I didn't leave the house for the first two weeks because of the reporters hounding me. I even had lawyers wanting me to sue you. But I declined."

"I appreciate that."

"You still owe me a steak dinner and chocolate pie."

"Well, I might have to send you a gift card on that. So, what made you leave your sanctuary?"

"I ran out of toilet paper and had no choice."

He laughed. "That'll always get you in the end."

She thought about what he'd said and laughed with him. "I see you've developed a sense of humor." She thought of the earlier call and asked if it had been him.

"Nope, today's the first time I've called."

"They wouldn't say anything. It could've been a wrong number."

"If you have any more calls, let me know. I hate to do this, but I need to run. You still coming to Kansas for Christmas?"

"That's the plan."

"Maybe I'll invite myself to Marcy's Christmas dinner. Take care, Sarah. Bye."

"Bye, Braden."

Sarah couldn't stop smiling. He'd called. It was a start. Though Christmas was months away, at least it gave her something to look forward to. Maybe he'd call again or have a reason to come to Memphis.

An hour later her phone rang. Like before the caller was listed as unknown. Still, she answered it. "Hello."

But no one spoke.

The first name that came to mind was Selena. This time she knew it wasn't Braden. She remembered his warning about her sister. A slight chill ran down her spine.

◆◆◆

Sarah stared out the window at the falling rain. The leaves had turned yellow and red and had started falling. The dismal weather had her mood thermometer way down. It was nearing the end of September, yet she hadn't heard another word from Braden.

Marcy tipped her off that he was planning to fly down a weekend in October. That would never happen. Though Sarah longed to see him, her news would give him cause to cancel the trip. News of her pregnancy needed to be shared now. It couldn't wait until October. What she had to tell him would destroy any chance of a relationship. Braden didn't want any more children. His responsibility would go no further than being financially involved.

But the life she carried inside was dear to her. She'd been tempted to tell Marcy but hadn't because of the chance of Braden hearing it through the grapevine. Despite all her big talk about how she'd never tell him, he had a right to know.

She stared at the phone and contemplated calling him. She didn't have his email address. A text didn't seem personal enough. Then she decided a letter would work best and sat down with pen and paper and wrote from her heart.

◆◆◆

Braden waited until he was at his desk before eagerly ripping the envelope and unfolding the letter. He'd meant to call Sarah all month but had stayed busy. At the end of October he planned to surprise her with a visit.

Dear Braden,

I've decided you should know. I discovered the cause of my exhaustion and nausea. I'm pregnant. I can't tell you how happy it's made me knowing our child is growing inside me. It's given me a new reason to live and a little part of you to keep. I'm not trying to pin you down and make you play daddy or do the so-called right thing and propose. I just thought you had the right to know. Other than throwing up each morning I'm fine. Hope you're doing well.

Sarah

Braden crumpled the letter and tossed it in the trash. His throat knotted as images of Andy ran through his mind, causing a jolt of pain to explode in his chest. He thought of the last day they'd spent at Worlds of Fun's Camp Snoopy.

That was the mostest fun ever. I love you, Daddy.

Braden never wanted to love that deeply again. Never.

His breathing became irregular.

He grabbed a legal pad, ripped the page out, and proceeded to write. His message took all of one minute to jot down.

Shit. Son-of-a-bitch.

A fine sweat beaded across his forehead as he envisioned Andy lying in his little coffin. No way in hell did he want another child. He didn't want to live with the fear of always being afraid something would happen.

Wanting to get the note in the mail, he left his desk and hurried to drop it in the outgoing mail. He glanced up at a deputy. "Has the mail gone out yet?"

"Nope. Postman should be here any minute."

After mailing his note to Sarah, he returned to his desk. He wanted to feel the surge of anger once more to justify the icy note he'd sent. He pulled his trashcan over to his desk to retrieve her letter. Surprisingly, his trash had already been emptied. He thought about catching up with the cleaning staff to get it back but didn't.

Not even ten minutes later, the custodian came by with his cart. Braden glanced up. "You've already emptied mine."

"No, I haven't been down this way."

Braden wondered who had been interested in his trash. Whoever it was would know about Sarah and the baby. Could it be the same person who'd sold out to Dagastino?

Later in the outer hall, he bumped into Marcy.

"Why didn't you tell me?" he asked.

"Tell you what?"

"About Sarah's news."

"Braden, you're not making sense."

"I'm sure Sarah confided in you before writing me."

"I don't know what you're talking about."

He lowered his voice. "She hasn't told you she's pregnant?"

Marcy's face paled. "Oh my. Poor Sarah."

Poor Sarah?

"Hell, she seemed damn pleased about it."

"And you're not? Braden, it's a wonderful thing."

Braden didn't reply.

◆◆◆

Marcy read Braden like a cheap mystery novel. His stormy eyes and deep furrowed forehead clued her he wasn't thrilled with Sarah's news.

His face turned to stone. "I don't want children."

"But, Braden, like it or not you're going to be a daddy."

"Shh. Don't say that. Not to anyone. Understand?"

"Yes, of course I won't. Are you still visiting her next month?"

"That's not happening. Her news is a deal breaker. I don't plan to see her or the kid."

The man has to face reality here.

"Your kid, you bastard. She had a little help making it."

Braden fled the room in a rage.

Why had she told Sarah about Braden's vacation plans? Maybe she'd take a few days off and visit Sarah. Tell her in person Braden had changed his mind about coming.

That evening when Marcy entered her house, carrying an extra large pizza, Brittany and Erica greeted her with smiles.

"Hey, Mom. Dad's in the shower," Brittany said. "He said not to start without him."

"Go change clothes and wash your hands."

"Yes, ma'am," they both murmured.

Marcy picked up Alex's phone off the counter and couldn't resist checking his calls. Tiffany's name showed up five times. Shock and disbelief racked Marcy, causing the phone to slip from her hands and hit the floor. She staggered to a chair and sat down.

Alex entered the room and stared at her. "You don't look well. Everything all right?" His gaze moved to the floor and focused on his cell phone. "You checked my calls, didn't you?"

She nodded while staring into the empty space around her.

"Marcy, she called me. I told her on the first call that we were back together. If you don't believe me, check the length of the calls. After the last call, I blocked her number. So far she hasn't tried calling again. I swear."

"What's wrong?" Brittany asked from the doorway.

"You're not leaving us again, are you, Daddy?" Erica asked, following her older sister into the room.

"No, sweetheart. There's just a problem your mom and I need to work out together."

"What problem?" Brittany asked, her eyes fearful.

"How we can get rid of an unwanted telemarketer."

Marcy liked Alex's explanation. "And if blocking the number doesn't work, what then?"

He shrugged. "You're the deputy, what do you suggest?"

"I'm not sure. I'll give it some thought."

The girls' faces relaxed.

"I thought you guys were having problems again," Brittany added.

Marcy glanced at Alex, then back to her daughters. "No, like your father said, we have a problem to solve together."

◆◆◆

Michael waited for Amy to enter the City of Elizabeth Library as she did every morning. She'd cut her long red hair to her shoulders, and her face seemed thinner. Once she was inside, he turned off his engine and hurried across the street. The cool air stung his face. At the top of the steps, he turned to see if anyone had followed him before entering the brick building.

He had tried to talk with his uncle about returning to school. But his uncle reminded him of his obligation and that from the moment those men in Alaska died, he was forever a part of the family business. Michael feared their conversation had made his uncle suspicious of his loyalty.

As he approached Amy's desk, she stood from the chair. She didn't appear happy to see him. "Michael, what do you want?"

"We need to talk." Paranoid, he glanced behind him before looking back at her. "Can you meet me later?"

"You walked out of my life, dumping me four weeks before our wedding and after six months, you expect me to meet you?"

"It's important, Amy. I'll explain why I had to call it off."

"I don't care why you did it. You're history. Do you realize how many people my mother had to call? How much money my parents owed that couldn't be refunded?"

"I'm sorry. I had a good reason for doing it. If you'll just hear me out."

She gave a surrendering sigh. "My lunch break is at one. Where should I meet you?"

"At the AMC on Garden Street."

"I only have an hour."

"It's the perfect place."

"I'll be there."

"See you then." Michael walked over to a computer and sat down, pretending to be searching for a book. A few minutes later, he stood and walked by Amy without giving her a second glance.

At one, Michael stood in the theater lobby. After fifteen minutes, he considered leaving.

She's changed her mind. She's not coming.

As she entered the theater, his heart lifted. He waved at her.

Amy crossed the lobby and stopped beside him. "Start talking."

Michael glanced over at the concessions. "Want anything?"

"I'm not hungry. Let's just get this over."

"Not here. I bought tickets for a movie that won't start for another thirty minutes. Let's go in there." He escorted her into the empty theater. The screen remained blank in the dimly lit room.

"We're the only ones here. What time does it start?"

"We're not watching a movie. We're talking."

Once seated at the top, Michael breathed in her scent of spring flowers and realized how much he missed her. "Amy, I never stopped loving you. But being married to me would've placed you in danger."

"Danger? How?"

"I made a deal with the devil."

"You're not making sense." Amy slipped from her coat.

"My uncle is a mob boss. He runs the show in Jersey and New York. When I had all the debtors on my ass to pay Mom's hospital bills and had been kicked out of school, he offered to clean up the financial mess including my student loans." He explained how his uncle screwed up his college.

"Oh, Michael, you didn't take his money. Please tell me you didn't."

"I did. I had to. I couldn't bring you into that kind of life."

"So why tell me now?" she asked, her voice softer and more patient.

"I was offered a deal by Deputy U.S. Marshal Braden Wolfe. I'm thinking about taking it. He's already working on it and running it by federal prosecutors."

"What kind of deal?"

"I plan to turn federal witness against my uncle."

Her face paled. "The Witness Protection Program. Michael those people have to give up their identity. They have to leave everything they've ever known and live where the government chooses. From what I've read they can't have any contact with their family and friends."

"I'm glad to see you're already familiar with it."

"Michael, you can't just disappear from the face of the earth. Think about this. Have you tried talking to your uncle?"

"Yeah, he wasn't too understanding. That's why I think he's having me followed. Look, Amy, unless I want to be a coldblooded killer always afraid someone will kill me before I kill them, I have to do this."

"So what are you leading up to?" she whispered.

"Come with me. We can get married and disappear together."

Her face looked numb. "Michael, I'd never see my family again, none of my sisters or brothers, not my parents, and aunts and uncles. I can't just leave them and never see them again."

"Do you still love me, Amy?"

"Yes, Michael, but you're asking too much." She stood and stared at him with an expression of horror. "After you walked out on me, I wanted to die. I'm just now getting my life back together. Please, if you love me, leave me alone."

She scooted down the aisle and left.

Michael closed his eyes and breathed in the sweet scent she'd left behind. Her reaction hadn't come as a surprise, so why'd it hurt so much? He'd contact Braden Wolfe and make the deal without her being a part of it.

◆◆◆

Sarah set a Jack O' Lantern on her porch then hung a scary witch above it. She walked to her mail box. Dead leaves crunched under her feet. She checked her mail and removed an envelope with a return address for the Kansas City Federal Marshal's Service. Her heart swelled with excitement. Back in the house, she sat at the kitchen table and carefully peeled open the envelope. Then pulled out the ragged piece of yellow legal pad paper.

She turned it over and read.

Sarah,

Don't do me any more favors. We're done. Send me a bill. Braden.

She stared at his icy words and read them several times, each time feeling like she was swallowing something sharp. Tears stung her eyes. She'd expected him to be upset but not so cruel in his reply. Obviously, he didn't plan to spend his vacation with her.

If Braden hadn't lost a child, she wouldn't tolerate his insensitive behavior. But the man had never been able to move past his son's death and the role he believed he'd played in it. Despite what Braden said, she'd send him a picture of their baby and keep him updated.

◆◆◆

The phone rang late one night. Andy was crying. *Daddy, I left Freddie Dinosaur in your car. I can't sleep without my Freddie dinosaur.*

At midnight, Braden banged on his in-laws' door. When it opened, he shoved past his father-in-law, took the steps two at a time, and delivered the toy in person. After a few hugs and kisses, he left.

The memory squeezed his chest. Braden thought of Sarah and the child she carried. He regretted what he'd written. He'd been angry at the moment and tried to be as hurtful as possible. He grimaced as a headache pounded behind his eyes. After a night of drinking, what had he expected?

Just as he was about to call Sarah, his phone rang. It listed the caller as unknown.

"Wolfe, here."

"Marshal Wolfe, it's Michael Dagastino. I'm ready to talk."

"Are you on a secure line?"

"Yes."

"Good."

Braden discussed the procedure of how everything would go down and scheduled a time to talk again.

"How's Sarah? Have you heard from her?"

"I've spoken with her a couple of times. She's fine."

No sooner than Michael disconnected, Braden got the ball rolling and called the necessary people to turn Michael into a federal witness. Due to the information being leaked to Dagastino, Chief Deputy Marshal Reiner remained the only person aware of it in Braden's district. If the mole discovered what was about to go down, it'd be a death sentence for Michael.

Chapter Fourteen

Sarah raised the garage door, drove inside, and lowered it. Grandma Sofia had always considered it bad luck to buy anything for a baby until after the sixth month of pregnancy, but Sarah hadn't been able to resist the DaVinci oak cradle.

Wanting to change into comfortable shoes before she brought her groceries in from the garage, she entered her house, then made her way from the kitchen to the den.

She came to an abrupt halt.

Her own image stood from the chair.

Sarah drew in a sharp breath. "How did you get in my house?"

"You should never leave a key under a flowerpot." Selena had a distinct Latino accent. "That's a really dumbass thing to do you know."

"But my alarm was set."

"Piece of cake for Reggie." She walked over to Sarah. "It took him two minutes to disarm it." Without warning, she slapped Sarah. "That's for having a better life than me."

Sarah slapped Selena even harder. 'That's for. . .'

Selena's fist popped Sarah's face.

The men with her sister laughed.

Sarah held her jaw for a moment and forced back tears. Pain radiated through the right side of her face. There wasn't any doubt who the dominant twin was.

Selena stood confident, looking amused. Then she glanced around the house at the furnishings. "It sucks to be you. I can tell."

The Latino man took Selena's arm and spoke to her in Spanish. As he talked, the fire in her sister's eyes smoldered, and her posture became more relaxed. She turned back to Sarah. "You don't have one fuckin' thing in this house to eat."

"I have groceries in my car."

"Carlos and Blade, go get the shit out." She turned to the man sitting at the computer. "Reggie, you can close your mouth."

"It's wicked looking at you two together."

Selena scowled at Sarah while answering the guy. "We're identical twins, dumbass."

Sarah's jaw still hurt. She wondered what Selena's purpose was for the visit. Did she plan to harm or kidnap her? There wasn't any way to reach either phone to call for help. She figured her best bet was not to show how terrified she was, but her stomach kept rolling.

She studied the men bringing in the groceries. Blade, the big, white, bald guy had tattoos and piercings. Carlos the Latino wasn't bad looking with ebony hair and dark eyes. Then there was the wiry, skinny, white guy called Reggie. She wasn't sure what he was doing at her computer. But after they left, she'd change her passwords.

The men made several trips. On the last trip, Carlos brought in the enormous box from her trunk. "That's everything."

Selena's eyes widened with acknowledgement when she saw the picture on the outside. "A cradle? What the hell do you need that for?"

Sarah smoothed her shirt over her rounded stomach. "I'm due in March."

"I read your husband was killed."

"And also my son."

"So you're fuckin' around?"

"It was bad judgment on my part."

Sarah cringed when Blade opened the mint chocolate chip ice cream and then double dipped from the carton. *Disgusting.* Carlos peeled a banana and ate it. He tossed the peel at the trashcan and missed, not bothering to pick it up.

"Pitch that bag of chips over," Reggie shouted from the computer desk.

Blade tossed it across the room.

Selena frowned. "I don't want junk food. Fix us something to eat."

"I can make spaghetti?"

"Sure," her sister replied. "We have an hour."

"Then there's time."

Sarah's best bet was to remain relaxed and calm. She didn't want to appear hostile or a threat. As a nurse, she'd learned if you spoke in a civil tone to someone, they'd usually reply in a similar way."

Sarah removed a pot and skillet and started preparing the meal.

She reminded herself Selena couldn't be trusted. Still, the fact remained that her sister was the only person who could tell her about their biological family. Good or bad, she wanted to know about them. Who were her parents? Were any of them still living? Had Selena known she had a twin?

"I've never let myself become fond of one man. A good fuck is all I'm after."

Sarah shuddered at her sister's harsh language. Rather than appear appalled, she kept a solemn expression. There was so much she wanted to ask, but would it send Selena off the deep-end again? Sarah didn't want to end up with another fist in her face.

Take the chance. Ask her.

"Were you adopted like me?"

"I'm pretty sure I wasn't. We were shit-ass poor."

"Why do you think our mother gave me up?"

"She didn't do it to give you a better life. She sold your ass. I'm surprised she didn't sell me too."

When Selena moved closer, Sarah flinched. But instead of slapping her again, her double leaned against the counter. "Did you know you were adopted?"

"I never knew until the arrest." *Keep her talking.* "What was our mother's name?"

"Teresa Rosalia Menendez."

"Do you know who our father was?"

"Don't know and don't fuckin' give a shit."

"What was she like, our mother?" Sarah poured the tomato sauce over the meat and added spices.

"A crack whore."

"Oh, I see."

"No, you don't. Hell, she screwed five men or more a night. And if that wasn't bad enough, she started me in the business. I gave my first blow job at the age of twelve. She had me spreading my legs for a few bucks by the time I was fourteen."

Sarah swallowed hard. "I'm sorry."

Carlos smiled. "Selena's the best. Her momma taught her right."

"Did she have any redeeming qualities?" Sarah asked, hoping for one nice thing that could be said about the woman who'd given her life. "What I'm asking is, did she ever do anything special for you?"

Selena appeared in deep thought. "Usually Santa never came to see me. But one year, Momma made sure I had some presents. She shoplifted a doll, some coloring books and crayons, and a little tea set. Then she convinced the department store Santa to deliver them in person in exchange for a blow job behind the store."

"How'd you learn the truth?"

"Because it was one of Mom's favorite stories to tell when she was high. Her favorite punch line was, 'Everyone knows Santa comes once a year.' That was my best Christmas."

That's horrible.

Though Selena still terrified her, Sarah's heart ached for this woman. Her sister. And she couldn't explain the connection between them, but one existed. Did Selena feel it? Or had years of being a ruthless killer robbed her of any real emotion?

"You don't seem like the type who'd fuck just anyone."

"I'm not. But I slipped up."

Still at the computer, Reggie butted in. "Deputy U.S. Marshal Wolfe."

"What about him?" Selena asked.

"She did the nasty with him in Alaska."

Sarah's mouth dropped open for a minute before she found her voice. "The information on my computer is private. That's none of your business."

"Wolfe. You did it with Braden Wolfe? Shit. That's fuckin' unreal. Does the bastard know he knocked you up?" Selena asked, still appearing taken back.

"He knows," Reggie replied. "From what she told her friend, he wasn't exactly thrilled by it."

Selena frowned. "Always knew he was a prick. Cocky asshole."

At the moment, Sarah would agree.

"Why Wolfe?"

"I'm not sure. Mark, my husband, was my prince charming, and Braden Wolfe is more like a evil troll."

For the first time, Selena cracked a partial smile.

Keep her amused. Keep it light. Slapping her sure didn't work.

Sarah returned to the stove and turned the heat down on the boiling pasta. "It's almost done."

Since Selena hated Wolfe maybe Sarah could use this to make her sister see her as one of Braden's victims. Maybe give them a common ground that'd give Selena some kind of emotional response.

"I'm not seeing Wolfe anymore. He doesn't want anything to do with this baby."

"Men. The bastards are all alike," Selena said.

Get her talking about family. Maybe there's an aunt or uncle, maybe even grandparents still alive.

"Actually, my father who raised me was a good man. But you're right. They're few and far in between. You go through a lot of frogs before you find a prince."

"I had a lot of creepy uncles. They were all animals. Always trying to pull me on their laps or cop a feel."

"Do you have any family still living?"

"Somewhere Mom has a sister and brother. But she never visited them." Selena glanced toward the den. "Get your ass up, Carlos. The food is ready. And you shitheads use some manners."

"Let me nap another ten minutes," Carlos mumbled.

"I'm ready to eat," Blade announced. He made his way to the kitchen.

"We're leaving in thirty minutes whether you've eaten or not," Selena said.

Clearly her sister ruled the group. Sarah wondered what she intended to do with her. Did they plan to take her?

Carlos rose from the sofa and walked to the kitchen. "All right, Selena, but when I'm too fucking tired to drive all night, remember this."

"Bitch, bitch, bitch. You sound like an old woman. Blade can drive"

Sarah served the food at the table. The men carried their plates to the den without asking. But she wasn't about to complain.

"Care for any bread," Sarah offered her sister.

"No, I don't eat bread. This is good."

Sarah set the bread down. "So you didn't know about me?"

Selena had her mouth full and shook her head.

"You're my sister. Being with you feels right. Don't you feel it?"

Selena stared at her for a moment. "I'm hungry other than that, I don't feel shit."

Sarah reminded herself that being sisters wasn't enough to protect her from Selena. After all, Cain killed Abel. But her heart went out to this woman who'd lived a horrid childhood. While Sarah had been playing in piano recitals, her sister had been whoring herself out so their mom could buy drugs. She had never felt lucky until now. She'd been the fortunate one.

Selena stood and rattled Spanish words off the tip of her tongue, speaking to the men.

Sarah's spine tightened.

Carlos joined them and spoke soft Spanish words to Selena. He placed his hands on her arms and held her steady before him. Again he spoke as though trying to reason with her. When she nodded in agreement, he let her go.

Sarah sensed it concerned her. What did one want to do that the other didn't? Murder her?

"Will you return?" Sarah asked, wanting to learn Selena's intention.

"I'll be in touch."

Sarah reached a hand out and touched Selena's arm. "Be safe."

Selena jerked back and narrowed her eyes into icy slits. "I just wanted to see you. I don't have time to be part of the fuckin' Brady Bunch." She paused and shifted her gaze to Sarah's stomach. "And if you're smart, you'll get rid of that evil little bastard."

Sarah held back the tears she wanted to shed for Selena. Yes, Selena had felt the touch all the way to her heart, and now she was protecting herself the only way she knew how by being hateful. But she couldn't fool Sarah. The magnetic force between them could only be described as powerful.

"Goodbye, Selena."

Selena spit on her. "Don't talk to me like we care about each other. I don't fuckin' care about you."

Sarah couldn't hold back the tears. "I'm sorry you feel that way. It's your loss."

"What? You gonna be there for me when I get executed? Come hold my hand and pray for me? Forget it. I was born with a ticket to hell in my hand. And I don't need anyone asking God to forgive me, not even you, princess."

Again Selena gave the orders, and the men followed her out the back door and across the yard where they disappeared through a neighbor's yard.

◆◆◆

Selena scolded herself for staying too long. She'd wanted to take Sarah with them. *Why wait?* But Carlos insisted taking her before he could set a deal up with Dagastino would be a mistake. Her abduction would make national news, and then there'd be no chance of passing Sarah off as herself.

"Back roads only. No highways or interstates," she told Blade, who drove the van.

She turned to Reggie. "Okay, dickhead. You mouthed off too much. Now she knows you hacked into her email account."

"Don't sweat it. Most she'll do is change her password. I fixed it where any email she sends out or receives will come to my computer also."

"Good, I was afraid you'd screwed up." She extended her hand over the seat. "Pass me the bottle of rum on the floor."

God, I don't want to feel anything for her.

Selena turned the pint size bottle up, hoping the liquor would help her fight the emotions churning inside her. She found herself angry with Wolfe for what he'd done to Sarah. *Shit.* She'd actually felt protective over her sister. She couldn't let that happen. She had to keep her heart cold and hard.

Sarah served one purpose, and emotions would only get in the way. Of course, she'd have Blade do the dirty work. He had no qualms with killing women. With Sarah's identity, she could have a new life.

Dagastino would be a happy man as well, thinking he'd killed her. And it all came with a bonus. Wolfe's child would die with Sarah.

◆◆◆

When the phone rang, Braden grabbed it without checking the caller ID. "Wolfe here."

"This is Don Hisky with *America's Most Wanted*. Just thought you'd want to know, we got another call on Selena Menendez. She was spotted in Little Rock, Arkansas. A service station attendant recognized her and heard her mention Memphis."

Have you notified the Memphis authorities?"

"Yes, absolutely. Problem is the caller didn't notify us right off. Quite a few hours passed before he recalled where he'd seen her and called it in."

"Thanks for the tip." Braden dialed Sarah's number. No answer. He found Marcy. "Keep trying to call Sarah. Tell her, Menendez might be headed her way. Tell her to lock the doors."

"Why don't you call her? Hey, where are you going?"

"Memphis."

Though he had his pilot's license, Braden didn't care for flying. Something about it lulled him to sleep. He'd never had a problem behind the wheel of a car. The earliest commercial flight to Memphis didn't leave for three more hours. He considered hitching a ride on a J-Pat jet out of the Missouri district. Rather than wait, he rented a Cessna 172. Too much was at stake. He doubted Selena would feel any sisterly love toward Sarah.

There had to be a reason other than curiosity behind Selena's desire to meet Sarah. The worst case scenario—kill Sarah and pass her body off to Dagastino as herself.

Shit. Stay calm.

He reminded himself a deputy was guarding Sarah's house. And by now, officers should be on the scene to back him up. Some rookie could get trigger happy and mistake Sarah for Selena.

After landing, he signed the needed papers for the rental car, then sped off using the GPS to locate Sarah's home.

By the time Braden drove up, the Germantown Police Department, the Shelby County Sheriff's Patrol, and a couple of Memphis marshals had arrived. Several FBI agents pulled up behind him.

Selena Menendez was on every agency's most wanted list.

Braden flashed his badge and introduced himself to the law enforcement already on the scene. "Is Sarah Mason all right?"

"Yes, she's fine," a Germantown police officer said.

Thank God.

Relief whooshed through Braden.

"Menendez wasn't apprehended. We were too late," the Memphis marshal stated. "We put out a BOLO on Selena and part of her gang, covering a hundred mile radius."

Another U.S. Marshal stepped up. "We set up people on all the interstates and main highways and collapsed the perimeter."

"Well, that's all fine and dandy, but she never escapes on main thoroughfares. Be sure the BOLO reaches the smaller towns," Braden said. He knew more about Selena than all of them put together.

Braden made his way through the law officers to the walkway leading from the driveway to the front door. The house wasn't as ritzy as he assumed it'd be. The gray brick house surrounded by tall oaks and beautiful flowers had more of a cottage look. He entered without knocking, knowing her house was full of police.

The aroma of rich spices and tomato sauce filled the air, making his stomach growl.

When Braden walked into the kitchen, Sarah sat in a chair, giving her statement to a female officer who jotted the information down. She stood and walked into his arms, pressing her face against his chest.

My Sarah is safe.

And he saw Sarah not Selena. He leaned his head against hers and tenderly embraced her for a few moments, letting her sob against his chest. He stroked her back gently, whispering words of encouragement.

"Calm down, angel. It's all right. You're safe." He turned to the marshal who'd followed him inside. "I was told someone would watch her house 24/7. Why wasn't that being done?"

"Ms. Mason told the deputy she didn't want him out front."

"Sarah, is that true?"

She nodded. "Yes. It only drew more attention from the news media."

"That's all right." His temper boiled when he noticed her cheek. "Who gave you that bruise?"

"Selena. But that's not why I'm upset."

"Then why all the tears?"

"Because I love her. I really do."

"Selena?"

"Yes, I can't help it. I felt close to her. And for a moment, I know she felt it too. Then she became so defensive and hateful. She argued with Carlos in Spanish, so I couldn't understand, but I know it was about me. Selena finally gave in, and they left."

"Do you remember any of the Spanish words?"

"No. But I had the feeling she'd planned to take me with them, and he was against it."

Sarah moved back, putting some space between them. She placed her hands on her stomach.

Braden eyed her rounded belly, and his breath left him. He didn't want to think about it being his child.

"At least, you and Selena would agree on one thing."

"What's that?" Braden asked her.

"She told me if I were smart, I'd get rid of the little bastard."

Braden stared at her stomach a moment, recalling what Marcy had said.

You're a daddy whether you like it or not.

"No, I don't want any harm coming to your baby."

"Our baby, you shithead," she said, looking outraged. "I love this child. If you don't, it's your loss."

"Hell, if you can love Selena, you're capable of loving almost anyone. Sit down and write Charles Manson a letter. I'm sure he'd like to know someone cares after all these years."

Several law enforcement officers chuckled.

"Selena's right. You're a bastard."

"Yeah, but you're glad to see me," he said, giving her a grin.

She nodded, and tears swelled in her eyes.

Again he cradled her in his arms, then kissed the crown of her hair. "I was worried sick about you."

"I thought they'd kill me."

"They didn't, and you're going to have protection."

"I don't want a house full of police officers watching everything I do."

He chuckled. "You won't. I packed a bag."

"You're staying with me?"

"You bet."

He faced the officers who stood in awe, as if they'd just been told Martians had landed. "Everything is all right now. If your officers spot Selena, they should call for backup. Keep in mind, her so-called family all have outstanding warrants and should be considered dangerous. Two were former members of Satan's Disciplines."

"She only had three of her gang with her," one officer mentioned.

"I could post several deputies out front," the Memphis marshal offered.

"No, that'd drive Menendez off. Since she wanted to take Sarah today, she might talk her gang into swinging back by. If that happens, I *will* call for backup."

"Is your goal to protect Ms. Mason or be the one to capture Selena?" the marshal asked.

Son-of-a-bitch.

Anger swirled through Braden's head and shot through his veins. He controlled his response. "Both. How long can the protection go on? Months? Years? This won't end. Sarah won't be completely safe until Selena Menendez is captured."

The marshal nodded. "We'll keep you updated."

Braden realized he appeared like a selfish, arrogant bastard, but on the flight to Memphis, Sarah had been his only concern. "You and your men can make your way out. Thank you for all your help. And I *guarantee* you that I will not try to singlehandedly take on Menendez or her gang. I'm still wearing a scar she left."

This time the Memphis marshal didn't comment.

After the house cleared, Braden glanced at the stove. "Is there any spaghetti left?"

"Yes, a little. You can have it. I'd rather have salad."

"I'm starving. Would you mind heating it up, while I wash up."

She nodded, then walked to the stove and turned on the burner.

During his dinner, he couldn't help but think how good it was to be back with Sarah. It felt right.

It wasn't until bedtime he realized Sarah had plans to change his mind about the baby. He had been assigned to Tristen's old room.

Yep, she has a purpose for doing it.

He sat on the edge of the bed and studied the picture on the desk of Tristen holding a trophy and soccer ball. Beside the picture stood the trophy he'd won. A *Star Wars* poster hung over the desk.

Strange, he hadn't kept any of Andy's things except pictures. His favorite toys had been buried with him. Now Braden regretted he hadn't kept Freddie Dinosaur or Silly Willy Bear. But they had meant so much to Andy that it'd only seemed right to keep them with his son.

After turning off the lamp, Braden eased beneath the comforter and stared at the glow-in-the-dark stars on the ceiling and the airplanes dangling on strings. He knew her motive for placing him in Tristen's shrine. She wanted him to see that she'd lost a son also and had felt the unbearable pain, yet she was willing to open her heart and give her love to another child.

Daddy, why can't me and Mommy live with you instead of Paw Paw and Grandma? Corey's mommy and daddy live together.

How do you tell your kid that his mother would choose drugs over him or that your job had to come first? Before Andy died, Braden had requested a transfer and a position that wouldn't require as many trips out of town. He'd also filed for full custody, taking his in-laws back to court. But all of it had come too late.

Braden grimaced.

◆◆◆

Sarah glanced at the wall clock. It was almost noon.

A lot of protection Braden is.

She hoped to use the time alone with him to change his mind about the baby. She hated to admit the strong effect he had on her. She recalled his total dominance over her in Alaska. Her body reeled with excitement.

No, it's not that. It's just my naughty little hormones going wild.

He meandered into the kitchen, rubbing his eyes and yawning. "Morning."

She glanced up and smiled. "You're just in time. I'm trying to figure out how this thing goes together."

Spotting the cradle, Braden frowned as he walked over and poured a cup of coffee. He sat at the table and glanced away from her project.

She ignored Braden and held the piece of wood in place and tried to screw it down. Her hand slipped causing the screwdriver to scar the wood with a nasty scratch. "Oh, fudge."

Braden looked up. "Hurt yourself?"

"No, but I scratched the blasted wood. I'm not any good at this kind of stuff." Sarah stared at the diagram. "There must be a piece missing. I can't do this."

Braden kept reading the paper not paying any attention to her. And she'd deliberately worn a knit shirt that emphasized her baby bubble. She wasn't about to let Braden get away with ignoring their child. He was the daddy-baby whether he liked it or not. Or was it baby-daddy? *Whatever.*

"I give up," she said and stood. She threw everything into the box and then pulled it into the garage. "I'll hire someone to do it."

"What's for breakfast?" Braden asked, not lifting his eyes from the paper as she came back into the room.

Is he for real?

"For your information, this isn't a bed and breakfast. If you want something, cook it or go out somewhere and eat."

With that said, she stormed to the rear of the house to the room she intended to convert into a nursery. She drug things out into the hall so she could paint it first. Her stomach churned. *Oh, fudge.* She stopped and ran for the bathroom, then leaned over the toilet and gagged several times before throwing up, followed by a series of dry heaves. *Holy crap.*

When Sarah looked up, Braden stood in the doorway. "Anything I can do to help?"

"No thanks. Just go back to the kitchen. This is something I've dealt with every morning by myself. I can handle it without you."

Despite what she'd said, he dampened a cloth and offered it to her.

Afterwards, she felt better. "Thanks. This isn't fair. Marcy has had very little morning sickness."

"Life's not fair." He helped her up and escorted her to the bedroom.

She crawled in bed and covered her eyes with her forearm. "I've always been told morning sickness wasn't as bad with a second pregnancy. Maybe I'm so sick because it's been so many years since my first one."

◆◆◆

Braden found Sarah asleep when he returned. He left the room quietly closing the door behind him. He walked to the kitchen, pulled out a skillet and proceeded to fry three sunny-side-up eggs.

Daddy, I want two sunny eggs. Don't break the sun.

Andy had been real particular about his eggs. Braden had never understood why since Andy smashed the hell out of them before he ate them.

After breakfast, Braden showered and shaved. He thought about the cradle but pushed it from his mind. His conscience kept nagging him to put the damn thing together.

He touched basis with the FBI to make sure Sarah's calls traced. It had already been set up with her service provider. Then he surrendered and pulled the cradle box in from the garage and sorted out the pieces by the diagram. He went to work and assembled it. He pushed the cradle causing it to rock back and forth. He couldn't help but envision a sleeping baby lying in it. His heart squeezed with pain when he thought of Andy as an infant.

He glanced up and discovered Sarah standing in the doorway.

Her eyes sparkled. "My cradle. Braden, it's lovely. Thank you for putting it together."

"Where do you want it?"

"I planned on cleaning out the middle bedroom, but I ended up sick."

"What has to be done?"

"Everything has to go to the attic."

"Let's get started." Braden didn't want to be a part of this child's life, but he couldn't have Sarah lifting heavy things and possibly hurting herself.

By noon, the nursery had been cleared of the sewing machine, a futon bed, and a small desk.

"I couldn't have done it without you. Thanks."

"I owe you for taking care of me in Alaska, that's all. Don't get any grand ideas that I'm going to play daddy."

"No, I'm not expecting anything from you." She turned away from him and scanned the room. "Once I clean the cobwebs, I'll be ready to paint."

"What color?"

"I went with yellow. It's bright and cheery. I have an animal border to put around the top. It works for a girl or boy."

Braden exhaled in frustration. "Have you bought the paint?"

"Yes and the border. It's in the garage."

"After lunch, I'll paint the room. You don't have any business breathing paint fumes. It could hurt the . . . never mind, you know what I mean."

"Baby."

His breath left him. "Yeah, that."

She smiled warmly.

Yeah, she can lay the bait, but I'm not biting that hook.

◆◆◆

Amy stared at a picture of Michael and thought about why he'd called off their engagement. At the time, she assumed he'd met someone else or had decided marriage wasn't for him. But the truth wasn't any better. How could he have allowed himself to be wooed into organized crime?

Why didn't you come to me first?

Then she recalled the sacrifice he asked her to make for him. She would have to leave behind her *life* and start over with a new name. She'd never be able even call her mother and father. When she thought of Christmas and all the other times that were special, she couldn't imagine her family not being a part of it.

She couldn't deny she still loved him. She hated how she'd stormed out of the theater without hearing him out.

Her heart ached for Michael, to be with him and be a part of his life, but could she make the sacrifice? And if she were willing to leave her life behind to go with him, how would she reach him? Then she remembered the name Braden Wolfe. The man who'd offered Michael the deal. But how in the hell, would she locate him.

And when she found him what would her decision be?

♦♦♦

Marcy hadn't found her desk job as exciting as going with Braden to track down fugitives, but she'd been home every night in time to fix dinner for her family.

Her mother had taken the girls for the night. Marcy wanted to make the evening romantic. Of course with her stomach protruding like a basketball, it wouldn't be easy. Maybe romance was pushing things a bit. Perhaps she should just hope for quality time with Alex.

On her way home, she picked up the items to prepare his favorite meal. When she pulled into the garage, his car wasn't there. She glanced at the wall clock and wondered where he was. She tried to keep the invasive thoughts of Tiffany from her mind.

An hour later, she had his dinner ready, but he still hadn't arrived.

She sighed as she surrendered and picked up the phone. First she called his office number, but only the recording answered giving business hours. Finally, she dialed his phone and discovered it'd been turned off.

Another hour passed without hearing from him. After putting the food away, Marcy walked to the front window and stood, staring into the darkness.

Déjà Vu.

He's with Tiffany just like before.

The thought squeezed at her throat until it burned.

◆◆◆

Braden stood admiring his work. *Not bad.* He'd spent all evening working in the room.

Sarah entered the newly painted nursery and smiled. "It looks nice."

Braden's heart warmed. "Now that you've seen it, stay out until the fumes clear."

"Yes, sir," she said, saluting him. "I've made dinner."

"Good, I'm hungry."

"After that huge lunch you ate?"

"Yep. What'd you fix?"

"Smoked salmon."

He grimaced. "Just hearing those words makes me ill."

"I'm teasing," she confessed. "I made a chicken pasta dish. Come eat."

Looking relieved, he nodded, then followed her to the kitchen.

After sitting and being served, he glanced across the table at her. "Thought I was supposed to fend for myself?"

She shrugged. "You're working around here. The least I can do is feed you." She stopped eating and stared at him. "I was thinking about what that officer said. Braden, are you here to protect me or catch Menendez? Which one means the most to you?"

He started to answer but stopped, questioning his true motives. Would he place Sarah's life on the line just for a chance to apprehend Selena? An imaginary weight sat on his shoulders as he considered his answer. Finally, he hesitantly shrugged. "I'm not sure."

The light in her eyes dulled, and her face paled. "Not sure or afraid I'll kick you out before Selena returns?"

"Catching her is important to me, but I wouldn't want to see you hurt to achieve that. You were my primary concern in coming here."

The phone rang, making her flinch.

Braden leapt from his chair and stood near the phone. "Answer it."

Sarah switched it to speaker phone before picking up the receiver. "Hello."

"I see you didn't waste any time calling the police."

She gave Braden a nod. "Actually, I didn't call them."

"Bullshit, you little backstabbing bitch."

"You were spotted in Arkansas," Braden said. "If you'd stayed a little longer, we'd have you right now."

Selena laughed. "Doubt that." She paused. "Wolfe, I don't like the way you've treated my sister. You knocked her up and then walked away. You're only willing to toss a few bucks her way, like she's your puta."

Rage rocketed through Braden's brain. He hated Menendez.

"Wolfe, when you fucked Sarah, did you think of me?"

"You're going down, Menendez. And I'll be the one making the arrest."

"You might have to choose," Selena said.

"Choose what?"

"Between Sarah and me? You can't have us both."

The line went dead.

Sarah's gaze met Braden's in a suspended moment. Then he averted his focus to her stomach.

Shit.

Chapter Fifteen

Alex still wasn't home. Marcy finally decided to drive past Tiffany's house. But as she was about to leave, her phone rang. She recognized the number. She hesitantly answered it. "Hello, Tiffany. What do you want?"

"I thought you might like to know why Alex didn't come home for dinner."

Marcy's jaw clenched. "I don't care to hear anything you have to say."

Tiffany laughed. "He's been here. We had some unfinished business to discuss and things got out of hand, and we ended up in bed. The sheets are still warm."

Tears ran down Marcy's face as she held back the sobs. She wouldn't let this woman hear her distress. "Go to hell, you bitch."

No sooner had she hung up the phone, Alex came through the door.

He dropped his keys and wallet on the kitchen counter before glancing up at her. "Marcy, I should've called. But my phone wasn't charged."

"Where have you been," she glanced at the clock, "for the last three hours?"

"With Ron Davis, the owner of Vistaview. He called as I was leaving the office and invited me to join him at the Morton House. We talked at the bar, but then he insisted we eat dinner. He is now officially my new client. We went back to the office and filled out the necessary papers. Now we can afford for you to quit."

"I don't believe you."

"You're kidding, right?"

"No, I'm not. You were with Tiffany. Don't deny it."

"If we can't live without you accusing me every time I step inside the door, our marriage won't work."

"She called."

"She what?"

"Look at the caller I.D. if you don't believe me."

He crossed the room and checked the numbers before turning to her. "What'd she say?"

"Basically, that the sheets were still warm."

"I didn't. I was never with her. Marcy, go to the restaurant. They'll tell you I was there. Our waiter's name was Tom. And if you need more proof, give Ron Davis a call. I'd rather he not know our dirty laundry, but if it's the only way to prove I'm innocent, call him."

Marcy didn't answer. Instead, she grabbed her keys and jacket. "Let's go."

"Where?"

"The restaurant."

Marcy and Alex waited in the restaurant's lobby for the waiter to appear. The aroma of the food made her feel ill.

When the waiter saw Alex, his face lit up with recognition. "Hello, sir. Was there a problem tonight?"

Her cheeks heated. Nevertheless, she stood her ground and thought of how to phrase her question. "You waited on my husband tonight?"

"Yes, ma'am. He and his guest."

She crossed her arms and glared at Alex.

"He was with an older gentleman," the waiter added.

Alex smiled.

"Not so fast." She looked back at the waiter. "How long would you say he was here?"

"Two hours at least maybe longer. They sat and talked after their dinner."

Alex eyed her with amusement. "Satisfied. Or do you need to speak with my newest client?"

Marcy shook her head, then glanced at the waiter. "Thank you. Sorry for bothering you."

"No problem."

Back in the car, she sighed. "Why would she say something like that? And how did she know you've been gone all evening unless she's following you? If she's insane enough to do this, she's dangerous."

Alex started the engine. "I'm sorry I brought this on us." He backed from the parking space. "I really don't think she'd hurt anyone."

"Don't bet on it." An eerie sensation of being watched washed over Marcy. Somewhere nearby, she would almost bet Tiffany sat in her car, watching them like a tigress waiting for her prey.

◆◆◆

Michael climbed in the limo and sat beside Uncle Leon. The long limousine pulled away from the cemetery. His mother's death made him more determined to turn on his uncle. Her last dying wish was for him to break away from the family business.

Don't appear angry.

Uncle Leon studied him intensely. Maybe his uncle would mistake the show of emotion as grief.

When he left, he didn't plan to take anything with him. He'd disappear with only the clothes on his back and a few pictures of his family and one of Amy. His testimony against his uncle would clear him from any charges concerning the Alaskan helicopter crash. He wouldn't have to do any prison time and would eventually be able to return to school.

But Amy's reaction still hurt.

"Let's talk, Michael."

Michael's shoulders tensed. He nodded.

"Chase says you've been edgy lately. Any particular reason?"

"I keep thinking about Alaska. And how I let you down." If he ever needed a poker face, it was now. He quickly thought about what else he could say. "I keep waiting for the shit to hit the fan, thinking any minute the Feds will arrest me and the others."

"If they do, you've got to trust me. I can get you out of it. I have a few politicians and judges in my back pocket." His uncle continued to brag, naming several of the people—judges and senators among them.

Michael nodded, trying to stay calm.

Remember the names.

"My sources tell me Braden Wolfe is in Memphis. Seems Selena paid a visit to that woman he mistook for her. She managed to give the Federal marshals the slip again. Sooner or later, Selena will pay her sister another visit. I want the Mason woman's house watched."

"Where'd you get your information?"

"Let's just say, I've made the right connections in Wolfe's office. How do you think I knew about the DNA?"

Michael gave a slight nod as if he approved.

If his uncle knew about Selena, what would keep this informant from tipping his uncle off about him turning federal witness? Another thought occurred to him.

What if he already knows?

♦♦♦

Braden didn't think Selena would show up any time soon. The call had come from a prepaid phone and was untraceable.

When he walked in the nursery, Sarah stood upon a ladder, putting up the border—a wide multi-colored print of zoo animals. He eased up behind her not wanting to frighten her. His gaze followed the curve of her back over her shapely bottom. He recalled how wonderful it felt lying with her curled up against him. His desire for Sarah made him restless. He wanted her and had since Alaska. No other woman had interested him. But he had to resist.

"It looks good," he said. She flinched, and he placed his hands on her waist to steady her. "Don't fall."

"You scared me."

"Sorry, angel."

"You can move your hands now. I'm fine."

"Climb down. I'll do that."

"No, I can manage. You painted the room, so the least I can do is put up the border."

"But I don't want you falling."

She turned and gave him a questioning look. "Why, Braden? If I lost the baby wouldn't that make your life much easier?"

"Sarah, that's not fair. I don't want you to lose the baby."

And he realized he really meant it. The child she carried was his—just as Andy had been. Had painting the nursery and putting the cradle together given the child more significance than he wanted it to have?

"You almost look sincere."

"I am." He placed a hand on her elbow. "Now carefully step down and let me finish it."

"Just hold the ladder for me."

Enjoying his view, Braden grinned. "All right."

Not only did he hold the base of the ladder, he ended up moistening the strips of border and handing them to her. An hour later, the border encompassed the room.

Sarah stepped from the ladder and pivoted around, taking in the nursery. "It's really cute. I want to buy some jungle animals. Hang a few monkeys around. Thanks for helping." She wiped her hands on her jeans. "Let's have some cake. And I'll brew a fresh pot of coffee."

"Sounds good."

Braden sat at the table, wondering about Selena. Was she heading toward Phoenix where she had friends? The doorbell brought him to his feet. "Stay here."

He walked to the front door and peeked out. Amazement rippled through him when he saw Michael. He opened the door. "What are you doing here?"

"I needed to speak with you and let Sarah know my uncle wants her house watched. I left the others sleeping at the hotel. Seems my uncle gets his information as quickly as you do. He mentioned he has someone working in your office who tips him off."

"I suspected it when you already knew we had Selena's DNA." He opened the door wider. "Come in. Sarah's brewing a pot of coffee."

Michael glanced behind him before entering the house. "Can't be too careful."

Braden closed and locked the door. "It's risky for you to be here." In the kitchen, he said to Sarah, "Look who's here."

Sarah turned from the stove. "Michael." She crossed over and gave him a light hug. "What are you doing here?"

"My uncle wants to get his hands on Selena, so he plans on having your house watched. He believes sooner or later she'll return."

Sarah shrugged. "She might, but I don't think it will be anytime soon." She paused. "Want cake and coffee."

"Sure. I haven't eaten." Michael slipped from his leather jacket and hung it over the back of a chair.

Braden didn't like seeing Sarah with her arms around anyone, even if the hug was just a friendly gesture.

Michael sat at the round table and accepted the cup and plate Sarah handed him. When he eyed Sarah's stomach, his face revealed his shock. "I'm glad you both made it back. I reported your location to authorities, but you'd already been rescued." He glanced at Braden. "And how's the leg?"

"I had surgery on my knee. No broken bones."

Michael nervously cleared his throat. "So you're going to be parents. Congratulations. You guys excited about the baby."

Braden sipped his coffee and set it down. "Sarah's thrilled."

"And you're not?"

Braden shrugged. "I have mixed feelings about it." The last thing he needed was Michael making him feel guilty. "Did your uncle say who his informant was?"

"No. He's been suspicious of me lately. I didn't want to push the issue." Michael finished off the cake. "What if this person tells him about my deal with the Feds?"

Braden ran his hands over his hair. "No one in my immediate district knows except Chief Deputy Reiner. Of course that will change the closer the time comes for you to disappear. Right now, it's being handled on a federal level."

"Uncle Leon asked me what was wrong. And I told him I was nervous about the possibility of being arrested for the helicopter crash in Alaska."

"What'd he say?"

"Not to worry. He had judges in his pocket."

"I hope you've been taking beneficial notes on your uncle's business."

"Every chance I've had, I've copied incriminating documents. I jotted names and dates down. I also recorded my uncle bragging about how he had that New York judge and police chief whacked."

"Holy shit. You heard him?"

"I did," Michael boasted, "and recorded it."

"That's too risky." Braden grinned. "Having this information, I don't think you'll have a problem being accepted into the program. They tried to charge him with those murders, but couldn't get enough evidence."

"I placed everything in my gym locker at Fit Above Fitness Center on Chestnut Street." Michael handed Braden a key. "Take the key in case something happens to me before I disappear. I have one also. Here's a list of judges and politicians who are on Uncle Leon's payroll." He slid the list over.

Braden took the list from Michael. "Put your key in a secure place."

"I keep it under the insole of one of my old jogging shoes in my gym bag."

"Does anyone know about the locker?" Braden asked.

"I never use it when anyone's with me."

"How soon can he be taken into protective custody?" Sarah asked Braden as she joined them.

He looked at Michael while answering her question. "Now that I know exactly what you have, I'll file a Witness Security Program application. I've already spoken with someone from the Department of Justice. They want your uncle. He's at the top of organized crime and racketeering."

Michael paled. "God, I can't believe I'm doing this."

Braden had been a little slack on his effort to help Michael. He'd been too concerned over apprehending

Menendez. Sarah would never forgive him if he let something happen to Michael. "Final decision whether a person can be accepted into WITSEC comes from the Federal Attorney General. One factor in your favor, you won't be a threat to any community we relocate you to. Have you spoken with the girl you mentioned?"

Michael's eyes dulled. "Yeah, she wouldn't even hear me out before she stormed out. Guess that's the end of it. Also, my mother passed away. It'll just be me going into the program."

"I'm sorry about your mother," Sarah said, placing her hand over Michael's.

"Thanks. Mom was very ill. She's better off now."

Sarah offered him a sympathetic look. "I hate Amy isn't going with you."

"I understand about her family, but if she really loved me, she'd come."

Braden swigged his coffee down. "Now that the initial shock of what you told her is over, maybe you should approach her again."

Michael shrugged. "I'm afraid I'll lead my uncle to her. For several days now, I think someone's been following me."

"Send her a letter," Sarah suggested. "I would have been willing to go anywhere with Mark. Maybe she's given it some more thought."

"I doubt it. Bottom line, she doesn't love me enough to make the sacrifice."

"I'm sorry. It hurts to love someone who doesn't return that love."

Braden's muscles tightened. For some reason, he had the idea Sarah was speaking to him instead of Michael. "And some people are too smart to become tangled up emotionally with another person." Braden turned back to Michael. "I think you need to disappear soon."

"I'm ready." Michael stood. "I'd better get back before they wake up. We're at the Hilton East." He glanced at Sarah. "Thanks for the cake and coffee."

"I'm glad you enjoyed it. Be careful. Don't take any more chances. Now that you've got the eggs just sit on the nest."

Braden laughed. "I've never heard it put like that. But she's right. Don't take any more chances. Just keep the information you have safe. It's enough."

"I will." Michael averted his attention to Sarah. "Do you have any family to help you when the baby comes?"

Sarah shook her head. "Nope, I'll be on my own. But I'll manage."

"Maybe Braden will stick around."

Braden frowned. "Once I get my hands on Menendez, I'm on my way back to Kansas."

"It was good seeing you, Michael, but I need to lie down. Braden will see you out." She retreated to her bedroom.

After Michael left, Braden walked down the hall and stood outside Sarah's bedroom door. He considered knocking but didn't. Instead, he wandered into the freshly painted nursery. The paint fumes still lingered in the air. He stared at the small cradle in the corner and felt an odd sensation—an unwanted warmth of caring and loving. Hardening his heart was becoming more difficult. He would stay until someone replaced him at the end of the week. He had to get out of Sarah's life *now*.

◆◆◆

Sarah stared at the bedroom ceiling. Braden walked past her door several times. The sooner he went back to Kansas the better. The longer he stayed, the more she hoped he'd change his mind about her and the baby. It was a fantasy. She sat up and swung her legs to the floor, then stood. After brushing her hair and washing her face, she left the sanctuary of her bedroom.

She found Braden in front of the television watching wrestling, of all things. How barbaric. It suited him. She grabbed the remote and switched off the television.

"Hey, I was watching that."

"Not anymore. We need to talk."

Braden sat on the edge of the sofa. "Shoot."

"I want you to leave."

His expression revealed his surprise. "And here I thought you liked having me around."

"No, I don't. I need to move on, and I can't do that with you under my roof. If you want someone posted here, I won't ask them to leave this time."

"Will Friday morning be soon enough?"

She nodded, then flipped the television back on and walked toward the hall. Could she stand having her heart toiled with for two more days? She stopped in the doorway and faced him. "I have a doctor's appointment this afternoon, and I plan to do some shopping. I'll be out a few hours."

"What time do I need to be ready?"

"You don't. I don't want you coming with me."

"Angel, you're not going out alone."

"In that case, we leave at two."

That afternoon at her obstetrician's office, she finally found two seats together in the crowded waiting room. No sooner than she sat down, she noticed how many fathers had come with their wives. One young man placed his hand on his wife's stomach and smiled. It made her remember how wonderful and supportive Mark had been during her pregnancy. But another part of her was jealous of these women for having someone to share the experience with.

Her evil troll hid behind a magazine.

Coward.

Sarah had hoped he'd come around. But he hadn't, and she doubted he ever would. She had to remember the impact losing Andy had caused. Not just his death, but the fact Braden believed he could've prevented it.

"Sarah Mason." The nurse waited at the door with Sarah's file.

Sarah turned to him. "Do you want to come?"

"No, you go ahead. I'll wait here."

◆◆◆

After she had gone back, Braden scanned the waiting area. He didn't realize so many husbands would be here. Again his heart tightened over the thought of Sarah being alone.

Then he did something really stupid. He stood and walked to the front window. "I'd like to join Mrs. Mason."

"And you are?"

"The baby's father."

She buzzed the door, and he entered.

"Examining room three."

"Thanks."

At the door, he inhaled a huge breath before turning the knob. He paused in the doorway and saw a nurse and doctor. "May I come in?"

The doctor looked at Sarah, and she nodded her approval.

"This is my baby's father, Braden Wolfe."

"Nice to meet you. I'm Dr. Olson. I feel it's always important for the fathers to be involved. Stand beside her please."

Braden stepped by the examining table.

"We were just about to listen to the heartbeat," the doctor said. He carefully raised her gown but kept a sheet over her only revealing her nice round pooch. He positioned a small device on her stomach.

"Let's see what we hear," the doctor said.

A whoosh of air accompanied each heartbeat, causing Braden's knees to buckle. "It's fast."

"All babies have fast heartbeats around 90 to 100 beats per minute. We won't know until I do an ultrasound, but I'm guessing it's a boy."

Sarah's face blossomed into a smile from the moment the heartbeat had been heard.

Instead of feeling joy, terror consumed Braden.

"Dr. Olson is old school. He refuses to do an ultrasound until the second trimester. We'll have to wait to find out for sure."

"I'll be back in Kansas by then."

Sarah gave him a cool glare.

The doctor ignored Braden's unenthusiastic attitude. "The baby sounds healthy, your weight and blood pressure are good, so I'll see you next month. Still having any morning sickness?"

"A little."

"That's probably from the iron in the vitamins. Be sure you don't take them on an empty stomach."

The doctor glanced at Braden. "If you plan to be in the delivery room with her, you'll need to take the classes offered by the hospital."

"I live out of town. Doubt I'll make it back for the big event."

The flame of happiness in Sarah's expression vanished and was replaced with humiliation as the doctor's expression revealed empathy for her.

"And when you're discharged from the hospital, will someone be there to help you?" the doctor inquired.

"No, but I am a nurse. I'll manage. Don't forget this isn't my first child."

"I haven't." The old doctor started to say something but stopped, and instead, he offered her a caring smile.

Sarah shifted her attention to Braden. "Dr. Olson delivered Tristen."

"Lovely infant. He had a head full of dark hair. And did he have a set of lungs. He made himself heard immediately."

Sarah laughed softly. "Mark thought something was wrong with him and started freaking out. It was an epic moment."

"Thought I was going to have to sedate Mark to keep him calm." The doctor paused. "I hate you don't have a man like Mark to stand with you this time." The doctor flashed a stern condemning look at Braden before he turned to the sink to wash his hands. "Get dressed, Sarah, and don't forget to make that next appointment on your way out."

Guilt washed through Braden as he thought about what the doctor had said. Without saying another word, he returned to the waiting room.

An image of the ultrasound film Valerie showed him when she was pregnant came to mind. He'd been out of town when she had it done.

It's a boy, Braden. If you're okay with it, I'd like to name him Andrew Braden Wolfe. Call him Andy.

He ground his back teeth and pushed the memory aside.

When Sarah walked out, he stood and met her at the door. She smiled, causing his chest to warm. He didn't want to feel this *deep* caring for her or their child. But he couldn't deny that he did. He hadn't treated Sarah right. Now he had to decide what he was going to do about it.

No longer did he see Selena when he looked at Sarah. Her facial expressions were softer, and many times her eyes spoke for her, expressing her mood.

At the car, he opened her door and allowed her to sit, then walked around to the other side. Before starting the engine, he looked at her. "I'm taking you out tonight."

"That's not necessary. I have a roast thawing."

"Cook it tomorrow."

She nodded without an argument. "What do you have in mind?"

"Somewhere expensive and quiet. I owe you a steak dinner."

"Jim's Place East. But it's a drive from my place."

"That's not a problem." Braden turned into her neighborhood and headed for her house. "Sounds perfect. I'll make reservations."

After they reached Sarah's house, Braden took a nap. When he woke, he walked out to the den and found Sarah going through her old picture albums. He sat beside her on the sofa. "May I see one?"

"Sure. Take your pick. I was big on pictures."

Braden picked up the white photo album and flipped it open, then thumbed through the wedding pictures. Sarah had made a beautiful bride. Her eyes sparkled with happiness in each picture. Mark had been a nice looking man, and his expressions showed how in love he was with her.

"Nice pictures."

"I think so."

Braden picked up another album. He realized he'd made a mistake when he saw pictures of Sarah in the delivery room. Mark stood by her side. In the last picture, it showed one of Sarah and Mark admiring their new son.

He hadn't been there for Valerie. He'd been working on a special task force in St. Louis.

A thick lump formed in Braden's throat. He finally swallowed it down before he turned to Sarah. "How can you look at these?"

"I couldn't before my Alaskan trip, but now I see it from a different perspective. Instead of dwelling on my loss, I think of how blessed I was to have them in my life even though it was only for a short time."

"That's better than living with anger."

"It is. And if you're sure you don't want any part of our child, I'd like for you to sign all parental rights away."

Her request knocked the freaking breath out of him.

Hell, I didn't see that one coming.

"Why?"

"Because, I'll probably remarry someday. I'd like for my new husband to be able to adopt this baby."

"You mean my kid will never know about me?"

"Exactly. Why let him know he has a dad who could care less about him? Especially if I meet someone who's willing to be a real father to him."

Braden's neck ached. "Let me think about it."

A coil of tension worked its way through his chest and then moved into his stomach. He hadn't expected this. This was his chance to walk away.

Chapter Sixteen

Marcy called Sarah and told her all the sorted details about Tiffany, then waited to hear her opinion.

"She sounds psycho. You obviously have a *Fatal Attraction* issue. What she's doing isn't normal, especially since she knows you're a federal marshal."

"That's what I thought. I might place a restraining order against her. It's not a guaranteed solution. But it's a start."

"Marcy, one thing I know is Alex loves you. That was apparent in Alaska. You've got to trust him."

"I'm trying." Marcy twisted the phone cord around her hand. "How are things between you and Braden?"

"Terrible. He's taking me to a nice restaurant. I thought he might come around, but I finally realized he's not changing. So I've asked him to sign his parental rights away."

"Oh my God. What did he say?"

"That he'd think about it."

"I can't believe he'd even consider it."

"He has his reasons. I can't say any more than that, but he has some demons to overcome. And he might never recover from his past."

"Sarah, he really cares about you."

"Ummm. . .maybe but not enough. I bet you're huge by now."

"You're changing the subject." Marcy paused. "By looking at me, you definitely know I'm pregnant. I need a sign that says, 'Wide Load'."

Sarah laughed. "You can't be that big."

"I am. And you?"

"I have a baby bubble."

"You mean baby bump?

"I prefer bubble. It sounds happier. Braden and I listened to the heartbeat today. Dr. Olson thinks it's a boy."

"That's great. He actually went with you?"

"Yes, but he turned and walked out without saying anything. I don't want him if all he feels is a responsibility to do right by me. This isn't the Dark Ages. I want him to love me for all the right reasons. And he doesn't. I think what happened in the cabin was a case of lust on his part. Stupidity on mine."

"It can't be easy having him under your roof."

"No, so I asked him to leave. Seems he'd already planned his escape. He's returning to Kansas on Friday."

"I'm sorry. Thanks for listening about Tiffany and being a friend. I can't discuss it with Alex or my mother. Are you still coming for Christmas?"

"Yes, if you want me."

"Of course. I can't wait to see you."

"Same here. Just do me a favor. I don't want to see Braden while I'm there. So please don't play matchmaker and invite him over."

"I wouldn't dream of it." But she had thought about doing exactly that. She said her goodbyes and hung up, feeling sorry for Sarah.

Marcy decided to contact a private investigator. Tiffany would be so busy following them that she wouldn't realize she was being tailed. Once Marcy had proof Tiffany was tampering with their lives, she'd take it to the police.

Later that evening, she shared her plans with Alex.

"Let me speak with her. Maybe I can reason with her."

"No, that's what she wants. Please trust my instincts on this. There's a saying in law enforcement."

"What's that?" Alex asked.

"The female is deadlier than the male."

◆◆◆

Braden helped Sarah into her chair, then sat beside her in the classy restaurant. As she'd promised, the place provided an elegant setting that was quiet. No kids. *Joy*. He waited until after they'd ordered to say anything. "You look lovely tonight."

"Thank you. You're not so bad yourself."

After the waiter took their orders and left, the man across from them eyed Sarah with interest. The muscles in Braden's face became rigid and profound as he glowered at the man. The admirer turned away.

But the man's interest reminded Braden of what Sarah had said about her wanting to remarry eventually. She wouldn't have a difficult time finding anyone who wanted the role of husband. The thought of Sarah being with anyone else but him made him so jealous he thought his veins would explode.

"Braden, that man could've been my future husband. You had no right to scare him off with that bulldog face."

"Bulldog?"

"Yes, like you're guarding a bone. You've made it clear you aren't interested in me. Which leads me back to the question I asked earlier."

"I'm still thinking about it."

"I deserve an answer. I'd like to start dating if the opportunity arises once *my* baby is old enough to leave with a sitter."

"I'll give you my decision tonight."

"Just don't forget."

"You'll get your answer."

Shortly, a server came with their steaks, ending the polite conversation Braden had felt obligated to make. Neither spoke for the next ten minutes. After the waiter refilled his coffee, he asked about Marcy, but Sarah remained very tight lipped.

"Look, I knew Alex and Marcy were having marital problems. She didn't tell me, I just picked up on it at a cookout at their house. I overheard them talking at the lodge. I figured out he'd left her for someone else."

"Actually, they separated for a short time." Sarah sighed. "I'll feel like a traitor telling you, but I'm going to for one reason."

"And that is?"

"I think the other woman wants revenge. Marcy believes she's dangerous."

She told him what the woman had done.

"When I fly back Friday, I'll tell her I heard the gist of what she said, maybe she'll open up. I think she needs my help."

"And Michael?"

"I've spoken with a federal prosecutor about him. Before we go any further on it, I need to find out who Dagastino's mole is. I don't want to put Michael in front of a firing squad."

Braden insisted they order a dessert. They selected a hot chocolate fudge cake with ice cream in the center and requested two spoons.

It wasn't until they were in the car that she brought up the subject again. "So what's your answer? Are you willing to give up all rights to this baby?"

Anger heated his blood. "Hell, no!"

"No? But that's not fair. You don't want anything to do with this child. And I want him to have a real father. A man who will be a part of his life."

"You heard me. And furthermore my child's not going to be a bastard."

"And what's your solution for that?"

"We'll get married."

"And just how will that work?"

"You'll live in Memphis, and I'll continue my life in Kansas. I'll pay for everything. A few months after he's born, we'll divorce. Then at least, our child will never be called a bastard. There's no way I'm giving up my rights."

◆◆◆

Sarah started to tell him where he and his proposal could go when another thought popped in her mind. For Braden this had been a giant step toward accepting the child as his. At least now he was referring to it as *his child*. Was she willing to gamble with her heart? Would Braden be able to stay away from his own son once he'd seen him?

Never.

"Under one condition," she declared.

"Name it."

"I want you with me when I deliver."

"You're kidding? I have a job in Kansas. I can't be here to take classes and do all that lame stuff."

"Then my answer is no."

"You don't care if our kid is considered a bastard?"

"People don't have to know. Besides, no one really cares these days."

"You're impossible." Braden stopped suddenly at a red light. "All right. I'll do it if I can arrange to be in Memphis at the time."

Sarah held back a smile. Braden Wolfe had a heart. And whether he wanted to outright admit it, he cared about their baby. Though the marriage could end in divorce, she wanted this opportunity so their child had a chance to know his father. There was only one kink in the entire plan. Sarah didn't believe in divorce.

Despite her principles, a marriage wouldn't work with him in Kansas and her five hundred miles away. Then she considered something else. She could move to Kansas. For now, she'd keep that to herself.

There will be a prenup, but I'll bring it up later.

"So when do you want to get married?" she asked.

"Anytime before the baby comes. A courthouse will do."

"No, I insist on a church."

He turned into her driveway and parked. "Sarah, when I said we'd get married it was in name only. I don't plan to change my life one bit."

There were limits to how far she'd go. She wouldn't tolerate him being with other women. "You plan to date?"

"Give me some credit. I don't believe in adultery even if the marriage isn't for love."

The idiot doesn't realize he just said something hurtful. Men.

Why did she love this insensitive jerk? She considered calling it off.

"Sarah, I don't want you to read more into this than there is."

"Trust me, I don't."

Braden hopped from the car, hurried around to Sarah's side, and opened her door. "Watch your step."

She waited until they were inside to say anything. "I'd like to get married at Christmas in Kansas. I want Marcy and Alex there."

"I didn't want them to know about it."

"And I'll ask Darrel to give me away."

"You'll do nothing of the sort. Hell, those are my people."

"I doubt Selena will attend considering you're not on her friends list."

"Marcy and Alex but not Darrel."

"Agreed. I'll have Marcy locate a small chapel."

Braden nodded. "Sure, have at it."

She rested her palm across her stomach.

This is for you, kiddo.

Because I'd like to tell him where he can put his star shaped badge.

Somewhere painful.

She smirked.

♦♦♦

Selena stared through the window of the large, comfortable house that had become her prison. She longed to go dancing at a club or anywhere fun. Again she'd been featured on, *America's Most Wanted*. She looked across the room at Carlos. "Once we kidnap the bitch, and you make a deal with Dagastino, I'll be free to go anywhere I damn well please."

"Think she'll trust you?" he asked.

"No, but I'm working on that. I sent her some pictures of our mother. And one has a man in it that might be our father. That'll get to her."

211

"You know Wolfe's staying with her, and word on the street is that Dagastino has her under surveillance too. So just how do you plan to contact her? You know her phones are monitored."

"That's why, asshole, we should've taken the bitch with us when we were in Memphis. Now I'm not so sure we can get close to her. I'm mailing her a prepaid phone. No wire taps. They can't trace it."

"Do you think she'll tell Wolfe?"

"Not after receiving the pictures. She feels some kind of bond between us. She eats up that sisterly love crap you know. Hell, I'd cut her heart out myself if it'd buy my freedom."

"And her baby?"

"I don't give a shit about it."

◆◆◆

Thursday afternoon, Sarah pulled the large manila envelope from the mailbox. It didn't have a return address on it. As she walked to the house, she ripped open the envelope and peeked inside. Someone had sent pictures but of what?

When she entered the kitchen, Braden sat at the table, drinking coffee. She let the pictures slide out on the kitchen counter. It required several moments before she realized what she was looking at. "Oh my God." Then she saw a handwritten note from Selena.

I came across some pictures and had copies made for you. I'm in some of the shots. I think the tall white man in the picture with Mom might be our father. Thought you'd want these. She wrote on the back that his name was Ralph Jenkins.

Selena

Sarah couldn't stop staring at the woman who had given her life and then sold her.

"You realize you're the lucky one, don't you?" Braden asked.

"I do, but it still hurts. When I think of the life Selena had, I feel very blessed I was the one sold. Our mother's boyfriends abused Selena sexually, even as a child."

"That still doesn't justify all the horrific crimes she's committed. A lot of people live abusive lives, but they don't turn to a life of crime."

"I know. I still feel sorry for her."

"That's because you're softhearted and kind." Then Braden kissed her forehead as he gathered her in his arms. Sarah's heartbeat accelerated. His mouth nuzzled her ear, "Even if you had been raised under the same conditions as Selena, you'd still be the way you are."

"Strange, because we look so much alike. When I look at my reflection, sometimes I see her. It's like the mirror has a dark side."

"Your reflection will always be light and pure. Selena was born bad. She's the dark side of the mirror. Not you."

He kissed her lips lightly, then gazed into her eyes.

At moments like this, she believed he cared about her.

As if realizing he'd made a mistake, Braden picked the note up from the counter and read it. Then he browsed through the pictures. He lifted the one with the tall man in it. "You have his high cheek bones, height, and slender build. Do you want me to run a search and see if he's still around?"

Sarah shrugged. "I doubt he'd care whether I'm his child or not."

"Maybe he never knew about Selena and you."

Sarah couldn't think about the man who'd fathered her now. Her heartbeat still surged from the affection Braden had shown her. The kiss had been simple yet sincere. She didn't want him to be loving and affectionate not if he planned to walk away after the baby was born.

"I wouldn't mind knowing if he's still living."

"I'll check it out when I get a chance."

"What time do you fly out?"

"About nine. U.S. Marshals will be keeping an eye on you. And this time, don't tell them they aren't needed. Selena is playing you."

"Playing me? How?"

"These pictures. She sent them to gain your trust. If I didn't have to take care of Michael's situation, I'd stay. She has something cooking."

"You're being extremely paranoid. Besides, you have cops watching my house. And don't forget Dagastino's men are keeping a vigilant eye as well."

"She's clever and has no conscience or soul."

"Are you worried about my wellbeing or the fact I might protect Selena and let her slip through your fingers?"

"No, Sarah. I'm worried about you. I'm sure she's hoping you'll trust her and feel some kind of bond."

"She is family."

"She's a heartless murderer. Did you know it was the Unabomber's brother who turned him in? He did it because his brother was killing innocent people. And Selena makes Kaczynski look like the Pope."

"I'd never protect her. You should know me better."

"If I'm right, her next move will be trying to contact you somehow."

"Why do you think she wants to stay in touch?"

"So you'll trust her enough to meet her somewhere."

"Maybe, she feels what I feel."

"I'm afraid that's not it." Braden frowned. "She wants to be you."

"Be me? How?"

"Think about it. If she killed you, then she could pass herself off as you and steal your identity. Selena could be reborn and free as a butterfly.

Chapter Seventeen

The next morning Braden stood in the nursery, taking one last look before he left for the airport. His son or daughter was becoming all too real to him. He didn't know why in the hell he didn't just sign his rights away. As much as he hated to admit it, he already loved the child Sarah carried and wanted the kid to have his name. But was it fair to walk out of the kid's life for good?

He wished he could be brave like Sarah. Didn't she fear losing this child and having to face that God awful pain again?

Sarah joined him beside the cradle. "It looks good in here. Thanks for your help."

"It amazes me how excited you are. Doesn't that make you feel like you're betraying Tristen?"

"No. But you and I have some differences in the way we view things. I'm Christian and truly believe my child is in heaven, and someday I'll see him again. You on the other hand, believe Andy—heart, body, and soul are in a coffin at some cemetery. We've never talked about religion or God."

"I used to believe in God."

"So you blame God for Andy's death?"

"Not just God, I take a large part of the blame. I could've let Valerie die, or if I had turned down the assignment, my son would have been with me instead of her. He'd be alive."

"God didn't cause that man to beat Andy to death. You're not responsible for what happened either. Things happen out of our control." She turned and left him with his demons.

He followed her to the kitchen.

Sarah stood at the counter, pouring a cup of coffee. "Do you have time to eat? I could fix eggs or make French toast?"

"No, coffee's fine. It's a short flight to Kansas." He took the coffee, blew across its surface, and sipped it carefully. "You have all of my phone numbers?"

She nodded.

"Memorize them. I want you to be able to reach me any hour of the day or night. Understand?"

"Yes, I do." She sipped her orange juice, then picked up her toast and nibbled it. "How soon before Michael enters the program?"

Braden shrugged. "There's a lot of red tape involved. If he's in immediate danger we'll take him before completing the preliminary requirements."

"It's almost Thanksgiving now. Do you think it will happen before Christmas?"

"I'm not sure. Have you spoken with Marcy yet?"

Sarah nodded. "After you went to bed, I called her. She's looking for a minister and a small chapel. And I told her you didn't want anyone to know."

He nodded. "Makes it less complicated."

"I'll have my attorney draw up a prenup just in case things turn ugly," she commented.

Braden gave a sarcastic snort. "Ugly—how?"

"Mark left me quite a bit of money. Also, he carried a very large life insurance policy which doubled because of his death being an accident. Greed can make the human heart do unpredictable things. I can't chance it."

"Sarah, I'd never do that to you."

She didn't look convinced. "As far as I can tell, your interest in me has been lust and a way to reach Selena. Why should I trust you?"

"I've always been honest with you." Braden sighed. "I'll sign." He stared at her for a few moments, wanting to pull her in his arms and hold her, assure her he cared about her—but didn't. "Take care, Sarah. Call me if you need me."

Braden didn't look back. Instead, he grabbed his bag and exited out the front door. Once inside his rental car, he headed for the airport.

A few hours later, he landed in Kansas then drove to headquarters. While at his desk, he pulled up records for Selena Menendez. She'd been born in El Paso, Texas. It stood to reason their father had lived there. He googled Ralph Jenkins. Three popped up in that vicinity. He jotted down their addresses. For now, he wouldn't mention any of this to Sarah. Remembering Marcy's problem, he decided to hunt her down.

He didn't have to search for long. Marcy waddled down the hall toward him. She looked like a barrel with two little legs.

He grinned. "Hey, Marcy. You look like you're ready to go over Niagara Falls."

She stared at him for a moment before realizing what he meant. "You're not funny."

"You sure you're not having twins?"

"Positive."

He followed her inside the deserted breakroom and poured a cup of coffee, then leaned against the counter while Marcy sat. "You should've known I'm monitoring Sarah's calls. So, since I know about your problems, let's discuss your options. Has that woman done anything else?"

"No. I hired Peter Anderson to keep up with her."

"Smart girl. Pete's a good PI."

"If I can prove she's stalking us, I can get a restraining order. That's a start. I hope she'll give up, lick her wounds, and move on."

"Maybe." He shifted his weight and glanced at the door to make sure no one was entering. "Marcy, there's someone who's been selling information to Dagastino."

"Here?"

"From what Michael told me, it's someone who works here. I'm thinking someone in the front office. I've considered it for some time."

"No freaking way. How will you find out who it is?"

He shrugged. "You notice anyone spending a little more money than usual? Such as showing up with new jewelry or cars."

"No, I haven't. But I'll keep my eyes peeled."

Braden sighed. "I need to know who's had access to all the information coming in about Selena."

"That might weed it down."

"It's a start. I have some important business to deal with, but I can't until I find out who's working for Dagastino."

"And Sarah? What the hell are you doing about her?"

"I'm marrying her."

"Just so your child has your name listed on the birth certificate. That's so medieval. It's not good enough. Have you stopped to think what it'll do to Sarah? She loves you, you asshole."

"Look, Marcy. My life is complicated."

"Yada Yada yada, bullshit. Cry me a river. Why don't you just sign the papers and give up any rights to her child?"

"My child."

"Let me get this straight. You plan to marry Sarah just long enough that the child has your name, but you don't plan on being a part of his or her life. Can't you see that there's something very wrong with that?"

"I don't recall asking for your opinion. See, this is why I didn't want any of you knowing."

"I figured you didn't want anyone knowing what an uncaring shithead you are."

"I just can't give up my child legally."

"How do you feel about Sarah?"

"I'm not sure. Torn."

"Then do a little soul searching between now and Christmas."

Braden stopped talking when the blonde he'd had dinner with entered the room. "Hey, Patricia. How's it going?"

"Good. Glad to see you're back."

"Glad to be back."

She paused in the door and smiled. "I have two tickets to Sunday's Chief's game. Interested?"

Marcy flashed him an eat-shit look and walked out.

Braden offered Patricia a courteous smile. "I'll pass. I'm behind on all my work. Maybe another time."

"I didn't expect you back this soon. Did you give up on Menendez?"

"No, I seriously doubt she'll show up in Memphis for a while. Besides, she's not the only case I'm working on."

Later that afternoon, he stopped by the receptionist's desk. "Hey, Marsha. Who usually takes the calls from AMW when I'm out?"

"Gee, Braden. It'd probably be Patricia or Cathy."

He remembered Patricia being the one who'd handed him the DNA results on Selena, who turned out to be Sarah. Patricia had asked about his stay in Memphis. Still he couldn't rule Cathy out.

♦♦♦

The next day, Cathy pulled in the parking lot driving a new Lexus.

He waited for her to step out of her car. "Did you strike oil while I was gone?"

"Early Christmas present from Nick. If we'd waited, all the end-of-the-year deals would've been gone. Do you like it?"

"What's not to like? It's gorgeous."

"Thanks, Braden."

Around ten he bumped into Patricia. Before he could target Cathy, he had to rule Patricia out. "You still have those tickets?"

"I do."

"Is it too late to change my mind?"

"No."

"What time should we leave?"

"The game's at noon. Pick me up at ten."

"We can grab a bite there before it starts."

Guilt edged its way into his mind. But his intentions weren't social. He had to know who kept Dagastino informed. He suspected Cathy, but it was Patricia who brought up Selena anytime they talked. Though it bruised his ego, maybe that's why she'd shown an interest in him.

◆◆◆

Sarah hadn't heard from Braden. She finally called Marcy at home and asked about him. She thought she'd misunderstood her. "He's what?"

"He has a date with a woman in the front office. They've seen each other before from what she says."

"Oh." It took her a minute before she could speak. She swallowed back the hurt. "This changes things."

"I'll be honest. I think marrying Braden is a mistake."

"I agreed to marry him for the sake of our child. But his seeing someone pushes the envelope too far. Do me a favor and cancel the chapel."

"I shouldn't have mentioned it."

"No, it's all right. I needed to know. How's your problem?"

"I meet with Peter Anderson today to see what he has on Tiffany. So far she hasn't bothered us again."

"Good. Maybe she's given up."

After Sarah hung up, she thought about Braden dating another woman. Knowing about it upset her, but like she'd told Marcy, it opened her eyes to reality. She'd daydreamed about the spontaneous kiss Braden had surprised her with in the kitchen. She'd read too much into the single kiss.

Sarah walked to the edge of the driveway to get the mail and waved at the officer parked in front. A small package rested atop the stack of junk mail. Once inside, she eagerly opened the box. The contents turned out to be a black TracFone and a recharger. Under the phone lay a note.

I'll call you. Don't tell anyone about the phone. It's our only way of staying in touch. Selena.

Braden had been right. Selena was smart. And Sarah's womanly intuition told her this didn't have anything with Selena wanting to be sisters.

Later that evening, she decided to tell Braden. She keyed in his personal cell number.

◆◆◆

While eating Gate's barbecue at Arrowhead Stadium, Braden noticed the diamond bracelet on Patricia's wrist. She also sported a large Coach handbag. He remembered Marcy commenting they were expensive.

"Nice bracelet."

"Thanks. I decided to treat myself to an expensive birthday present."

"That had to set you back a few grand."

She laughed. "Yeah, but I'm worth it."

Instead of saying more, she made a return trip to refill her Coke.

During the game, there hadn't been a chance to discuss anything with the crowd shouting. He'd hoped she might let something slip if he could get her talking. But, so far it'd been a date. A date he felt guilty as hell about. He'd enjoyed the game and her company.

When they climbed in his car, Patricia leaned against him, letting her hand slide over his crotch while she nibbled his earlobe. "Let's go back to my place and play our own game."

A painful erection pushed against his jeans.

His phone rang. "Let me get this."

"Don't answer it," she whispered while her fingers became more aggressive on his crotch.

The ringing stopped. Seconds later, his work phone rang. He pushed her hand away and answered the call, but in doing so, he accidently hit speaker phone.

"Braden Wolfe, here," he answered breathlessly.

"Are you busy?"

"No. I'm backing from a parking space." He motioned for Patricia to back off, but instead, she slithered her tongue down his neck, and her hand continued to squeeze his erection. He gasped. "I'm here. What's up?"

"Selena mailed me a TracFone." She paused. "Is this a bad time?"

"Patricia, stop. This is business." Finally, she quit. He switched off the speaker phone. "Sarah." But the line was dead. "Sarah, are you there?"

He punched in her number and listened to the phone ring until the answering machine picked up. "Sarah, call me back."

But she didn't. Sarah had obviously figured out what was going on. He gave Patricia a harsh glare. "I'll take you home."

"That's Selena's sister, right?"

"Yep."

"I heard her say Selena sent her a phone."

Patricia hadn't let up on seducing him until she realized the call was about Selena.

At her house, he walked her to the door. "I enjoyed the game. Thanks for inviting me."

"I'm sorry about your call. Do you want to come in and finish what we started?"

What you started, not me.

"No, I'd better try to reach Sarah."

Patricia appeared a little disappointed. She waited for his kiss. But instead, he turned and left. There was only one woman on his mind, and that was Sarah.

He'd make the necessary calls and obtain a warrant to have Patricia thoroughly checked out.

Braden tried several times to reach Sarah, but she wouldn't answer. Finally, he called the U.S. Marshal's office and had someone deliver the message to her door.

It wasn't long before a call came in. He answered it quickly without even checking the caller ID. "Sarah."

"No this is Marshal Stallcup. I spoke with Ms. Mason, and she asked me to inform you Selena sent her a phone but hasn't contacted her yet. She's expecting a call and asked what to do."

"Tell her to hold a small recorder near the phone and record what Selena says. Also, she's not to leave the house unattended. Please mention that I really need to speak with her."

"I'll tell her, but she's adamant about not talking directly to you."

After hanging up, he closed his eyes and let his head drop. Sarah had to be disappointed he'd returned home and taken a woman on a date his first week back.

◆◆◆

Tuesday morning, Braden waited by Patricia's desk with several marshals and FBI agents. She entered her enclosed work area and looked at him with uncertainty. "What's going on?"

"We pulled your computer data and phone records. Both show you've been in contact with Leonard Dagastino. We've also subpoenaed your bank account information. You had two large amounts wired to your account through a corporation connected with him."

"It was no big deal. I passed on what AMW told us. That's all."

"It was a big deal to the men who died in the helicopter crash." Braden stepped back and let Chief Deputy Marshal Reiner and the special agents take it from there. Patricia glanced back while being escorted away.

Now it's safe for Michael.

Back at his desk, he keyed in Ralph Jenkins to the DMV. Three photos showed up. Could one of these older men be the young man in the photo Selena sent Sarah? Only one was still active. Two had expired. He'd look into it later. Right now he wanted to try calling Sarah again.

This time her home phone rang endlessly. She'd disconnected her answering machine.

Marcy stepped in his office. "How'd you know about Patricia?"

"She always seemed to have questions about Selena. She had access to everything, and she was sporting a hell of a bracelet Friday night." He stood and pinned a hard look on Marcy to emphasize his point. "That's the only reason I went out with her. I swear it. Have you talked with Sarah?"

Marcy nodded. "She's upset."

"It's not what she's thinking." He explained about Patricia attacking him in the car. "Sarah hung up before I could say anything, and she hasn't spoken to me since. Well, she has to come around before Christmas. Hell, we're getting married."

Marcy looked guiltier than hell.

Braden scowled. "Out with it. What are you not telling me?"

"Sarah needs to be the one to tell you."

"She's not taking my calls."

Marcy let out a frustrated breath. "You idiot. I don't think Sarah's coming Christmas. She asked me to cancel the reservation on the chapel."

"She told you to do that?"

Marcy nodded. "Braden, do the decent thing and stay out of her life."

That evening at his house, he discovered an overnight Fed-ex envelope on his porch. It was from Sarah. He waited until he was inside to remove the letter. He sat down, turned on a lamp, and popped a top on a beer before reading it.

Dear Braden,

I have no desire to marry you at Christmas or any other time. We're back to the original plan. Please sign and return it to me. Sarah.

Braden read the three page document, giving up all legal rights to his child. He tossed the papers into the trash. Okay, maybe Sarah wouldn't marry him, but she couldn't stop him from seeing his child and being there when he was born. He reminded himself it could be a girl. The thought of a little girl wrapping her chubby little arms around his neck warmed him.

◆◆◆

"Sarah, please listen," Marcy pleaded.

"I don't want to hear his name."

"Just hear me out. Please."

Sarah finally surrendered. "Go ahead. I'm listening."

"Braden only went out with Patricia to find out if she's the mole working for Dagastino."

"From what I heard, he was taking the assignment all the way to the bedroom. Isn't that a little beyond the call of duty?"

"They were in his car, leaving the stadium." Marcy explained about the woman manhandling him. "I believe him, Sarah."

Sarah recalled his telling Patricia to stop. "I don't know. It sounded like he was enjoying it."

"Did he moan?"

"No, he gasped and had a difficult time controlling his breathing."

"That doesn't sound like he was necessarily enjoying it."

"Marcy, I sent him the papers to sign and told him the wedding was off. I was only marrying him in hopes there'd be a chance he'd want to be a part of his child's life."

"I was wrong about him. I think he really wants to get married. And his date with her couldn't have meant much. He had the FBI confiscate Patricia's phone records and computer. She was arrested the following Tuesday."

Okay, maybe she'd overreacted. "I've got to run, Marcy."

"Please come for Christmas. We were counting on you being here."

"You won't tell Braden I'm in town?"

"I won't."

The moment Sarah hung up, the TracFone on the counter rang. She pushed the record button on the digital recorder before answering the phone. "Hello."

"Sarah, it's Selena. How's little momma?"

"Getting bigger."

"Did you like the pictures?"

"Yes, thank you. Braden offered to find our father."

"He probably died years ago. Is Wolfe still there, hoping I'll waltz back into town?"

"No, he returned to Kansas. You're not his only case."

"I'm sorry I was nasty with you. It's just I don't like how helpless emotions make me feel. They scare me."

"I didn't take anything you said to heart."

"You haven't told anyone about this phone, have you?"

"No," Sarah lied.

"It's our only way to stay in touch. I'd like to see you again. I thought of some things about Mom and our relatives I should've mentioned. Maybe we can meet somewhere when things die down. I could take you to meet some of mom's family."

"Maybe. I'll think about it." Though she knew she wouldn't. "Listen, I can't talk right now. Take care, Selena."

After hanging up, Sarah pushed stop on the recorder. Braden's suspicions had been on target. Selena was up to something. Just as he'd predicted, she'd found a way to contact Sarah and as he'd also warned Selena wanted to meet with her. Could Selena have some bizarre plan to take Sarah's identity as Wolfe had suggested?

She had the deputy contact Braden concerning the call.

Later that afternoon, the doorbell rang. Sarah glanced through the peephole and saw a delivery person. She opened the door.

A teenage boy stood holding a vase of flowers and a huge lion with a wild mane and a silly face. "Sarah Mason?"

"Yes."

"These are for you." He had her sign the clipboard, then handed her the floral arrangement and bear. Inside, she set both down and removed the card.

Sarah,

I'm sorry. I wish you'd let me explain. It's not how it seemed. I threw away the papers you sent. I have no intention of giving up my child. The roses are for you, and the lion is for our baby. My best wishes. Braden.

Sarah warmed from his apology. Why did this man have so much control over her heart, body, and soul?

An image of Braden dragging her through the Alaskan diner, wearing chains flashed in her mind. Then she recalled him strapping her to the headboard.

No, it's doesn't have anything to do with that.

But she couldn't deny the sensual heat the images caused. She refused to explore the dark side of her sexuality.

♦♦♦

Marcy stared at the photographs Peter Anderson placed before her. It appeared Tiffany followed Alex around after work and parked in front of their house at night and had done so often. Marcy had more than enough reasons to place a restraining order against her. After she shoved the photographs in her purse and paid the investigator, she glanced at her watch. No doubt the traffic on Quivera, especially near the medical center, would be backed up. She'd be late picking the girls up from school.

She drove through the Pleasant Ridge Elementary loop looking for her daughters. She parked and walked inside the school office and inquired about them. Their teachers had gone. The office told her the girls hadn't returned inside to wait. The principal called the teacher who did dismissal. She returned to Marcy. "Mrs. Baker said she looked up, and they were gone. She assumed you'd picked them up in the car lane."

Marcy's heartbeat sped up. She dialed Alex to see if he'd picked them up. The panic in his voice caused fear to explode inside her.

Oh, God, please let them be safe.

She drove home, pulled into the driveway, and jumped out, not taking time to pull into the garage. She ran up to the front door, unlocked it, then hurried inside. The TV blared from the den, and she headed towards the noise. Brittany and Erica sat on the sofa, watching cartoons.

Marcy called the frantic principal and Alex to let them know the girls were all right. Then she walked in the den and hugged them both. "Did you walk all the way home?"

"No, Mom," Brittany replied. "A friend of Daddy's gave us a ride. And I used the spare key."

"Did you get his name?"

"It wasn't a man. Her name was Katie."

"I don't know a Katie." Then deep anxiety plunged through her. She removed a picture of Tiffany from the envelope the detective had given her. "Is this her?"

Erica smiled. "Yep. She's nice."

"And fun," Brittany added. "I like her."

Marcy's breath left her for a moment.

I'll kill the bitch if she comes near my kids again.

Chapter Eighteen

Braden had things underway for Michael's departure. Due to his life being in jeopardy, the OEO decided to handle the preliminaries after he was in protective custody. The federal attorney's office had given the okay. When Michael called, they'd set up a time and place for him to disappear before Dagastino was arrested. Then Braden would go after Chase and Lenny for the men's deaths in Alaska.

"Braden, there's a woman who insists on speaking with you on line two. Ms. Noland."

"Thanks, Marsha."

He lifted the receiver to his ear. "Marshal Braden Wolfe speaking."

"Marshal Wolfe, I'm Amy Noland." Braden thought for a moment. The name seemed familiar. "And you're calling about?"

"Michael Dagastino. We were engaged. When we spoke, he mentioned your name. Has he entered the program yet?"

"Give me your phone number, and I'll call you right back." After verifying her identity and number, he returned her call. "You asked about Michael. He should be entering very soon. I'd say before Christmas."

"Why so soon?"

"Because if his uncle gets so much as a whiff of this, he's dead. He informed me you weren't interested in entering the Witness Security Program with him."

"It's just that I have such a close family. The thought of giving them up forever seems so impossible. I love them. But I also love Michael."

"I need an answer soon."

"Can you give me more information about the Witness Protection Program?"

After giving her the ins and outs of the program, he asked her again. "Have you changed your mind?"

"I'm not sure. I need more time to think about it. I have two sisters expecting. I can't imagine never seeing their children or them seeing mine. It's almost like dying and coming back as someone else."

"Amy, we tell you never to contact your family, but I will say not everyone follows the rules. The chance of being discovered increases the more communication you have with your family. The most threatening time will be for the first couple of years after the trial. Make a decision soon. I can't promise that you can be included once he's relocated."

"Yes, sir. And thank you."

Shit. He shouldn't have said anything about staying in contact with her family, but it was true. If the girl saw any hope of communicating with her family in the future, she might decide to go with Michael.

After Braden hung up, he leaned back in his chair and thought about Sarah. Did she like the flowers? He'd missed being with her. He thought of her often and found himself thinking of the baby as well. He'd been extremely depressed without her.

He wanted to make the trip to Memphis now, but couldn't because he'd promised Michael he'd see him through the process. And he couldn't be in two places at the same time. He couldn't blame Michael for not feeling safe with just anyone considering who his uncle was.

Marcy stopped beside him. She rested one hand on her back while the other pressed against his desk for support. "I'm exhausted."

He jumped up and brought a chair over. "Sit."

She eased into the chair. "Braden, we filed the restraining order against Tiffany."

"Good, it might help. Of course, it might just make her go beyond the limits for spite."

"She already has."

His gaze locked with hers. "How?"

She told what Tiffany had done with the girls. "I can't believe she did something so bold. This was more like sending a warning or testing the waters. She could be planning something bigger."

"Stay alert."

"We've red flagged Tiffany at their school and told the girls not to let that woman come near them again. Alex is so sorry he brought this on us. We just hope this is all over before the baby comes."

"I hope so too. I sent Sarah flowers and a gift for our baby. Has she mentioned it?"

"I haven't spoken with her." Marcy offered him a warm smile. "You miss her, don't you?"

He nodded. "Yeah, I do. But I think the only way she'll speak to me is if I fly to Memphis and knock her door down."

Marcy laughed. "The big bad wolf is going to huff and puff until she lets him in. From what Sarah tells me, you have ghosts that interfere with you loving another woman and child. You need to get past it, or you'll lose Sarah."

Had Sarah shared his deepest secrets with Marcy? A lump formed in his throat. "Has she been specific?"

"About your past? No."

"I've only shared it with Sarah."

"That should tell you something. You wouldn't have if you didn't feel some kind of special bond with her."

He shrugged. Of all the women on the planet, why did his soul-mate have to be Selena's sister? He reminded himself he'd basically moved past that problem. The only obstacle standing in his way now was moving past the fear of losing someone you love.

"Once I get Michael squared away, I'll pay Sarah a visit. I think what I need to say should be said in person."

"Just be sure you say the right things. So far you've been a verbal screw-up. Instead of thinking of yourself, think of Sarah."

Marcy had pegged him for what he was. A selfish bastard. Had he ever once considered what Sarah was going through? He recalled all the loving husbands at the doctor's office, supporting their wives. Sarah had to face that waiting room each visit. Alone.

A mountain of regret tumbled down on him, making him wish he could be with Sarah. He actually understood how hard it'd been for her and wanted to protect her from any more sorrow or pain.

"I plan to say the right things, but I'm afraid it'll be after Christmas before I can make the trip to Memphis."

Marcy rested her hand on her belly. "I'm gonna tell you because Sarah's happiness is at stake. She's still coming to our house for the holidays."

"Well hell, why didn't you say something sooner?"

"She made me promise I wouldn't tell you."

"Am I invited for Christmas dinner, or do I just have to barge in on you?"

"I'm not sure. Maybe it'd be best if you just happen to drop by. Let me get back with you on it. I'd hate for Sarah to know I broke my promise. You better not screw this up."

"I won't. Trust me."

"Despite your sincerity, I think you'll muddle things up, and Sarah will end up not talking to me. You mess up our friendship, and you'll be on my shit list forever."

Braden grinned at Marcy's threat.

He waited for her to leave before calling the Ralph Jenkins who still had an active license. It turned out he'd been born in Vermont and had been transferred to Texas. After some searching, he found the second Ralph Jenkins in the La Tuna Federal Correction Institution. He checked this Jenkin's DNA on file against Selena's. It wasn't a match. *Thank God.*

◆◆◆

Sarah stared at the fluffy brown lion wearing a huge yellow bow that sat in the cradle. It represented Braden's desire to be a part of his child's life. Whether she married him or not, she realized he cared about their baby. The crazy looking lion proved it. Any idea of moving to Kansas had vanished. With them living so far apart, she mused over the type of arrangement they'd have for visitations. Of course, that wouldn't be a problem for a while.

Someone knocked on the door. She left the nursery and walked toward the front. She peeked through the small hole and saw a deputy. Sarah opened the door. "Can I help you?"

He smiled warmly and flashed his badge. "I'm U.S. Marshal David Connors. Marshal Wolfe told us you'd been in contact with Selena. He wanted me to examine the prepaid phone."

"Sure, come in."

He followed her to the kitchen. "Nice home, lady."

"Thanks. Care for a cup of coffee?"

"Coffee sounds great."

"Have a seat at the table. Do you want to listen to the recording?"

He appeared confused for only a moment. "Yeah, the recording. Sure. I need to detect how much of a threat she is to you."

He sat down, and she handed him the phone and the digital recorder.

"Has she called back?"

"No. I think Marshal Wolfe might be onto something. She's been nothing but peaches and cream since her visit, which is a total turnaround from how she acted in person. As much as I'd like to, I'm not buying her sister act."

Sarah found the deputy attractive and pleasant. After pouring the coffee, she walked over and set it before him. "It's hot."

"Thanks for the warning." He stirred the spoon around the steaming liquid before glancing back at her. "So Wolfe thinks. . ."

"That Selena plans to make people believe I'm her and then murder me and steal my identity."

"Sounds like her. The girl doesn't have a conscience."

"It's sad, because I've always wanted a sister, and she's what I ended up with." She glanced down at his coffee. "Would you like a piece of cake to go with that?"

"No thanks. I'm cutting back before the holidays. Getting back to Selena, has she suggested a place for you guys to meet yet?"

"No. She talked like it might be a while."

Sarah escorted the deputy to the front. He had an easygoing relaxed manner she liked. Not like Braden, who stayed keyed up like a feisty dog that needed to be neutered.

An hour had passed when someone rang the doorbell again. She flicked the dishwasher on, then headed to the door. Again she peeked through the hole and recognized Marshal Stallcup, who'd delivered a message from Braden earlier in the week. She opened the door and waited for him to speak.

"Ms. Mason, I need the TracFone and recorder from you."

For a moment, she thought someone was playing some kind of practical joke on her. "Marshal Wolfe just sent another marshal to examine it."

"Not that I'm aware of."

"Marshal Connors. He wore a jacket and had a badge just like yours."

"Ma'am. There's not a Connors working with us."

She told him what the man had said and asked. "Surely, the deputy out front saw him."

Marshal Stallcup frowned. "It seems he received word to relocate and thought I'd sent the order."

She started to mention the cup Conners had drunk from but realized any DNA had been rinsed off by now. "Dagastino has someone watching me."

"Apparently, he's growing impatient waiting for Selena to return.

After he left, she closed and locked the door.

How'd they know about the phone?

Then she remembered Patricia, the woman who'd been with Braden. She'd probably tipped the crime boss off before her arrest. As much as she hated to do it, she needed to speak with Braden herself. Too much was lost in translation when she sent messages.

She dialed his work number.

"Sarah, you're speaking to me."

"This isn't a social call. I believe you referred to me as 'business' when I last spoke with you."

"I was just trying to make her leave me alone."

"I didn't call to discuss that. I called for a reason." She explained about Marshal Connors.

"Stallcup called."

"Oh, so you already knew this."

"Yeah, and I agree with you. I think Dagastino sent someone to see if you knew any more."

"He appeared authentic. He even wore the U.S. Marshal jacket you have."

"Hell, you can buy those on e-bay. I'll have Stallcup see if they can find this character. Sarah, we need to talk. But what I have to say needs to be said in person not over the damn phone."

"Braden, I appreciate the lovely flowers. And the lion is in the nursery. But I don't want to marry you. I was marrying you for all the wrong reasons. I don't want to be with someone who doesn't love me. If you insist on being present at the birth, that's your right. If you still want anything to do with this child, we'll work out a visitation schedule."

"Sarah, please don't make any final decisions until I speak with you in person."

"I don't see how anything has changed. There's nothing you can say that—"

"I love you."

The line remained silent for a moment.

Sarah held back showing any enthusiasm over his confession of love. "Why this grand epiphany now?"

"I've always loved you, but I was just too hardheaded and foolish to admit it. I can't live without you."

"I see. It's still about you, and what you need. You've never once thought of my needs. You've managed to make me feel used and cheap. I promised myself I won't let you hurt me again."

"But it's not just about me. That's why I wanted to wait and say these things in person. I knew I'd screw it up over the damn phone. And I have, haven't I?"

"I'm not sure. I need time to think."

"Take all the time you need. I just want you to promise me you won't etch your decision into stone until I've had a chance to fly down."

"I won't write you out just yet. Is that good enough?"

"More than I deserve."

"I'll toast to that. Give me a little notice before you show up on my doorstep. At least twenty-four hours."

"I'll try. Take care of yourself."

"I will." She hung up.

♦♦♦

All the next day, Sarah hadn't been able to stop thinking about Braden's confession of love. Though he'd said the words, she wasn't sure it would lead to anything. Things had changed.

When the doorbell rang, she pushed away from her computer. Remembering the imposter who'd paid her a visit, she peeked out the door and saw Marshal Stallcup.

She opened the door. "Are you bringing me roses?"

"No, but I intercepted these from the delivery boy." He handed her the tall crazy giraffe. "This goes with it."

"Thanks." She waited until he walked away before closing the door and taking the flowers to the table. She opened the card and read it.

I'm not good with words. But, I do love you.

Braden wasn't a quitter. She'd give him that.

The shrill ring startled her. It came from the phone Selena had mailed her. She hurried into the kitchen and pushed record on the small digital device. "Hello."

"Sarah, are you alone?"

"Yes, but I'm being watched 24/7. How are you?"

"Bored. Where I'm cooped up would be considered paradise to some, but to me it's sheer hell. Heard from Wolfe?"

Sarah didn't see the harm in talking to her sister. She still had the unexplainable desire to be near her. Also, she hoped to learn more about her mother's relatives.

"Yes. He sent a toy lion last week and today he sent a giraffe with a dozen pink roses for me."

"Sounds serious."

Sarah changed the subject. "I've been looking at the pictures you sent. Do you think our dad knew about us?"

Selena sighed. "I'm not sure. The kind of people Teresa hung around with, it wouldn't surprise me if he skipped out when she told him."

"Where is our mother buried?"

"I had her cremated."

"Did you place her ashes in a cemetery, or do you keep her in an urn?"

Selena laughed. "I flushed her down a toilet."

"That's dreadful."

"Not really, just consider it a burial at sea. Christ, why would you fuckin' care?"

"I'm not sure, but I do." Sarah couldn't believe her sister could be so cold. Maybe if she'd been treated like Selena, she'd have done the same thing.

Let this be a wakeup call.

Like Braden said, Selena was a killer without a conscience. Sarah had hoped to get information about her mother or learn something of her family's heritage. Rather than continue, she redirected the conversation. "I heard they're featuring you on *America's Most Wanted* again."

"That's just fuckin' great. Thanks for the tip."

"Have you ever thought about surrendering?"

"Hell, no. You think I'm fuckin' mui loco?"

"At least Dagastino wouldn't be able to reach you."

"You're clueless on how things work. He'd pay someone to whack me on the inside. It's too bad we can't spend some time together now that we know about each other. But I can't come back there. Maybe we can meet. Are you going anywhere for the holidays?"

"With the pregnancy, I can't really get away," she lied.

"I just thought it'd be cool. You know, see how we're alike and different. Like I'm allergic to chocolate, are you?"

"No, but we have the same birthmark."

"Shape of Florida." Selena paused for a moment. "I've got roses tattooed on my butt. It's like a vine that goes across my ass."

Sarah laughed. "Apparently, Wolfe doesn't know everything about you, or he would've made me drop my pants to verify he had his fugitive. I should go. I have a doctor's appointment today. They're doing an ultrasound."

"I'll call later."

"Goodbye, Selena."

Sarah played the recording. Selena's voice sounded gentle and caring at times. Her accent wasn't as strong. Without the accent, it amazed Sarah how much they sounded alike.

If Selena ever slipped up and gave away her location, Sarah would have no choice but to give the information to Braden. The thought of Selena being killed by lethal injection saddened her. But Selena would go on killing innocent people. There was little hope of redemption for her sister.

Later that day before her doctor's appointment, she made her airline reservation for her trip to Kansas. Visiting Marcy would make it easier to get through another Christmas without constantly dwelling on Mark and Tristen's deadly Christmas Eve accident.

◆◆◆

Braden was about to hang up when an older woman answered. He introduced himself, then told her about Sarah and Selena. "I think your son might've been their father."

"He was serious about a little Mexican girl from high school. He wanted to marry her, but his dad told him he should wait until he got back from his deployment to make such an important decision. But, he died in action and never came home."

"I'm sorry. Was her name by chance Teresa?"

"Yeah, it sure was. I never knew what became of the girl."

"Did he know she was pregnant?" Braden asked.

"If he had known, he would've married her. My son was a good boy. He was on the USS Stark when it was hit in the Persian Gulf. He received a Purple Heart."

He talked to the lady a little longer about Sarah.

After he hung up, he made the three hour trip to the cemetery where Andy was buried. He walked through the graves until he came to the one with a little lamb statue resting on top of headstone. He read the words etched into the gray stone.

Andrew Braden Wolfe. Andy. God's Little Lamb.

A small picture of Andy hugging his favorite teddy bear was centered above his name. The same bear that had been placed in his coffin at the funeral. The same bear now snuggled in Andy's arms along with Freddie Dinosaur.

But Daddy, it's my weekend to stay with you.

Andy, I can't help it. I'm being sent out of town this weekend. I'll make it up to you.

But Braden never got the chance.

He knelt beside the grave and set the small stuffed toy beagle at the base of the headstone along with a bouquet of white daisies.

"Sorry I was never able to give you a real puppy."

Tears clotted his throat and burned his eyes.

"I should've been a better father. I tried. But I let you down." He placed his hand on the grave above his son, but only felt the coldness of the earth.

For a brief moment, he heard Andy's giggle.

That's not a real mouse. It's a toy mouse. Daddy, you're funny.

It'd been an April Fool's joke. But Andy had been a step ahead of him and hadn't fallen for it.

A sharp, crushing pain ripped through his chest, causing Braden to do something he *never* did. Hot tears flowed freely down his face, and he sobbed uncontrollably.

"Oh, God. Why Andy?"

The image of Andy's battered little body at the morgue invaded Braden's thoughts. One thing that made his pain and guilt even worse was the fact Andy had suffered before dying. His death had been brutal and painful.

Braden wept aloud as the onset of tears and pain continued like waves pounding the shore. Finally, he wiped his eyes.

"I loved you so much. I'll always love you."

He stood and stared at the headstone a few more moments, then walked away knowing he could never make it up to his little boy.

Now life had given him another chance with the child Sarah carried. Though he'd tried not to care about it, he did.

◆◆◆

Selena looked at her gang. "She's not interested in meeting. She used the pregnant thing as an excuse. I get the feeling she's lying about going out of town Christmas."

Reggie checked Sarah's emails. "You sure nailed her. She received a confirmation from Delta. She'll be flying into Kansas on December eighteenth. Flight 225 lands at five-twenty-five. Her return flight is booked for December twenty-seventh."

"That might be our opportunity. Is she staying with Wolfe?"

Reggie continued reading Sarah's emails. "Nope, her friend Marcy is picking her up."

"That might be our only chance," Selena said.

"You're talking about a fucking airport, Selena," Carlos reminded. "How do you propose we kidnap her with a bunch of T. S. A. cops around?"

Travis added his take on it. "More likely, a marshal will drive her to the Memphis airport, and her friend will pick her up."

"Grab her on her way home," Carlos suggested.

Blade snorted the coke on the table before him. "No, because Wolfe will have a car waiting at the airport."

"We need to keep her friend away from the airport. Then when she steps out of the airport and gets past security, she's all ours," Roberto added. "Outside the building, they mainly have people directing traffic. They won't notice us."

"That isn't much of a plan," Carlos said. "Too many holes in it."

"Her friend is a federal marshal," Selena said.

"Off duty and off guard," Roberto reminded.

"She's also pregnant from what I've read in Sarah's emails," Reggie said.

"I'll have to approach the subject carefully. My sister isn't estupido."

"You're not starting to like her, are you?" Carlos asked.

"She's my ticket to freedom. Once Dagastino kills her, I won't have to live underground like a freaking blind mole."

"How will you hand her over to Dagastino without her convincing him she's not you?" Roberto asked.

"It'd be simpler if I slit her throat and then Carlos delivered her body to Dagastino," Blade said.

"After the arrest in Alaska, he's gotta know about Sarah," Travis mentioned.

"If I have to, I'll have her tongue cut out. You'll go to him the week before Christmas and tell him I've been fuckin' around on you, and you're tired of taking orders from me. Especially since I carry another man's baby."

"And what's keeping him from hearing Sarah's been abducted?" Roberto asked.

Selena sighed in frustration. "I'm taking her place. I've been practicing the way she talks. I'll call her friend and tell her I'm not coming."

"Get a new phone in her name with the same number, and then hers won't have service, so she can't reach that Marcy bitch. Then when you call her friend, Sarah's name will pop up," Reggie suggested.

"But you need the serial numbers from her cell," Travis argued.

"Leave the phreaking to me," Reggie said. "There's nothing I can't hack into."

"You're a genius." She turned to Carlos. "We'll need a plane waiting in Kansas, so we can fly her straight to Dagastino."

"I'll take care of it. Don't forget she'll need roses tattooed on her ass."

"Find someone there to handle it," Selena ordered. "Wolfe will look like the world's greatest screw up if we abduct her in his own backyard."

Chapter Nineteen

Amy sat at the dining room table with her family. She barely touched her Thanksgiving dinner as she listened to the conversation and the light teasing and laughter that followed. If she went with Michael, she'd never experience times like this again.

Later in the kitchen, she waited until she was alone with her older sister who was married with two children. "I heard from Michael."

"Mom told me."

"How much did she tell you?"

"All of it. Are you thinking about going with him?"

"I've been considering it, but I haven't made up my mind. And after today, I don't know if I can walk away from all of you and never look back."

"Do you love him?"

"Yes, that hasn't changed. I spoke with a U.S. Marshal who told me that some people stay in touch with their families even though they're told not to."

"Wouldn't that be dangerous?"

"Yes. The most crucial time would be the first couple of years following the trial. I'd have to change my name and live wherever the government decides."

"Sounds scary."

"I know, but once he goes into the program, I'll never be able to see him again. Even if I've changed my mind, they wouldn't be able to tell him. So what should I do?"

"Amy, no one can make that decision for you. I will say if it were Ben, I'd choose him over my family."

"I have to give the marshal my answer."

"When?"

"Soon. At any time, they will make him disappear. One minute I'm sure I want to go with him, but then I have second thoughts and back out."

"I love you, Amy, but I want you to be happy. When things are safe maybe we can work out a way to stay in touch. If you decide to do it, take my school email address. Then when you're ready, contact me there." She smiled. "Sign it Mrs. Roadinger and talk about your little boy, Mikey Jr."

Amy laughed before growing serious. "Is Mom worried that I'll do it?"

"She is, but you have to pick what's best for you. I know how much you love Michael. I truly believe he's what you need most in your life."

"Thanks for being honest. If I go, I won't even be here for Christmas." Tears clouded her eyes, and Amy hugged her sister.

◆◆◆

"She thought you were a marshal?" Leon Dagastino asked, wanting to know all he could about Selena's sister.

"Marshal Conners. She never questioned it. It's amazing how much they look alike," Chase said. "But that's as far as it goes. Other than looks they're as different as day and night. Ying and yang. Sarah is a class act. Gracious and refined."

"But what did she say about Selena?"

"Wolfe thinks Selena is up to no fuckin' good. Thinks she plans to kill Sarah and walk away with her identity."

Leon had to hand it to Selena. She had brains. "Good plan. I'm surprised she hasn't already done it."

"That'd be a little hard to do. Wolfe has Sarah's house watched. "

"If you distracted the deputies, so can Selena. And when a body turns up with Selena's face how am I supposed to know the difference?"

"Remember, Sarah is pregnant."

"Yes, that's right. Deputy U.S. Marshal Braden Wolfe's gonna be a daddy. Fathering a kid who has Selena's genes." Leon laughed. "The man hates her as much as I do. When my informant shared the news, I didn't find it useful then, but now it might be good to know. From what Ms. Green said, Wolfe wasn't pleased."

"That might've change judging by the flowers delivered. Both times, the roses came with a big toy for the baby. I figured Braden Wolfe's been sending them."

"What are you saying?"

"Think about it. Who goes to that much trouble for someone they don't care about?"

"So, maybe he cares after all."

◆◆◆

The doorbell rang Thursday morning, and Sarah sighed with frustration and set the screwdriver down. She peeked out the peephole, expecting to see Marshal Stallcup. Her breath left her.

She yanked the door open. "Braden, what are you doing here? You promised to give me a twenty-four hour notice."

"I couldn't wait to see you. I knew I screwed things up on the phone."

"How'd you get here?"

"I rented a small plane and flew down. I didn't have time to give you notice. I have to fly back Sunday."

She eyed the bag in his hand. "There are several hotels in the area."

"I want to stay here."

Sarah glanced at the patrol car in front of her house. "It's Thanksgiving. You can stay if those men can go home and enjoy the holiday with their families."

"I can arrange that."

"You can stay in Tristen's room again."

"Now, angel, I'd hoped to stay in your room."

Sarah rolled her eyes. "Fat chance. We have a lot to work out, Braden. I don't think that'd be a good idea." She started to tell him the news but decided to wait—at least until he was sitting down.

Without any further arguing, he deposited his bag in the room and returned to the kitchen. "Damn, what smells so good?"

"I have lasagna in the oven. It's not homemade."

"No traditional turkey and dressing?"

"Too much work. Without any family, this just seems like any other day. How's Marcy?"

"Bigger than a horse." He glanced at her stomach. "Hell, you're almost as large."

She smiled. "She's only a month or so ahead of me. I'm on my fifth month. I went to the doctor yesterday and had an ultrasound. And something unexpected popped up."

His expression changed to concern. "Are you all right?"

"I'm fine. Rather than explain it, let me show you." She hurried to the dining room and pulled the large envelope from a drawer, then returned to the kitchen. She removed the dark sheet of film and held it up in the light. "Do you see his head?"

"Yeah, I see it."

"And there are his testicles."

Braden grinned. "That's my boy."

Sarah expected that grin to fall off his face within the next few minutes. "Now see the shape to the right."

"Yeah, it looks like another head."

"You know what they say, two heads are better than one."

"It's another head?"

"Our little girl."

Braden's smile vanished, and his face grew pale green. "What'd you say?"

"I'm having twins. A boy and a girl. Dr. Olson had suspected it, but didn't want to tell me until he did the ultrasound and was absolutely sure."

"I need to sit down. And I could use a stiff drink."

"I have some wine."

"Not strong enough. Whiskey would be better."

"You're out of luck. I was going to call and tell you tonight. I didn't expect you to be overjoyed about it. Just consider this payback for Alaska."

"You sure know how to get even. Let me see that film." He held it up in the light and did something totally unexpected. He traced his finger over the outline of each baby. A huge smile eased across his face. "Twins. Have you told Marcy?"

"No, I wanted you to know first."

Braden pulled her into his embrace. "I love you, Sarah. I know I've been a jerk, but I had some demons to battle."

"And have you?"

"I think so. I visited Andy's grave. I left my hate and anger at the cemetery gate. I want you in my life."

"And the children?"

He smiled. "Them too. I still want us to get married at Christmas like we'd first planned."

"Oh, I see. Does that mean we divorce after the babies are born?"

"No, and I truly doubt we'd have gone through with it. I don't like being without you. I want to stay married."

"I don't know, Braden. I love you, but sometimes love isn't enough. I'm not sure it would work between us. I'm still Selena's sister."

"I know. But I no longer see her, I see you, Sarah."

"I'll consider it."

"Consider it?"

"I'm not making any hasty decision. These children need a mother and father who get along and have no regrets about marrying one another. Right now I'm not so sure you wouldn't resent me later for tying you down."

"Then think about it. When can you give me an answer?"

"Christmas. I'll do some soul searching between now and then. But even if my answer is no, you're welcome to be present when they're born."

"That's a month away. And if your answer is yes, how soon can we get married?"

Sarah shrugged. "Maybe New Year's Day."

She could tell by the way his eyes dulled he wanted it to be sooner, but she didn't care. Though she loved him, she had to make sure it was the best thing for them both.

He blew a surrendering breath. "If you say yes at Christmas, we can at least pick out rings and look at houses."

"You want me to move to Kansas?"

"Yep, I'll pay to have your furniture moved. I'll even help decorate a nursery in the new house just like the one here."

"You're getting ahead of yourself. I haven't said yes."

◆◆◆

Braden didn't like her answer but had to pull back and give her the time she asked for. He couldn't think of any way to prove he really loved her.

After dinner, he cleaned the kitchen while Sarah soaked in the tub. He decided to make her a cup of hot chocolate.

He opened the bathroom door and found Sarah still in the tub.

"What are you doing in here?" she asked.

"Room service," Braden announced. "I brought you hot chocolate."

"I'm naked."

"So."

"Set the cup down and get out," she ordered.

His gaze raked over her breasts and down her body. Desire whirled through him. He wanted her. But to push the issue might make her more reluctant to marry him. This was all for Sarah. He wanted her to see it wasn't always about him.

He dropped to his knees on the mat beside the tub and took the washcloth from her hand. "I'll wash your back."

"That's not necessary."

"You took care of me in the cabin. Let me spoil you this weekend."

She sat up and first took a sip of the chocolate before setting the cup out of the way. "Pamper me all you want."

Braden lathered soap on the cloth and ran it over her back. She closed her eyes and made a sigh of pleasure. He dipped the cloth in the tub and squeezed the water out, letting it run down her back.

After rinsing her off, he stood and offered his hand. She came out of the tub with beads of water running down her smooth olive skin. It shimmered in the light. He had a hell of an erection. "I'll dry you."

He blotted the towel over her, then wrapped it around her. He paused a moment thinking about the life inside her. His children.

"You're beautiful, Sarah. My Sarah."

"With my stomach swelling up."

"Even more so." He sprawled his large hands over her belly. "I can't wait to see them."

"You might change your mind when they're both screaming to be fed at the same time. Or when they both have dirty diapers."

"Did I ever mention that I'm a pro at changing dirty diapers?"

She smiled. "No. Let's see you handle two at a time."

"Exactly why you need me in your life. Handling two isn't like handling one."

"You sound like a used car salesman trying to give me a sales pitch."

He grinned. "Yeah, I am. But I'm low maintenance and high performance."

She laughed. "Probably a lemon."

He wanted to draw her into his arms and hold her but didn't. Doing something irrational could ruin everything. Instead, he would pamper her all weekend and ignore the sexual urges pulsing through him like mini torpedoes.

She reached for her gown, and he stopped her. "Not until I've rubbed you down with body lotion. You don't want any stretch marks."

"Braden, this is silly. I can do it."

"But I want to do it." He nudged her through the bathroom door to the large bed. "Lie down."

He applied the lotion she kept beside the bed and smoothed it over her skin, rubbing his hands over the rise of her stomach.

"Maybe I should do it."

"Shh...I'm not trying to seduce you. This is for you."

He applied more lotion. He lightly stroked her breasts and stomach. Once her skin had absorbed it, he eased her gown over her head and helped her pull her arms through it. "Anything else I can do for you?"

He hoped she'd make the first move. Instead of appearing aroused, she stood and returned to the bathroom. "I need to brush my teeth. I can handle that one on my own."

He grinned. "Well since you don't need my services any more, I'll leave you. I think I'll watch a little television before turning in. Good night, Sarah."

"Night, Braden Sleep well. And thanks for the bath and massage."

Walking across her bedroom, he zoned in on a wedding picture of Sarah and Mark setting on her dresser. Did Sarah have more of an issue with letting go than she let on? Maybe her hesitation about marrying him had more to do with Mark.

If she did marry him, he didn't plan on keeping Mark's picture around. He couldn't expect her to get rid of them, but at least, she could keep them in a drawer. Better yet, a chest in the attic. He'd be more than willing to dig a hole in the backyard and bury them. He grinned. Sad, being jealous of a dead man.

On his way to the den, he peeked inside the nursery and saw the large crib partially put together. It'd be a bigger job to assemble than the cradle. Not wanting to disturb Sarah, he closed the nursery door and went to work.

◆◆◆

The next morning, Sarah walked past the nursery and noticed the crib. Braden had obviously stayed up much later and put it together.

She eased Tristen's bedroom door open and peeked inside. Braden lay sprawled out on the twin bed, his arm and foot hanging off the side. Her gaze lingered on him a moment, before she closed the door and made her way to the kitchen.

She sat at the computer and emailed Marcy. Now she could tell her about the twins. She also told her how loving and thoughtful Braden had been. After she hit send, she stretched and walked into the kitchen to start breakfast. No sooner had she removed the eggs from the skillet, the TracFone rang, and she quickly answered it before Braden woke up. "Selena?"

"Who else did you expect to call you on this phone? Santa Claus?"

Sarah laughed. "I have company. I can't talk loudly, or I'll wake him."

"Don't tell me. Deputy U.S. Marshal Braden Wolfe."

"Yes, he flew down for a visit."

"Let me ask you this, if Braden had a lead on me, would you tip me off?"

"You're my sister. I don't agree with the things you'd done, but at the same time I don't want anything bad happening to you, so I'm not sure."

"A little birdie told me you're having twins—a boy and a girl."

Sarah paused. "How'd you know?"

"I'm fuckin' psychic."

Sarah had changed her password after Reggie had tampered with her computer. There wasn't any other explanation. Somehow, he still had access to her emails. She'd have the entire hard-drive erased.

Don't act weird. Keep talking.

"Braden actually handled it pretty well."

"I'm surprised he didn't head for the border."

"He's coming around. I've got to go."

After clicking off the phone, Sarah slid it in a drawer, hoping Braden had forgotten she had it. The urge to stay connected with her sister was overpowering. She hoped Braden was wrong about Selena's motive for calling. But clearly there had to be a reason why she read Sarah's emails.

Braden entered the kitchen. "You're up early."

"I have a lot to do today. Thanks for finishing the crib. I'll keep the cradle in my room, and when they're older I'll move them to the bed. "I just realized I'll need two of everything."

"You're grandmother will be thrilled about the twins."

"Grandma Sofia is dead."

"True, but your biological grandmother is still living. I found your father's mother. Ruth Ann Jenkins. She lives in Texas where you and Selena were born."

"Oh my God! And my father?"

Braden told her what he knew.

"I'm glad he wasn't just some john my mother tricked for a few bucks." She hugged Braden. "Thank you. I'll give her a call."

She did and talked for an hour. Now she had a real family.

♦♦♦

Friday evening at a nice Chinese Restaurant, Sarah couldn't stop talking about her new grandmother. She figured Braden was tired of hearing it. "I promised we'd visit once the twins are old enough. I have aunts, uncles, and cousins to meet."

"And you still have my family to meet. I never could face them after Andy died. His little cousins always asked about him. Mom couldn't give it a rest either. So, I stopped visiting them."

"I'm sure if was painful. Since I didn't have anyone left, I wasn't faced with that issue."

Back home, Braden pampered her again and waited on her hand and foot. The man was laying it on thick.

Sarah couldn't help but be disappointed when he tucked her in and gave her a quick peck on the cheek. She wanted a real kiss. A deep meaningful kiss. Her blood boiled with needy passion any time he touched her. She wanted him.

Most of Saturday, Braden fixed and repaired things around her house. He raked leaves and bagged them. Then he took her car and had the oil changed. Sarah had forgotten how handy having a man around could be.

That evening, Braden once again bathed her. When he helped her from the tub and wrapped the towel around her, she couldn't hold back. She slipped her arms around him and pressed her nude body against him. "Braden, I want you to sleep with me."

His eyes lit up. "You sure?"

"Yes. I know you're trying not to crowd me or make me feel pressured. But I want this as much as you do."

Braden lowered his head and kissed her deeply, letting his tongue search for hers. After the kiss, he held her face between his hands and kissed her forehead, above her eyes, her cheeks, and around her mouth before centering his lips over hers again. "God, Sarah. I love you."

He guided her to the bedroom. She walked over to Mark's picture and flipped it around before climbing in the bed. "Make love to me, Braden."

"My pleasure, angel."

She pulled the comforter back for him, and he joined her. His kisses lit her body with a passionate fire. Heat radiated off his skin as he melted against her. Every nerve ending in her body burned with sensual need. He was all male—hot and powerful.

For the next hour, he used his mouth and hands to bring her body off the bed. Then he rolled her on her side and pressed his erection against her bottom.

"With every single breath, I smell you. I taste you. And now I want you."

"Oh, Braden, I want you to."

He eased inside her and stroked back and forth. His hard muscles flexed with each movement.

"You won't hurt the babies. Don't hold back."

"You sure."

"Positive."

He nuzzled the back of her ear and neck, then kissed her shoulder. She pulled away from him, separating their bodies. "You're holding back."

"Am I?"

"Yes, roll over on your back." She straddled him, taking him inside her. She closed her eyes as the friction of their flesh built an unbearable heat between them. He grasped her hips and raised her up and down on his masculine flesh. Her inner muscles tightened, and he cried out.

For a moment she sat on him, staring at his face. She thought about what Selena said earlier. "Who do you see when you look at me?"

"My Sarah. No one else."

She stretched out on top of him, embracing him, and resting her head against his shoulder.

"Are you sure I didn't hurt the babies?"

"Braden, I love my children. I wouldn't risk losing them."

Sunday afternoon, Braden entered the den, carrying his tote bag. "I have to leave. I don't like flying at night if I can avoid it. Remember you promised me an answer by Christmas."

"I know."

"I'm going to be busy between now and then. I won't be able to call you often." He explained what was going on with Michael and Amy.

"You think she might go with him?"

"She still sounds reluctant."

"When Dagastino's arrested, that will take some of the heat off Selena."

Braden's brows drew in a frown. "Has she called lately?"

Sarah nodded. "But I forgot to record it."

"Promise me you won't trust that bitch. She'll only use you."

"She is my sister."

"She doesn't feel anything for you but contempt and jealousy. Whatever you do, don't trust her. Swear to me you won't."

Sarah swallowed hard. "I swear."

"Don't ever forget, she's a killer. She wouldn't blink an eye at killing you or our babies." He gathered her in his arms and drew her into his embrace. His heart pounded against her. After several deep kisses, he whispered in her ear. "I love you."

"I know. I love you."

With one more kiss, he headed toward the rental car.

"Call me when you've landed safely," she shouted from the door.

He nodded and waved, then climbed in and drove away.

Her heart sank to the pit of her stomach. She'd be miserable without him.

A phone rang from Tristen's room. Braden's phone lay on the nightstand. He'd left it. She'd overnight it to him. She answered his phone. "Hello."

"Sarah?"

"Yes, Alex?"

"I need to speak with Braden. It's an emergency."

"He just left for the airport. What's wrong?"

"I can't find Marcy anywhere."

Chapter Twenty

Marcy opened her eyes and scanned the ordinary bedroom, wondering who in the hell had her. It smelled flowery like the scent of cheap room spray with an underlying smell of mothballs.

Her head pounded from the blow she'd taken, and her wrists ached from the rope that bound her hands behind her back. All she remembered was being in the parking garage that connected to the mall—with her arms full of Christmas packages.

She glanced down. Someone had removed her clothes and slipped a flimsy hospital gown on her, leaving the back open. Was her baby all right? When she felt movement, she sighed with relief.

At least whoever abducted her hadn't tied her feet. She considered it being Tiffany, but didn't think the slutty twit had the strength to lift her.

Of course the criminally insane possess an extra dose of adrenaline.

As she rose from the bed, she grimaced from the head pain.

There had to be some way of freeing her hands, and she had to do it before her abductor returned. She'd seen cases where people killed pregnant women near term and harvested their infants.

The thought petrified her.

She studied the chairs and furniture in the neatly maintained room but didn't see anything that could cut the rope. Placing her feet on the floor, she stood and took a few steps. The room swayed back and forth like a carnival fun house, and she thought she'd vomit.

She backed up to the door and placed her fingers around the knob and turned it. Apparently, it'd been locked from the other side. Perhaps the closet had something useful in it. She crossed the room and again with her back against the door maneuvered her fingers around the knob. This time she was successful.

The door creaked loudly.

Oh, God. I hope no one heard that.

Her heart accelerated for a moment.

The closet mainly contained women's clothes. With her hip, she pushed the door closed.

She managed to open the nightstand drawer and spotted her salvation. An opened plastic disposable razor lay in the heap of junk. After dropping to her knees, she lowered her head in the drawer. As though bobbing for apples, she grasped the razor handle with her mouth.

A door slammed from somewhere in the house.

Footfalls came her way.

She stood and pushed the drawer closed, dropped the disposable razor in the center of the bed, and lay back down on her side facing the door.

Her fingers fumbled behind her, searching for the plastic handle.

Where is it?

Finally, she gripped it.

Please let it be sharp enough to cut the rope.

The door opened.

Tiffany stood in the doorway. She wore a sinister frown. "I hoped you'd stay knocked out until I had a chance to tie your feet and properly secure you to the bed. Unfortunately, my nosy neighbor came over and wouldn't leave."

"Release me right now. I am a federal marshal."

Tiffany laughed. "That doesn't impress me."

"Why are you doing this?" Marcy asked.

"Isn't it obvious?"

"The only thing it proves is that you're crazy."

"No, I'm in love with Alex. And the only reason he went back to you is because you're pregnant. He felt obligated to you."

"He didn't know about the pregnancy until after he'd called it quits with you."

"I'm sure you found some sly way of letting the information leak out."

"And you think killing me will solve the problem?"

"Yes, but I don't want you dead. Not yet. First, I plan to rip that fetus from your womb and kill it with a hammer."

"What?"

"The only thing connecting Alex to you is an umbilical cord, and I plan to cut it."

Marcy's heart did a triple beat. But if she wanted to get the upper hand on Tiffany, she had to stay calm.

"That's murder."

"No, it's gratification and my only chance to be with Alex."

While Marcy tried to think of ways to keep Tiffany talking, she worked on freeing her hands. She could feel the rope wearing down. Threads began to break. She had to be careful not to cut her wrists.

Just a little more and I'll have it.

Madness flamed in Tiffany's eyes. "When he realizes you and the baby aren't an issue, he'll come back to me. Your daughters won't be a problem. They like me."

Marcy held her breath as the razor sliced through the few remaining threads.

Her hands were free.

Pick the moment carefully to make a move.

No doubt, this woman's mental state gave her superhuman strength.

I'm too weak. Now isn't the time.

"So far you haven't done anything. Don't you see if you kill my baby and me, you'll go to prison? You still won't have Alex. I won't press charges for the abduction if you let me go now. I swear."

◆◆◆

When Braden stepped from the small plane, Darrel waited for him on the tarmac. "You must've really missed me if you drove over to meet me."

Darrel didn't smile.

Braden frowned. "What's up?"

"It's Marcy."

Fear crept up Braden's spine. "What about her?"

"She's missing. She was last spotted in the mall and hasn't been seen since. Her car was found with the door open and her purse left in the seat. Christmas packages were left on the ground."

"Have you pulled surveillance from any cameras in the garage?"

"They're getting it now."

"I need to speak with Alex."

"He's a basket case," Darrel said. "He admitted he had an affair, and he thinks the woman is involved."

"That'd be my guess. You got a name?"

"Tiffany Ellis, 555 Westington Drive. Shawnee."

"Old neighborhood but nice. Let's go pay Ms. Ellis a visit. I'll follow you in my car."

◆◆◆

Tiffany wheeled a cart into the bedroom.

Marcy swallowed back her fear.

The top shelf held gauzes and shiny instruments that looked like something a doctor would use. Immediately, she knew what Tiffany intended to use the long knitting needle for.

"I'm going to need you on your back with your legs spread. Let me think how I should do this. I could knock you out again, but then you'd miss all the fun." She paused as though studying the situation. "It might be wiser to secure your feet before I try to reposition your hands." She held out her hand. "Give me your foot."

"Look, I've decided you can have Alex," Marcy said. "I'll take the girls and my baby and move somewhere."

"I like your girls, and I want to be their mother." Tiffany laughed. "It's just you and the baby that need to be disposed of." She reached for Marcy's foot. "Don't be difficult."

She jerked her foot away.

"If you don't cooperate, I'll have to take drastic measures. See that bat in the corner? I'll beat the baby out of you if I have to."

Marcy had to act now.

God, help me find the strength.

Tiffany reached again for Marcy's right ankle.

Marcy pulled her knee into her chest, then kicked. Her foot made contact with Tiffany's stomach. "You're not killing my baby, you stupid bitch."

Marcy stood, but her head spun and dizziness wrapped her in a foggy haze.

I've got to do this. Don't fall. Don't black out.

She steadied herself.

Tiffany grabbed the bat and swung but missed.

Marcy yanked the nightstand drawer out and flipped it over, dumping its contents. Then she shielded her stomach.

Again Tiffany swung the bat.

It made contact with the drawer. The splintering of the wood caused Marcy's heartbeat to race. She gasped for breath.

She threw the drawer at Tiffany, but her attacker dodged it and swung the bat a third time. Marcy gripped the end of the bat and wrestled for it. Her knees buckled slightly.

I'm going down. No, I can't pass out.

God, help me. I don't know if I can do this.

As Tiffany tugged the bat with all her strength, Marcy simply let go, causing Tiffany to fall backwards. The bat hit the floor. Her abductor crashed into the rolling cart, knocking it over. The clatter of metal tools hitting the hardwood floor rang out.

"Three strikes. You're out." Marcy made her way through the door and down a hall, willing herself not to pass out. She opened the front door and fled the house. The sight of familiar cars made her stop in the middle of the yard. "Braden!"

She ran toward him.

He took her in his arms and hugged her for a moment. "I was scared shitless when they told me."

"I'm glad you're here."

Other patrol cars pulled in front of the house. Darrel hurried over and informed the Shawnee officers of the situation.

Marcy didn't care that she stood in the middle of the yard half-naked. Her baby was safe now. She was safe. That's all that mattered.

"Are you all right?" Braden removed his jacket and draped it around her.

"I feel like I'm going to faint."

"Lean on me. Is she still inside?"

"Yes."

"I want you to lie down on my backseat while we bring her out."

"Braden, she's insane. She has a baseball bat, but I don't think she has a gun."

He assisted Marcy inside his car. "Rest. You're safe now. You'll need to call Alex." He reached in his jacket pocket. "I must've left my work phone at Sarah's. And my personal phone is at home."

"Please ask Darrel to give Alex a quick call. I love him, but I'm angry with him. He's the one who brought this on us."

"Sure, you rest."

Marcy closed her eyes and slipped into the darkness of sleep.

◆◆◆

Braden's adrenaline dropped knowing Marcy was safe. He loved her like family. After making sure Alex was notified, he joined the others. He and two other officers entered the front door at the same time Darrel and the others burst through the back door.

"U.S. Marshals. Tiffany Ellis, come out with your hands in the air," he shouted. In the den, he met up with the men.

"Lead the way," Darrel said.

With his gun in ready position, Braden walked through the house. The other officers followed behind him. "Clear." He rounded the corner into the den. "Clear." He edged down the hall, then entered a bedroom.

Christ almighty.

Braden checked the woman for a pulse. "She's gone." He stared down on Tiffany's lifeless body lying on the bed. She'd used a surgical knife to slit her wrists.

Darrel stood beside him. "Oh, sweet Jesus. Man that's a lot of blood."

"Call the ME."

Braden returned to his car and opened the back door, waking up Marcy. "I found your clothes. You want to go back inside to change?"

"No, I just want to go home."

"Sorry, but we're meeting Alex at the hospital. You and the baby need to be checked out."

"I'm all right. Did you make the arrest?"

He placed his hands on his hips and shook his head. "She's dead."

"You killed her?"

"No, she took her own life. At least you won't have to worry about her walking back into the picture again."

Marcy sat in a daze. "Call Alex and tell him you've decided to take me home."

"Sorry, kid. You probably have a concussion. Also, you're pale. You look like you spent the night with a vampire. Now lie down and close your eyes until we get there."

Once Marcy was quiet, Braden thought of Sarah. About how his entire world would collapse if anything happened to her or the twins.

Darrel remained behind for the ME while Braden drove Marcy to the Overland Park Medical Center not far from her home.

He stayed with Marcy until Alex showed up.

Once he arrived home, Braden needed to hear Sarah's voice. He pulled out his personal phone from the kitchen drawer and called her.

"Braden, have you found Marcy?"

"She's safe."

"Where was she?"

"Tiffany abducted her." He explained everything that had happened. "She suffered a slight concussion from being clunked over the head, but other than that, she's doing great, and the baby seems fine."

"Thank God. I'm so glad."

He sighed. "Sarah, what happened to Marcy has me terrified. Selena poses an even greater threat. Tell me again, you'll never agree to meet her anywhere without me."

"I won't."

"Marcy came close to being murdered. I don't want the same thing happening to you. I wish I could be with you, so nothing can harm you."

"Michael's going to need you."

"I know. Maybe you should stay with Marcy."

"I'm fine here. You have my house watched day and night, so don't freak out. Hey, you left your phone."

"I know."

"I sent it Fed-ex. You should get it tomorrow."

"Thanks. I love you, Sarah." He paused, but she didn't echo the term of endearment. "Well, I guess I should go. With Michael turning federal witness Friday, I have a lot to do. Bye, Sarah."

"Braden, wait. I love you. I'm just not sure it will be enough."

"It's more than enough."

Braden didn't plan to take *no* for an answer. He'd do whatever it took to prove his love.

◆◆◆

Sarah tried not to think about Braden, but she couldn't keep the arrogant marshal from her thoughts. He hadn't called since the Monday after Thanksgiving to let her know Marcy was safe. She missed him, but knew he was working diligently on Michael's transformation into the WITSEC.

Selena hadn't called either. While it came as a relief, she also missed feeling that internal thread that bound them together when they talked.

Packing for her Kansas trip kept her busy. One bag contained just Christmas presents for Marcy and her family. For Braden she had a nice fishing rod, hoping he'd take the hint and start relaxing and enjoying life. Thank goodness it folded down into a zipper bag that fit perfectly in her suitcase.

There was one last thing to do. She packed Tristen's room. She kept the things that were the most important to her son in a nice wooden chest and gave the rest to Goodwill. It was time.

◆◆◆

Michael had spoken with Braden several times since Thanksgiving. It lifted his spirits when Wolfe mentioned Amy had called. Now it was a waiting game to see if she'd choose him over her family. But with the Christmas season in full swing, her decision might be more difficult to make. No one celebrated it like her family. It'd be hard for her to walk away. Each carol that played would hit a soft spot in her heart for her family and would remind her of what she was giving up.

He wanted to contact her but couldn't risk it. His uncle could be following and monitoring his every move. Michael had spotted cars tailing him.

Braden promised to contact him if Amy agreed to be a part of the program. As for Michael, family didn't mean much. With his mom gone, there wasn't anyone left he cared about.

Once taken into protective custody, his uncle would be arrested.

Michael had been summoned to his uncle's office. His stomach knotted up. Had Uncle Leon become suspicious of him?

Breathe slowly. Relax.

Michael entered the office and waited for Uncle Leon to acknowledge him.

"Michael," he'd said, "you're as jumpy as a mouse. What's with you? The boys mentioned you seem jittery."

Michael shrugged, trying to appear calm. "Nothing much. Just undecided about buying my own house. It's a big step."

"You want a house, I'll buy you one."

"You've done too much already. I guess I should consider a condo since I don't have a family."

"You just need a place to fuck the women. You are into women, aren't you, Michael?"

"Definitely. I've just been too busy to become involved with anyone."

"Involved. Hell, there are plenty of bitches to screw without them expecting a commitment. I'll give you a number to call. You tell the lady who answers what you're into, and she'll fix you up."

"Thanks."

"Call her now. Set it up for tonight."

"I don't have the condo yet."

His uncle threw him a set of keys. "Use my penthouse in town."

"You sure about this?"

"Yeah, now call and set it up."

Michael had no choice but to do it. There wasn't anyone he wanted to sleep with but Amy. If he didn't set up the appointment, his uncle would definitely think something was wrong and might suspect Michael was involved with a woman.

He couldn't chance his Uncle Leon learning about Amy. Because he might go as far as threatening her family.

◆◆◆

Friday morning, as he had done every day, Michael made his way to the gym. Signing a contract on a condo had put Uncle Leon's mind at ease. Why buy a condo if you're about to walk away? It'd been a long night, waiting to hear from Braden. Obviously, Amy decided not to join him.

Regardless, he couldn't live his life the way Uncle Leon wanted him to. He wasn't a killer. The bottom line was he had a conscience. Something he doubted his uncle had ever possessed.

As far as the hooker, he paid her extra not to blab that nothing had happened. From the way she grinned, she probably assumed he was gay and his uncle didn't know.

Michael entered the locker room and removed his old shoes from his bag. As he was about to remove the key, Chase entered the room.

Michael's heart leapt in his chest.

Damn it.

He drew in a slow easy breath.

Remain calm. Look natural. Slip the damn shoes on.

Michael forced a smile. "You come to work out with me?"

"Shit, no. Your uncle wants you to watch over your shoulder. Something's goin' down. Lenny spotted the Feds tailing your uncle. We're not moving that shipment today. Don't go anywhere near the warehouse. Take the day off." He looked at Michael's feet. "What's wrong with the shoes you had on?"

"Not broken in yet." Michael picked up one of the old shoes and tilted it slightly to put on. The insole gapped, allowing the key to slide to the heel. Then it dropped to the floor.

His breath hitched.

Chased offered him the key. "You dropped this."

He took it. "Thanks." He finished putting on the old shoes and lacing them up, then stood to leave. "Time to workout."

"Aren't you gonna put your bag in the locker?"

"Yeah, sure." Michael put the key in the lock and opened the door wide enough to slip his gym bag on top of the box of information. God, he hoped Chase hadn't noticed it. Michael slammed the door and placed the lock back on. He took his towel and water bottle and headed toward the equipment. "See ya round."

Chase nodded. "Don't bust your hump."

Michael stepped on a treadmill and walked. Walked until he knew Chase had left the building.

Once it was clear, he returned to the locker room, grabbed his shoes, placed the information in his gym bag and headed for the club's back exit.

He stood at the door. What if his uncle's men were waiting for him instead of Wolfe? Had he been careful?

He glanced behind him before opening door.

Deputy U.S. Marshal Wolfe stepped from the car and met him at the bottom of the steps in back of the fitness center. "You ready? We've been waiting. What happened?"

Michael filled him in on Chase's unexpected visit. "He scared the living crap out of me. I expected him to question me about the key or notice the box in my locker. At that point, I wasn't so sure I'd make it at all."

"So maybe your uncle wasn't as suspicious of you as you thought. You got everything?"

"Everything I care about is in this gym bag. Since you didn't call last night, I don't suppose you've heard from Amy."

Wolfe shook his head. "No, I haven't."

Michael's throat tightened. But he understood how she felt about her family. He didn't begrudge her for it.

"What about my uncle?"

"FBI agents and other law enforcement agencies are on their way to take him into custody."

"He'll probably make bail."

"Wouldn't surprise me. But he'll be watched around the clock. He'll wear a monitoring device. If he tries to leave town, he'll be picked up."

"I doubt you have to worry about that. He's so damn cocky he'll believe his fancy attorneys will get him out of this without any prison time."

"With your testimony and recordings, that won't be happening." Braden smiled.

"Where will I be living?"

"I've heard a few cities tossed around. The OEO will go over it with you. I know you're disappointed about Amy. I'm sorry."

"It's what I expected."

While Wolfe drove toward the safe house, his phone rang. "Braden Wolfe." He paused. "Amy?"

Michael's spirits lifted. Had she changed her mind?

"No, it's not too late. Got your bags packed?"

Michael couldn't believe it.

"Give me your address and I'll have someone swing by within the hour."After hanging up, Wolfe glanced at him. "She'll be at the safe house tonight."

Michael's heart soared. "I can live anywhere so long as she's with me."

Braden grinned. "I included her in the applications I filed. I thought she might come around."

"I'm speechless."

"It's about damn time I saw you at a loss for words."

The Pennsylvania safe house was referred to as Camelot, probably because the house constructed from gray stone had a tower in front. Later that night, Braden waited on the porch while Amy and Michael had a chance to talk. He couldn't help but worry about Sarah. He stared up at the stars. Those same stars were over her house. He wished he could be with her.

Something felt off tonight. His shoulders muscles tightened.

The air held a sweet scent from the laundry coming from a neighbor's dryer vent, but the smell made him nauseated. He paced back and forth across the porch of the old house.

God, he hated he'd promised Michael he'd be with him through the initial process.

He couldn't stop the uneasiness eating away at him. He sensed trouble—like the heaviness in the air before a storm.

Chapter Twenty-one

Leon Dagastino glared at the FBI agents arresting him. "You sons-of-bitches."

"Get your hands behind your back, sir," the little dickhead said.

He let the young agent handcuff him. "You dumb shits. I'll be home before dinner."

"Maybe, but you're still a federal arrestee and coming with us."

He had several judges and police officials on his payroll. Still he hated to waste the time. He'd planned to play a round of golf. Not to mention he was in the middle of a deal with Carlos Torres that'd finally give him closure over his son's death.

"You'll never make the charges stick. No federal jury will hang anything on me, because you can't prove shit."

None of the FBI agents, Federal Marshals, or local New Jersey cops responded. But they all wore cocky expressions.

Bastards.

Before they escorted him from the house, he instructed his secretary to call his lawyer.

Leon assured himself they had no witnesses or ways of making anything stick. No one was stupid enough to go against him, not if they valued their life. He thought of some of the men working for him and wondered if any had betrayed him.

Then he recalled how edgy Michael had been for the last several weeks.

Surely not.

But he had to face the possibility of it being his nephew who'd turned into a federal rat. How? Who'd approached him? He remembered Michael's trip to Alaska. Obviously, Michael had lied concerning the events there and had made a pact with Wolfe.

He'd never live to see his twenty-seventh birthday.

That night after he was released and back home, Leon called Carlos Torres. "Can you talk?"

"Si, Senor Dagastino."

"I want to double our deal."

"Double?"

"Yes, I still want Selena, but I want her sister, Sarah as well. Don't harm Sarah Mason in any way. The money will double."

◆◆◆

"Son of a bitch," Braden shouted at the news that Dagastino had already posted bond. Braden sat down with Amy and Michael and informed them of his uncle's release. "And by now, he's figured out you're the one who turned on him."

"I can't believe he's out already. I thought it'd take a little time."

"From this point on, you'll be kept under tight security. No going outside, even in the back area. There are four deputies working twelve hour shifts at all times. When you're transported, you'll be in a bullet proof vehicle. We have several we use. Each time you go to the courthouse, a different route will be used."

"You think your uncle would have you killed?" Amy asked Michael.

Braden knew he'd also kill Amy for the hell of getting even.

"Yes, if he finds me."

"That's not going to happen," Wolfe assured the young couple. "We've taken every precaution to keep you safe. Until the trial, we're keeping you here. Once the trial is over and he's sentenced, then we'll relocate you in your permanent dig. They'll give you a choice of three of four cities. You'll keep your first names and be assigned new last names with the same initial as Dagastino. Now you'll go in the conference room and review your immunity agreement with FBI Special Agent Lancer. He's your handler. He'll make you aware that you're a non-custody witness."

"What does that mean?" Amy asked.

"That you volunteered, and you can sign out of the program if you want."

Amy's face lit. "We can?"

Michael placed a hand over hers. "No, we can't. It'd be like committing suicide. My uncle would have us killed."

I've already covered a lot of what he'll say, so just pretend you're hearing it for the first time. I don't want to piss off the FBI."

Michael laughed. "I think we can manage that."

"After that, Marshal Parker, the supervisor, will review security details. "

Braden didn't tell them he was returning to Kansas for Christmas Day. He'd be gone a couple of days. He wanted to propose to Sarah the right way. He had a ring and had practiced his proposal.

A deputy escorted Michael and Amy to what they referred to as the tracking room. Braden decided while he was off duty, he'd take a nap.

Marshal Howard caught him by the arm. "Hold up. Thought you should know Dagastino has already put a contract on Michael."

"Shit. That's not good."

◆◆◆

While on the flight to Kansas, Sarah debated on whether Braden would make it to Marcy's for Christmas. She hadn't heard from him. With so much going on, she didn't expect him to contact her. Dagastino's arrest had made the national news.

Her thoughts shifted to the call from Selena the previous evening. Sarah had already gone to bed. In a foggy haze, she almost informed her sister that she had to be at the airport early but caught herself and said doctor at the last minute.

But the call disturbed her. It was like listening to a recording of her own voice. Selena had totally dropped the accent. Now Braden's theory didn't appear unreasonable. She should've never continued having conversations with Selena.

She exited the Delta flight and followed the signs to the luggage pickup inside the terminal. Marcy and Alex planned to meet her outside in the pick-up zone.

Marcy had taken a leave of absence. The ordeal with Tiffany left her exhausted and shaken. Since Sarah was arriving four days before Christmas, they'd be able to do things together. They planned to shop for baby clothes.

After grabbing her luggage, Sarah ventured outside in the waiting zone and stood under an awning. She doubted she could relax until she reached Marcy's house. She pulled out her phone and hit Marcy's number.

Dead. *Oh, fudge.* She'd just recharged it the night before. If Marcy and Alex didn't show up soon, she'd flag a taxi. Something unexpected probably came up. Had Marcy had gone into early labor?

She hadn't thought to ask Marcy what kind of car she drove.

A light blue sedan with tinted windows slowed down as it approached.

She waved.

It pulled to the curb. The back and front passenger doors opened simultaneously. It required a moment to comprehend it wasn't Marcy's car.

Before she could run or scream, two men she'd never seen jerked her in the backseat. She struggled but couldn't break free. Her heart raced, freezing out her ability to think clearly. One of the men covered her mouth. The tobacco odor on his hand made her sick.

"Grab her fucking arms, Roberto," Blade ordered.

"Travis, you ass-wipe, get her luggage," Selena said. "An airport cop is walking this way. Carlos, drive!"

The sedan pulled from the curb and left the airport. The man removed his hand from her mouth.

She breathed in several deep breaths, allowing her heart to slow down. She processed her situation. "You won't get away with this. I have friends expecting me. They should be here any moment."

"I hate to tell you, but I canceled your plans," Selena said. "Marcy, Sarah. I hate to do this to you at the last minute, but I'm not coming. I'm not ready to face Braden."

Selena sounded exactly like her.

"You bitch," Sarah said. "Marcy's too smart. She'll know the call didn't come from my phone."

"Considering I have all the needed identification to become you, it was surprisingly easy. I purchased a phone in your name, kept your number, and ended your service." Selena smiled. "And since it's a no show for Marcy, I think she bought it. Technology doesn't lie. It was your name and number she saw on her phone when I called. "

When the cloth covered her nose, Sarah tried to hold her breath, refusing to breathe in the ether. Finally, she gasped for air. Her throat burned and brought tears to her eyes. Her mind swam in a pool of blackness.

◆◆◆

One thing Marcy knew for a fact, Sarah wanted to marry Braden. Why had she changed her mind at the last minute? Something didn't seem right about it. She dialed Sarah's home phone and didn't get an answer. Then she keyed in the number for Sarah's cell phone.

"Marcy, if you called to talk me into coming—don't."

Traffic sounds blared in the background.

"I didn't call for that."

"This isn't a good time. I don't feel well. I was just lying down for a nap."

"Before we disconnect," Marcy said, "sing the song we sang at the lodge. I was trying to remember how it went."

There was an extended pause.

"I'll call you back after my nap. Then I'll sing it for you."

"Sorry, I bothered you."

Resting my ass! Unless she's napping on the side of an interstate in rush hour.

Marcy disconnected immediately and dialed Braden's cell, but it was turned off. Then she remembered he'd disassembled it, so it couldn't be traced. She paced back and forth. Her phone rang. The number was unknown. Thinking it could be related, she answered it. "Hello."

"Marcy, it's Braden. Did Sarah's flight make it all right?"

"Braden, something is wrong." She explained what had taken place. "It sounded like Sarah, but then again it didn't."

"Call Darrel and have him track down her movement and see what tower her phone last pinged from. Call security at the airport and see if a Sarah Mason was on that flight?"

"I'm on it."

"I'll call you back. I can't leave until I speak with the supervisor and he finds a replacement for me."

Marcy disconnected, then called Darrel and explained what had happened.

In less than an hour, he phoned back with the information to pass on to Braden. "The T. S. A. verified Sarah was on the flight from Memphis to Kansas. I spoke with a traffic handler in the pick-up zone. She thought something was going on in a blue Toyota sedan. Before she could get to it, the driver pulled away. She managed to get a plate number."

"Have you run it yet?"

"Yes. Turned out to be a rental car from Budget near the airport."

"That's a dead-end. Have you spoken to the rental manager?"

"That was my next step. Manager said a white male rented it. The identification he used turned out to be stolen."

"Should you post someone there in case they bring the car back?"

"No. I guarantee they'll dump it," Darrel said. "What did you find on Sarah's phone?"

"The first two calls pinged off a tower in Kansas near the airport. The last location pinged off a tower near the old Desoto county military base. Then nothing. Selena must've ditched the phone."

"The only thing out there is an old hangar, a few boarded up buildings, and landing strip," he stated. "It hasn't been used in years. I'll take some deputies and check it out. Tell Braden, we'll find Sarah and bring her home. "

"Also, there's another possibility we've overlooked. If Braden's theory about Selena is correct and they're heading to Jersey, you guys might be dealing with Selena and Dagastino.

◆◆◆

Sarah woke and vivid images played in her mind of what had happened at the airport. She opened her eyes and discovered she was stretched out in the backseat of the car. She sat up and scanned her surroundings. The car appeared to be in an airport hangar. But this one looked as though it had seen better days.

Birds flew in and out of the broken windows at the top of the high walls. Their chirps and whistles echoed in the vast empty space.

Shivering, Sarah pulled her long coat over her legs. She glanced at the ignition. No key. Too bad. To escape, she would willingly plow down her abductors, even her sister.

Selena and the men stood in the wide doorway. Selena paced back and forth, bitching at Carlos. He hot-boxed a cigarette, puffing one draw after another while defending himself.

Sarah opened the door and pushed it a fraction, allowing her to hear what they said. Hopefully, they'd speak English.

"He's not coming," Selena shouted. "He should've been here an hour ago."

"He's coming. I talked to him this morning."

"Shit for brains, Wolfe is probably looking for us. Why don't you call him and give him directions?"

"And whose fault is that?"

"You should've ditched the phone at the airport," Reggie said.

"Stick to your computers," she snapped.

"Chill," Carlos said. "You're too hyped up."

Sarah thought about Braden. His job came *first*. He wouldn't be coming for her. He would stay with Michael, but she didn't see the need to tell them.

The sound of an airplane landing broke through her thoughts.

"He's here." Selena looked at Travis. "Get Sarah." She turned to Reggie and Carlos. "Load up. Let's get out of here."

Instead of following Selena's orders, Carlos waited until the small jet taxied into the hangar and the pilot climbed down.

Travis opened the car door and helped her out. "Watch your head."

She ducked then stood. She dipped her hands into the pocket of her coat. Still her fingers ached from the cold. Her thin gloves were no match for the frigid temperature. The wind whipped around her.

"It'll be warm on the plane," Travis said. "You go on over. I'll grab your bag."

Reggie carried several suitcases along with a computer bag. Blade toted long rifle bags to the plane.

Sarah stopped beside Selena and looked at the pilot. Did the pilot know about their plans to kill her? If she said something, they might kill him. She'd try to write a note and leave it in the plane asking him to report it.

"I'm Craig Miller."

Before Sarah could reply, Selena grabbed her arm. "Let's get on the plane. We might be having company soon. Your friend was suspicious. She called back wanting me to sing some stupid song."

Thank you, Marcy.

"Where are you taking me?" Sarah asked Selena.

"To a fucking ball, Cinderella. After tonight, your life won't be so charmed anymore. It'll be my turn to be princess."

While small, the jet held them all. Sarah sat in the plush leather seat by the window. Selena joined her. With her sister watching, she wouldn't be able to leave the pilot a note.

After a quick preflight check, the pilot started the engine and taxied out onto the runway.

Several sirens blared from nearby and grew louder.

They craned their necks to peer out the jet's windows.

Two large black SUVs headed toward them with their blue lights flashing.

"Get us up," Selena shouted to the pilot.

He revved the engine and started down the runway. The SUV followed and closed the distance. The plane sped up.

"Shit man, they're catching up with us," Carlos said.

"Not for long," shouted the pilot.

The jet lifted upward leaving the police cars behind.

Sarah's heart sank to her stomach. When the pilot took off without a gun aimed at his head, it meant he knew exactly what was going on. The creep.

◆◆◆

Braden joined Michael and Amy in a small eating area off the kitchen. "Selena has Sarah."

Michael's face paled. "Are you sure?"

Amy looked at Michael. "Who are Selena and Sarah?"

"Identical twins." He filled her in on the details.

Braden took over. "I think Selena is going to try passing Sarah off as herself. That'd mean they're taking Sarah to Dagastino. To pull that off, they might dump her corpse on his doorstep."

Amy's eyes widened with fear.

"Selena doesn't realize Uncle Leon has been indicted," Michael said.

"It's been on national news. That wouldn't change her plans since he's back home."

"If he agrees to meet her, there are two places where he conducts his business. He has a lake house in upper state New York and a warehouse on Johnson Street in Newark. What about the monitoring bracelet?"

"The tether allows him to move about the city. His travel is limited. So, that'd make the warehouse the better choice."

"Interstate 78 will take you right into Jersey."

Braden wanted to go after Sarah more than anything, but he hated breaking his promise to Michael. "I requested to leave. My replacement will be here soon."

"Go, Wolfe. We'll be fine," Michael insisted.

Braden pulled a chair closer to the couple and sat down. "Until I can leave, let's talk about what's going to happen next. Now that they have worked out the terms of your protection, two federal attorneys will review all the evidence you gathered. It'll be extensive questioning for a couple of days. But they have to have all their ducks in a row. They don't want your uncle's fleet of attorneys getting him off the hook."

While Michael was with the attorneys, and Amy took a nap, Braden walked around the outside perimeter of Camelot. In case someone had discovered the location, he had his Glock .40, a S&W.357 Magnum with hollow point bullets, a Beretta nine millimeter semi-automatic, and his favorite—a pump action shotgun he called The Terminator.

Though Darrel would do everything in his power to save Sarah, she needed *him*.

Back inside, he used a secure line to call Darrel. "Give me an update. Have you found Sarah?"

"Sorry, man. We just missed them. They were taking off when we arrived. They pulled out in a Falcon 10 SN 166. Identification number November-4057. Looked like an older model. Maybe early eighties."

"Any flight plan filed that match it?"

"Nope, the guy is flying under the radar."

"When they got airborne, which direction did it fly?"

"He banked a one-eighty and flew due east."

"That's what I figured. New Jersey is due east."

"At least she's heading your way. I'll book a flight now and call the marshal's office there."

"Explain to them this hasn't been confirmed. We're acting on a hunch," Braden instructed. "My replacement just arrived. I'm out of here as soon as say goodbye to Michael and Amy. I'll meet you at Newark Liberty. I'm not that far from the airport. I'll be expecting you on the next flight."

"Marcy threw out the possibility that once we get there, we could be dealing with Dagastino and Menendez."

"If that's the case, we'll get more than we bargained for. Let's hope we can stop Selena before she harms Sarah or tries to deliver her to Dagastino."

"Do you think he'd harm her?"

"Not if I give him what he wants."

"Shit. You're talking about Michael."

"This could go in that direction if Dagastino gets his hands on Sarah.

Braden left Camelot with regret. While driving, he considered Marcy's scenario. Then he thought of Sarah and his two children. He considered the possibility of being put in the position of having to choose between Sarah and Michael.

After placing his sim card back in his phone, he contacted the supervisor and requested Michael and Amy be transferred to a different location. If he didn't know their twenty, he wouldn't be able to sell Michael out. He'd never forgive himself if anything happened to Sarah or the twins, but at the same time, he wouldn't step across the blue line and screw Michael over.

The drive to Jersey took less than two hours. At the Newark Liberty International Airport, he flashed his badge and bypassed the security checkpoint. Then he walked to the terminal and sat, waiting for Darrel's flight to land.

Marcy needed to be kept in the loop, so he called and updated her on his and Darrel's plans. "Before I hang up, there's something I need you to do."

"Sure. Name it."

"See if you can find who owns a Falcon 10 SN 166 with the identification number November-4057. Also, call every Jersey airport and see if it's landed."

"Will do. I'm praying for Sarah."

"Me too."

◆◆◆

Sarah studied her sister's face.

Selena appeared tired and weary. When Sarah spoke to her, she wouldn't look her in the eye. She had to feel some remorse for what she planned to do.

"I wonder which of us is the oldest," Sarah said, trying to engage Selena in a conversation.

"Don't you know that tonight I'm going to screw you over and then send what's left of your body to Dagastino. After he thinks he's killed me, I'll walk away with your identity. So shut the fuck up. I don't want to talk to you."

Sarah stared out the window. Who was she kidding? d Selena didn't care about anyone but herself.

Carlos twisted in his seat and glanced back at Selena. "I told you I'd handle everything. I rented a warehouse down by the bay. You can hide out there while I set things up with Dagastino."

"What about the tattoo? She's got to have my tattoo."

"I got a tattoo guy who said he'd put the roses on her ass. He said cutting out her tongue wouldn't be a problem for an extra five thousand."

"He understands I don't want her dead?"

"Si. You can get Cinderella ready for the ball while I'm gone."

Sarah gasped for air.

I have to find a way out of this.

Her stomach rolled, making her nauseated.

Dear Holy Father, forgive me of my sins, please save me and my babies. Protect us. In the name of the Father, Son and the Holy Ghost.

She made the sign of the cross.

"But they'll still be able to tell us apart," Sarah said. "They'll know one of us isn't Sarah Mason when we both have roses on our ass."

"But he won't be looking at my ass, just yours."

"Selena, thinks of everything," Carlos added. "But this time, I made our plans." He looked at Selena. "Wait till you see this warehouse."

"How'd you find it?" Selena asked him, a distinct sharpness in her eyes that showed what an alert predator she was.

Carlos couldn't stop fidgeting. A nerve above his right eye twitched. "Just like I found the pilot—on Craig's list. I've rented a van also."

Selena didn't look completely convinced.

"You can find everything on the Internet," he added.

Her sister made eye contact with Reggie. He grinned. "He's right. People even try selling their kids."

The tension eased on Selena's face.

"Fasten your seat belts," Craig Miller, the rented pilot announced over the intercom. "We'll be landing in about twenty minutes."

Suspicion lingered in Selena's eyes. "You hired a pilot named Craig on Craig's List?"

"Yeah, So? He was the only one willing to wait and fly us back."

"And you've already paid him?"

"Si, he didn't trust me."

"Shit for brains, you never pay more than half. Then he gets the other half when the job is done."

"I trust the guy."

Selena rolled her eyes and shook her head, but didn't reply.

Sarah couldn't explain it, but the emotions Selena felt ran through her as if they were her own. Her sister sensed something was wrong, but being in mid-flight she was helpless to confront Carlos.

The landing gears lowered with a whining sound. Thinking back on the helicopter crash, a trace of fear rushed through Sarah for a split second. She looked out the window.

They landed on a private landing strip outside the city in a deserted area. In the distance, huge smoke stacks filled the sky with twirling black smoke. And as Carlos had promised, a white van had been parked nearby.

Once the plane stopped, Selena held a tight grip on her while the others exited. She motioned for Reggie to stay. "Google Craig Miller and see what comes up."

Reggie pulled out his phone and keyed the name in. "His name actually pops up a lot. Of course, Craig Miller's a common name."

"Are any of them our pilot?"

Reggie clicked on one. He turned his phone so she could see. "That's our guy."

"Is he really on Craig's List?"

"Yep, right here."

"Let's go. Don't mention this to the others."

"Wouldn't dare." He winked at her.

Outside at the van, Selena cornered Carlos. "Why is the pilot coming with us?"

"He can't wait out here alone."

"He's just going to leave his jet?" Selena asked. Craig Miller approached her. She drew her gun and aimed it at him. "Stop, right there."

"Hold up, sweetheart," Craig said. "If you don't feel comfortable with me going, I'll stay with my jet."

Selena studied him for a moment. "Carlos has already paid you. What's to keep you from leaving us stranded?"

"Better reason to keep me with you. No one will bother the jet. It's not that easy to tow away."

"Okay, you come with us. We'll need you to fly us to Memphis. I have some bank accounts to close out."

"No problem. But we'll need to refuel there."

Sarah didn't trust Craig Miller either. Something seemed off about him and so did a van left this far out for their use, but considering Selena's heinous plans, Sarah didn't plan to share her suspicions. Somewhere in the midst of whatever was about to happen, she hoped she could escape.

Chapter Twenty-two

Braden called Marcy. "Come up with any names?"

"The plane belongs to the Zentirtron Corporation out of Newark. I did a little more searching, and it turns out Dagastino owns the company."

"But why would Selena get on a plane with one of his men?"

"She obviously doesn't know. One of her men has sold her out."

"That would mean the pilot works for Dagastino. I know where they're taking her."

"You do? How?"

"Michael mentioned his uncle conducts his business, in a warehouse on Johnson Street. If he's orchestrated this, that's where they'll stash her."

"Actually, I found a warehouse across town owned by Zentirtron on Garfield. He just purchased it recently. Maybe Michael didn't know about it."

"I'm not sure. It's worth checking."

"Braden, be careful."

"I'll do whatever it takes to get Sarah out safely."

After ending the call, he waited for Darrel. His plane had landed and people exited the gate. Darrel came out, and Braden joined him. "Good flight?"

"Not really. Too much turbulence."

Braden told Darrel what Marcy had discovered. "Looks like Selena is caught in the web she weaved for Sarah."

"Couldn't happen to a nicer psychopath. Dagastino will have them both. With them being twins, it's sort of like a two-for-one sale."

Braden frowned. "Not amusing. Let's go."

"Sorry, man. "

In the parking lot, Darrel whistled at the decked out sparkling blue Chevy pickup. "Nice wheels. Where'd this come from?"

"It's on loan. It was confiscated from a drug bust." After fastening his seatbelt, he zipped out of the parking lot. "Where's the command post?"

"Where ever you want it. It's mobile. Where we going now?"

"To the U.S. Marshal's headquarters in Newark. FBI will want to be in on this. I want to make it clear that Sarah is a pregnant hostage and is not to be harmed in any way."

◆◆◆

Travis escorted Sarah from the van. She studied the outside of the warehouse. No distinct features separated it from the other industrial buildings in the area. Three loading docks stood on the front and another one on the side of the building. A tall chain link fence with barbed-wire around the top enclosed the grayish building. In the near distance, a train rumbled by.

Even if she managed to reach a phone, she wouldn't know how to explain her location. She hadn't been able to see any street signs. And the warehouse didn't have any numbers, but it did sit near a railroad track. Maybe that could narrow down the search.

Carlos climbed from the van and opened the wide garage doors, then Reggie drove inside and parked.

The vast warehouse had two sections. On one side, it was opened to the top. In back, rows of metal shelving filled a large section from floor to ceiling. Several forklifts had been parked to the side. The second half of the warehouse had offices and stairs leading up to other floors. Along the wall, two offices and a conference room were sectioned off and enclosed with glass across the front.

"It's cold as hell in this place," Selena complained.

"We can use the offices. They have heat," Carlos said. "All the rooms should be unlocked. Roberto, find the switch to turn the surveillance cameras on so we can watch for visitors."

Selena turned back to the others. "Reggie, go pick up some food. The rest of you can hang out in the end room." Then she looked back at Carlos and flashed him a seductive smile. "You and I have some business in the middle room." Selena opened a bottle of water and took a big swig. "First, lock her in an office."

"The tattoo guy should be here within the hour."

Selena screwed the cap on the bottle. "We'll bring her out when he arrives. Make sure there isn't a phone she can reach."

"No problem."

Inside the office, Sarah sat on the sofa.

Carlos looked at her. "Don't try to leave this room, or I'll gag you and tie your hands. Comprenda?"

She nodded.

"You have a busy night ahead of you so rest."

At first, Sarah considered different escape plans. Where could someone hide in this building? There had been several hallways branching out. Surely one of them led to an exit. She remembered the tall metal racks. If she climbed to the top would they be able to see her? The silly notion faded from her mind.

In the office beside her, Sarah listened to Selena and Carlos. Her sister didn't hold back with the profanity in the heat of passion.

This was Sarah's chance. She figured the others were in the conference room, and Reggie had gone for food.

Marcy and Darrel will have no way of knowing where they took me. I've got to do this on my own.

She stood up and tiptoed to the desk. Ever so slowly she pulled each drawer out, looking for a telephone or something she could use as a weapon.

Nothing. Zilch. Unless she could shoot her way out with paperclips and note pads. Death by sticky note.

Before venturing into the warehouse, Sarah opened a door inside the office. It turned out to be an empty closet. The second door she opened squeaked, and Sarah held her breath. The heavy bumping against the wall coming from the next room drowned out the noise.

This room contained a toilet and sink. Trying to be quiet, she removed her shoes, then crossed the room and opened the main door. She looked both ways. Not seeing anyone, she ran through the vast space. The cold pavement stung her feet. Her heart pounded in her ears as she ran. She turned down a hall and tried several doors. All were locked. She followed the maze around another corner and spotted her salvation. A door that led *outside.*

Heavy footfalls could be heard, but Sarah couldn't tell where they were coming from?

She walked with urgency toward the door. She placed her fingers around the doorknob.

Just as it started to turn, a strong hand gripped her shoulder and pulled her back.

Her fingers slipped off the doorknob.

One of the shoes she held dropped to the concrete.

"Let me go," Sarah said as she turned to hit the person. She gasped when she realized it was Craig Miller, who had a hand on her. It didn't stop her from slamming the heel of her other shoe against his head.

He snatched it from her, then pressed her against the wall. "Lady, you're not going anywhere."

Something occurred to her. He had the same accent as the man who'd pretended to be a marshal, the one sent by Dagastino.

"You work for Dagastino?"

"Why haven't you told your sister?"

"With what she plans to do to me, why would I tell her? After he has Selena, will he let me go?"

"You're the prize. Selena's just a bonus. Now slip your shoes on. I'll walk you back."

Sarah didn't understand. Why would the mob boss want her? It was Selena he was after. "I can pay you a large amount of money."

"Really? How much?"

"Five hundred thousand. Get me out without a rose tattooed on my ass and my tongue still in place and it's yours."

"Tempting, but I have other plans."

"I might be able to cash in some stocks and get you another hundred thousand."

"Sounds good, but I won't betray the boss."

"I'll tell Selena you're in cahoots with Dagastino."

"Just to be on the safe side, I think I'll gag you."

"She'll kill you." Then it dawned on Sarah why Dagastino wanted her.

God, no.

◆◆◆

In the briefing room of the Newark Police Station, Braden had to play nice with the other cops if he wanted to save Sarah's life. They all had their own idea of how to get her back. But he would have the final say or at least he hoped so. And as usual the FBI thought their plan was the best. But this wasn't going to be a FBI show.

"Finally found a judge who'd sign the warrant," FBI Special Agent Proctor stated.

A New Jersey marshal added, "We'll take that warehouse apart if we have to. Our mobile command post can set up on Hermon or Pennington."

"Vesey's better," quirked the FBI agent. "Watch it from the rear."

"Do they intersect Garfield?" Braden asked.

"Shit. Garfield. Hell, that's over on the other side of town," stated the older, gray haired NPD Captain. He was a large man who looked like he'd never missed a doughnut break and spoke with a thick Jersey accent.

"My information came from a reliable source."

The captain looked at a list of properties belonging to Dagastino. "Doesn't show him owning a damn thing on Garfield."

"It wouldn't be listed," Braden stated. "It's owned by Zentirtron. Dagastino is the prime share holder."

FBI Agent Proctor looked disheartened. "Shit. That judge was hell to reach. He'll be pissed when I tell him we targeted the wrong place."

Braden folded his arms. "Go ahead with the raid."

"You fuckin' serious?" the Jersey marshal, Deputy Spence said. "Why waste time?"

"I want Dagastino to feel safe. Send enough cars to make it look like you're casing the place. The rest of us will focus on Garfield. Anyone know the area?"

"I know it." NPD Metro Captain pointed to the map on the table. "It's near the bay. Take the turnpike and get off at exit fourteen."

FBI Agent Proctor joined in. "We'll have an unmarked vehicle cruise by the place. See if there's any movement."

The agent came across as cocky and arrogant, but right now Braden needed all the help he could get.

"The mobile unit can set up on Ocean View," Marshal Spence said. "We should be able to monitor activity from there."

"No. Keep it near the warehouse on Johnson." Braden frowned. "I don't want them to panic and kill Sarah. Because if you're spotted, they might feel boxed in."

"We stay on wise guys all the time," Agent Proctor mentioned. "They never make us. We're like flies on the wall."

Braden doubted it, but didn't want to insult any of these local guys.

The NPD Metro Captain folded his arms and grinned. "You know what every dumbass wise guy says that's brought in?"

The special agent and the deputies waited for his answer.

"They say, we know the Feds have been watching us." The captain looked at Agent Proctor and smirked. "So you're not as invisible as you think."

The men started arguing, slinging insults and cursing at each other.

Their accents ground on Braden's nerves. He glanced at Darrel who was grinning.

Braden lifted a paper weight and banged it on the desk. "I'm going in alone. Once I have Sarah out safely, I'll give the green light, and you can do whatever you want to the others."

"Definitely out of the question. It's too risky," Agent Proctor said. "We'll bring in a hostage negotiator."

"I can have our swat team on standby," said the NPD Metro Captain. "Toss in some flash bangs or gas."

"I don't want any of that crap used until Sarah's out," Braden stated. "Dagastino wants me. So if you bring in a negotiator, he'll insist he only speaks with me. As far as a swat team, I think Sarah would end up dead. You see there's a slight problem. Selena and Sarah are identical."

"Can you give him what he wants?" Deputy Spence asked.

"No, but I don't plan to wait around and chat with him." He explained about Michael. "He wants me to give him the twenty on his nephew. I won't sell the kid out. I'll sneak in the back door, grab Sarah, and leave."

"This is some deep shit," the police captain stated.

"Clash of the Titans," Agent Proctor said. "Dagastino against Menendez. Seems like one of her men has pulled a double bang on her."

"Go in on Johnson Street with the warrant," Braden stated. "At the same time, I'll go in on Garfield. Dagastino won't be expecting it. Is there a way you can pull blueprints on the Garfield warehouse?"

"Getting them now," the NPD Captain said and left the briefing room.

"We'll have some choppers on standby in case anyone jets out of there and tries to escape," Agent Proctor said.

The captain returned shortly with the needed blueprints. "Got an aerial view of it and the building's blueprints."

"Thanks." Braden leaned over the building plans, studying the layout of the warehouse. He needed to pinpoint the best place to enter. He studied the aerial view to see where to cut through the fence. "I'll cut through the wire in this corner because it'll be easier to find if I'm leaving in a hurry. There's a door here. From what I can tell, there are two floors. The bottom floor is divided into two sections—warehouses and offices." He straightened up. "One more thing, don't leak any of this to the media. I don't want cameras flashing when I squeeze my ass through that fence. It'd ruin the element of surprise."

The others laughed.

♦♦♦

Miller escorted Sarah to the office where she'd been earlier. He duct-taped her mouth and tied her hands and feet, then bound her with rope to a straight back chair. "Front row seat. You'll get to see all the action."

She couldn't move. All she could do was stare out the glass into the warehouse. If he hadn't caught her, she'd have escaped. Now, she couldn't imagine how she'd get out of this. More than likely, she wouldn't. It was her babies that concerned her most.

He tapped on the glass. "Bulletproof. Dagastino had it installed in all the rooms. He never knows when a drug deal will go south."

After he left, Selena joined her. "You didn't get very far. I owe Miller one."

She slapped Sarah a few times for trying to leave. "Since you went and got your mouth taped up, you won't be able to eat. Consider it your punishment for trying to bail."

Knowing Sarah couldn't go anywhere, they left the office door open and went to eat. Breathing in the aroma of the Asian food created hunger pangs in her stomach that wouldn't let up.

She had more important things to think about instead of food—like how to free her hands and feet.

♦♦♦

Sarah's hands and arms ached from being tied. None of her attempts over the past hour to wriggle out of the restraints had worked.

The acoustics magnified any noises or words spoken in the empty space. She listened intently.

"Van's here," Roberto shouted. "Let him in."

"It's the tattoo dude. Get Cinderella," Carlos said.

Selena glanced her way, then looked back at him. "Wait until Travis and Roberto bring in the work table from the warehouse. Tell him to do the tattoo first. She might not be in any condition after her tongue's been yanked out."

A white van rolled inside. The side panels advertised tattoos and body piercings.

Sarah's appetite disappeared at the realization that she was going to have her tongue cut off to appease Selena's fear of her talking to Dagastino.

The man who stepped from the van had body art up his arms and neck. Not just black ink, but red, yellow, and blue as well. He was balding with piercings on his lips and ears. He made Blade look like a Boy Scout.

Sarah hated tattoos. But the tattoo was the least of her worries. This same man was willing to cut her tongue out. She doubted she'd survive such an ordeal.

Travis pulled a water hose over to the steel table set up in the warehouse.

Sarah didn't like feeling this helpless. She blamed herself for being in this predicament. Braden had warned her about Selena. Had she really believed they could have any type of relationship?

Hopefully, the tattoo would come first, so she could use the time trying to talk Selena out of it. If she could convince Selena that Dagastino would never fall for this scam, she might have a chance.

The tattoo artist set a case on the table opposite of Selena and opened it.

Next, he whipped out a huge assault rifle.

Men jumped out of the van. Miller joined them.

Bullets sprayed the room.

Sarah's breath caught.

Travis crumpled to the floor.

Several bullets pounded the office wall.

Sarah's heart sank to her stomach.

Tied to the chair, she could only watch the scene unfold and pray. She prayed for Selena. Then she prayed for herself and her unborn children to make it out safely.

Bullets pinged the glass in front of her, but the glass didn't shatter.

Miller had told the truth. Thank, God.

None of it seemed real—more like she was watching a shootout on some television crime show.

Selena and Roberto squatted low and shielded their heads.

Blade ran out from the conference room. He sprayed a line of bullets at the men, taking down two.

Dagastino's men opened fire, and Blade's body jerked as it toppled over.

Sarah gasped and closed her eyes for a second.

Roberto drew his gun and fired off a round.

The next pop hit Roberto's forehead. He dropped to his knees and fell over, face first.

Sarah's breath froze in her lungs.

Her heart had never pounded so hard.

Selena grabbed Roberto's gun, but before she could load it, Craig Miller pointed a gun at her head. "Drop it, Selena."

Reggie stepped from the conference room with his hands up. "Don't shoot. I have valuable skills."

"You fuckin' shitheads." Selena handed the automatic over, then stood. Her gaze landed on Carlos. "You bastard. You sold me out, you piece of shit."

"Si, I was tired of you calling me shit for brains and treating me like I have no feelings. Dagastino respects me."

Their voices echoed, letting Sarah hear everything.

A man stepped through the office door. "Sarah."

A degree of disbelief came over her. Marshal Conner. She remembered him.

"You'll be okay." After untying her from the chair, he freed her feet so she could walk, leaving her hands bound.

"This is goin' to hurt." He yanked the duct tape from her mouth.

She flinched from the pain.

"Dagastino wants to meet you."

Sarah walked into the warehouse, stepping around Roberto's body and the puddle of deep red blood that had seeped from his head.

The garage door opened and a white limo drove into the warehouse. A dignified, handsome, older man stepped from the car. He studied the bodies lying on the cement. He looked at Reggie. "Why isn't this one dead?"

Craig Miller walked over to Dagastino. "He can hack into any computer. He's a whiz-kid."

Dagastino smiled. "How long did you work for the ice queen?"

"Six months."

"You have any loyalty to her?"

"No, sir. She treats us like dogs. I'd already been putting out feelers looking for a new gig. I'm tired of working for the bitch."

"Crime is turning toward the Internet. Number one target—the IRS. I can use a kid like you."

Reggie grinned. "I can hack any system or penetrate any firewall. No one can keep me out."

"We'll work out an agreement later."

Finally, Dagastino turned his attention to Carlos. "You pulled it off. I had my doubts."

"Si. I brought you both women as you requested," Carlos said "So you see I'll serve you well working with your South American connections. I have people in Argentina and Brazil who can be trusted."

"If you turned on Selena, then you'll turn on me if a better deal comes along for you. I don't work with fucking gangbangers."

"If I don't have a place with your organization, I'll take my money and leave for Argentina tonight."

"The only way you'll be going back is in a body bag." Dagastino nodded at the tattooed man. "Take care of him."

Sarah turned her head. Three loud pops rang out. She didn't understand people like this, people who thrive on greed and power. She knew Dagastino would kill her if he didn't get what he wanted—Michael.

She turned around in time to see Selena spit on Carlos's body.

Dagastino crossed over to Selena. While two men held her, he punched her in the stomach. Selena groaned. Then he backhanded her. Blood oozed from her nose.

"Stop it!" Sarah shouted.

"I'm just getting started." He grinned at Selena. "I've dreamed of this moment. I think of what you did to Frankie. I assure you, you'll be begging to die and go to hell before I'm done with you. I plan to torture you until there's nothing left, then I'll fucking cut out your damn heart." He glanced at one of his men. "Put the flex cuffs on her."

Chase escorted Sarah closer to Dagastino. "This is Sarah Mason."

The mob boss lowered his gaze to her stomach. "You're expecting Deputy U S. Marshal Braden Wolfe's child. True?"

She wouldn't answer. He'd said child, so apparently he didn't know about the twins.

"So, I'm right."

"Don't get your hopes up," she said. "He's not thrilled about the baby."

"He wanted her to get a fucking abortion," Selena shouted.

"Gag her."

"What Selena says is true. I doubt he'd lose much sleep if something happens to me," she lied.

"We'll get back to Wolfe in a minute. I'm curious. Are you fully aware of what your sister had planned for you?"

Sarah nodded. "I can't explain it, but I care about her. I don't believe she'd really would've gone through with it."

"Trust me. She would've and not missed a moment of sleep."

Sarah glanced at Selena. Her sister's face softened for a moment. Her eyes appeared regretful.

"Selena only cries crocodile tears," Dagastino said. "If she cried real tears, they'd be for herself not you. She is without remorse."

"And I suppose you're remorseful?" Sarah boldly asked.

"Yes, you see it will trouble me deeply if I have to kill you and your unborn child."

"Braden Wolfe will not come for me."

"He's already in town. My informant told me he's setting up a task force to get you back. The fucking idiots have a stakeout near my Johnson Street warehouse miles from here." He grinned. "When they arrive with their warrant, they'll only find a night crew working. I'm sending you to a cabin I have. Then I'll contact Wolfe to come alone to my office if he wants you to live."

Craig Miller joined them. "Where do you want Selena?"

Dagastino's brow dropped in a moment of thought. "I need to settle this thing with Wolfe and deal with Michael before I have my fun with Selena. For now, bind her feet and put her in one of these rooms."

"The boys have dinner ready," Chase commented. "Do they eat?"

"Sarah does but not Selena. Since she loves her sister so much put them in a room together after Sarah eats."

"Cuffs?" he asked.

"I don't see the need."

Craig Miller frowned. "Sarah tried to escape earlier. She managed to find the back door. I think she needs restraints."

Dagastino smiled at Sarah. "If I thought I was going to have my tongue cut out, I'd try to escape too. She has nothing to fear from me, so long as Deputy Wolfe cooperates." His gaze dropped to her stomach. "No restraints. Post Lenny by the door. I'll be upstairs in my office. Take shifts watching her."

Craig didn't look pleased.

"I'll send Wolfe a message after we get her moved. Once I take that ass-wipe of a nephew for a ride, I'll be able to beat the rap."

"Braden will not give you what you want," Sarah said.

"They all sing if the price is high enough."

Chapter Twenty-three

Sarah forced herself to eat the cheesesteak sandwich and fries. The smell of onions and peppers made her nauseated. She tore off a portion of the sandwich and wrapped it in her napkin, then slipped it in her coat pocket while no one was looking.

She studied the small room off the same hallway she'd been down earlier. She looked for any type of utensil she could use as a weapon, but there wasn't anything but a plastic spoon.

Drop your weapons or I'll spoon you to death.

Though her situation was grim, she smiled wryly.

"I asked if I could accompany you to the lake house. Dagastino agreed to let me go," Chase said. "I don't trust the others."

"And if Braden doesn't give him what he wants, will you be the one to kill me?"

Chase didn't respond. "You done eating?"

"Yes." She stood and followed him to the little office where she'd been before.

Selena sat tied in the chair with her hands and feet bound.

If Sarah had the opportunity again, she'd escape. Now she had a better understanding of the warehouse and where to go. She hated leaving Selena, but she wouldn't have time to free her. It's not like she owed Selena anything.

Sarah settled on the sofa.

Chase returned with a pillow and a small blanket. "Sarah, I thought you could use these."

"Thank you. It's chilly in here."

He pinned a harsh look on her. "Dagastino is being nice by not cuffing you. There will be a guard out front all night. If you try to run, you'll be bound from head to toe in chains. Am I clear?"

Sarah nodded. "I won't. Thanks, Chase."

After he left, Selena grinned. "He clearly likes you. When did you two become friends?"

Sarah told her about him pretending to be Marshal Conner and visiting her house to get information.

She went in the bathroom, wet a paper towel, then returned to the office. She blotted the damp towel over Selena's face, wiping the dried blood from it.

"My lip hurts."

"Think you can eat?" Sarah removed the sandwich.

"I don't feel like eating."

"You need to keep your strength up." Sarah tore it into smaller pieces and fed her sister.

"You know I hate you. I despise everything about you, you know. Why be nice to me?"

"Like I told Dagastino, I care about you. I feel a link with you I can't explain. And I think you've felt it before. Be honest."

Selena shrugged. "It's your fuckin' imagination."

"Are you cold? I can wrap the blanket around you."

"No, you fuckin' bitch. Leave me the hell alone."

"Now you're becoming defensive."

"So."

"It proves you do feel the connection between us." Sarah placed the pillow on the sofa and stretched out, then tossed the blanket over her since her sister hadn't wanted to use it. "This sofa hurts my back."

"All you do is whine and complain. At least you get to lie down. If you hadn't gotten yourself knocked up, your back wouldn't be hurting."

Sarah huffed. "Like you've never been knocked up."

"Many times. But I always took care of it."

Sarah changed the subject. "I haven't had a chance to tell you this, but Wolfe found our father's family."

"For real? Was it that Jenkins man?"

"Yes, and he loved our mom. But before he could marry her, he was killed in a military skirmish. He received the Purple Heart and had a military funeral. I wonder how different our lives would've been if he had married her?"

"My life couldn't have been any worse. Life for me has always been one major fuckup. I thought I'd be on an airplane to Europe tonight. A new life as Sarah Mason. But the devil pulled a fast one."

"I forgive you, Selena, because I know you were just desperate."

"Dagastino's right. You're an idiot."

Lenny slumped in a chair just outside the door. She considered sneaking up behind him and strangling him. Now she was starting to think like Selena.

"Pretend you're asleep, Sarah."

"Why?"

"He'll get sloppy on the job. Then we can escape."

"I wasn't planning on taking you with me. You've convinced me that you hate me, so why would I waste valuable time trying to free you?"

"If we get out of here, I'll surrender to Wolfe. I'd rather die by lethal injection than what Dagastino has planned."

"I don't trust you. I think you'd kill me and switch our clothes out to make him think I killed you, then you'd escape."

"That wouldn't work. You never got the rose tattooed on your ass."

Several times Lenny glanced back at them.

Sarah decided she'd try to take Selena if she could free her hands and feet. Could the plastic restraints around Selena's wrists and ankles be removed easily?

Someone walked up to Lenny, and Sarah closed her eyes, then feigned sleeping.

"Hey man, too bad you're stuck here. We're about to start a poker game."

"They're asleep. I can check on them between hands."

"You'll just be a couple of doors down."

"Sure, let's go," Lenny said, anxious to give up his assigned duty.

Sarah waited until the two men walked away. She first untied the ropes that bound Selena to the chair. "What now? How do we get these restraints off?"

"We need a needle or something that will reach the pin control."

Sarah reached in the desk, pulled out a paperclip, and straightened it. "I hope this works."

"Get my ankles first. See the little yellow box."

"Yes."

"Slide the paperclip down the side. If you can trigger the pin, I can slide the strap out."

"I've got this. It isn't brain surgery." Sarah poked the clip several times while glancing over her shoulder like a nervous deer. The clip broke. "Crap."

"We need a needle."

Sarah glanced back to see if anyone was coming. Lenny would be returning soon to check on them. She tried another paperclip. This one sprang the locking mechanism and loosened the strap.

"I can walk. Now do my wrists."

A door closed nearby. Footfalls came toward the office.

Sarah made it back to the sofa and closed her eyes.

She assumed it was Lenny. Once she heard the door down from them open and close, she jumped up and started working on the flex cuffs. "Hold still."

"Don't stick me."

"Talk about me whining."

"Just get my hands free."

Sarah slid the paperclip down and poked around for the locking mechanism. After several attempts, she found it.

Selena slid it off her hands. "Let's go."

"Shh! Remember, the least little sound is ten times louder."

Stepping into the main warehouse, they didn't see anyone. Only a few dim lights lit the area. The white limo remained parked where it had been. Down the hall, light shined from the conference room, and the men's voices sounded muffled as though they were trying to be quiet.

Sarah followed Selena as they inched from the room.

"Stay behind me," Selena ordered.

Not a problem.

"There has to be a way out of here besides through the end loading doors. That'd make enough noise to wake the dead," Selena whispered.

"I found one earlier. There's a hallway up ahead. You go down it, then make a right. There's an exit door not far."

"What stopped you from leaving?"

"Craig Miller. That's why he taped my mouth. He thought I might rat him out." But at the time, Sarah hadn't planned on tipping her sister off. Not with Selena's party plans for her.

Selena grabbed an empty whiskey bottle from a counter. Large enough to crack someone's skull, which is what Sarah thought her sister had in mind.

As they turned into a passageway branching off the main room, the power in the building shut down with a thud. Total blackness engulfed them.

"The poker game is over. They'll be looking for us." Selena said. "Let's find that door."

"Who cut the power?"

"Who gives a shit? Let's go."

Sarah nodded. It took a moment for her eyes to adjust. "This way."

They turned the corner, and someone grabbed Selena's wrist, squeezing until she dropped the bottle.

"Son-of-a-bitch," whispered a man. "The damn thing hit my toe."

Sarah recognized the voice immediately. "Braden?"

"Sarah." He pulled her into his arms and hugged her against him. "God, I was so afraid for you." He kissed her forehead and her cheeks before moving his lips over hers.

"Enough of that shit," Selena ordered softly. "Let's get the fuck out of here. Hell, Sarah. The man acts like he loves you." She extended her hand. "Wolfe, give me a gun."

"Think I'm crazy?"

"You want to make it out with Sarah?"

"Yeah, but you're still not getting a gun. Now move it."

"They'll kill you, Wolfe."

"So long as Sarah makes it out."

He handed a small .38 to Sarah. "Don't let her take it from you."

Sarah nodded. "I won't."

"Remember how to use it?"

"I can do it."

"If she tries anything, shoot her. If you don't have the stomach for it, at least shoot her in the damn leg."

"I will."

"I doubt it." Selena laughed softly. "Wolfe, how'd you get in here?"

"We disarmed the alarm system through their security contractor and the FBI shut off the power. Then it was a matter of picking a lock. They have generators. The lights will be back on soon."

A loud sound made Sarah jumped, but she recovered quickly when she realized it was noise in the venting pipes.

"Generators are working," Selena warned.

A row of dim lights came on as well.

The shouts and footfalls of Dagastino's men could be heard.

From a side door, a man stepped out with his gun aimed at them, but Braden fired first. Even with the silencer, a small pop rang out.

Sarah's breath left her for a moment.

Braden opened the back exit door and stepped out first before motioning for them to follow. He remained against the building beneath a fire escape. There was only one dim light over the door they had exited. Beyond that the area remained dark. He pulled out a small radio. "This is sixty-two, do you copy?"

"I copy, Wolfe."

"I have the women. Move in. Over."

"Copy that. We're ready to clean house."

Braden slipped the radio in his pocket. "We have to make a run for the left corner. I clipped a hole in the fence. If

I don't make it, run down the hill toward the river. Help will be waiting."

They started across the open space between the building and fence, but bullets plowed a path in the grass in front of them. They stopped short.

"Drop your gun, Wolfe! "

Braden glanced up. The silhouette of a man stood at the top of the fire escape with a semiautomatic rifle aimed toward them. "While I distract him make a run for the fence. Now!"

"But they'll kill you," Sarah argued.

"You have our kids to think of. Now go."

Selena grabbed Sarah's arm and jerked her toward the fence. Before they could run, Dagastino and his men exited the same door they had just come through. "Stop right there."

Standing side by side, Selena and Sarah froze and faced the mob boss.

Dagastino stood with two of his thugs. "Drop your gun, marshal or your lady dies."

His men aimed their weapons on Sarah and Selena.

Chase had his gun on Braden. Craig Miller climbed down the fire escape and joined the others.

Braden dropped the gun and raised his hands.

"Now toss your other guns over."

Braden pulled one from inside his jacket and a small one from his boot and slid them over.

Selena whispered to Sarah, "Give me the gun."

Sarah hesitated for a moment, then inched closer to Selena. Sarah had to *trust* her sister. The gun would do more good in Selena's hands than her own. While everyone's attention was on Braden, Sarah slipped her sister the .38.

"Marshal Braden Wolfe. Your visit is a real surprise. I was just informed your task team served a warrant on my Johnson Street warehouse. So how'd you know about this place?"

Braden didn't answer.

"You're one cocky asshole to think you can come in here alone. I hadn't expected you to be so heroic. Sarah must mean a great deal to you. I understand the child she carries is yours."

"Braden, don't do anything stupid," Sarah begged.

"Listen to her. Tell me what I want to know, and I'll gladly let you both go once I've got my hands on that worthless piece of shit nephew of mine."

"I don't know where he is," Braden said. "As soon as I left the safe house, they relocated him."

"I don't believe you. Which is more important? Honor? Or Sarah and your child? Is the life of my nephew worth more?" Dagastino stepped up to Braden. "You realize I'll find Michael before the trial. Why put off the inevitable?"

"You'll be making a deal with the devil, Wolfe, "Selena shouted. "He'll never let you and Sarah leave alive. He'll pay you off with a bullet in the forehead just like he did Carlos."

"Your answer, Marshal Wolfe."

"I can't tell what I don't know."

A helicopter flew over spotlighting the area.

Dagastino frowned. "Seems I need to speed this up. I'm going to count to five. If you don't tell me, Lenny here is going to shoot Sarah."

"Braden," Sarah whimpered.

"One, two, three, four, five."

"Shoot her," Dagastino ordered.

Oh God.

Selena darted in front of Sarah. Two bullets hit Selena. At the same time, she fired off five quick shots at Dagastino.

Sarah screamed.

The mob boss grimaced, then fell backwards and hit the ground.

Braden grabbed the gun Selena dropped and fired on Craig Miller, taking him out.

Selena.

Sarah tried to hold her sister up, but couldn't. "Hang on, Selena."

"Drop your weapons and put your hands over your head," a loud voice ordered over a megaphone. When the helicopter landed, officers jumped out and ducked beneath the twirling blades. They ran with rifles aimed.

Dagastino's men fired on the officers. The darkness lit up with gun fire.

The smell of gun powder filled the air.

Braden pulled Sarah from her sister, forced her to the ground, and shielded her with his own body.

When the gunfire stopped, Braden helped her up. She glanced at Selena and swallowed back the tears. Then she stared at the bodies of Dagastino's men. Chase and Lenny lay dead. She regretted Chase hadn't surrendered. There had been something different about him. He still had a shred of conscience the others lacked.

"We need a bus!" Braden shouted.

Sarah gathered Selena in her arms. Blood oozed from two holes in her chest, soaking her shirt. Her sister's breath was shallow. Selena gasped for air.

"Selena, I love you."

"I don't deserve it."

"You saved me and the twins."

"Because I'm fuckin' loco."

"Hang on, an ambulance is coming."

"Name the girl after me."

"You want me to name her Selena?"

Selena's voice was a whisper. "No, Marie."

Her sister grimaced and closed her eyes. Then her head dropped to the side. In death, Selena's harsh lines softened, making her look at peace.

Sarah made the sign of the cross on Selena's forehead and prayed that God would have mercy on her soul. She looked up at Braden, who had joined her. "I want to give her a funeral. Even if it's just a graveside service."

"I'll make the arrangements for her body to be returned to Kansas." Braden pulled Sarah up and held her in his arms. "Are you all right?"

She couldn't answer. Instead she clung to him and cried. Her sister had sacrificed her own life to save her. Why the change of heart?

Oddly enough, Sarah felt like a part of her had died. She finally composed herself and lifted her head from Braden's shoulder. When she wiped her eyes, she realized Darrel had joined them along with other law enforcement officers. More officers and deputies came from the front and had rounded up the thugs inside, including Reggie.

"Satan is a happy old fart," Darrel said. "He reaped Dagastino and Selena's souls in one evening."

Sarah didn't find it humorous and scowled. "I loved her."

"Apparently, she felt something for you." Braden offered his hand. "Let's go home, Sarah."

◆◆◆

Sarah stared at her baby bubble in the mirror. If it hadn't been for Selena, she and the twins would've died. They buried her sister two days after Christmas in a small Kansas cemetery. For a moment, her reflection reminded her of Selena—the dark side of the mirror.

A knock on the door brought her out of the trance. She turned around as Braden entered the bedroom. "Braden. When'd you get here?"

"Just now. Marcy said it'd be okay to come back."

"I'm ready. Let's join the others."

"Wait, there's something I want to say. You may want to sit down."

She sat on the edge of the bed. "I thought you had to return to Michael and Amy. What happened?"

"Since Dagastino and all of his closest men died, the hit-man who has the contract on Michael knows he won't be paid the balance owed him. He'll go after another mark. Long story short, Michael and Amy dropped out of the program. There's no need for him to testify. The recordings in Dagastino's own voice will get several judges off the bench, some police officers fired, and a couple of politicians will be sweating. But none of them will be able to connect the evidence to Michael, because it never came out who our witness was."

"Will Amy and Michael be safe?"

"I think so. After they get married, they're moving to Vermont to be close to one of her sisters. It's a small town where a stranger stands out and neighbors watch out for one another."

"I'd like to write him. Maybe send a wedding—"

Braden interrupted. "Don't say anything else. I have something to say."

"Okay. You've got my full attention."

"I'm gonna try not to screw this up." He paused a moment. "I've been a number one asshole. I don't deserve you. But I don't want you to return to Memphis. I want you here. I want you in my life every day. I love you, and I do love our twins. I want to be more than just a part of their birth." He dropped on one knee and pulled a ring box from his jacket pocket. He flipped it open revealing a gorgeous ring. "Sarah, please do me the honor of marrying me."

"You started off a little rough around the edges, but you've made up for it. Since I'm helplessly in love with you, I have no choice but to say yes."

He removed the ring and slid it over her finger. "Can we get married tomorrow?"

"Can you find a church that fast?"

"Marcy never canceled the chapel. We're all set. I've taken a week off, so I thought we could fly somewhere warm like Aruba for a honeymoon."

Sarah stood placing her hands over her stomach. "I'm huge." She walked in front of the full length mirror. "Do you know what I'll look like in a swimsuit?"

He joined her and smiled at her reflection. "Beautiful."

"Environmentalist will be trying to return me to the ocean."

"Angel, you have no idea how absolutely sexy you look." He placed his arms around her, then kissed the side of her face. "Don't argue. You're my fugitive. You're on my most wanted list."

Sarah smiled. "And if I resist arrest?"

He winked. "I still have the cuffs and chains."

"You might want to take them to Aruba in case I make an attempt to escape."

"You just try it, lady. You're my catch of the day. " Braden took her in his arms and kissed her deeply.

Epilogue

Braden arrived at the Easter egg hunt at Marcy's house. Sarah and his two toddlers were already there. He gave her a quick kiss. "Sorry, I'm late. Have I missed the hunt?"

Sarah hugged him. "You're just in time."

Braden took the coffee Alex offered. "Thanks. It's chilly out here."

He angled the lawn chair in the sun and zoned in on his two year old toddlers scouting for colored eggs. It didn't seem to bother them that it was cold.

Marcy's little girl kept handing the eggs to Marcy instead of putting them in her basket.

"No, Emily," Marcy instructed. "Put it in the basket."

The Easter egg hunt brought back memories of Andy.

Look, Daddy, I found the prize egg.

That makes you the egg king. You get to rule over all the bunnies.

Andy giggled. No, I'm not. You're playin' with me.

Yeah, I am.

I love you, Daddy.

I love you too.

Braden no longer felt the hate and bitterness. Instead, the memory warmed his heart.

"Grandma Jenkins sent them each a big toy bunny. Your mother sent two crazy looking ducks and a bunch of candy," Sarah told him.

"We'll help them with the candy."

Samantha and Simon wobbled through the yard, picking up Easter eggs. Every time Simon looked away, Sam snatched one of his eggs and placed it with in her basket.

Next, she placed her hand on Simon's blue egg. His son finally wised up and caught her. Simon tried to take his egg back, but his unruly daughter knocked her twin brother down into the spring grass. Simon's face puckered, and he wailed loudly.

"Samantha, give Simon back his eggs right now," Sarah demanded.

Instead of doing as she was told, his mischievous daughter shook her head and ran as fast as her chubby legs would go across the yard. Her black curls jiggled as she ran. She plowed down Marcy's little girl who started crying. Alex lifted his daughter and consoled her before passing her to Marcy.

Braden shook his head and stood. Though he thought it often, he'd never outright admitted to anyone, he feared his daughter possessed Selena's defective genes. It was bad enough she was her namesake. He'd felt a little better after the twins were christened in the church, but it still hadn't tamed his daughter. Simon on the other hand behaved like an angel.

"Samantha Marie Wolfe, you better do what your mother told you to do," Braden ordered.

Brittany and Erica laughed at the sight of Sam running from him.

"Run, Sam," Erica shouted. "He's right behind you."

When Braden caught up with her, he snatched her Easter basket and whisked her up into his arms. She smelled sweet like marshmallow bunnies and jelly beans.

She kicked and screamed all the way to the deck where he sat on the steps and placed her in his lap. Her forehead lowered in a frown, her bottom lip puckered out.

"Sweetheart, you can't take your brother's eggs. That's not nice. You hurt him and made him cry. And he loves you so much. Daddy wants you to give him back his eggs, and I'll help you find some more."

She pouted a few more minutes, then climbed down the steps and held her hand out. She took the basket of eggs and toddled over to Simon.

She returned the stolen eggs to her brother. Next, she did the unexpected. She dropped her basket and wrapped her arms around Simon and planted a big wet kiss on his cheek. "Wuv you, Simon."

Everyone *ahhhed and ooohed* over it.

"They are so cute," Brittany said. "I wish Mom had had twins."

"Bite your tongue," Marcy said.

Braden crossed the yard and joined Sarah. "That's our girl. She's got an acute case of the terrible twos."

Sarah laughed. "If it will put your mind at ease, my mom told me I was a holy terror as a toddler."

He grinned, knowing she'd seen right through him. He gathered Sarah in his arms and kissed her deeply. "I love you, angel. And I love our son and daughter more than you'll ever know." He paused for a second, his gaze on Samantha. "With our love and guidance, I know she will turn out to be as wonderful as her mom." He kissed Sarah's cheek, then joined Sam.

Braden took his daughter's plump little hand and guided her to some flowers and pointed to several dyed eggs. "Look, Sam. There's three eggs."

She quickly placed them in her basket, set it on the ground, and clapped her hands together, giggling.

Braden smiled down on his daughter, then glanced over at Simon before meeting Sarah's gaze. The woman had made his life complete by loving him and giving him these two beautiful children. He loved Simon and Samantha as much as he had Andy.

No longer did hate and anger fill his heart and control his actions. He was a man content with life and at peace with himself.

But most importantly, Braden had learned to love again.

The End.

When Death Calls – Coming next.
Romantic suspense with a paranormal twist.

Before Ryan could say another word, Madam Francesca hung up. He shook his head. "Damn, I hope she doesn't call back."

Though he admitted her prediction had been dead-on about his dad's surgery and the 97/A scored on his criminology exam. A parlor trick of some sorts or a damn lucky guess.

He returned to bed and climbed between the sheets, then closed his eyes. He couldn't sleep nor could he stop thinking about the whacky fortuneteller's warning. If the serial killer's next victim turned out to be Amber Hatfield, he'd never forgive himself. "Oh hell."

Ryan reached over and googled the name on his Android. There were two Amber Hatfields in New Orleans. One of the women lived only a couple of streets over from the last victim. She'd be the one he checked first. But exhaustion from the full day he'd put in made him groggy and tired. He considered staying in bed.

Damn it to hell.

When he reached Amber Hatfield's Lake View house in district five, he eyed a black car parked out front beneath a streetlight. The residence stood dark.

A shadowy figure turned the corner and disappeared around the side of the house.

He killed the engine and called for backup before leaving his car. He removed his gun and held it in a ready position, then ran to the front of the house. From there he edged along the side to the back corner and stopped. He should wait for backup, but what if this was the serial killer and the bastard got away?

Ryan's heart pumped hard. He turned the corner. "Police. Stop or I'll shoot!"

The perp stopped. The guy wore dark sweats and a hooded sweatshirt, preventing Ryan from seeing his face. Something shiny dropped to the ground. If lucky, it'd be the murder weapon used to butcher the other three women.

Ryan approached the suspect with his gun aimed. "Turn around. Drop to your knees and put your hands over your head. Now!"

"I'm not armed," a female shouted.

He recognized the voice. *Shit.* Disbelief washed over him.

She dropped to her knees and placed her hands on her head.

He stalked over to where she crouched and grasped her arm, then jerked her to her feet. "Madam Francesca?"

"Detective LaBarre?"

While he didn't think she had murdered the women, he thought maybe she had an accomplice. "You're under arrest for the murder of Candice Gore."

"I'm what? I didn't kill Candice."

"I see what your game is. You're building yourself up as a famous psychic. You predict their deaths, then kill them to validate your so-called psychic abilities."

"That's ridiculous. Think about it. I'm in front of a crystal ball from five till ten every night. I don't have time to kill people. I'm sure I'll have an alibi for each night a woman's been killed."

"You're too busy taking their money with your razzle-dazzle bullshit."

"That's great coming from a blockhead who can't see anything but black and white. Besides, I don't have the equipment to sexually assault them."

The fact that the women had been sexually assaulted had been kept quiet. How did Madam Francesca know unless the man working with her had told her?

"No but your partner might've." He'd planned to keep that to himself, but he wanted to watch her reaction.

"The only partners I have are cats. Do you think one of them did it?"

"If you're not involved, then what the hell are you doing here?"

"I knew you were patronizing me when I called earlier. I wasn't expecting you to do anything. So I felt I had to save Amber Hatfield."

"The killer's using a damn machete, and you thought you could save her," he leaned over and picked up the letter opener she'd dropped on the ground, then dangled it before her. "with this?"

She nodded. "Don't under estimate a good letter opener."

When he escorted her to the front, a patrol car pulled up, and an officer stepped out. "Everything under control?"

"False alarm. You can go. I can handle her."

After the patrol car pulled away, Ryan walked her to the black car. She stood under the streetlight. The light filtered down on her, revealing enormous blue eyes. She pushed back the hood, uncovering short blond hair.

His gaze stayed fixed on her for a moment. She smelled like honeysuckle on a summer night. He thought about kissing her for a brief second before he remembered her profession.

Shit. Maybe I'm the one who's nuts.

She was the last person he wanted to be attracted to. He despised her kind. Had ever since a fortuneteller convinced his wife he was running around. His marriage ended in divorce. What really angered him, he'd never looked twice at another woman.

"Lady, you need a straightjacket."

"I knew it. You think I'm crazy."

"Yeah, for coming here alone."

"Oh, admit it. You think I'm a crackpot because I talk to the dead."

"Yeah, but I couldn't stop thinking how stupid I'd feel if you turned out to be right. So here I am. Maybe we both need a straightjacket."

"Make mine a size seven." She giggled.

"Lady, stop wasting my time."

"Grumpy ass," she mumbled as she climbed in her car. She smiled slyly.

Ryan waited until she pulled away to leave. If she called again, he'd recommend she spend her next vacation in the psych ward at the River Oaks Hospital.

About the Author

Elaine Meece writes romantic suspense novels. She is an active member of RWA and belongs to the River City Romance Writers, Music City Romance Writers, and Malice of Memphis. She has been a finalist and won many contests sponsored by RWA chapters for best romantic suspense.

She resides in Bartlett, Tennessee with her husband, Geoffrey. Elaine is a former school teacher.

Besides writing, she loves to sing, hike, and go inner tubing on the Current River in Missouri. She also has spent two weeks kayaking the icy waters of Alaska and tent camping in the Alaskan wilderness.

She is a member of the Memphis Scottish Society and Bartlett United Methodist Church.

Join her Facebook page: author Elaine Meece

37632075R00177

Made in the USA
Middletown, DE
02 March 2019